BEFORE HE KILLS AGAIN

ALSO BY TADHG COAKLEY

Novels
The First Sunday in September
Whatever It Takes

Non-Fiction
Everything: the Autobiography of Denis Coughlan (co-author)
The Game: A Journey into the Heart of Sport

BEFORE HE KILLS
AGAIN

TADHG COAKLEY

MERCIER PRESS

To the victims of domestic,
sexual and gender-based violence.
And to those who protect
and look after them.

© Tadhg Coakley, 2023

978-1-78117-825-6
978-1-78117-826-3 Ebook only

Cover design: Sarah O'Flaherty

A CIP record for this title is available from the British Library.

Printed and bound in the EU.

Part 1
HELEN'S EYES

CHAPTER 1

COLLINS PARKED in the Supervalu car park beside St Mary's on The Hill. It was one of those low sized almost circular modern churches of which he didn't approve. Getting out of his car, he looked at the spire made from metal bars and a simple cross. The blue sky and sunshine seemed to mock the waste of a young life.

He took the funeral wreath from the boot of his car. The flowers were red and white, with the emblem of a liver bird in the centre circled by the words 'You'll Never Walk Alone'. He'd only found out the previous year she was a Liverpool supporter like him.

He gave the wreath to one of the undertakers beside the hearse on the Harbour View Road. The man said: 'Thanks'.

Some of her friends were smoking near the front door of the church. He stopped and glared at them. Only one, Chloe, held his gaze. Her eyes looked lifeless.

As he stepped inside the church he heard the word 'Pig'.

He walked on. Another funeral because of you.

WHEN HE had phoned Jackie the previous week to check up on her, she picked up on the second ring.

'If it isn't Batman himself,' she said. 'The lone hero dedicated to saving Gotham City.' There was too much gaiety in her voice, she was high on something.

'Hi, Jackie, how're things? Can we meet up?'

'So you can point out the error of my ways? Give me a lecture? I am *so* tired of all that, Collins.'

'No, I just wanted a chat, bit of a catch up.'

'You're some fucking liar.'

'Come on. The hot chocolate is on me.'

'*She* rang you I suppose.'

'Nobody rang me. I just called for a chat.'

'You did in your hole.'

Collins wanted to avoid talking to her while she was high, there was no point.

'Come on, Jackie, I can pick you up now, bring you to McDonalds. Where are you? I'll be there in ten.'

'Haha, nice try. See you around, Collins.'

'I can get you back into Cuan Dé, Jackie,' Collins said, but the line was dead.

He looked her up on the Garda PULSE system and saw a charge of soliciting against her. That confirmed it. *Why hadn't you kept a closer eye on her?*

He tried to phone her back twice. He tried again the following day.

He went to her mother's house. Jacqueline had moved to a small social housing development in Carrigtwohill.

There were steps up to the front door of the new red-bricked maisonette. In the sunshine children played on a green area nearby.

Collins pressed the bell and waited. Already the heat was pulsing down even though it was only June. Two baskets of flowers hung on either side of Jacqueline's door. Thriving pots of flowers on the ground by the railings to either side – which he took as a good sign.

Kyle – Jacqueline's son and Jackie's brother – opened the door and slammed it in Collins' face. He rang the bell again. This time Jacqueline did answer it. She looked healthy, she was clearly off the drink. Collins tried not to show his relief.

Her face was flushed and her hair was tied up. From the sports top, leggings and bare feet he guessed he had interrupted a yoga session.

'Hi Jaqueline,' he said, smiling. 'How are you?'

She watched him closely without speaking. He hoped the smile had reassured her. She opened the door for him to enter.

'The kitchen is straight ahead, there,' she said. They went through. He stood awkwardly by the fridge.

'Sit down, sit down, you're making me nervous,' she said. 'Tea or coffee?'

'Black tea, thanks.'

He sat down. She filled the kettle and switched it on. She sat at the table opposite him, her face a mask of worry.

'Is it Jackie? Has something happened?'

'I phoned her the other day, I was worried. Is she okay?'

Jaqueline shook her head and her eyes filled with tears.

'No,' she managed to say. Collins got up and removed two cups from the stand by the kettle. He took a tea bag from the tin. The kettle boiled.

She stood up and faced him.

'What happened?' she said. 'And sit down, it'll give me something to do.'

'I looked her up on the system the other day,' he said. 'I saw that there was a charge against her from a few weeks ago.'

'What is it now?' she said. Collins noticed her hands were shaking. She wouldn't meet his eyes.

'I'm sorry to say it is soliciting,' he said.

She shuddered and put a hand to her mouth. She looked out the window.

'My therapist in rehab prepared me for this,' she said. 'You know what she told me?'

'No.'

'She told me that I can't look after anybody else until I can look after myself.'

'And how are you doing?'

She sniffled. 'Some days I think I'm only hanging on. Other

days I think I'll be okay.'

'But,' she said and she turned to make the tea. 'I know now that I can't look after Jackie and look after myself too. And I'm no good to her or Kyle drunk.'

She placed the two cups of tea on the table and took a jug of milk from the fridge. She sat down and shrugged.

'I can't do it for her any more,' she said and her voice was flat. 'I just can't.'

'I was hoping if I could get to her, I might be able to do something. Do you know where she is?'

She shook her head. 'No. She was living with her boyfriend somewhere near Douglas Street, but I think he threw her out when she started using again.'

'I spoke to her last Tuesday,' he said. 'But I can't get through to her since. I'll try to trace her phone, we might get a location for her using that.'

'I know I'm a bad mother,' Jacqueline said, her voice breaking. 'I should have stopped Dinny and I should have done better with Jackie. And now Kyle is hanging around with those pups.'

As if in response, the sound of the front door slamming quietened her.

'I'll find her,' Collins said.

HE NEVER did. The call came through later that day when he was chatting with his new partner, Deirdre Donnelly, in the station. He looked at the phone before answering; it was a colleague, Aisling Crowley.

'Collins?' she said.

'Hi Aisling, what's up?'

'I thought you'd want to know. We found the body of Jackie Buckley in a flat off Evergreen Road just now.'

Collins winced. *Again.* He closed his eyes. *You useless fuck.*

'Collins? Are you there?' Aisling said.

'Yeah, sorry. Was it an overdose?' he said.

'Looks like it. There were two of them. The other is critical in CUH. There's a very pure batch of heroin doing the rounds right now, there was another death last week.'

'Definite ID?'

'Definite, Collins. I'm sorry, I know you did your best for her.'

My best.

'Thanks for letting me know, Aisling, I appreciate it,' he said and hung up.

'Bad news?' Deirdre said.

'Yeah, an overdose,' he said, standing up. 'I have to go to Carrigtwohill and tell the family.'

'Want me to go with you?'

'No thanks, girl. Appreciate the offer.'

COLLINS SAT near the back of the church at the funeral. The usual platitudes from a young priest, although he did seem to be genuine. There was no eulogy and Collins was glad. Jackie would have hated it.

She was buried beside her brother Dinny in Curraghkippane Cemetery. The graveyard was on a hill with stunning views of the River Lee Valley and rising hills to the south. There wasn't a cloud in the sky. A blackbird sang throughout the entire ceremony from a nearby sycamore.

Collins stood at a distance from the grave but in a place where Jacqueline had a clear view of him. Kyle had grown tall since Collins had seen him last. He had given up his boxing and sold his dogs, Collins knew, and was dealing for the McMahons, who were steadily taking over the drug trade in Cork since Mickey had returned from Spain.

Collins had been moved from the Drugs and Organised Crime

Unit after Dominic Molloy's murder the previous winter, so he didn't have much contact with the drug gangs in Cork any more. He was furious when he heard there was a new gang operating out of his home patch, West Cork, and he had made enquiries about who might be dealing the pure batch of heroin. Then he let it go, what would be the point?

After the prayers had ended, two young women stepped forward and sang the hymn 'I'll Fly Away', which Collins knew from the film *O Brother, Where Art Thou?* They were obviously sisters, probably twins. They were both small. One wore a blue summer dress and black Doc Marten boots. Her hair, in a bob, had been dyed purple and grey and her long drop feather earrings were the colours of a rainbow. The other singer had her hair in the same bob but it was jet black. She wore a Nirvana t-shirt and baggy khaki pants. Their singing and their harmonies were clear and slow and beautiful and soft.

At the final chorus Collins lowered his eyes and looked at the ground. When he realised there would be no other songs, he joined the queue before the family and shook hands with Kyle, saying: 'I'm sorry for your loss, Kyle, I was very fond of her.' Kyle looked at him and blinked once but did not speak.

'Jacqueline,' Collins said and held out his hand. She embraced him; she was surprisingly strong.

'I'm sober thanks to you, Collins,' she whispered in his ear. 'And I know how much you did for Jackie, and Dinny too. I'll never forget it.'

She released him.

'I'm so sorry,' he said and he laid his hand on her arm. He turned away.

'I know,' she said quietly.

After the funeral, he drove to Bandon to visit his mother, who had tripped over her new dog and broken her hip. Being infirm didn't suit her and she hated the walking aid she had to use around the supermarket. She hated having to explain to friends and neighbours how she had fallen, so she never mentioned the dog to people.

He had dinner with her and left when the home help arrived.

Just outside Cork, Deirdre phoned him on a station number.

'Where are you?' she said. 'There's been a murder in Blackrock.'

'I'll be there in ten minutes,' he said. 'I'll meet you out front.'

CHAPTER 2

DETECTIVE SERGEANT Deirdre Donnelly glanced at the clock on the Audi's dashboard: 21:15, but it still wasn't anywhere close to being dark. She looked in her mirror as the car headed out the Blackrock Road. The beginnings of a blazing sunset had begun in the western sky behind.

She glanced at her new partner, Tim Collins, in the passenger seat. He was pale. She'd heard about his squeamishness around dead bodies but she hadn't believed it. There were so many rumours and myths built around Collins she didn't know what to believe. Her first month in Cork with him had been uneventful, which was disappointing. She was almost glad when word had just come through of a body being found in Ardlea Drive, an estate off the Blackrock Road in the south-eastern part of the city.

'Do you know where this place is?' she said. It was her first stationing in Cork and she hadn't yet gotten her bearings. She knew Páirc Uí Chaoimh was nearby, but that wasn't much help.

'You'll be taking a left in a few hundred metres,' Collins said. 'I'll tell you when we get there.' His phone rang and he held the screen out at arm's length to check the caller. That was another thing: he looked so old. She'd expected somebody … well, hotter, for starters. He looked more like her father than her boyfriend Jake. All in all, she felt let down. When Superintendent Frank O'Rourke told her she would be partnering Collins and that he wanted her to rein him in and to report anything 'dodgy', she'd been expecting fireworks, fighting gangland crime at the coalface. Collins seemed to be more interested in his precious coffees or sitting at his desk than being out there on the streets in the battle ground.

Collins answered the call.

'We'll be there in one minute, superintendent,' he said. 'I understand, superintendent.' He hung up.

'O'Rourke?' Deirdre said.

'Yes. Next left here, after the trees.'

'What did he want?' Deirdre said and resented having to ask. That was another thing about Collins, she could hardly get two words out of him.

'He said he wants this investigation handled with "kid gloves" and "by the book",' Collins said and grimaced when he saw the mass of blazing lights ahead. Vehicles and people were blocking the entrance of the well-to-do looking estate.

She pulled the Audi up on a footpath. Much quicker to walk. Somebody at the station had clearly leaked the news of a body to the media, there were two camera crews setting up with two well-known local broadcasters, Amy Geary and Martin Smyth.

'Collins! Collins!' they called out simultaneously and headed straight for the detectives.

'Collins, has the woman been identified? Is it murder?' Smyth asked, sticking a microphone in front of Collins' face.

'Collins, is the husband suspected?' Smyth said.

Other reporters also held out phones, trying to get a quote. Collins walked past them all without an acknowledgement. A press photographer took a photo. Deirdre wondered if she resented the focus being exclusively on him.

A huddle of neighbours stood on a lawn across from the house which was now cordoned off. Collins looked closely at them and a few other people standing around. He approached the first two gardaí in uniform in front of the yellow and black incident tape.

'Donal, can you get a video of all the people around, including the media? Theresa, can you organise somebody to go around and get everybody's name and details, please? Straight away, before they disperse? Thanks.'

Collins held up the tape for Deirdre to go under. She felt she was being too passive. She had investigated several murders in her time in Pearse Street in Dublin; she wasn't some rookie thrown in at the deep end.

'Dr Gubbins,' she said, approaching a tall stooped bearded man in a green polypropylene boiler suit about to enter the small marquee covering the front door. He was head of the Technical Unit in the Cork Division and she had met him only once, at a retirement function the previous week. He had been approachable even though he seemed to be fixated about being referred to as 'Doctor' rather than Paul. He wasn't even a real doctor, somebody told her it was a PhD.

'I'll inform you when you can enter the building, detective,' Gubbins said and walked away.

'Won't be long,' Collins said to her. 'He's always cranky when there's a dead body in the vicinity. We can suit up in the meantime.' He walked to the Technical Unit van and took the plastic bag that was handed to him by a woman in the same suit and cap as Gubbins. She was talking animatedly into a mobile phone. She handed Deirdre an identical bag, and ended the call.

'This is my new partner, Deirdre Donnelly,' Collins said to the woman. 'This is Blessing Nzekwe, Deirdre, the best forensics analyst in Cork.'

'You are such a charmer, Tim,' Blessing said. 'Very nice to meet you Deirdre, I wish it was in happier circumstances.'

'Nice to meet you too, Blessing,' Deirdre said, knowing better than to shake hands – TU people hated any bodily contact.

Two young gardaí approached Collins. One of them looked sick with nerves. Clearly they were the ones that had discovered the body.

'Do you know Michael and Seán?' Collins said to Deirdre. 'This is Detective Sergeant Deirdre Donnelly,' he said to the men. 'Start at the beginning, leave nothing out. Remember what O'Malley taught ye.' He was referring, Deirdre, knew, to Cathal O'Malley, Ireland's most famous detective and now a teacher at the Garda Training College in Templemore.

The taller of the two, Michael, exhaled and looked at his notebook.

'We were in the squad car in Ballinlough at a dispute between two neighbours, when we got the call …'

'Time?' Collins said, pulling the boiler suit over his right foot.

'Oh, sorry,' Michael said. 'Just after eight.'

Collins glared at him.

'Ten past eight,' Michael said, quickly. He glanced at his colleague, who licked his lips. Deirdre didn't know whether they were nervous because they had found a dead body or because they were reporting back to Collins.

'Eight minutes past eight. I checked my watch when the call came in,' Seán said. To Deirdre he looked young enough to be in secondary school, but that was happening a lot lately.

Collins nodded. He was fully suited up now and he stood facing the two young gardaí.

'We arrived here soon after … we arrived here at 8:13,' Michael continued. 'And were met by the neighbour who had made the call. She was very agitated.'

'Name?' Collins said.

The garda looked at the notebook. 'Orlaith Moloney, from number 43, just across the road. She had been phoning the … victim's phone number for over an hour. They were supposed to go for a walk and the car was outside and there was no answer at the door or to her phone calls and texts. There was no sign of the dead woman's eight-year-old son, either. She had phoned the husband and he rang her back and said to phone the guards that something must have happened.'

Collins glanced at Deirdre. The husband was always the first suspect until he wasn't.

'Name of the deceased?' Collins said.

'Helen O'Driscoll,' Michael said and paused.

'Another neighbour, Hugh Delaney, had a spare front door key and we entered the house at …' he hesitated. Every garda knew that these times could be the making or breaking of a case and he didn't want to get it wrong. '8:18 p.m.' He looked at Seán, who nodded, checking his notebook.

'There was no sign of any forced entry, front or back, or any window. We checked them all. There were two open windows to the side, they could have been used for entry, but there were no marks or sign of disturbance around them. We didn't touch either window – we could have used them to get in but we knew there was a spare key by then. The alarm was turned off. No sign of life or anything downstairs. We saw her body on the bed in the bedroom when we went upstairs. She was clearly dead but we checked for breath and pulse. Neither. So, we called it in at exactly 8:21.'

Collins turned to the Technical Unit woman who had given them the protective suits. 'How long more, Blessing?' he said.

'Not long, maybe ten minutes,' she replied. 'He is just finishing off a few things. But he will want you straight out, we have a lot more to do.'

'Can you go back to the moment when you opened the front door?' Deirdre said to Seán. He seemed to be the more perceptive of the two. 'What was the first thing you noticed?'

'It was quiet in the house,' he said. 'Somebody was cutting grass in the distance. And some children playing further down the park. And some music, there's a concert in the Marquee.' This was more like it.

'But nothing inside the house. There was total silence. The sun was streaming into the living room on the right. The TV was turned off, the radio in the kitchen too. There were two windows open in the sitting room and the blinds were blowing a little. No smells in the kitchen of cooking or coffee or anything. Kettle was cold. A few pieces of ware on the drying rack, no plates on the table or island or anything like that.'

Deirdre knew better than to interrupt him, the kid was on a roll and seemed to have a photographic memory.

'We went upstairs together,' he said. 'And there was no sound or smell there, either. Oh, Michael called out when we entered the house first. I forgot to mention that. No response. So, we weren't expecting to meet anyone or find anything. I pushed open the bathroom door, that's the first door on the right. Nothing. Clean toilet. Nothing.

'Then Michael pushed open the main bedroom door and we saw the body. A woman, mid-forties I'd say, blonde hair. Face up, partly on the bed. Contusions around the neck, naked from the waist down, clear signs of sexual assault.'

'What clear signs?' Deirdre said. This was no time for him to be embarrassed.

Seán exhaled.

'There was blood around her … midsection and thighs,' he said. 'Blood on the bed cover, too.'

'Thanks Seán,' Collins said. 'We'll see that ourselves when we go up. Was the blood still wet? Could you tell?'

'No. Dried.'

'Anything else?' Collins said. 'What happened then?'

'We rang for an ambulance and for backup. The first squad car arrived in ten minutes and the super about ten minutes after that. We cordoned off everywhere and set up a perimeter down the road.'

Gubbins came out of the house and approached them. He

peeled off a green plastic cap and the hood of his suit.

'You can go in now, but don't touch anything, we're not finished,' he said to Collins. He didn't acknowledge Deirdre, which rankled.

'Are we looking at asphyxiation, doctor? Sexual assault?' Collins said to Gubbins.

'Superintendent O'Rourke will get my report in due course,' Gubbins replied. He took a phone out of his pocket and turned away.

'Two things,' Collins said to the gardaí. 'The boy? Any sign? Did ye search for him?'

'Oh, yeah,' Michael said. 'No sign, we searched the house, top to bottom. A few of the lads are going door-to-door in case he's with a friend.'

'And the father?' Collins said. 'Who's following up with him?'

'Superintendent O'Rourke told us to give the phone number to Detectives Clancy and O'Regan.'

Collins didn't react. Deirdre watched him closely. The chances were that the husband did it, so Clancy and O'Regan would get to arrest him and take lead on the case and close it out. This was the dirty end of the stick, examining a dead body and a bloody bed.

Collins looked at her, glumly.

'You ready?' he said.

'Yeah,' she replied. She put the plastic cap over the top of her head and headed for the door.

CHAPTER 3

DEIRDRE AND Collins passed through the forensics marquee and into the front hall. It was almost dark now and the house lights were turned on. The décor was tasteful; beautiful, even. A good oak floor behind the sunken welcome mat and colourful tiles. Pale blue and off-white paint on the walls, in two tones. A large mirror on the left by the door. Small paintings and family photos on the wall of the stairs and on a console table to the right.

Money and good taste, all for nothing now. Deirdre could hear the thrum of the concert going on in the distance in the Marquee. It seemed strange that so many people so close by were having fun at a time like this. She wondered what kind of music Collins liked. She pushed it out of her mind. *Concentrate*, she told herself.

Collins took the stairs in bounds ahead of her, as though he were eager to see the grisly scene. She followed on quickly, she wanted to see his reaction and his modus operandi. *Look, listen and learn,* her father used to say. *Every day is a school day.* Even if it was the husband and he had taken the boy with him, it had to be proven.

Collins paused at the top of the stairs, as though listening. He moved around a Technical Unit marker on the landing floor. A woman was taking photographs of the body and Collins entered the room and stood at the end of the bed. He moved his gloved hands to his face and pressed them to his mouth and nose.

'Jesus,' he said, through gritted teeth and he seemed to sway. Deirdre wondered if he might topple over. He went to the window and looked out.

The photographer made eye contact with Deirdre and shrugged.

'Okay, okay,' Collins said and he turned. His face was drained of colour and his eyes were wet.

'Nail this bastard, Collins,' the photographer said. She faced Deirdre and said: 'I'm Alison Cronin, Technical Unit. You the new partner? Good luck with that.'

'Deirdre Donnelly,' Deirdre said.

'Did you get Helen's knees and elbows?' Collins said.

'I got it all, Collins, as you well know, and don't touch that body or anything else,' Alison said and left the room.

Collins approached the body and looked into the dead woman's eyes as if that old myth were true: that the killer's face would be reflected there.

'What colour would you say Helen's eyes are?' Collins said and Deirdre didn't like the way he kept referring to her first name. It seemed affected, as though they weren't already committed to catching her killer. Or as though Collins cared more than she did, than anybody else did.

'Does it matter anymore?' she said. Surely something left behind by the killer was more important, some piece of DNA or something to prove who did this horrific thing.

'It does matter. Whoever did this can never take away the colour of her eyes,' Collins said. 'They are green. Look at them.'

Deirdre found herself leaning over the body and looking into Helen O'Driscoll's blood shot, bulging, soft green eyes – lifeless now.

'What do you see here?' Deirdre asked him, moving away. *Every day is a school day.*

'Rage and pride,' Collins said. 'Rage and pride. Enough pride to drown in, a sea of it. This is a display. He thinks he's a great artist leaving his masterpiece for us to admire.'

'Will you take upstairs and I'll do downstairs?' Deirdre said. 'We can compare notes later.'

'Sounds good,' Collins said. He walked to the other side of the room, by some sliding door wardrobes.

'Before you go,' he said. 'What do *you* see? What can we take with us?'

She thought for a moment.

'I see myself,' she said and Collins' head shot up.

Deirdre stared back at him. 'I see every woman who was ever born and had to endure either the threat of violence from men or the violence itself. And you know what? I'm fucking sick of it.' She turned and left the room.

'Well then,' Collins said.

CHAPTER 4

COLLINS LOOKED at the body again. The worst of the nausea was over, he felt in control again. Even his therapists couldn't explain or help him with his reactions to the bodies of murdered people – women and children, especially.

The face was red which was an indication of asphyxiation, and the pinpoint haemorrhaging in and around her eyes. There was a thin red mark around her neck, it looked like the killer used some type of ligature. A vivid bruise on her temple. No marks on her hands or face, why didn't she fight back? Maybe she was unconscious.

Collins looked at the two dressing gowns hanging on the back of the bedroom door to see if a belt was missing. Both were intact.

He worked the room from the far corner on the right, anti-clockwise. He opened every drawer and examined every inch of it. He looked underneath every surface. The laundry basket contained leggings, a sports bra and some children's clothes.

In the wardrobe, he went through her clothes, feeling and looking his way through every stitch. He thought he heard a muted noise, like a phone on silent. He checked his own phone: nothing.

He went into the next room, a study. Blessing was in there, bagging a laptop.

'Any sign of her phone, Blessing?' Collins asked.

'No, but we have the number, we will get the provider to do a location sweep.' This was standard practice after any major crime, to track people's whereabouts, but the killer might have taken the phone since it often contained incriminating evidence.

'We phoned it, upstairs and downstairs. Nothing.'

'Okay. Were there any clothes on the ground or anything?'

Collins said. 'A towel? Any sign of a ligature?'

'No. Nothing. We noticed the mark around her neck, we'll test everything suitable.'

'I checked the dressing gown belts, in case one was missing.'

'Yes, we noticed them too.'

'He must have taken some of her clothes as a trophy,' Collins said. 'It didn't look like she was coming in from a shower or anything like that.'

'That's what Dr Gubbins said.'

'We might be able to confirm what she had been wearing if somebody met her earlier,' Collins said. 'When is the pathologist due?' The body could not be removed until then.

'She is due in a few minutes, she was in CUH doing something when we called her.'

'Good,' Collins said. He didn't want Helen's body to be displayed like that for any longer. 'What's your sense of Helen O'Driscoll?' he asked. He knew that Blessing had trained in psychology as well as forensics.

She labelled the clear bag and took a photo of it. She thought for a moment.

'Very methodical, very organised. Not one thing out of place in the house. But a strong personality, too. Apart from the room downstairs with the big TV and the fridge with beer, the whole house is her personality. Look at the presses in the kitchen and at the bookshelves in the living room. All the books are alphabetical by author. I never saw that outside a library,' she said.

Collins looked at a small child's painting framed on the desk, a self-portrait with the letters E-V-A-N scrawled at the bottom. He shuddered.

'The boy's name is Evan, is it?'

'What?' Blessing said, distracted. 'Yes it is – he's eight.'

Collins went back and continued his search through Helen's

clothes and then her husband's. His name was Gregory Murphy, he had noticed from the framed degree on the wall of the study. Science, if Collins' Latin wasn't too rusty. He was probably called Greg, they always used the birth certificate name in university. His clothes were good quality, a lot of Tommy Hilfiger and he had three Paul Costello suits. No shortage of money, but killings like this were never about money.

So, Helen kept her own surname after they got married. Nothing strange in that.

Collins looked at the floor of the wardrobe and noticed it was different from the good oak wood outside it. He sensed a presence and turned quickly to the body.

He went to the first wardrobe he had checked and took out the long stick with the hook to pull down the folding stairs to the attic.

Nothing apart from a stifling heat. It was neat and orderly around the door. Some suitcases and several large plastic boxes, stacked in two rows. All labelled. The rest of the surface was deep with blown insulation.

When he got downstairs, Deirdre beckoned him outside.

'The super wants us to head back and have a team meeting,' she said.

'Any news of the boy?' Collins said.

'No,' she replied. 'Not yet. Looks like that will be the focus of the investigation for now.'

They stood aside as the Assistant State Pathologist, Alice O'Callaghan, arrived with Inspector Tom Brennan, who had driven her from CUH. She was carrying a big old medical bag and she smiled when she saw Collins.

'Hello, handsome,' she said. 'Are you never in Dublin, at all? You promised us you'd call.'

'Hi Alice,' Collins said. He noticed Brennan's face set in anger, he hadn't known that Alice and Collins were friends. 'I don't get out of the real capital much, any more, I'm afraid. How are you? How are Rose and Suzie?'

'We're fine, Collins. Don't be a stranger,' Alice said. She waved and entered the house.

'You *know* her?' Deirdre said.

'Yeah, when I was stationed in Store Street I got friendly with her partner, who's a garda. Long story,' Collins said. 'Listen, let you head back in, I'm going to stay around here a while. We need to find Evan.'

'The super said he wanted us both back for a briefing,' Deirdre said, shaking her head. Collins could see she was uncomfortable about going against instructions.

'Tell him I'll follow on, I just need to check something here but I have to wait until they remove the body.'

'Up to you,' Deirdre said and walked away.

COLLINS LOOKED around. It was quieter, except for gardaí coming and going. All the neighbours were gone and the perimeter on the street had been moved further back, all the way to the Blackrock Road. That should have been done immediately, he thought. He took out his phone and found the number of Kate Browne, the most senior of the Family Liaison Officers (FLOs) in Cork.

'Hi, Kate? This is Collins, can you talk? Are you up to speed on the murder on the Blackrock Road?'

'One second Collins,' she replied. Then he heard her talking to somebody, excusing herself.

'I'm with some of the family there, the husband's parents. They're distraught, needless to say. What do you need?'

'I'm worried about Evan, do they have any idea where he could be?'

'No, they phoned various people, friends and neighbours, but nothing. They're just down the road in Ballintemple. They even searched around their own garden, apparently he walked on his own down there a couple of months ago, without permission.'

'Can I come down and talk to them? There's something wrong here, but I can't put my finger on it.'

'What is it?'

'I just want to see if the grandmother would be strong enough for something. Can you let me talk to them for five minutes?'

COLLINS WALKED to Maryhill from Ardlea. The concert in the Marquee had finished and there was gridlock on the Blackrock Road. Throngs of people, mostly young, passed by, giddy in their post-gig high. Many stopped at the barriers by the entrance to Ardlea and gaped at the garda flashing lights.

The light outside 16 Maryhill, an old bungalow, was on and two gardaí were standing outside in high viz jackets. Collins said hello to them and rang the doorbell. Kate opened the front door and stepped outside.

'What's this about?' she whispered. 'Is the husband suspected? I thought he had an alibi.'

'No, it's not about him, it's the boy. I think he's hiding in the house and won't come out.'

'Hiding? I thought they searched it from top to bottom, and all around the estate?'

'It's just a feeling, but I think it's worth a try. They can remove the body now that the pathologist has been there ...'

Kate thought about it. 'Five minutes,' she said. 'And don't upset them.'

Collins nodded. 'Surname is Murphy, that right?'

'Yes,' Kate said. 'Jim and Nora. Jim doesn't seem fully with it.'

Collins followed her through. There were classical books lining both sides of the hall and he realised this was Professor Nora

Murphy, who had taught him in UCC, several years previously, not that she would remember him.

'Jim. Nora,' Kate said, when they entered the sitting room. 'This is Detective Tim Collins, he's one of the investigating team and he wants a quick word.'

'Is there news?' Nora said. She was in her mid-sixties. She was thin and fit looking, tanned from being outdoors. Her eyes were rimmed with worry. Her husband looked a good ten years older but his face was strangely passive, almost serene, as though he were on medication.

'No, professor, I'm sorry,' Collins said. 'There isn't. I wanted to talk to you about Evan. I think he's hiding somewhere.'

'Where? Where is he?' Nora said standing up. Exactly the response Collins had wanted.

'I think he might be in the house,' Collins said. 'But I want him to come out of his own accord and I need you for that.'

Nora wanted to go to Ardlea immediately but Collins explained to her that Helen's body had to be removed first, that Evan couldn't possibly see it. Then he went outside with Kate and phoned Superintendent O'Rourke, outlining his plan.

Collins was glad that O'Rourke was in charge of the case. He was conservative in his approach and a devout Catholic, but he let his Detectives get on with their work and didn't micro manage, which suited Collins just fine.

O'Rourke was sceptical and put him on speakerphone to the group. Then he patched in Lorraine Crowley, one of the station's counsellors, who was a child psychologist, and she swung it – she thought it was essential that a stranger didn't find Evan. A man, especially, in the circumstances.

Collins told them that he thought Evan was hiding under the wardrobe in the bedroom, which was why he hadn't searched further. He didn't want him to see his mother's body.

An hour later, Collins, Deirdre, O'Rourke and Brennan were standing on the footpath outside the house in Ardlea as Lorraine Crowley, Kate Browne and Nora Murphy entered through the Technical Unit marquee.

Temporary lights had been set up on the lawn and insects were flying in wide circles around them. The heat was still oppressive, no sign of any breeze.

The blinds had been lowered and the curtains closed in the bedroom where Helen had been found. The window faced to the front and all four gardaí looked up at it. Some uniformed gardaí were also gathered by the taped exclusion zone, watching expectantly. Alison, Blessing and Gubbins from the Technical Unit stood by their van, in their green overalls.

'You better be right about this, Collins,' Brennan said.

Collins ignored him. Was there a possibility that Helen's murderer could have killed Evan, too, and taken his body, as another trophy? Surely not, the TU would have found something to indicate that and how would the killer remove and transport a body?

He heard Nora call out Evan's name inside the house.

'Evan? It's Granny Nora, you can come out now, love.'

Nothing.

'Evan? It's okay, love, it's all over. You can come out now.'

The only sound was traffic from the Blackrock Road. Collins stared at the window and willed the boy out.

There was a sound like a sob and the unmistakable crying of a child. Collins closed his eyes.

'Thank God,' Deirdre said, quietly.

A few minutes later Kate emerged from the marquee. Nora was behind her, carrying the boy, who was crying loudly, his face pressed against his grandmother's neck. Lorraine was next, holding a bottle of water. She escorted Nora to a waiting car and opened the door.

Kate made for the group of gardaí and spoke to Superintendent O'Rourke.

'Collins was right,' she said. 'He was hiding in the wardrobe. There were some loose floorboards and he must have been able to wriggle his way under them. When Nora called out his name in the bedroom, we heard a sound and he shot out of the wardrobe like a bullet.' She looked at Collins.

'Did he have her phone?' Collins said.

'Yes, I saw it in the wardrobe where he was hiding. I didn't touch it.'

'I'll retrieve it,' Paul Gubbins said and walked towards the house.

O'Rourke turned to Collins. 'How did you know?' he said and Collins shrugged.

'Just a feeling, but I might have heard something, too, when I was going through the wardrobe,' he said. 'I'm not sure.'

'Well, it was a good idea to get the grandmother and not to have the child see the state of his mother,' O'Rourke said. 'Although what he heard is another thing. We can't do much more here, we should head back and plan our next steps.'

Collins walked over to the Technical Unit van where Blessing Nzekwe and Alison Cronin were standing.

'Want a coffee or anything, lads?' he said.

'He's looking for something, Blessing,' Alison said.

'I am not! Jesus, you're after getting fierce cynical, Cronin.'

'I'll have a cappuccino,' Blessing said. 'The phone, right? You want us to do that first? It is always the phone.'

'That would be great, Blessing, thanks. One cappuccino coming up. Alison?'

'Vodka and tonic would be nice, Collins. No ice. Failing that, I'll have a large latte.'

Chapter 5

It was 23:22 according to the clock on the wall of Meeting Room 3 of Anglesea Street Garda Station, but nobody was complaining about not going home. They all knew the importance of quick action and moving in the right direction immediately.

Deirdre looked around the room. She felt that usual thrill of excitement at the beginning of a murder inquiry, the sense of focus and energy. It was enjoyable, she had guiltily confessed to another detective while celebrating cracking a case one night in Dublin after too many glasses of wine.

O'Rourke sat at the head of the table, with Inspector Brennan to his left. Beside him, Sergeant Mick Murphy, who didn't get on with Collins, but who had been nice to Deirdre since she moved to the Cork Division. Beside him Jack Clancy and John O'Regan; Clancy was another famous detective, his work in the Drugs Squad in Dublin in the 1990s and his battles with 'The General' were legendary. O'Regan seemed to be winding down to retirement, Deirdre thought, and she wondered if she could be paired with Clancy if Collins didn't work out.

Deirdre sat opposite Brennan, with Collins next to her. Beside Collins the veteran detectives, Tom Kelleher and Jim Murphy, old cronies of Collins' apparently.

'Okay,' O'Rourke said. 'Will you sum up where we are, Collins?'
Collins straightened up in his chair.

'Here's what I know,' Collins said and he cleared his throat. 'A call was made to Anglesea Street Station shortly after twenty hundred hours this evening about Helen O'Driscoll, 39 Ardlea Estate, Blackrock Road. A neighbour, Orlaith Moloney from 43 Ardlea Estate had become concerned about Helen's well-being. Two gardaí in Ballinlough, Michael Kingston and Seán Murray got a call from the station at 20:08 and arrived at 39 Ardlea Estate at 20:13.

'They entered the house at 20:18 by the front door using a spare key that another neighbour Hugh Delaney had. We need to talk to him, too. Soon after entering the house by the front door, Kingston and Murray found no sign of forced entry or a struggle in the house. However, they did find the body of Helen O'Driscoll – who hasn't been formally identified yet. Presumably sexually assaulted and murdered by asphyxiation – to be confirmed by the pathologist.

'The area was cordoned off and the Technical Unit have been carrying out forensic examinations since. The Assistant State Pathologist, Alice O'Callaghan, arrived at the house sometime around 21:50 and made an initial examination. The body was removed to CUH for a full post mortem soon after. Evan Murphy, aged eight, the son of the deceased was found hiding in a wardrobe of the house by his grandmother Nora Murphy at around 22:45. The husband of the deceased, Gregory Murphy is in Belgium working at present. He works for a pharmaceutical company and spends a lot of time travelling.'

'One thing I should add: there was a concert in the Marquee tonight and Ardlea is used as a short cut by people heading down towards the Marina, so there could have been a lot of people walking through the estate earlier, the killer among them. It seems he picked his moment well. That's it so far.

'Did I miss anything?' he asked Deirdre.

'No, that's it,' she replied. 'The crowd going down to the concert complicates things but there might be some video cameras outside some of the houses that might show something. One other thing: no sign of a break-in or no indications of a home robbery. Her purse was intact in her handbag hanging up in the hall.'

'Okay, good enough,' O'Rourke said. 'We're doing door-to-door already and we'll be doing more of that tomorrow, first thing. I won't keep ye too long now, tomorrow is going to be a long day. Collins and Donnelly: I want ye to look into Helen O'Driscoll. Contacts, friends, known and unknown associates, the works. She either knew the assailant or she didn't. I'm inclined to believe she did.

'Clancy and O'Regan: concentrate on the husband for now. Is he really in Belgium, could he have organised this, how were things between them? The whole story, top to bottom. If ye rule him out, I'll reassign ye.

'Kelleher and Murphy: gather every bit of detail from the neighbours, passers-by, cameras, dash cams. Review any information from last night first, and ye can have as many people as ye need in the morning to continue the door-to-doors. The crowd going to the concert complicates things but something might turn up. And why was the neighbour so concerned in the first place? Everything.

'Mick, can you set up all the comms systems we need, organise the press stuff and all that? The media are going to be all over this in the morning, they're already reporting it as a murder and the victim has been named on social media, before some of the family were even told – the bastards.'

O'Rourke looked around the table. He let the silence linger for a moment, which impressed Deirdre. That bound the team together and knitted them into a unit. She vowed to remember that trick when she would be a superintendent, leading such teams.

'We're going to get this guy,' O'Rourke said. 'We owe it to that woman and her family. Make it happen, people. Let's meet at 07:00 for a quick briefing in case anything turns up. We can review at 18:00 also unless you hear otherwise. Phones fully charged and close by at all times in case something happens during the night. Get some sleep. Ye're going to need it.'

CHAPTER 6

IN THE corridor outside the meeting room Deirdre asked Collins if he fancied a pint. She was wired and wanted to talk to him about the following day, to plan it out. Collins looked at his watch.

'Sure,' he said. 'Crane Lane is still open. The quickest way is to walk.'

Anglesea Street was quiet when they left the station. The night was balmy. They crossed the road.

'Where should we start tomorrow?' Deirdre said as they were passing the old school that had been converted into a courthouse.

'You mentioned you have a sister, are ye close?' Collins said.

'Very. Will we start with Helen's sister? What's her name again, Kathleen?'

'Yes, I think so. Kate said she's in CUH now formally identifying the body. We could talk to her first thing.'

'Sounds like a plan,' Deirdre said. 'Female friends, too, but the sister will know them. That woman who called it in, Orlaith Moloney. She seemed a good friend. That other neighbour, too, the man.'

'Hugh Delaney,' Collins said. 'Might be more of a friend to the husband.'

'We shouldn't rule anything out at this stage,' Deirdre said. It was a cliché, but still true. 'It could have been a break-in gone wrong. We should check previously unsolved rapes or near-misses from break-ins.'

'Sure,' Collins said. 'But that killing looked personal, to me.'

'I agree. A lot of anger. But you never know, no harm in checking.'

Collins took out his phone on Parnell Bridge. 'This is a long shot but I'm just ringing Blessing.' He rang the number but she didn't answer. He left a message for her to call him asap, he wanted a look at the phone and laptop.

'If the killer knew her,' he said, 'there might be something on the phone. She must have given it to the child before she hid him in the wardrobe.'

Deirdre bit her lip. She should have thought of that. *It isn't a competition,* she thought. *Get with the programme.*

'We might ask IT to compare what's on the phone versus the laptop,' he said. 'It was a Mac, so the chances are everything is backed up on her iCloud account.'

'As long as the laptop isn't the husband's.'

'I doubt that, he's working abroad, he'll have his with him.'

Deirdre nodded. Of course, it's hers. Collins was looking for the big sources of information first, so he can eliminate what he doesn't need. Impressive.

Collins' phone rang as they were crossing the South Mall and he answered it.

'What?' he said. 'You do? Already?' He stopped on the footpath and looked at Deirdre. 'Okay, thanks a million, Blessing, you're a star. We'll pick it up in ten minutes.' He closed the call.

'We're in luck. TU did the phone first so we can get in, we can pick them up now. Blessing said they already downloaded all the data so we don't have to worry about losing anything.'

Deirdre was disappointed about the pint. But the sense of excitement was powerful, too. They were going to get this fucker, she was sure of it.

CHAPTER 7

COLLINS AND Deirdre set up in a small meeting room on the first floor of the station to trawl through the phone and laptop records. Collins had been impressed with Deirdre earlier, especially her anger at seeing the body. He believed in the power of anger to motivate people. As long as it didn't cloud her thinking, but there was no indication of that. She appeared ambitious, too, which could be good or bad.

They looked at the most recent phone calls on the phone first. Her husband had called at 18.04 and left a voice message. There were two calls from her friend Orlaith, after that, again leaving voice messages. Another unanswered call from the husband, another voice message. It looked like the last actual phone conversation was at 15:23, when Helen had phoned Orlaith.

'Reasonable to assume the attack took place between 15:23 and 18.04,' Deirdre said.

'Yes,' Collins replied. 'And the blood was dry by 20:18. Let's see if there's anything on WhatsApp or social media after 15:23.'

Deirdre had just opened WhatsApp on the phone when it began to ring. A phone call, they could both see, from 'Kathleen'.

'Her sister,' Collins whispered.

'Should we answer?'

'No. But she knows. Why is she ringing?'

'She wants to hear her voice, maybe,' Deirdre said. They both looked at the phone vibrating on the desk, it was still on silent. Eventually it stopped. Then there was a text indicating a voice message had been left.

Collins clicked it on and put the phone on speaker. He felt like he was hearing something intimate between two people. Something he shouldn't be hearing. The message came through.

The woman was weeping.

'Helen. Oh, Helen. We love you. We always loved you. I'm so sorry.' The crying turned into a high pitched keen and was ended. Deirdre put her hand over her mouth. Collins looked at the window. A bluebottle was butting itself against the glass. He went over and opened it. The bluebottle flew out and there was quietness.

'What do you make of that?' Collins said, sitting back down.

'Let's keep an open mind,' Deirdre said. 'I'd like to hear it again.'

They listened to the message again.

'Could be anything,' Collins said. 'Maybe they had a row or Kathleen said something angry to her the last time they spoke.'

'Still, we should ask her tomorrow,' Deirdre said.

As if on cue, Collins' phone rang. He didn't recognise the number but on instinct he answered it.

'Is that Detective Collins?' A woman's voice which Collins recognised immediately.

'Speaking,' he said. 'Who is this?'

'This is Kathleen O'Driscoll, Helen O'Driscoll's sister. I know it's very late, detective, but I wonder if we could talk. It's about her death. I have some information.'

'It's not too late at all, Kathleen, I'm actually at work now. Where are you right now? I can go there.'

'I'm in the Kingsley Hotel, but I'd prefer not to meet here. I can go there.'

'I can have a squad car at the door in ten minutes to bring you here. I'm at Anglesea Street Garda Station.'

'That would be fine. I'll be at the door of the hotel in ten minutes.' She hung up. Collins looked at Deirdre.

'That who I think it is?'

'Yep,' Collins said. 'She says she has some information.'

KATHLEEN O'DRISCOLL stepped out from the back of the squad car in the rear car park of the station. She was in her late forties, with long dark hair. She was wearing an overcoat, which seemed incongruous to Collins during a heatwave. Under that a black trouser suit, cream blouse and black low-heeled shoes. Her eyes were rimmed and red and she held a tissue in her right hand.

Collins and Deirdre approached her. They had agreed in advance that Deirdre take lead on the interview.

'Kathleen, my name is Detective Sergeant Deirdre Donnelly and this is Detective Tim Collins. We're so sorry for your loss.' Deirdre shook the woman's hand.

Collins did likewise. 'My condolences,' he said. 'Please come this way.'

They led her to the lift which opened immediately.

'Can we get you anything?' Deirdre said as the door closed. 'Tea or coffee? A glass of water?' Collins pressed 3, they were bringing her to a quiet room at the front of the building. He stood aside from the two women.

'No, thank you. A cup of hot water, if you don't mind. I think I'm coming down with something.'

They had left two windows in the room open to try to cool it down, but it still felt stuffy to Collins when they walked in. It was called 'the good room' because it was where VIPs were brought by senior gardaí for discussions. It was not a formal interview room with the usual tone of adversarial confrontations and the paraphernalia to record them. It was carpeted, and on the right there was a small coffee table surrounded by three armchairs and a bookcase containing legal books and statutes. On the left was a good quality long table surrounded by six matching chairs. Collins led Kathleen O'Driscoll to the second chair from the end. He and Deirdre had left their notebooks and folders opposite her. Deirdre had placed a box of tissues on the table.

Collins was trying hard to get a read on the woman. She appeared impressively self-assured, despite the circumstances and the earlier phone call. He guessed a medical or legal background; professional and successful. The clothes, the posture, her height – she must have been close to six feet – all spoke of capability and drive. Even the fact that she had taken the initiative to be here at 1:15 in the morning spoke volumes to him.

'Can I take your coat?' he said to her. She thanked him and he hung it on a coat-rack near the door. With his back to her, he opened the Voice Memos App on his phone and pressed the red 'record' button. He picked up a landline phone on a console table and pushed three digits.

'Hi Katya, this is Tim Collins, and I'm in the good room. Can you send up a cup of boiling water, please, and a strong coffee and …' He looked at Deirdre and she shook her head 'no'. 'And water for three please? Thanks very much.' He sat beside Deirdre and placed the phone face down on the table.

Kathleen cleared her throat and began.

'I want an assurance that nothing of what I tell you here will be attributed to me and will be kept as quiet as possible. I'm only speaking to you with that guarantee.'

Deirdre gave a mock wince.

'We'll do the best we can on both counts, Kathleen,' she said. 'But if we are asked on oath or in a trial situation we can't lie. I'm sure you understand that. I can guarantee you that we will keep this conversation as quiet as possible. Anybody who doesn't absolutely need to know about it won't know about it. You have our assurances on that.'

Kathleen closed her eyes and exhaled.

'Very well. When Helen was young, she made some mistakes. She … had some issues in college. She became addicted to alcohol and drugs. By the time we found out, she was under the control of a man who was manipulating and coercing her. He was involved in the sale of drugs. My mother was so upset about it. Nothing like that ever happened to the family before, needless to say.'

Collins noticed the distaste in Kathleen's expression as she spoke. He wrote three words on his notepad: 'Addresses', 'Dates' and 'Record'.

'Anyway, things came to a head when we found out she was pregnant. I am five ...' she closed her eyes momentarily. '*Was* five years older than Helen and I was living in Dublin at the time with an aunt. Helen came to live with us and she went into rehab and got cleaned up and she had the baby given up for adoption some months later.'

Kathleen exhaled loudly. 'And I'm thinking now that her murder might have something to do with that. That the drug dealer she was involved with came looking for her and killed her. Or it had something to do with the baby, who would be twenty-one now.'

Deirdre gave her some space in case there was anything else she wanted to volunteer before the questions began.

'I suppose you have some questions,' Kathleen said. She directed this at Collins for some reason. He let Deirdre begin. He did have one question but there was no rush.

'Can you give us the name of the man who Helen was involved with in college?'

'His name was Robbie Wilkins. I don't know anything else about him.'

Collins wrote down the name. He didn't know it.

'Did he stay in touch with her or did something happen recently?'

'Helen told us he didn't stay in touch. He wanted nothing to do with the baby, which was probably just as well. It made the adoption easier for Helen, I think. But I do know she felt very guilty about it. When she met Greg a few years later, it got easier

I think; and then when Evan came along ...' At this she gasped and lowered her head and began to cry. Deirdre moved the box of tissues closer to her. Kathleen took one.

'Thank you,' she said. 'I have one question, myself. It's about Evan actually.'

'Go ahead,' Deirdre said.

'How much would Evan have heard?' Kathleen said. 'How much would he have known?'

Deirdre glanced at Collins. She wanted him to answer. He quickly decided not to dwell on Helen's death.

'Very little,' he said. 'I did think about that earlier, but I believe he would have known or heard very little. We brought one of our counsellors, Lorraine Crowley, in on this earlier when we were deciding how to get Evan out of the house in the best way. She is also a child psychologist, I can give you her number if you want. If you want to talk with her.'

'Thank you,' Kathleen said. 'Yes, I'd like to talk to her.'

'Can you give us some details about Helen and the baby?' Deirdre said. 'When would this have happened, where she was living, the date of birth etc.'

"Em, it was in 1997 when Helen came to live in Dublin. I had just qualified as a doctor and was doing a rotation. I think the baby was born in late October. I can get the exact date, I'm sure.'

'A boy or girl?'

'A boy, God he was beautiful. It broke Helen's heart, but she was still very vulnerable, in no position to bring up a child.'

'And where was Helen living before that?'

'Oh, in some dump around Barrack Street with *him*. We weren't even sure where, she didn't want us to know, to be honest. I think deep down she was ashamed.'

Shame, Collins thought. *How often that comes up.*

'Do you know if Helen was ever in trouble with the gardaí,

around this time?' Collins asked. He didn't want to go on a wild goose chase, but it could be useful.

'I … I'm not certain. We never knew anything at the time, but Helen did tell me a few years later about being in trouble. About being arrested. It was horrible, she said, but she didn't say much more.'

'We have a few difficult questions we have to ask you,' Deirdre said. 'They are purely routine, we must ask them, I'm afraid. Can I go ahead with them?'

'Yes.'

'How were things between Helen and her husband? What's he like?'

'Oh. I was wondering what you meant,' Kathleen said. 'Greg is a lovely man. We were delighted when they got together. He was a very steadying influence on her, but he's very kind, too, and great with Evan. He dotes on him.' She paused.

'As far as I know things were fine between them. He's away a lot, he works for a pharmaceutical company with a base in The Netherlands, so he's over there a lot and in China. But Helen never said anything and I think we'd have known.'

'Do you know of any problems she was having?' Deirdre said. 'Any threats or any worries about anything?'

'Not that I know of. I'm living in Dublin and she's in Cork but we talk regularly. Could this have not been a stranger, somebody who broke in?'

'We're not ruling anything in or out at this stage,' Deirdre said. 'We're investigating every possibility.'

Collins wrote the word 'regularly' on the notebook.

'Who were Helen's closest friends?' Deirdre said.

'Oh, she was very close to two old schoolmates Niamh O'Shea and Sara Bourke. And she's very friendly with one work colleague, Anna O'Leary.' Kathleen thought for a moment. 'And her neighbour,

Orlaith. Orlaith Moloney, they go walking a lot. They would be her main friends, I think. She was very friendly with Greg's sister, Paula, too.'

Collins wrote down the names. They had appeared on her Recent Calls and Messages.

'How about work colleagues?' Deirdre said.

'Apart from Anna, I'm not sure. She talks – talked – about her a lot. Jesus, I can't believe this is happening.'

'This is really helpful,' Deirdre said. 'We're nearly finished, actually.'

There was a knock at the door and Katya appeared with the drinks. She left the tray on the table and Collins placed the hot water in front of Kathleen. He poured three glasses of water and distributed them. He brought the coffee with him as he sat down again.

'Tim, do you want to ask Kathleen anything?' Deirdre said.

'Just a few questions, if you don't mind,' Collins said. Kathleen sipped from the glass of water.

'You live in Dublin, how did you get to Cork so quickly tonight?'

'Oh, my husband and I were visiting my mother, she hasn't been well.'

'When did ye get down, roughly?'

'We came down this afternoon,' Kathleen said. Collins noted the vagueness of that but he didn't want to pursue it, yet.

'And ye don't stay with your mother?'

'Oh,' Kathleen said and she looked flustered. 'My husband … we prefer to stay in a hotel, my mother's house isn't very big.' Collins noted the hesitation around who really wanted to stay in the hotel.

'You said earlier "when you found out Helen was pregnant",' he said. 'How did ye find out?'

Kathleen paused.

'We got a phone call telling us,' she said.

'Sorry, who got the call?'

'My mother. A man phoned my mother and told her Helen was pregnant and was a disgrace to the family. Can you imagine?'

'And did you think it was the father?' Collins said.

'We weren't sure. My mother didn't think so. The caller said some nasty things about Helen and the father. Helen especially.'

'Do you remember what kind of things?'

'He called her a slut and a whore. He called *him* a scumbag and a criminal. It was somebody educated, my mother said. That was the impression she got. But he was very angry, he was shouting down the phone.'

'Did she have any other boyfriends around that time? Somebody jealous, anything like that?'

'One or two, but nothing serious. Helen kept a lot of her life hidden from us at that time.'

'And before Greg, anybody serious, anybody who might hold a grudge?'

'No, Greg was definitely the first after the baby.'

'I have to ask this, I apologise in advance,' Collins said. 'But could there have been anybody else since Greg? Or recently?'

'No!' Kathleen said, angrily. Her face was flushed and she glared at Collins. 'No way! That's ... no way.'

'I'm sorry, but we have to ask these questions,' Collins said. He decided to change direction.

'Do you know any details about the adoption?' Collins asked. 'Did Helen ever follow-up or look for contact? Did the child – boy – ever make contact?'

'Not that I know of. Helen never said anything. Greg knew all about it, but I think they both just wanted to put it behind her.'

'You did the right thing in telling us,' Collins said. 'There may be no connection but it's always good to know these things. Now

I have a more personal question.'

'Personal?' Kathleen said, alarmed.

'Yes, when you phoned me we were actually going through Helen's phone. And we heard the message you left on the phone tonight, just before you called me.'

'Oh.' Kathleen reddened. 'I never thought.'

'So, what I wanted to know is why you made that call, and why you said you were sorry.'

'I'm her older sister. I was supposed to be looking after her. I never forgave myself for what happened her before, I ran away from all the conflict and went to Dublin. And now I've let her down again.' She lowered her eyes, her face set rigid.

'And why did you call her?'

'I wanted her to answer the phone. I wanted it all to be a bad dream.'

'But you had just identified the body.'

'That wasn't her! It wasn't her on that gurney, it wasn't my sister! My sister, my baby sister.'

Kathleen broke down in tears and Deirdre looked at Collins. He nodded. They had pushed her as far as they could. Anything else could wait.

CHAPTER 8

AT THE 7 a.m. briefing in Meeting Room 3 Deirdre informed the team about the late-night session with Kathleen O'Driscoll. She had practised on her way to work, getting the five main points right in her head.

Deirdre's favourite lecturer at Templemore Garda Training College had been Gavin Cuffe, a brilliant Glaswegian, who taught Information Studies. Everybody going into the class had expected some theoretical librarian rubbish that could never be applied in the job; how wrong they were. Cuffe managed to back up every aspect of the course by hard examples, some of them famous. She could hear him clearly, as she drove along the South Link from Ballincollig towards the station: 'Information is your fuel as a garda. You can't do one single thing without it, so treat it like manna from heaven.'

He had also taught them how to relay information and he believed that people could only take in between three and five pieces of information at a time. She put that in practice whenever she could and she wanted to impress O'Rourke, Collins and the others in situations like these.

'Did I leave anything out?' she asked Collins when she'd finished.

'No. Well done,' he said. 'Great summary.'

'What do you think we should do about it?' O'Rourke asked. She had prepared this, too.

'Myself and Collins can check up on it. The drugs, this Robbie Wilkins and the adoption. Shouldn't take too long. Maybe after we talk to her friends. It seems a long shot in fairness.'

'I agree. You okay with that, Collins?' O'Rourke said.

'Yeah. But I'd like to look a bit deeper into Kathleen O'Driscoll, too. I'm not convinced about her answers for bringing this all up. Seemed a bit of a red-herring to me.'

This surprised Deirdre. Collins had said nothing the night before. She would have to find out his rationale for this conclusion.

'Be careful with that, Collins,' O'Rourke said. 'She's just lost her sister, people react in all sorts of ways after a trauma like that. Be very discrete, okay? Kid gloves. And keep me informed.

'Forensics will be giving their initial analysis at the 6 p.m. briefing, they probably won't have much yet. Clancy and O'Regan have gone to Schiphol Airport to meet Greg Murphy, the husband, to bring him home. Dutch police escorted him from his hotel in Amsterdam to the airport and will be handing him over.'

O'Rourke checked his watch. 'That might have happened already. We can't rule anything out at this stage so everything by the book, people. All Is dotted and Ts crossed. I'll see you all here at eighteen hundred hours.'

DEIRDRE WAS hungry after the briefing and suggested they get some food at Tony's Deli around the corner and plan their day. It was too early to begin phoning people.

She never could eat first thing in the morning, which isn't ideal when you're a garda.

Outside the deli in the queue on the street, she broached the subject of Kathleen O'Driscoll.

'Why do you think that was a red-herring last night?'

'I dunno. It was all a bit odd. A few hours after she finds out her sister has been killed, she rings us with something that happened over twenty years ago? Why not wait until today to talk to us? Makes no sense.

I couldn't sleep last night so I came in early. I went through Helen's phone. Guess how many times Helen phoned Kathleen in the last six months?'

'I dunno. Twenty? Thirty?'

'Once. One phone call to an only sister in six months. Nothing on her WhatsApp or Messages. Guess how often Kathleen phoned Helen?'

Deirdre looked at him.

'Never, not once,' he said. 'She told us she phoned Helen "regularly" but there's nothing about all this which seems regular. We have to find out more about her.'

'The friends might know more,' Deirdre said.

'That's what I was thinking. I made up a list from last night and I have the phone numbers ready.' Collins checked his old battered notebook. 'I think Niamh O'Shea is in Waterford and Sara Bourke is in Dublin so we might phone them. We should meet Anna O'Leary and Orlaith Moloney, they're both local.'

'Jesus, Collins, do you ever sleep?'

Collins shrugged. He leaned closer to her and lowered his voice.

'I've been suffering from insomnia for a while. It comes and goes. Long story but it's one of the symptoms of PTSD which I've had since a case a couple of years ago.'

'The Butcher. I heard about that.' Deirdre was surprised that Collins was being so open.

'Yeah. For some reason he couldn't kill his victims while they were awake, only when they were asleep. I think it was a form of torture. He told all the victims that when they fell asleep he'd kill them, including me. Seeing Helen's body triggered another sleepless night.'

Deirdre didn't know what to say to that, so she said nothing. They were at the top of the queue. Collins ordered a double espresso and a croissant. He said he'd eaten earlier. Deirdre felt self-conscious so she ordered a small breakfast roll, even though she felt like a large one. This Collins was beginning to surprise her, maybe the partnership wouldn't be a washout after all.

The Safe Place Chat Room 22/Strictly Members Only (LOL)

Rodger: *Haha, I see another Stacy has bitten the dust.*

Meeks1964: *That the Cork one in Blackrock?*

Rodger: *Yeah, any info, Meeks?*

Meeks1964: *No apart from it's the way all foids have to go unless they play ball and give us what we want.*

Rodger: *4sure, but they WILL play ball if that's the alternative. Anybody know anything about that Stacy????*

Carlow Stud: *Hope she died roaring, the bitch*

Detroitstud: *Kill them all!*

Swordsman: *Fuck them all!*

Rodger: *Any info? Anyone????*

Rogue1: *Might do but hush hush.*

Grand Gentleman (admin): *I'm shutting down this stream. Go to <<The Very Safe Place Chat Room 12>> if anyone wants to chat about this.*

Stream closed for comments now ...

Chapter 9

It was difficult to get anything useful from Niamh O'Shea. Helen's name had not yet been given to the media so Collins, who was taking lead, had to break the news to her. She was so upset that she couldn't talk. Her husband came on the phone and demanded to know what was going on, and who Collins was. Collins told him about Helen's death and how they needed to talk to all her friends about her, that he and Deirdre would ring back at 4 p.m. and interview Niamh then. The husband said he would be there and take the call and they could talk on speaker, that they weren't to talk to Niamh without him being present.

With that in mind, Collins phoned Sara Bourke and broke the news to her as gently as he could. She, too, was distraught. A housemate of hers, Trish, came on the line and Collins explained the situation and said they would phone again at 5 p.m. to talk to Sara.

Deirdre phoned Orlaith Moloney and she agreed to meet them immediately at her home in Ardlea.

There was garda tape around Helen O'Driscoll's house as they passed. The blinds were down in all the windows. The marquee had been removed from outside the front door. Two gardaí were sitting in a squad car outside. Collins and Deirdre saluted them. The street was empty of children or neighbours. It was not a day for play or gardening. Deirdre pulled in outside Number 43. The front door opened as they were walking up the path. *Orlaith had been looking out for them*, Deirdre thought. *Of course she was.*

Orlaith was a low-sized woman. She was in her late forties, Deirdre guessed. Fit looking and deeply tanned. She wore pale blue slacks and flats; a loose Spanish-looking patterned top. She was wearing gold and silver earrings and a simple necklace to match. Her hair was short and she had allowed the natural grey to come through. Her eyes were puffy from crying.

Deirdre shook hands with her first at the front door. Then Collins.

'My deepest condolences,' he said. 'Thank you for agreeing to meet us.'

Deirdre winced. She should have sympathised, too. She had a lot to learn from this old guy, PTSD or not.

'Not at all,' Orlaith said. 'Whatever I can do. Helen is ... was ...' She teared up. Having to change that tense gets people every time. Deirdre had seen it too often. She felt tired. *Get your game face on, girl.*

A man entered the room. He was well-groomed, wearing a white shirt, navy trousers, and black brogues. It looked as though his hair had been dyed, but his moustache was well on its way to grey. The skin on his face looked so shiny that it could have been buffed. A Rolex on this left hand completed the picture of affluence.

'This is Jim, my husband. Is it okay if he sits in?' Orlaith addressed the question to Collins who said: 'Not at all. It's just a chat, we want to get a picture of Helen.' He and Deirdre refused tea or coffee.

The living room was spotless and sunny. A large L shaped room. Pictures of three children, two girls and a boy at various ages on the dresser and mantelpiece. The most recent looking photo was of a young woman's graduation with a beaming mother and father. Deirdre and Collins were directed to two armchairs. Orlaith and Jim sat opposite in a two-seater sofa with flowery upholstery.

'We won't keep you long,' Collins began. 'First off all, my name is Detective Tim Collins and this is my colleague Detective Sergeant Deirdre Donnelly and we are part of the investigating team.' Deirdre noticed Collins' wording was very careful not to upset Orlaith.

'Can you tell us a little about yourself, Orlaith? Just to get going.'

'Myself?' she said.

'Where you're from, a little bit about your family, your and Jim's family, when did ye move here, that sort of thing.'

Orlaith took a deep breath.

'I'm from Douglas originally, my maiden name was O'Toole. My father was an engineer at the airport, my mother was a teacher. They're both retired now. I have one brother and two sisters. My brother is in Canada, my sisters both live in Cork.'

Collins smiled. He just wanted to get her going, Deirdre realised, on comfortable topics.

'After my leaving cert I went to UCC to study languages, I've always loved them. French and German; then I did the HDip and became a teacher. I met Jim in college and we've been together since. Jim did Commerce and works in finance on the Mall. We got married in 1993 and Sue came along in 1997. That's her, there,' she said pointing to the graduation photo.

'She looks like you,' Collins said. Orlaith nodded.

'Then James in 1999 and Ellen in 2002. She'll be doing her leaving cert next year. James is in Third-Med, he's the brainy one.'

'And when did ye move here? It's a fairly new estate, I'd say.'

'2002,' Jim said. 'Just before the Celtic Tiger. We were lucky in that.'

'Is that when you met Helen?' Collins said, putting the attention back on Orlaith. She sighed.

'Yes. She and Greg moved in a few years after us. We hit it off from the beginning. I got her to sign up for St Michael's Tennis Club and now we ... more recently we used to walk a lot together. Hill climbing, we joined the Blackrock Walking Club.' Jim put his hand on Orlaith's arm to steady her.

'I know this is very hard,' Collins said. 'But how would you describe Helen as a person?'

'She was so kind and thoughtful. I always said she put other people before herself. Like, whenever we went out, she'd go to where I wanted to go. And when I got tennis elbow, she gave it up too, even though she was a far better player.

'She was a great mother, needless to say. She worshipped Evan – God that poor child.' She put her head in her hands.

'Take your time, do you want a break?'

'No. Thank you.'

'She was a teacher like yourself.'

'That's right, history and English. Saint Anne's.'

'Were you aware of anything bothering Helen? Anyone she was in conflict with or any worries she had?'

'I didn't know whether to tell you this or not, but she didn't get on with her family. Her sister and her mother. They had some kind of a falling out.'

'Do you know when that happened?'

'I think it was a few years ago, she never liked to talk about it, but then Evan couldn't get to meet his cousins or anything and she'd mention it. Apparently something happened and her mother took her sister's side.'

'Do you know what it was?'

'Not really, but it had something to do with her brother-in-law she told me, once.'

The skin on Deirdre's neck began to tingle and she tried not to change her demeanour. She could sense Collins doing the same.

'That's Kathleen's husband.'

'Yes.' Orlaith looked at her husband and he nodded. 'Helen told me when we were walking in Italy and we'd had too much wine to drink. There was a waiter and she said he looked very like Kathleen's husband. His name is William, I don't know his surname.'

Collins did not react. Deirdre could sense him willing her to continue.

'Helen suggested … she never came right out and said it … that something happened between herself and William. Years ago, now; before she met Greg. She felt terrible about it and she told him that it could never happen again, but he wouldn't accept it. He wanted to have an affair with her and he was blackmailing her into it. If she wouldn't agree he'd tell the family everything.'

'Go on.'

'I don't know the details but I think he was pressurising her again lately and she got some legal advice. This was about four years ago when we went to Cinque Terre.'

'Did she say anything since?'

'No. I brought it up once or twice, and she said she had exaggerated everything in Italy but I was sure she didn't.'

'Did Kathleen know?'

'I think so. I was over in Helen's house one day a couple of years ago and Kathleen phoned her and I could hear the screaming down the line. It was terrifying, I must say. Helen didn't want to talk about it. It's the first thing I thought of last night.'

'When was this phone call? Can you remember?

'It was the summer before last. I remember because we were planning a trip to London for some Christmas shopping. We used to go to London on the last week in November every year for Christmas shopping.' Orlaith closed her eyes and left out a sob.

She stood up and left the room. Jim followed her.

Collins looked at Deirdre and raised his eyebrows.

After a few minutes, Jim returned to the room. Deirdre and Collins stood up.

'She's very upset,' Jim said. 'She said she might be able to talk later.'

'That's fine,' Collins said. 'Please tell her we said thanks. She did the right thing, telling us. I know how difficult it must have been but we need to know these things. She has Deirdre's number, if there's anything else, she can contact us any time.'

'She blames herself,' Jim said. 'She's wondering if there was something she could have done.'

'Please tell her she has nothing to blame herself about,' Collins said. 'There was nothing she could have done. She was a good friend, at least Helen had that.'

CHAPTER 10

WHEN THEY returned to the station, the car park was shimmering with heat and Collins could smell melted tar. He reckoned he would have to change his shirt before the day was through. He was impressed with Deirdre, she seemed to be naturally cool.

He would have preferred to go to the Kinglsey Hotel immediately and speak to Kathleen O'Driscoll before she and her husband had time to prepare their stories further. What he really wanted was to get stuck into William Hughes, but that would have to wait.

O'Rourke had called a briefing for noon, so Collins had just enough time to get a coffee from across the road. The coffee in the station was undrinkable. Deirdre had kept a chair for him beside her.

There was a palpable air of excitement in Meeting Room 3, that heady mix of purpose Collins tried to detach himself from whenever he could. His father had tried to interest him in fox hunting when he was young, but the blood lust he felt from the riders and hounds repelled him. Or perhaps it was his natural affinity for foxes, their beauty and lore. He wasn't sure. But there was a big difference in chasing a vixen with thirty huntsmen and a pack of hounds than hunting down a brutal murderer who could kill again if they failed.

'I told the super what Orlaith told us about Helen's brother-in-law, William Hughes,' she said as he sat down.

'And what did he say?'

'Helen's husband confirmed it too. Clancy is going to fill us in on that, now.'

Collins sipped his coffee and waited. As far as he was concerned, Jim Clancy was the best detective in the station, maybe the division. He glanced over to Clancy and O'Regan at the far end of the table. O'Regan saluted him and Collins saluted him back.

Clancy's head was stuck in his notes and he was writing frantically.

O'Rourke entered the room with Brennan and sat at the head of the table. He looked cool and well-groomed in his superintendent uniform.

'Okay, everyone,' O'Rourke said. 'We've had some further intel this morning that I wanted to share with the group. Detective Clancy here will brief us on the interview with Greg Murphy, the victim's husband.'

Clancy cleared his throat and began.

'Myself and Detective O'Regan flew to Schiphol Airport from Cork this morning on the 06:05 flight along with Tony Murphy, Greg Murphy's brother. We met Greg Murphy at Schiphol in a room near the departure gate and accompanied him home. He came directly here with us from the airport, arriving at 10:17.'

'The main piece of information we received from him related to a William Hughes, Helen O'Driscoll's brother-in-law, married to her sister Kathleen. Mr Murphy alleged that Mr Hughes had pursued Helen sexually and had harassed her for years. Something had happened between them a long time ago, when Helen was vulnerable having had a baby and Hughes wanted to rekindle it, but Helen said no.

'Mr Murphy said that there was a rift in Ms O'Driscoll's family as a result of this. Her sister Kathleen took her husband's side and said that Helen had, in fact, sexually harassed Mr Hughes. Apparently, their mother also took the side of Kathleen.

'When asked if he knew if Mr Hughes had been in contact with Helen recently, Mr Murphy said he didn't think so, but that Helen was terrified of him. He had made sexual and violent threats to her in the past. He felt that if there had been any contact she would have told him.

'So, we're now following up on this William Hughes to see if there's anything on him. Any questions?'

Deirdre said: 'How was Greg Murphy?'

'He appeared very upset. He cried a lot in Schiphol when he met his brother and he cried a lot during the flight home. He was more composed in the interview and was livid about the harassment of his wife.'

'Okay,' O'Rourke said. 'Thanks Jim. We have another update from Detective Donnelly who, along with Collins, interviewed a friend of the victim this morning.'

Deirdre went to the podium and spoke without notes and gave an account of the interview. She didn't draw any conclusions or make any suppositions; she just gave the facts as they were presented to her and Collins.

'Thanks Deirdre,' O'Rourke said.

'Do you think there's anything in this baby and adoption connection, Collins?' Clancy asked. Collins was annoyed that he hadn't asked Deirdre, who was still at the podium but he didn't let it show.

'We need to look into it, obviously,' Collins said. 'But why would this Robbie Wilkins character turn up now after nearly twenty years? The sexual nature of the attack and its brutality points more to an obsession like the one we heard about Hughes. But we can't rule out some kind of opportunistic attack too, maybe we should look at older cases with similar MOs.'

'We're not ruling anything in or out,' O'Rourke said. 'All avenues of inquiry are open but this development about the brother-in-law has to be fully investigated. Clancy and O'Rourke will follow up with him immediately and check his whereabouts, etc. Collins and Donnelly will follow up with the sister, but be discrete, we don't want any drama. Kelleher and Murphy will look into the adoption and this character, Wilkins. Mick Murphy will arrange to get the details of any similar MOs. With a bit of luck, we'll have something from forensics at six.'

Collins was expecting that Clancy and O'Rourke would be assigned to interview Hughes and he and Deirdre would continue with Kathleen, having already met her. He looked forward to meeting this Hughes.

'Do we know when the removal is?' Collins asked the room. That would interfere with meeting Kathleen but it would also offer an opportunity to observe the family.

'Not for a couple days,' Mick Murphy said. 'The pathologist doesn't want to release the body yet.'

That suited Collins just fine. He and Deirdre could get to Kathleen that afternoon.

He made the call immediately after the meeting but Kathleen's phone was turned off.

At his desk, he got news that O'Rourke was looking for him. Deirdre was waiting outside O'Rourke's office.

'Did you phone her?' she said.

'Yes, the phone was off. I texted too. I think we should go out there and turn up the heat. Clancy and O'Regan will be on to the husband too.'

'Let's see what the super says. I think he's on a conference call with Dublin.'

Collins knew that Deirdre would not rock the boat, it was why they had paired her with him. But he was still disappointed. He looked at his watch.

Five minutes later O'Rourke's secretary called them in. He was busily tapping at his computer when they sat down opposite him.

'What do you think, Collins?' he said, without looking up.

'We need more information. That's either going to come from him – which is unlikely if he's guilty – or somewhere else. We need his movements, whereabouts, recent behaviour, phone access, any criminal record or any accusations against him, the works. He needs a wake-up call and quickly, before he can destroy evidence or create false trails. This is murder, no matter who they are.'

O'Rourke stopped tapping at the keyboard. He looked up and rubbed his chin.

'Okay, let's be clear, Collins. You are dealing with the sister. We need more information about the adoption stuff to rule out any connection. You can ask her why she didn't mention the links to her husband and the family fall-out. She will fob you off. You will report this back to me. Are we clear?'

'Yes, sir.' Collins said, knowing it was the answer he wanted. Ostensibly, anyway. If there was trouble, O'Rourke could now avoid any fall out and put all the blame on Collins.

'Stay away from the husband, Collins. Clancy and O'Regan have him.'

'Yes, sir,' Collins said and O'Rourke glared at him.

'Donnelly, keep an eye on him. I'll see you both at six, if not before.'

DEIRDRE DROVE them to the hotel which was on the western edge of the city. She parked right in front of the main entrance door and noticed Clancy and O'Regan sitting just inside it. The lobby behind them was busy, expansive and bright. People were eating late lunches; those by the windows overlooking the river. Collins pulled over two stools. Clancy and O'Regan had commandeered large armchairs.

'We tried the room,' O'Regan said. 'No answer.'

'Give us the wife's number,' Clancy said.

'Sure,' Collins said and he took out his phone. Clancy looked surprised but said nothing. He dialled the number.

'Turned off,' he said.

'What have you got on Hughes?' Collins said.

'He's connected,' O'Regan said. 'Big knob in Dun Laoghaire: yacht club, golf club, the works. His brother is a barrister, a former attorney general. We've already been warned by O'Rourke.'

'Really?' Collins said. 'He told us to go hard on the sister, give her the works, bring her in if necessary.'

'Haha,' Clancy said and then his attention was drawn to two people approaching. He stood up and the others followed his example.

A heavy-set man in an expensive suit and a younger woman approached. Collins recognised them. Frank Cremin and his daughter Patricia of Cremin, Halley and Foster Solicitors, the most prestigious and expensive legal firm in Cork.

'Detectives,' Frank Cremin said, not deigning to introduce himself. 'Excellent to have you all together so I don't have to repeat myself. For the record. My firm are now representing Ms Kathleen O'Driscoll Hughes and her husband Mr William Hughes in the matter of the tragic death of her sister and I am instructed to inform you that my clients will not be speaking to you about this matter until after the funeral. At that time, any interactions whatsoever between the gardaí and my clients will come through my office. Is that clear?'

There was a momentary pause. Collins took out his phone and held it out as through recording.

'For the record,' he said. 'Can you please identify yourself? Do you have a business card or some other means of identification, so we know which office to contact?'

'Detective Collins,' Cremin said. 'I'm aware of your reputation, but any intimidation of our clients or ourselves will be noted and reported with consequences. Am I clear?'

'Oh, this isn't intimidation,' Collins replied, calmly. 'But for the record, the death of Helen O'Driscoll was not a tragedy, it was a brutal murder and rape.' Collins looked at the woman. 'Or should I say a brutal rape, followed by a brutal murder.' He looked back at Cremin. 'And we will find out who raped and murdered that woman in her own home and we will bring them to justice. Whoever's office we have to go through and whatever the consequences. Am *I* clear?'

'You'll be hearing about this,' Cremin said and he turned on his heels. The daughter followed him.

Clancy laughed.

'Nice one, Collins. Don't think I ever saw a face go as red as that.'

'Fuck him,' Collins said. 'This isn't some property deal or a business transaction in the yacht club. He's on our turf now.'

CHAPTER 11

DEIRDRE DROVE them back to the station. She and Collins did not speak much on the journey. She put Collins' reaction to the solicitors down to macho bravado, but what if the anger behind it was something else? An anger aimed at the man who did the murder? She wondered why she, herself, was not as angry – should she be? She also wondered if she should react to the outburst, or do or say something about it. She decided not to.

They phoned Niamh O'Shea first and her husband did most of the talking. Deirdre asked the questions, keeping things calm and trying to cajole information from Niamh.

'Niamh, did Helen ever mention anybody who was threatening her?' she said.

'You don't have to answer,' her husband said on the speaker-phone. 'You don't have to get involved.'

'Jesus, she was my friend, Senan. My best friend. I'm already involved.'

There was a pause on the line. Deirdre looked at Collins and he gave her the thumbs up.

'Her brother-in-law was harassing her about ten years ago,' Niamh said. 'His name is Hughes. He was trying to force her into an affair. What a creep, not to mention being her sister's husband.

'When Kathleen found out, he said that Helen had seduced *him* and he was sorry about the whole thing. She went ballistic and blamed Helen. I don't know if I should mention this, but Helen was a bit wild in college and she had a baby she gave up for adoption. Kathleen threw everything at her, the whole thing, making out like she was some kind of slut, after every man who walked by, which she wasn't.

'Anyway, Hughes wouldn't let up, the bastard, even after she married Greg. He plagued her with nasty messages and he sent her pictures and videos, too. That he took when they were together. He was blackmailing her, basically.'

'What kind of pictures and videos?'

'You know, of them having sex and photos of her naked.'

'Did you ever see any of the messages or pictures?' Collins asked.

'God, no,' Niamh said.

'Do you know,' Deirdre said, 'if there was any recent contacts by him?'

'I didn't hear anything about that. But if I had to guess who did this, it'd be him.'

Another silence. The sound of crying.

'Niamh, this is Tim Collins here. Can you tell me a bit more about Helen's time in college, about the man she was involved with then, the father of the baby?'

'Oh, he was another creep, he had her wrapped around his finger. Me and Sara kind of lost touch with her around that time. I was in Mary I in Limerick and Sara was in St Pat's in Dublin. But we met him a few times, and he treated her like dirt. Dumping him was the best thing she ever did.'

'Did she ever look into the adoption details?' Collins said. 'Or try to make contact or anything?'

'No. Not that I heard, anyway. But she did say once that she would like Evan to get to know his brother eventually. We should do that, love. We should find out who the baby is. Shouldn't we?'

'We'll see,' her husband said. 'Maybe. In a while. I think we might wrap this up now, it's been a tough day.'

'Niamh, one other thing,' Collins said. 'Apart from you and Sara, are there any other people that Helen was close to, that we might speak to about her?'

'Áine O'Leary, she's very friendly with her at work and Orlaith, her neighbour. She phoned me earlier, she's lovely. And Helen was pally enough with Blake, too. Ye should talk to Blake.'

'What's his surname?' Collins said.

'Ormsby. Blake Ormsby. They used to be friends in college.'

'O-R-M-S-B-Y?' Collins said.

'Yes.'

'If there's anything else,' Deirdre said. 'Don't hesitate to phone. I'm texting you my number now. And once again we're so sorry for your loss.'

'Thank you. Thanks.' She hung up.

Collins wrote the words 'Blake Ormsby. College?' on his notebook.

'Well?' Deirdre said.

'More information,' Collins said. 'Him sending her those messages and pictures shows a loss of control, which I was hoping for. We have to find those, they will look good in court. Not to mention give us leverage when we talk to him – which we will, whatever Mr Cremin says.'

THE OTHER phone calls to Sara Bourke and Greg Murphy's sister Paula did not add anything. They searched Helen's phone and laptop for the messages and videos from William Hughes but couldn't find them.

There were messages, phone calls and WhatsApp messages from somebody in her Contacts List called BO. One contained a poor quality photo of a young Helen O'Driscoll and a blond young man in a bar with a table of drinks glasses in front of them. Helen was clearly drunk, her eyes were glassy and unfocused. The message from BO was: *Look what I found, we had great laughs.* The reply from Helen was: *God, I was out of it, so glad I don't drink any more.*

'That stood out for me,' Collins said. 'I wondered if it was somebody called BO or what. I guess it's Blake Ormsby. We should meet him and see what he says. I still want to get to the bottom of her links with this character Robbie Wilkins.'

AT THE 6 p.m. briefing Collins was sitting in his usual seat beside Deirdre. Word had gotten around of his interaction with the solicitors and he was being slagged about it. Deirdre didn't think the comments were funny, it was the usual laddish banter she had grown to hate.

When O'Rourke and Brennan entered the room there was a hush. O'Rourke scowled at Collins when he passed, Brennan ignored him.

Clancy reported that Cremin, Halley and Foster Solicitors were representing Kathleen O'Driscoll and William Hughes and were refusing interviews until after the funeral.

'I think we should talk to that pair, now,' Collins said. 'This is a murder investigation, we can't let this guy dictate what we can and can't do.'

'I agree with Collins,' Clancy said. 'Is there any hope of pushing for interviews?'

'Not for now,' O'Rourke said. 'Mr Cremin has been in touch with us and has made a complaint against Detective Collins here.'

Deirdre was surprised to see the superintendent smirking at this news. Looking around, she saw that several others were smiling too.

'I was present at that altercation,' Clancy said. 'And Collins only asked him to identify himself so we would know which solicitors' office to contact. Cremin is completely over-reacting.'

'Anything to add, Collins?'

'Not really, superintendent. What is the nature of the complaint?'

'The usual rubbish in legalese, but will you stay away from the family for now, like a good man?'

'Yes, of course sir. One important piece of information. A friend of Helen's, Niamh O'Shea, informed us today that Hughes had sexually harassed Helen for years and sent her threatening and sexually explicit videos and messages to blackmail her. We searched the phone and laptop but didn't find them yet. I think myself and Deirdre should follow up on that tomorrow.'

'Yes, of course,' O'Rourke said. 'Will you go through the system and get in touch with Dublin about Hughes, Mick?'

'Yes, superintendent,' Mick Murphy said.

'Those videos and photos would look good in court,' O'Rourke said. 'We're not giving up on Hughes, Clancy, rest assured on that. We just can't interview him yet.'

Deirdre was impressed that O'Rourke used almost exactly the same expression as Collins. They were both thinking in terms of what they needed for a conviction. She resolved to ask Collins about it later.

Tom Kelleher reported that nothing concrete had turned up from the door-to-door interviews. They had looked through five house videos and one dash cam video so far. He complained that he wasn't given enough gardaí to call around to all the houses and they would have to do more interviews on the following day.

The fact that dozens – if not hundreds – of music fans had walked through the estate before the Marquee concert made their task much more difficult and they were widening their search to the Blackrock Road and Monaghan Road, but they wouldn't be finished that for another two days.

'It occurs to me that the time of the murder isn't a coincidence,' Clancy said. 'Which could mean it was well planned in advance and not a random attack.'

'We need a good photo of Hughes and a physical description too,' Collins said. 'So, we can compare him to anybody on those dash cams and house videos.'

'We'll get those,' O'Rourke said. 'But we have to keep an open mind, too. We have to look at all leads and all lines of enquiry, even if they don't involve Hughes. Anything else?'

Mick Murphy reported that a hotline number had been set up as well as a Twitter hashtag but nothing concrete had turned up yet. They were still following up on some calls, but he needed more staff to work with.

O'Rourke stood up to close the meeting.

'Okay. As you all know, the first days in these kinds of investigations can be tough, without any forensics or major breakthroughs, but we need to keep plugging away at it. You all have your assignments, the main thing is we do everything thoroughly and by the book and we don't jeopardise our chances of a conviction when it comes to court.'

CHAPTER 12

THE FOLLOWING morning, Collins and Deirdre phoned more of Helen's friends, but nothing came of those calls.

The initial scene of the crime briefing by the Technical Unit at 2 p.m. was crowded. Paul Gubbins, Blessing Nzekwe and Alison Cronin were sitting at the top table. A projector was beaming the first slide of a presentation, entitled 'SOC 18 June 2018, Ardlea Court, Cork: preliminary findings'.

The Technical Unit people went through the presentation slowly and in great detail. There were thirty-five slides and it took over an hour. Deirdre found it utterly depressing, the sordid and useless death of another woman.

It looked like there wasn't much help to the investigation, yet. Gubbins was careful to preface the report that it was too soon to make any firm conclusions, that samples were still being tested and reports of DNA would take several more days to come back from the laboratory. There was no indication of semen on the body and they had tested several possible ligatures for blood or skin traces, without success.

Until they had samples of suspects, the family and a cleaning woman, they could not yet draw any conclusions about fingerprints.

At the end, Gubbins also reported on the assistant state pathologist's preliminary report. Toxicology tests were not yet completed, which made any conclusions premature. Cause of death was asphyxia, using a thin ligature, the thyroid cartilage and hyoid bone were both fractured. The victim had severe vaginal and vaginoperineal lacerations; the pattern of injuries had forensic significance in that they were caused by an object with a circumference of 2–3cm. No such object was found at the crime scene.

'For fuck's sake,' Deirdre said, quietly. She saw Collins close his eyes.

Ending the presentation, Gubbins asked for 'pertinent questions'. Deirdre was beginning to dislike this man.

Collins asked if there was any information about the nature of the object that caused the lacerations.

'If there had been information of that nature in the report, detective …' Gubbins said. 'I would have stated it.'

'Doctor,' Deirdre said, 'does the nature of this crime scene and the MO remind you of any other similar scenes in your experience?'

Gubbins looked at her appraisingly.

'That's a very good question. There was an unsolved attempted rape last year. The victim was unconscious and lived, but she could not identify her assailant. Her name is Thompson, as I recall. Any further questions?'

There were none. When the Technical Unit people left, O'Rourke stood up.

'Now, as you just heard, the report of the Technical Unit was disappointing given that very little usable evidence has turned up so far. But that, in itself, is usable and it means we have to work even harder to get justice for Helen.'

Chapter 13

Deirdre found out the unsolved rape case that Gubbins had referred to involved a woman called Lea Thompson, who had been assaulted in her apartment on Harty's Quay the year previously. No DNA, no fingerprints, no suspects, nothing. It was officially still under investigation but, in reality, it would probably never be solved.

She told Collins about it in the station's cafeteria. It was almost 9 p.m.

'I remember that case,' Collins said. 'The big mystery was how the attacker got in. It was on the first floor of an apartment block in Rochestown. He had to be able to get in the front door of the building and also into her apartment. The front door had swipe card access and the apartment door was by a key. The CCTV system had gone down an hour or two before the attack; they never found out how that happened. Only for a friend calling to the front door and ringing her buzzer and phoning her, they reckoned she'd have been killed.

'They suspected one of the building's security men for a while but he had an alibi and no record. They never charged him – or anybody else.'

'We need to read that file,' Deirdre said. 'I'm heading home now. We do that tomorrow?'

'Yeah, we need to look up that old case with the drugs, too. See you in the morning.'

Collins went back to his desk in the open-plan area on the second floor. He connected Helen's mobile phone to his laptop and made a call to Philip Hegarty, an unlikely computer genius, who owed Collins some favours and had been helping him with investigations for years. Hega had been pressured to take part in a computer scam by a low-life cousin and Collins pulled some strings to prevent charges against him. Now Hega was officially a consultant to the Garda Síochána, which meant he could charge for his time.

'Hi Collins, how's tricks?' Hega said.

'Can you download the hard drive of a phone to scan through it for me?' Collins asked.

'Sure, no bother, but a lot of the stuff on Apps are in the cloud and they wouldn't show up.'

'How would we get hold of them?'

'There's an App for that, too. Is it an iPhone?'

'Yes, an iPhone 7, I think.'

'That makes it a bit trickier. iOS is hard to get around. Can you connect it to your laptop and hook it up to Wi-Fi?'

'I've done that already.'

'Okay, I'm going into your laptop now through the system I told you about before. Are you keeping your software up to date, like I told you?'

'I think it did an update the other day.'

'Yeah, right. I can see the phone now. What are you looking for?'

'Text messages or WhatsApp messages, maybe. Or voice messages. The woman who owned the phone was called Helen O'Driscoll. A guy called William Hughes was sexually harassing her and I'm wondering if there is any proof. You might have to go back a few years.'

'Okay, this will take about twenty minutes. I'll ring you back when it's done.'

Collins unlocked his drawer and took out a sleeve of Nespresso capsules. He picked up a bottle of water from his desk and walked to the other end of the room, where Clancy was poring over sheets of paper. A stack of eight or nine files was on his left, all bound in brown folders held together with elastic bands.

Collins didn't ask Clancy what was in the files. They looked like legal documents. He waved the sleeve of capsules.

'I brought you these,' he said. 'I took a few of yours last week.'

Clancy looked up and scowled.

'Who else knows?' he said.

'That you have an Espresso machine? Clancy, you're surrounded by twenty-five professional detectives. Everybody knows, you always under-estimate people.'

'And they never fail to let me down.' He took the sleeve.

'Can I have a double?' Collins said. 'If you don't mind.'

'Make it yourself,' Clancy said and opened the drawer.

As Collins was making the coffee, Clancy said: 'Aren't you going to ask?'

'Okay. What are the files?'

'The last ten cases that the Cremins have defended. I want to get a feel for them, we're going to be going up against them soon.'

Good move, Collins thought.

'Anything from the phone or laptop?' Clancy said.

'Nothing much yet, I'm running a search programme there now. Do you want one?' Collins said, indicating the machine.

'No. I spoke to O'Rourke today. I told him I should be the one to interview Hughes and you should be there too.'

'What did he say?'

'He said he'd think about it, but he'll agree. You okay with that?'

'Yeah, but I think it's better myself and Donnelly do the sister. Better to have a woman there.'

'Fine.'

'What do you think of Donnelly?' Collins said.

'She's good. Tough enough, I'd say. A bit young but I think she has her eye on promotion before getting the job done.' Collins had suspected the same thing, but had decided to work on her, try to bring her on.

'What do you think of her?' Clancy said.

Collins chose his words carefully. He didn't want to be disloyal.

'She doesn't take it personally enough,' he said. 'Not like us.'

'A lot of good it does us.' Clancy said. 'You finished?'

'Thanks,' Collins said, putting the machine back in the drawer. He was aware he was being dismissed.

'Next time get the blue Indonesia ones,' Clancy said.

HEGA PHONED twenty minutes later while Collins was thinking about taking his last sip of coffee.

'Okay,' Hega said, all business. 'I found them on her iCloud account. They had been deleted from the phone but when I disabled the iCloud drive sync, I was able to restore them using her Time Machine. Had to go back a few years but got them eventually.'

Collins knew better to ask for any details.

'So, what do you have?' he said.

'Good few files, Collins. A lot of pictures and some sex videos. Lots of screen grabs of texts and WhatsApp messages too. Looks like he phoned her a few hundred times and sent her WhatsApp messages and texts, mostly cajoling her at first, telling her how much he loved her, then it gets nasty. Looks like she changed her phone number a few times, but that didn't stop him.'

'When was all this?'

'One second. The last one was two years ago, I'll get the dates for you.'

'Can you send them on?'

'I'll send you a link. Click it on your laptop and you can drag the folder over. I have to go, Collins, big day tomorrow.'

'What's on?'

'Me and Jen are getting married.'

'Seriously?'

'Yep. She's up the duff and all, man.'

Collins' eyes widened.

'Congratulations, Hega. Tell Jen I said congratulations on both counts.'

'Will do.'

'I'm delighted for you, Hega. Have a great day, boy. All the best with the baby.'

'Sound, Collins. Catch you, man.'

COLLINS CLOSED the call and looked at his phone. Hega a husband and a father; the idea was terrifying, but it felt right too. Might be the makings of him. He wondered what kind of a wedding present he should get.

He clicked on the link when it arrived and downloaded the files. He began to look through them. Spanning five years, it looked like. Threats of violence and sexual violence; threats to tell her husband and friends. Clear proof that he had been harassing her for years. Several breaches of the *Non-Fatal Offences Against the Person Act*, if not the *Criminal Law (Sexual Offences) Act*.

He brought the laptop over to Clancy. He showed him some threats and a video.

'Nice work,' Clancy said. 'That birthmark near his hip might come in handy if he hasn't gotten rid of it. Pity we can't charge him with sexual harassment, her being dead.'

'Hundreds of messages and calls,' Collins said. 'But it looks like it stopped over a year ago. So why kill her now?'

'Who knows with those bastards,' Clancy said. 'But it gives him a motive for sure, if she wanted to bring a case against him.'

Chapter 14

Collins texted Deirdre the following morning at 6 a.m.

Be in early if you can, want to show you something.

He got a reply in seconds.

Leaving home in ten.

He showed her the messages, videos and images.

'That looks like Helen O'Driscoll in the video,' she said.

'Yeah, that must be Hughes.'

'How did you find them?' she asked.

'Remember the IT guy I told you about, who is doing consultancy for us now? Philip Hegarty? He was able to do a remote search and he found it somewhere on her iCloud.'

'Were you up all night again?'

'No, I was home by one, slept like a log,' Collins lied.

He announced the finding of the documents and pictures at the 7 a.m. briefing and asked O'Rourke if this meant they could get access to Hughes now.

'He was clearly harassing her,' Collins said. 'And he knew she had these videos and threats which provides us with motive.'

O'Rourke said he would get legal advice about it. Collins was looking for a good way to break the news to Deirdre about him and Clancy interviewing Hughes – in fairness, it was Clancy put in the request and not him. He and Deirdre would have Kathleen to interview, she could take lead on that.

The Garda Records Office in Cork was known as the GRO. It was notoriously dusty and files often went missing. It was in an old industrial estate complex in the old southside city suburb of Ballyphehane.

It was very well protected. Many old criminals in Cork would love to have burned any evidence against them. Collins and Deirdre had to show their IDs at the gated entrance to the estate and again at the door, which was heavy and felt like cast iron.

The waiting area was crowded with gardaí in and out of uniform. Collins saluted a few of them and stood in line.

'You sit down,' he said to Deirdre. 'I want to talk to this fellow.'

The man turned and smiled at Collins. He held his hand out to Deirdre.

'Kevin Tuohig,' he said. 'I'm very sorry for your trouble, being partnered with this cranky old man.'

'Deirdre Donnelly,' Deirdre said.

'Howya, Kevin,' Collins said, putting out his own hand. 'The very man.'

'I hear ye're on the murder case,' Tuohig said. 'The brother-in-law do it?'

'That's what we're here to find out,' Collins said. 'How are they treating you in Ballincollig?'

'I'm a fucking messenger boy, now,' Tuohig said. 'Some gouger threw a punch at me on Saturday and I threw a few back. Now the super is trying to put manners on me.'

'He has his work cut out. Did the names ring any bells for you?'

'They did but I was drinking a lot that time.'

'It was Kevin who arrested Helen and Robbie Wilkins in 1997,' Collins said to Deirdre.

'What do you remember?' he asked Tuohig.

'Yer man Wilkins was full of himself, she was only doing what he told her. She got the Probation Act and he got a suspended sentence. It was a thing of nothing, really. He owed money to one of the Turner's Cross gang.'

'Do you know where he is now?'

'I do. He's running a gym and "wellness" centre in Bishopstown, whatever that is. Doing well for himself, he never got involved again.'

'Did you get a sense of her, at all?'

Tuohig winced.

'I think she was just rebelling a bit, and got in with the wrong crowd. She gave up the drugs when she got pregnant and I don't think she ever went back. She got the fright of her life when we locked the door on her in the Bridewell, I do remember that much.'

'Do you think there could be a connection?' Deirdre said. 'With her murder?'

Tuohig rubbed his chin.

'Hard to imagine after all this time. I think herself and Wilkins went their separate ways, neither of them wanted to dwell on it, I'd say.'

'Thanks, boss,' Collins said. 'We should probably have a look at him, in any case. The baby was put up for adoption.'

Tuohig nodded and his name was called out from behind the counter.

'How did you get to the top of the queue?' Collins said.

'What's that song about friends in low places, Collins?' Tuohig smiled. 'At least some people remember all I've done for this godforsaken county. And the state of that Cork hurling team? Ring must be turning in his grave.'

'Kilkenny aren't much better, the hiding Galway gave ye.'

'We'll clean them out in the final, they always shit themselves when they get near to it. I'll be seeing ye. Mind yourself, Deirdre. Don't take any lip from him.'

'I won't.'

THEY CHECKED out the drugs file and the one on the assault of Lea Thompson. Collins read the drugs one first and then they swopped over.

There was nothing in the file about the drugs case of any material value to them. A typical case of young people taking a wrong turn and learning their lesson. There had been a tip-off to the Bridewell Station, which initiated the search and arrests.

Collins felt he was getting a sense of Helen, though. It must have taken great strength to change the course of her life's direction. Putting herself through college, staying clean, getting a good job, meeting a good man.

She had rebuilt her life and gotten away from Wilkins – only to walk into the clutches of another bastard, maybe the one who killed her.

CHAPTER 15

DEIRDRE DROVE them back to the station. Turning left towards The Lough, she said: 'is that drugs file any use to us? Looks like she was in the wrong place at the wrong time.'

'I agree. But do you remember when we were interviewing Kathleen O'Driscoll about when they found out that Helen was pregnant?' Collins didn't tell Deirdre he had recorded the interview and listened back twice.

'What about it?'

'It was somebody they didn't know who phoned the mother to tell her. Kathleen said something about him.'

'She said that it was somebody educated even if he was using language and shouting down the phone at her.'

'Yes, well done,' Collins said. 'It says in the file that the man who rang the Bridewell that there were drugs in Helen and Wilkins' flat had a "funny accent".'

'That could mean anything,' Deirdre said.

'Yes, but what if it was the same man who informed the gardaí about the drugs and told the family about the baby? Somebody with a grudge?'

'It's still over twenty years ago, Collins.'

'That's true, but she's still friendly with one man from her college days.'

'Blake Ormsby,' Deirdre said. 'Even his name sounds educated and I bet he has a "funny accent" too.'

'Only one way to find out,' Collins said. 'Let's track him down when we get back.'

'I NOTICED one thing in the Thompson rape case,' Deirdre said.

81

'Right.'

'You saw it too?'

'What did you notice?'

'The doctor who examined Lea Thompson in the CUH Sexual Assault Treatment Unit said the damage to the vagina could have been caused by an object,' Deirdre said. 'Gubbins was right.'

'Unfortunately, because she was unconscious she can't corroborate it,' Collins said.

'No, but we should talk to her anyway.'

'I agree. What do we know about her?'

'Not much. She's thirty-five; lives in London now. I think the parents are in Kinsale so we can get to her through them.'

'In my experience these kinds of things over the phone are a waste of time and a lost opportunity. I think somebody should go to London, probably you.'

'You trying to get me out of the way, Collins?' Deirdre said, eyebrows arched.

'She won't want to talk to a man about that. She might not want to talk at all, it's probably the reason why she's in London in the first place.'

'Fair enough, but have I time?'

'Let's see. We can't do everything ourselves. There's a team there for a reason.'

'I have a question,' Deirdre said. 'Why does a man use an object for a rape?'

'I don't know, maybe we could get advice on that from a psychologist. Dublin might have access to an expert in the UK or US or somewhere.'

'We need a profile done on this guy, too. The Dublin Divisional profiler, Melanie Ryan specialises in sexual assault, I think we should bring her in.'

'I'm not convinced of the whole profiling system but I've heard good things about her, will you put that to O'Rourke, or do you want me to do it?'

'I'll do it, I want to make a list of actions, anyway.'

'Good stuff.'

DEIRDRE CONTINUED: 'The other thing is that if the same per-petrator raped both victims it reduces the probability of it being Hughes. He's based in Dublin and these two were in Cork, it's unlikely he had links with Lea Thompson *and* Helen O'Driscoll.'

Collins thought about that. It didn't suit the case against Hughes but it had to be considered.

'You asked the question of Gubbins at the briefing, that's the only reason we know about Lea Thompson. But what if there are more cases, in Dublin, for example, where Hughes lives?'

'We need to check,' Deirdre said at the Barrack Street traffic lights. 'Main thing is we put some serious pressure on Hughes as soon as possible.'

Collins cleared his throat.

'About that,' he said. 'Actually, two things.'

She regarded him, noting the change in tone.

Collins hesitated, trying to pick his words. She'd just have to put up with it.

'Clancy told me last night that he wants to interview Hughes with me and not O'Regan. He said this to O'Rourke and he was giving me the heads up. I wanted you to hear it from me.'

'Oh,' Deirdre said. There was a long pause which Collins tried to fill.

'You and me will still interview Kathleen, you might take lead on that.'

'What did O'Regan say?'

'I don't know. That's between them, none of my business, but I'd say he's used to it. A man once told me that Clancy is as ruthless and smart as a shithouse rat, but twice as nasty. But he's some detective.'

'Thanks for letting me know,' Deirdre said. 'So, what next?'

Collins' phone rang. He looked at the number, an 021 landline. 'Hello?' he said.

'Is that Detective Collins?' A woman's voice. Authoritative.

'Speaking. Who is this?'

'My name is Bríd Crean. I'm a solicitor and I work for Legal Aid Offices, a company specialising in family law. I advised Helen O'Driscoll and I have some information that may be pertinent to her death.'

'Thank you for getting in touch,' Collins said. 'When can we meet you?'

'I'm back-to-back all day, today, I'm afraid. Can I meet you at 8 p.m. in the Raven Bar? Do you know where it is?'

'Yes. Can you not talk over the phone? Now? Or we can go to your office.'

'I'm sorry, no. I have a client waiting now, I have to go, 8 p.m. in the Raven?'

'We'll be there, my partner, Detective Sergeant Donnelly and myself. Thanks again.'

Chapter 16

Before the 7 p.m. briefing, Deirdre dropped an A4 printed page on the desk in front of Collins. It was a list of actions for the team. He read it and was impressed.

'This is great,' he said. 'Just what we need.'

Deirdre said. 'Anything I'm missing?'

'Somebody has to talk to Evan Murphy about the attack, one of the FLOs or maybe Lorraine.'

'I'll put her name down for that,' Deirdre said, making a note. 'Oh, maybe you should read those ten case notes of the Cremins too, to prepare for the Hughes interview.'

Collins smiled.

'Good idea. I can't imagine Clancy missing anything, but you never know. Two heads are better than one.'

The briefing meeting was downbeat. Collins looked around the table and felt little energy.

It was clear that nothing had turned up from talking to all the neighbours – or from the home and dash cam videos. Nothing useful had yet come from the freephone number line that had been set up. The lack of any forensic evidence or anything circumstantial had stalled progress. Collins had seen this often in cases, but not usually so soon after the crime.

The pathologist had released the body to the family, which meant that the removal would be on the following evening and the burial the morning after. That meant the interview with Hughes was a bit closer, which was one good piece of news.

Collins thought the team looked tired and directionless. He felt that O'Rourke should rally the troops but he seemed almost in shock. The newspapers were calling the gardaí inept and a politician in the Dáil used the term 'Keystone Cops' and wondered if any woman in Ireland was safe in her own home. There had been forty-five candle-lit vigils for Helen around the country the night before including a march in Cork city by over 2,000 people. The media coverage was incessant.

Collins was proud of Deirdre when it came to her turn to report. Instead of speaking from a sitting position at the table, she stood and went to a flip chart near the head of the table that Collins suspected she had placed there for that purpose.

'Okay,' she said, clearly. 'Myself and Collins spent the day in the Records Office looking at the case notes for the rape of Lea Thompson that Dr Gubbins mentioned yesterday and the 1997 drugs case against the victim and Robbie Wilkins. I'll come back to that in a minute, but I just wanted to recap where we're at now and where we might go.

'The files we recovered from the victim's phone makes interviewing Hughes a high priority action.' She wrote a heading *Actions* at the top of the chart and *1. Interview William Hughes* underneath it.

Collins watched O'Rourke's reaction: he was making notes.

Deirdre continued. 'Because of the lack of control Hughes showed in his harassment of the victim, we thought there might have been other instances that should be looked into.' She wrote: *2. Investigate Hughes.*

'Obviously we need more information from Kathleen O'Driscoll, too, and other relations and friends of the victim. We will probably have to wait a few days after the funeral for some of these.' She wrote: *3. Interview Kathleen O'Driscoll, etc.*

'While we don't think there's a direct link between the murder and her drugs case in 1997, it still warrants further investigation. Collins and I noted that somebody informed the family about

Helen's pregnancy and the gardaí about the drugs in the house. Both were done over the phone. Kathleen O'Driscoll referred to the person who informed Helen's mother as being "educated" and the file notes said the person who rang about the drugs had a "funny" accent.' Deirdre made the quotes symbol with the fingers of both hands as she did this.

'It may be the same person in both cases, which would indicate a grudge. That doesn't prove any connection to her murder so we're suggesting that Robbie Wilkins who was Helen's partner at the time be interviewed, and we should also interview Blake Ormsby, a friend of hers at the time, who she has stayed in touch with.' She wrote these as items four and five on her list.

Clancy spoke up as she was writing.

'I suggest we investigate these two people fully before we interview them, so we can maximise the information from them and see if they could be implicated.' Deirdre made a note of that.

'Now,' she continued. 'The next item is delicate but it may be possible to get some information from Evan Murphy. This is probably a task by the FLOs or Lorraine Crowley.' She wrote this as item six.

'From looking at the Lea Thompson assault we were able to confirm that her sexual assault was carried out using an object. Also, there was no DNA, no prints, nothing else found at the scene as Dr Gubbins said. But ... she suffered similar injuries to our victim. So, we have a few suggested actions from this.

'She lives in London now and Collins suggested somebody go over there and talk to her in person rather than do it over the phone. He also suggested a woman does it.

'But the crime took place in Cork which makes a link with Hughes less likely given he's based in Dublin. So, we suggest to widen out any possible similar rapes to Dublin and even nation-wide.'

Collins looked around the room. Everybody was paying close attention, Deirdre really had a knack for presenting to a group.

'Today Collins got a phone call from a solicitor Bríd Crean, from the company Legal Aid Offices, who said she has information about the case. We're meeting her after this meeting. So that's the next item.'

'We also suggest looking for further information from the assistant state pathologist about the nature of the rape and the use of an object.' She wrote *10. Discuss with Assistant State Pathologist about nature of rape.*

'Collins tells me he spoke to Alice O'Callaghan so we can cross off No. 10 as done.' She did so. 'Do you want to report what she said, Collins?'

'Yes, she said the object was smooth and hard without any jagged edges. She wouldn't make any other conclusions about it. There were no remnants of the object found in the body and the nature of the trauma came from the force with which it was used in the attack, rather than the size or shape.'

Deirdre continued. 'Last item is a suggestion of mine. I worked with the Dublin profiler Dr Melanie Ryan on a previous case and she's the leading expert on sexual assault in Ireland. She did her PhD on the subject and I think it would be a big help if she read the file and had an input. That's subject to your approval, of course, sir,' she said addressing O'Rourke.

'I think it's a good suggestion,' O'Rourke said. 'We're getting slaughtered in the media and I'm getting slaughtered by the top brass. I've been promised every asset I need and I'm sure that includes Dr Ryan. What do you think, Tom?'

'I think we need to do everything we can,' Brennan said. 'And we have to been seen doing so. We have our own profiler in Cork, Seamus O'Connell, but he mainly works with the Drugs and Organised Crime Unit so I don't see a problem.'

Deirdre put it on the list.

'So, that's what we've come up with,' Deirdre said, putting the top back on the marker and placing it on the tray beneath the chart.

ACTIONS
1) *Interview William Hughes*
2) *Investigate Hughes for other events/issues*
3) *Interview Kathleen O'Driscoll, etc.*
4) *Investigate and interview Robbie Wilkins*
5) *Investigate and interview Blake Ormsby*
6) *Talk to Evan Murphy (FLO)*
7) *Interview Lea Thompson (in London) – talk to parents first*
8) *Check for similar cases nationwide with a similar MO*
9) *Talk to Bríd Crean, solicitor for Helen O'Driscoll*
10) *Bring in Dublin profiler Melanie Ryan*

'That's great work, well done, Deirdre,' O'Rourke said from the top table. Collins could see he was relieved.

'I think we can use this as the basis for allocating duties for the next few days and build upon the list following on what we heard earlier. As I see it there are some specific actions interviewing people, reviewing local cases and so on and more general actions broadening this inquiry out. So, we'll ask for assistance from HQ on items 9 and 10.'

Tom Brennan said: 'I think they can handle No. 2, as well, looking at Hughes. Much easier for them to get a handle on that in Dublin.'

'Good point,' O'Rourke said. 'Dublin Castle have far more resources than us, they can take lead on those actions. We can handle everything else ourselves. Myself and Tom will have a look at who is best suited to every task and we'll allocate them tonight and let you all know.' He looked around the room.

'Good work everyone. I think we've taken a major step forward in getting justice for Helen.'

COLLINS CRINGED inside at this expression, which he'd heard O'Rourke use before but it was always good to keep the victim in the forefront of the mind. Deirdre sat back down beside him and he tapped her arm with his elbow.

'Nicely done,' he said, quietly.

'Thanks,' she replied.

CHAPTER 17

ON THE way over to the Raven Bar, Deirdre asked Collins if he knew anything about Bríd Crean.

'I never met her,' Collins replied. 'But she's well known in the city. I think she set up Legal Aid Offices with another woman called Liz Roche who was sexually assaulted by a priest when she was young. He was convicted of that around 2000.'

'What does the company do?'

'They started out supporting victims of domestic and sexual violence but now they deal with separation, divorce, family disputes and childcare. I think they have five or six solicitors working with them and counsellors, psychologists, psychotherapists; they have a whole range of services. A lot of the people working there are volunteers. I think they get a lot of government funding and they work closely with the Rape Crisis Centre and the CRW – Cork Refuge for Women – and other services. I heard they're doing a lot of work for residents in Direct Provision now too. She's a formidable character by all accounts.'

THE RAVEN Bar was located at the corner of South Main Street and Liberty Street in the city centre. Collins knew it from the odd pint before or after a show in The Triskel Arts Centre or a film in The Gate Cinema. He had never eaten in the restaurant at the back of the pub.

They found her alone in a quiet booth.

'Det. Sergeant Deirdre Donnelly,' Deirdre said, shaking hands.

'Tim Collins,' Collins said, doing likewise. 'Thanks for meeting us, Bríd. I don't think we've met but I know about your work.'

'I know about you, too,' Bríd replied. 'Emily Creedon and CRW are my clients and she told me how you help her out.'

'Emily is a great woman, I do what I can.'

'A bit more than that,' she said. 'Sit down, sit down.'

Collins and Deirdre sat down opposite her. Collins sidled into the booth self-consciously. He looked at her. She was in her mid-fifties, he guessed. A pair of reading glasses on the menu. She looked tired but determined. Intelligence in the eyes. Her blonde hair was short, in a pixie-like cut. No ear rings. She wore a black blouse and understated lipstick. She assessed him openly.

'I won't offer you a drink, because I'm expecting somebody shortly.' She cleared her throat and looked around the restaurant. 'Helen O'Driscoll came to me several years ago. A mutual friend referred her to me. She wanted legal advice about a man who was sexually harassing her. They had previously been in a relationship but she had ended it. That's often how it begins.' She took a sip of water from an almost empty glass.

'Not long after she broke it off, she met him in her apartment in Cork and he raped her.'

'Is this William Hughes we're talking about?' Deirdre said.

'Yes.'

'Why didn't she bring charges against him?' Deirdre said.

'Why do you think? For the same reason that most women don't. Only 230 of 1,000 sexual assaults are reported. Of those, only 46 lead to a charge and nine lead to a prosecution. That's nine prosecutions out of a thousand. How many of those rapists go to prison, do you know?'

'No, I don't,' Deirdre said.

'Four. Four rapists out of a thousand. And when women do report it they are put through hell and their underwear is paraded in front of the court. Our legal system is completely unfit for purpose. Did you know that 26 percent of women in Ireland have experienced physical and/or sexual violence since the age of 15, and that 41% of people in Ireland know a woman who had been a victim of some form of domestic violence?'

Deirdre was momentarily flummoxed, so Collins spoke.

'Tell us about Helen O'Driscoll,' he said.

Bríd exhaled.

'She was brave and strong, trying to live her life and bring up her son. What should I call you?'

'Collins or Tim, I don't mind.'

'Okay, let's go with Tim. That surname thing is a bit macho for me. Helen was very brave and very determined to protect herself and Evan. Her family behaved despicably. That man is a monster and if he didn't kill her, I certainly think he'd be capable of it. He groomed her when she was vulnerable and he raped her when she stood up to him.'

'Was there any particular reason she didn't report the rape – besides systematic failure? In your opinion?'

'Yes.' She took a sip from her water glass. 'She felt very guilty about the affair with him in the first place. Of course, he gaslighted her and coerced her – she was at a low ebb at the time, really low. But she felt terrible about it later. And her sister and her mother found out and they cut her from the family. She moved back to Cork and got her life together – how, I'm not sure, it must have taken great strength. She worked nights in bars, which must have been very tough for somebody in AA. She put herself through college and got her degree and a teaching job and then she met her husband, Greg. He's a good man I must say.'

Bríd looked accusatorily at Collins as if asking him: *Are you?*

'What's your sense of Hughes?' Collins said.

'He's a narcissistic monster, clearly, but he can hide it brilliantly. He does that little boy, puppy big-eyed sad look very well. Male jurors fall for it every time. Helen told me he has total coercive control over his wife, Kathleen.'

'That would explain something I can't go into,' Collins said. 'Is he intelligent?'

'Very, I would say, but also cunning. These men can manipulate others and they pick their victims very well. They're like predators seeking out the weakest and most vulnerable.'

'But predators will try many victims before they find the right one, do you think he would have tried this with other women?'

'Without doubt. All the studies show this pattern. But it's very hard to find victims of domestic, sexual and gender-based violence who will come forward. Especially women who are already marginalised such as Travellers, Roma and migrants. There's a great sense of shame and a huge shortage of emergency accommodation, not to mention inadequacies in the law protecting witnesses.'

Collins looked at Deirdre to indicate her turn.

'Do you know of any contacts between Hughes and Helen recently?' Deirdre asked.

'No. If there were, I didn't know about it.'

Bríd looked her watch and then at the detectives.

Collins said: 'If Helen was being harassed again, what do you think she would do?'

Bríd paused before answering.

'I think she would have fought back, if at all possible. She was a brave woman. But you don't know what these men are like, what he would have used against her. If he threatened Evan, for example. A mother would do anything – anything – to protect her child.'

Collins nodded. He looked at Deirdre.

'Thank you for your time,' Deirdre said. She shook hands with Bríd and stood up. Collins sidled out of the booth.

'Thank you,' he said.

Bríd gripped his hand and locked eyes with him. Her look hardened.

'Get this bastard,' she said.

'We will,' Collins replied.

Chapter 18

In the morning, they decided to interview Robbie Wilkins. Collins checked Helen's phone for Wilkins' number which was listed under 'RW'. There was one phone call and one text about five months earlier. The phone call was first and lasted twelve minutes. The text the following the day said: *No. I can't. Sorry.*

He showed them both to Deirdre as they got into the car.

'What do you think?' he said, pulling out of the station.

'Could be anything but looks like he asked her for something,' she replied.

'Money, maybe. Did you hear anything from Tom and Jim, weren't they checking the bank accounts and finances?'

'Yeah, they said there was nothing funny. The husband is earning big money and she had her teacher's salary; they were secure and there was nothing major going in or out lately.'

'Let's see what Wilkins says about it. Good to have it in the back pocket, anyway,' Collins said. 'Helen seemed to have been on good terms with him from that text, the way she apologised.'

They got to Bishopstown quickly via the South Link. The fitness and wellness centre was a modified two storeyed house off the Curraheen Road. There was a small waiting room at the front with a young woman behind a desk.

'Can I help you?' she said, alarmed. Collins wondered if she knew they were gardaí and how she would have known that. He noticed a badly drawn bird on the area between the thumb and forefinger of her left hand – a prison tattoo.

'We're here to see Robbie Wilkins,' Deirdre said. Collins liked the way she took the lead in these situations, it meant he could loiter behind and take things in. The receptionist's relief was palpable. The gardaí weren't there for her.

'Do you have an appointment?'

'We're gardaí,' Deirdre said. 'It's a personal matter.'

'Can I say what it's about?' the receptionist said, lifting a phone. Collins was impressed by how quickly she had recovered her aplomb. Neither he nor Deirdre responded to the question.

Wilkins appeared, looking flustered.

'Come through,' he said and led them to a large bright room with a desk and three chairs and a treatment bed.

'Please sit down,' he said, closing the door. 'I was wondering when you'd get here, I presume this is about Helen.' His voice was soft and clear with only a trace of Cork pronunciation.

He sat opposite them. He was fit and lean, almost emaciated. He had greying hair cut very short and wore a type of teal coloured medical-looking uniform and white socks and clogs. His bare hands and forearms were strong and there was a document in Japanese framed on the wall which probably referred to some martial art.

'Yes it is,' Deirdre said. 'I'm Detective Sergeant Deirdre Donnelly and this is Detective Tim Collins. We're from Anglesea Street Garda Station. Can you tell us the last time you had any contact with Helen?'

'I phoned her about six months ago about Liam,' Wilkins replied.

'Liam?'

'Our son,' Wilkins said. 'Helen's and mine. Who we gave up for adoption.'

Deirdre paused for a moment, then recovered herself.

'He made contact with you?'

'He contacted me five years ago when he was fifteen. We've become close. He comes down to Cork four or five times a year and stays with us. My wife and I have two other children – Liam's brother and sister – and he's very friendly with them.'

'Was he close to Helen, too?' Deirdre asked.

'No. He tried to connect with her at that time, but she said she wasn't ready. She did meet him but her own son was still a baby and she said there was other stuff going on in her life.' He took a drink of water from a reusable bottle on the desk.

'We were in Fitzgerald Park in February and Liam was with us and I saw Helen with her husband and her little boy, Evan. I didn't say anything and Liam didn't notice her. But later that evening I mentioned it and he said he'd like her to be in his life. His adoptive parents have always been very open with him about the adoption and he's a lovely lad, really. He just wanted to get to know her. So, I phoned her and she wasn't sure. She said she'd talk to her husband and think about it. Then she texted me the following day to say no, she wasn't interested, or she wasn't able. I think she said she wasn't able in fairness. And I respected that and Liam got on with things, he's just finishing a business degree now so he has plenty on.'

'Can you take us back to 1997?' Deirdre said. 'When you and Helen were arrested and charged with possession with intent to supply.'

Wilkins took another drink of water and looked thoughtful.

'We were young and stupid, what can I say? We got into drugs and then we owed money to some dealers and they pressured us to deal for them. I did it mostly, Helen was too nervous and I told the guards that at the time. We weren't careful, either, and she got pregnant. Her family wanted her to get an abortion but she wouldn't. It was a wakeup call and although I'm still registered as a convicted criminal I never did time and that was a lucky break.'

'And have you dealt in drugs since?' Deirdre said.

'No! Jesus. I never touched a thing again. I went into NA and got clean and I've never had a drink or anything since. I have worked hard to put it behind me and now I have this business and a family so I would never jeopardise that. And Helen never looked back, either. It's tragic.'

This was the first time he had mentioned the murder and Collins wanted him to get closer to that.

'Where you Tuesday night between 5 p.m. and 7 p.m.?'

Wilkins glared at him.

'Give me a break,' he said. 'I was here until eight with clients and then I went straight home. I was home by 8:30.'

'Can you give us the name and contact details of those clients, so we can verify that?'

'Is that really necessary? Jesus, I had nothing to do with this.'

'We won't tell the clients what it was about. We'll make something up about a break in to the clinic.'

'Oh. Okay.'

'So, you don't have any contact with drug dealers or anything like that anymore?' Collins said.

'No, of course not. What's this about?'

'Only I noticed your receptionist seemed to realise that we were gardaí straight away and she had a prison tattoo.'

Wilkins opened the top drawer of his desk and took out a folder. He handed it to Collins. It was advertising a charity called '2nd Chance'. It was about rehabilitating criminals back into society and preventing recidivism.

'Look at the back page,' Wilkins said.

There were photos of the trustees and board members of the charity and their names were listed. Wilkins was one of the board members.

'I do counselling and vocational training with some of the prisoners in Cork and Limerick prisons. I never did time, but I could have, easily, so I want to give people the same second chance I got. When Claire was released a year ago, she signed up for a secretarial course and she works here as part of her placement.

She's a good kid, she had it very rough at home.'

Collins felt guilty and handed the folder back.

'When was the last time Liam was in Cork?' he said.

'Jesus, what are you implying?' Wilkins sat up in his chair. 'This is ridiculous!'

'I'm not implying anything,' Collins said. 'We need to know where all Helen's family and acquaintances were on Tuesday night.'

'Well, he wasn't in Cork, that's for sure. He's her son for God's sake.'

'Can you give us his contact details, so we can interview him?'

'Jesus, he's her son.'

'Did you break the news to him?' Collins said.

'Yes I did. Yesterday. It broke my heart and it broke his, too. Now he'll never get to know her. So, the last thing he needs ...' Wilkins stopped speaking and threw up his hands. He picked up the phone and spoke into it.

'Hi, Claire. No, everything's fine, nothing to do with the practice. Can you write down the phone numbers of Sheila O'Callaghan and Thomas Browne please and bring them in? Thanks.'

Wilkins took out his phone. He took a Post-It from a pile and wrote on it. He handed it to Collins.

'Anything else?' he said to Collins. 'Only I'm a bit busy here this morning.'

'Too busy to help us try to find the killer of Liam's mother?' Collins said.

'I don't deserve that. I told you everything I know.'

'Did you ever know of anyone with a grudge against Helen? Even in college, anybody there who she jilted or anything?'

Wilkins thought about that one.

'No. I don't think so. She had a few boyfriends before me but nothing serious.'

'If you think of anything or anybody, please ring us at this number.' Collins gave him his card, which had his name and number on it.

'Can you give me Claire's surname and PPS number, too? I just want to verify that. And if you think of anything else or want to change anything you have just said, you can ring me at Anglesea Street Garda Station. We might need you to make a formal statement.'

Wilkins glared at him again and opened the laptop on the desk. He began clicking and typing. Claire came in with a piece of paper and gave it to Wilkins.

'Anything else?' she said, blushing.

'No, Claire, that's fine,' Wilkins said. 'Thanks a million.' He wrote her name and PPS number on the paper, stuck the Post-It to it and handed both to Collins.

'Thanks very much,' Collins said, standing. He now believed Wilkins' story – all of it. 'I'm sorry we had to do this. And I'm sorry for your loss.'

Wilkins' eyes widened. He coloured.

'Thank you,' he said as Collins turned, followed by Deirdre, and left the room.

In the car, Deirdre asked Collins if he suspected Wilkins, if that's why he had been so hard on him. Collins thought a bit before replying.

'No, but I've made mistakes in the past. Assuming people were not guilty when interviewing them or assuming people didn't know something useful when they did. I wanted to make this as formal and pressurised for him as I could.'

'Do you think him or the son are involved in any way?' she said.

'I don't,' Collins said. 'But we should follow-up with those numbers about the alibi and phone the son, too.'

HELEN O'DRISCOLL's removal was held at a funeral home on the eastern side of the Boreenmanna Road.

Collins had been to several funerals of murder victims. The funerals of professional criminals who had been killed were full of loss and a sense of waste – with devastated mothers, wives and children. Full of anger and retribution from fellow gang members and hatred of the gardaí.

Funerals of innocent victims were different. A sense of shock, a sense of revulsion and horror along with the grief – the great wrongness of it all. The family and friends being numb and glad of the numbing, which would soon wear off.

Collins, Deirdre, Clancy and O'Regan stood on the grass outside the funeral home. It was up lit by evening light and Collins could hear the sound of a match from the GAA stadium just down the road. Groups had gathered on the grass and the car park, having gone inside and come out again, some of them looking ashen. Collins checked his watch, turned to Deirdre and said: 'I'm just going in for a second, be right back.'

He went in the main door of the funeral home nodding to the funeral director who nodded back. He did not sign the condolences book nor join the queue making its way to commiserate with the family and friends. Instead, he entered through the exit door on the left and stood to one side, by the back. There were the usual sounds of whispered sympathies and the odd sob. Women held tissues as they left. Helen's body was at the top of the room in the coffin on display. At least her face had not been so damaged as to warrant a closed coffin.

To the right at the top of the queue, Greg Murphy stood alongside his brother, both in black suits and ties. Greg Murphy was a tall, heavy man, but he looked shrunken into the suit. He was in shock, Collins could see, not really knowing what was happening. He shook hands with people and smiled but it was all fake, he was clearly in a bad place. His brother was a younger version of himself, not as tall or heavy and more in control. No sign of Evan.

Collins scanned the front row of the seating area, looking for William Hughes but he appeared not to be there. Given his history with Helen that was probably just as well. There was no sign of Kathleen O'Driscoll or her mother. *Imagine not attending your own daughter's funeral,* Collins thought. *What kind of a person would do that?*

He recognised Orlaith Moloney and her husband Jim in the third row. He assumed many of Helen's friends such as Niamh O'Shea, Sara Bourke and Anna O'Leary and their partners were also there but he didn't know what they looked like. Many of the mourners sympathised with and hugged women and men in the first few rows – Greg's family and Helen's work colleagues and friends, Collins guessed.

He looked around the room, scanning the faces looking for anything that stood out or seemed out of place. Eventually, he turned and left.

CHAPTER 19

THE NEWS that Hughes had an alibi for the murder spread quickly through the station. Deirdre heard it from a uniformed garda in the corridor and told Collins. A friend of Hughes, Fran O'Donnell, had presented himself at the front desk of the station with the solicitor Patricia Cremin.

O'Donnell claimed that he and Hughes had been together since 4 p.m. in the Mount Oval Bar on the day Helen had been murdered. Clancy and O'Rourke interviewed him and found CCTV footage at the bar to corroborate the claim.

Deirdre and Collins went to Clancy at his desk, later that night.

'It's definite, is it?' Collins said.

'Yeah, the CCTV proved it beyond doubt,' Clancy replied.

'Why were they at the bar in the first place?'

'They knew each other from school. Had a meal together and then watched a soccer match on television.'

'How convenient,' Collins said. 'I would have thought rugby would be more of his game.'

'I wouldn't mind, but we got a call earlier from Donnybrook about a sexual harassment claim against Hughes from two years ago.'

'Is it active?' Deirdre said, hopefully.

'No. The girl dropped it. Donnybrook thought the family had been bought off or intimidated. She was a neighbour and Hughes got hold of her phone number and started sending her messages.' Clancy shrugged. 'It doesn't matter now, anyway. We know he didn't kill Helen O'Driscoll.'

'Yeah,' Collins said. 'No point in interviewing the wife, either, whatever she was up to on the night of the murder.'

'Makes your list a bit shorter anyway,' Clancy smirked at Deirdre, which she resented.

'Those pricks have to get lucky every time,' she replied. 'We only have to get lucky once.'

Chapter 20

'WHAT KIND of a name is Blake Ormsby, anyway?' Deirdre said to Collins over coffee in the open plan area around their desks.

The morning briefing had been downbeat, focusing on Hughes' alibi. O'Rourke had given the team a pep talk, but Collins sensed desperation in it. They needed a breakthrough.

'English, I guess,' he said. 'Or Scottish, maybe. The only ones I could see on Google apart from our man were American.

'The mother is American, I think,' Deirdre said. 'We got that from Niamh O'Shea, who knew him in college with Helen. There was no father on the scene apparently.'

'What else did she say?'

'He's from South Tipperary, just outside Clonmel somewhere. Lives in Ballincollig, has some kind of a research IT company to do with cyber security. Seems to be a one-man band with a lot of contractors in Eastern Europe working for him.'

'Let's do it. Will I ring him or you?' Collins said.

'You do it. You're better at intimidating people.'

Collins looked for a sheet of paper on his desk, the one with the names and phone numbers on Helen O'Driscoll's contacts list. He tapped the number into his phone and it began to ring. He put the phone on his desk and switched to speaker mode. It rang out. There was no voice message option, but the phone wasn't out of service or turned off.

'You got the details of his company there?' Collins said. Deirdre passed him a print out. He looked at the contact phone number, it was a land line. He dialled it.

It was answered on the third ring.

'Hello, Blake Ormsby Research, Blake Ormsby speaking.'

'Hello Mr Ormsby, this is Detective Garda Collins. I'm ringing you in connection with the death of Helen O'Driscoll.'

'Oh, God. Yes, I saw it on the news. It's terrible. How may I help you?'

'Myself and a colleague would like to speak to you about Helen, could we call out to Ballincollig and do that now?'

'Yes, that would be fine. Anything I can do to help. Do you need the address? I'm in the office right now.'

'No, that's fine,' Collins said. 'We'll be there in thirty minutes or so. Thank you.'

Collins hung up.

'Are we on? What did he sound like?' Deirdre said.

'Yes. He sounded ... normal,' Collins said.

COLLINS AND Deirdre pulled up to the non-descript unit in the non-descript industrial park outside Ballincollig. There were six companies in the block, with their names above the doors. One framing company, one shoe importer; Collins couldn't tell what business the others were in. The name above Number 1 was 'Blake Ormsby Research' and underneath: 'Software Solutions'.

'I meant to ask you,' Collins said. 'Did anything come up on the system for him?'

'No,' Deirdre said. 'Some penalty points for speeding, that was all.'

Ormsby answered the door immediately. No doubt he had been waiting for them. He was about 5' 10" and physically strong looking. He wore a jacket over a polo shirt and chinos but his biceps and thighs looked bulked up by weights. He was wearing those tan pointed shoes that Collins hated. His glasses were rimless and thick, and his hair was thinning, which made him look older than his age of forty-one.

Not that appearances mattered, Collins knew that killers came in all shapes and sizes, many of them innocuous looking.

He led them through to a small dark office and offered them tea or coffee.

'We have a Nespresso machine,' he said, looking at Collins.

'Yes please,' Collins said. 'Just black for me.'

'The same for me,' Deirdre said. Collins knew she wouldn't drink it. She gave him a meaningful look when Ormsby had left. Collins nodded. Why had Ormsby mentioned Nespresso to him?

Collins opened the door quietly and went back to the desk near the front door. He could see a layer of dust on some parts of it, near the edges of a monitor and keyboard. But other parts had been wiped. He ran his finger along the top of the keyboard. Dust.

He opened a drawer and took out a small diary. There was a name on the front page: Lizzie Howard. He looked through the pages. It seemed to contain lists of names and phone numbers. He put the diary in his inside jacket pocket and went back to the office. Deirdre glared at him.

'Just looking for a toilet,' he said. He took out his phone, opened the Voice Memos App, and pressed Record. He placed the phone's screen on the table.

He took in the room. There was a series of framed pictures of computers on the walls, beginning with a human hand, then an abacus, a slide rule and on to modern computers and mobile phones. The last picture was a person, which Collins found disconcerting. There were two bookshelves, crammed with computer manuals and files. The table looked expensive. The chairs were leather.

'Sorry, I hope these are okay. My secretary is off today,' Ormsby said, placing the coffees on coasters. He left and returned with what looked like a sparkling water for himself.

'Thanks very much,' Collins said and sipped his coffee. 'It's very good.'

'Good,' Ormsby said. 'Now what can I do for you?'

Collins had seen this before. It was meant as a way of flagging status. That he was helping them but it was by his choice. They needed something and he was the provider.

'Can you tell us a bit about Helen?' Collins said. 'I understand ye were friends.'

'Well, we were friendly in college,' Ormsby said. 'God, it seems like ancient history now.' He stopped, as though waiting for another question. *He's trying to show superiority*, Collins thought. *He thinks this is a battle of wills.*

Collins found himself paying closer attention, his senses alert. He looked at Ormsby waiting for an answer. He was also looking for some kind of tell. Ormsby was acting very much like somebody who didn't want to be dragged into the death of an old acquaintance.

Ormsby took a sip of water, a classic delaying tactic.

'We were friends in first year in college,' he said. Collins picked the faint hint of a lisp in the words 'friends' and 'first'.

'But in second year she started hanging around with a different crowd. There were a lot of drugs and the fellow she was going out with was dealing, we all knew that.' Ormsby paused for a moment and his expression changed.

'Wilkins. It took me a while to remember his name. Then she left college and I heard she had a baby and gave it up for adoption. Then I went to Cambridge for a few years where I did an MSc and then a PhD – a doctorate.'

Collins nodded.

'Did you have any contact with her after the baby?' Collins said.

'No. As I say I was in the UK for six years in all.'

'And since then? In recent years?'

'No,' Ormsby said. 'I guess we move in different social circles. To be honest I don't socialise much at all. It's all work, work, work.' He said the last words light-heartedly, but Collins sensed something odd in the tone.

Collins didn't react, waiting for more. Ormsby looked at the clock on the wall, as if hinting.

'In college,' Deirdre said. 'Was your relationship sexual?'

Ormsby jumped at the word. His whole body shook strangely and his tone went up a notch.

'No, no, no, no,' he said and at that moment Collins felt his voice sounded strange and his accent became more Oxbridge and also 'educated' – the word Helen's sister, Kathleen had used.

'Never?' Deirdre said, archly.

'No, no,' Ormsby said. 'We were in the same class and we hung around in the same gang for a short while, that was it.'

'Only some of Helen's friends said it was more. A *lot* more,' Deirdre said.

'Who said that?' Ormsby replied and Collins could see a hint of anger, before he reined it back in. 'Well, they are mistaken, it was never like that. Will that be all? Because I'm due to join an important conference call.'

'One last question,' Collins said and he paused before taking another sip of coffee. 'You said you've had no contact with Helen in recent times, is that right?'

'No. No contact,' Ormsby said, looking him in the eye.

'You sure about that? It's very important and this will be your third time saying it.'

'Yes, I'm sure.' He shrugged. 'At least I don't recall any.'

'That's it,' Collins said, standing up. 'Thank you for your time, Doctor Ormsby. And for the coffee.'

Ormsby led them out. Deirdre thanked him again at the door. Collins just walked away. He saved the recording on his phone and turned off the App.

The Very Safe Place Chat Room 12/High Level Security

Grand Gentleman (admin): *I'm starting this chat room about the Stacy in Blackrock Cork. Is this the start of the incel Rebellion in Ireland?*

Carlow Stud: *For sure. Bring it on!*

Saville2: *Bring it on!*

Maynooth Loverboy: *Bring it on!*

UpTheYard: *Sex for all men! MeToo (LOL)*

Bondsman: *Pussy Galore (LOL)*

Meeks1964: *Bring it on, but we need more.*

Rodger: *More???*

Meeks1964: *One isn't enough for critical mass, we need 10, maybe 20 for them to get the message.*

Rogue1: *I agree, but every revolution begins with one significant action and follows from there. So, who will provide us with the next dead Stacy?*

Grand Gentleman (admin): *Maybe the brother who provided the first one? Haha.*

Rogue1: *Bring it on, brother. But we need something bigger, our own Elliot Rodger or Alek Minassian. We need the foids to sit up and take notice.*

Grand Gentleman (admin): *Watch this space. Literally (LOL)*

Rodger: *Woohoo, bring on the Rebellion! Can you share more, Grand Gentleman?*

Alex 22: *Bring it on! Bring it on!*

Saville2: *Bring it on!*

Detroitstud: *Kill the foids!*

Swordsman: *Fuck the foids!*

CHAPTER 21

'WHAT DO you make of that?' Deirdre said, when they sat back into the car.

'Dunno,' Collins said. 'Very intelligent and controlled until you brought sex into the conversation. That's something we might work on, next time. I think we have enough for a formal interview at the station, but I think we'll need a bit more for it to be any use. That Merc looks like it's his, I'll run the reg and see what comes up.'

'Something off about him,' Deirdre said.

'What?'

'I dunno. He gave me the creeps. Something odd.'

'I got the secretary's name, Lizzie Howard, we should talk to her,' Collins said. 'There was a lot of dust around her desk like she hadn't been there for a while.'

'He said she just had the day off,' Deirdre said.

'Just going to ring a contact in HQ there and she what she comes up with.'

'Wait a minute, how did you find out the secretary's name?'

'It was on a note on her desk near the front door.'

He took out his phone and rang his friend Rose O'Grady who worked in Garda Headquarters in Dublin and had a lot of information at her fingertips that Collins couldn't get near.

'Hi Rose.'

'Hiya Collins, I heard you met Alice, any developments?'

'No, nothing firm yet, we had to rule out a guy who was harassing her.'

'I heard about him, the brother-in-law, what a sleazebag.'

'Oh yeah, but looks like his alibi stands up. Listen could you run a name for me, there? Lizzie Howard, looks like she's a secretary to a company called Blake Ormsby Research or Software Solutions. Based in Ballincollig. Oh, will you run him, too, in case there's anything there?'

'Okay, will do.' She hung up.

'What are you thinking?' Deirdre said.

'Nothing, yet, but why would he lie about her having the day off? Anyway, she might give us some information about him. I agree with you, he's hiding something, but it might have nothing to do with the murder. Listen, will you pull around the corner and park? I want to talk to the people in the next couple of units, see what they have to say.'

She started the engine. 'I'll do it,' she said. 'In case your contact phones back. What's the secretary's name again?'

'Lizzie Howard,' Collins said.

'Okay, back in a bit.'

When she had walked away, Collins took the diary out of his pocket. It was soft-covered but he could see it was used as a notebook. Pages of contacts were handwritten neatly in the first few pages with phone numbers. At the back, there were a series of passwords for computers and online services. VAT numbers, bank account details and other financial information. In the middle what seemed like protocols for locking up, lists of things to check and other procedures for scanning her computer for viruses.

The phone numbers contained the names of some large manufacturing and service companies in the region – multinationals. Looked like Ormsby had some big clients, must be good at his job. Collins realised he hadn't asked Ormsby what he did for those companies. Something to do with IT security, he guessed, but he needed to know more. Probably to do with hacking. Hega might know about it.

Collins remembered reading somewhere that all the best hackers were eventually taken on by companies who prevent hacking. But if you knew how to protect systems, you could easily get around the firewalls, too.

He looked through all the names in the notebook again to see if any of them rang a bell. None.

Deirdre arrived back and sat into the driver's seat. Collins put the diary back in his pocket.

'The place next door was closed,' she said. 'But the owner of the next one over, the shoe importer, was mad for chat. Not a fan of Mr Ormsby *at all*. "Stuck up fucker" he said. He hasn't seen Lizzie in weeks – he called her Liz. One day he asked Ormsby if she was still working there and only got a grunt back. He says that Ormsby is there at all hours, the car is often parked overnight. He thinks he sleeps there which is in breach of the planning licence but he doesn't have any proof or else he'd report him. Of course, he was mad to know why we were around.'

'Any customers or any people ever call?'

'Very rarely, he said. Liz used to get visits by a friend or two but she'd go out and sit in their cars rather than them coming in.'

'Did he say what the company does?'

'Something to do with computers, he said. Hadn't a clue, really, but Liz told him it was to prevent hacking in big companies and cyber-crime.'

Collins' phone rang. It was Rose.

'Hi Rose,' he said. 'I'm just going to put you on speaker there so Deirdre can listen in.'

'Hi Deirdre, nice to talk to you.'

'Hi Rose thanks for the help.'

'No bother,' Rose said. 'Okay. Elizabeth Howard, I think it's her, I see her name here on a tax form as listed as being employed by Cyber Securities Ltd. which is listed down to Ormsby. He has eight different companies, it appears.'

'Do you have a home address for her?' Collins said.

'I do, I'll text that on now. I did a search on that and there was a suspicious activity reported two weeks ago by her next-door neighbour. A car was sent out by Bishopstown but they didn't find anything.'

Collins and Deirdre exchanged glances.

'Anything on record for her?' Collins said.

'No. One speeding ticket and two parking tickets. Oh, a car crash last year but not her fault.'

'But, listen to this,' Rose said. 'A Mr Blake Ormsby came up on a list of men in Ireland belonging to the incel movement. There was a guy trying to get a child into his car in Galway and when he was picked up he tried to trade a list of incel members for a non-custodial sentence.'

Again Collins and Deirdre looked at each other. Deirdre pumped her fists in celebration.

'Have you heard of this incel crowd?' Rose said. 'It's short for involuntary celibacy.'

'I think I read something about a killing in the UK. Is it on the proscribed list?' Collins said.

'Not as far as I know. But Dublin Castle are keeping an eye on them. I'll text you the number of someone you can ring about that. And that's it, really. Incel seem to be mostly online in chat rooms and stuff but this guy in Galway had a printed list. Ormsby has eight companies as I said, all to do with computer security, hacking and all that stuff. I have to go, Collins, bye Deirdre.'

'Okay, thanks a million, Rose,' Collins said and the line went dead.

'I told you he was weird,' Deirdre said. 'Involuntary celibacy, for fuck's sake. Like it's a human right or something that women have to give them sex whenever they want it. Jesus Christ!'

Collins looked at the two texts from Rose, one with the address and the other with the phone number of Melanie Ryan.

'That's funny,' Collins said. 'The person investigating incel is Melanie Ryan, the Dublin profiler.'

'I told you she was good,' Deirdre said starting the engine. 'Have you Lizzie Howard's address? We can phone Melanie on the way.'

Collins looked it up on Google Maps and directed her.

'This is our guy, Collins, I'm sure of it.'

Collins didn't reply. He was beginning to think the same thing but they needed more than a name on a list.

Chapter 22

Lizzie Howard's home was off the Model Farm Road and they were there in ten minutes. Deirdre had driven fast, angrily, as Collins read news from his phone about incel members who had shot, stabbed or harassed women in the US, UK and Canada.

He phoned Melanie Ryan and left a voice message.

The estate looked fairly new; detached and semi-detached houses, some backing on to the pitches of the Cork Institute of Technology. All the gardens were neat and well groomed, except one. Number 45 had three large flower pots out front but whatever had been growing in them was dead and shrivelled. The grass was uncut in the lawn and the blinds were drawn in all three windows on show. Bindweed was flourishing in bushes near the front gate.

'Long gone, I'd say,' Deirdre said as they approached the door, which didn't have a spy hole to look out through. There was opaque glass at either side but it appeared that newspapers had been stuck on the inside of the panes. Collins looked through the slot for post but there was a flap on either side and he couldn't see through.

Deirdre rang the bell. Nothing.

Collins bent and glimpsed under the large window's blind. He thought he saw movement.

Deirdre rang the bell again. Then she knocked on the door.

'Gardaí,' she said loudly. 'Detectives Donnelly and Collins from the Cork Special Detective Unit. We want to talk to you, Lizzie, it's very important.'

A woman opened the front door of the adjacent house and peered out. Collins beckoned her closer. He showed her his badge over a low wall.

'We want to have a chat with Lizzie,' he said quietly. 'Is she all right?'

'She never comes out any more, her food is delivered,' the woman said. She looked about eighty – well dressed and sharp.

'When did this start?'

'A good few weeks ago, I don't know what happened. She was so nice, very chatty and happy in herself but now she won't come to the door or anything. I can … I can hear her crying sometimes at night. I don't know what to do, I don't know any of her friends or family. I tried to call into her a few times but she won't let me in or anything.'

Collins nodded. Deirdre had joined them.

'She's been locked in there for weeks,' Collins told her. 'Are you the woman who rang the gardaí about something suspicious?'

'Yes, two weeks ago. I saw a man jumping over Liz's back wall. I'm a hundred per cent sure. It was nearly two in the morning and I couldn't sleep. I often can't since my husband died. I heard a noise out the back and when I looked, it was a full moon and I saw him clearly. He had a hood on and all black clothes. He hopped over the wall no bother even though it's over six foot tall.'

'Any sign of anyone since?'

'No,' she said and gave a quick head shake. 'And I keep a good eye out.'

'Did Lizzie talk to the gardaí on the night?' Deirdre said.

'Oh, she did. She didn't want to open up first but they made her. They said they were going to break it down.'

'What's your own name?" Collins said.

'Betty Kelly,' she said.

'Thanks Betty, you can go back in now. We'll call into you if we need you.'

The woman retreated behind her door. Collins looked again at Number 45.

'What do you think?' Deirdre said.

'I'm just going to drop in a card with my number and a note. Then we might stand by the gate to let her see us.'

He took out a card from his top jacket pocket. He wrote on it: 'You must come out Lizzie or we're going in. Phone me first.' He dropped it through the letter box and pressed the bell several times.

They walked out the gate and stood on the footpath. There was the sound of a training session from one of the pitches in the distance. After a few minutes, Collins' phone rang. It was an 021 number.

'Don't say anything, he's listening,' a voice whispered. 'That card could be fake. Anyone could print one.'

'Okay,' Collins said. 'I'm giving you more ID now.' He walked to the door. He pushed his wallet and his badge through the letter box. He returned to the path and waited. He and Deirdre could see movement through the glass. After a few minutes, he heard the line go dead. The front door opened.

They walked through. The air was fetid and hot in the hall. He could see dust motes swirling in the sunlight that was streaming through the door.

The door to the side of the hall was closed but another door straight ahead was partly open. Collins could see the curtains at the top of on the stairs were closed.

'Close the front door! Close the front door!' a woman's voice said.

Deirdre closed it and the room was cast into shadow. Collins pressed a light switch to his right. There was dust on the wooden floor. There were spiders' webs on the banisters.

Collins pushed the door open and walked into a kitchen/ living room area. He couldn't see her in the gloom. The air was stifling and there was the smell of rotten food. He could hear the buzzing of flies. It looked like they were behind the blinds of both windows, which had been pulled down. There was some kind of black plastic sheeting covering the glass in the back door.

'Where are you?' he said.

She stood up. She had been sitting in the corner on a two-seater sofa.

'I can see and hear everything from here,' she said. She held out her hand with his wallet and badge. He moved forward and saw her cower. He stopped.

'You can put them on the table there,' he said. 'If you like.'

She did so and slinked back into the corner.

'This is Deirdre and my name is Tim,' he said. 'We'd like to talk to you, Lizzie. Is it okay if I call you Lizzie?'

'Liz is fine,' she said. 'But ye'll have to turn off your phones first. Otherwise, he'll be able to hear everything.'

Collins took out his phone. Deirdre did the same.

'Off, off?' he said.

'Yes, totally off. Otherwise, he can get inside it. He can get inside any computer.'

Collins and Deirdre turned off their phones.

'I'll have to make sure,' she said and she pointed at the table. They put the phones on the table. Collins noticed how thin she was. She was wearing a dark Adidas track suit and dark runners. Her hair was tied up in a ponytail. She moved to a drawer and took out a narrow long box. She unspooled about three feet of aluminium kitchen foil, put it on the table, laid the phones in the middle of it and folded the foil over them, again and again.

'People think aluminium can't block signals, but it can,' she said. She had a slight Cork accent but her voice was clear and without emotion. When the phones were fully wrapped she put them in the fridge. Collins looked at Deirdre and gave a slight nod.

'The freezer is better but it damages the phone after a while. Ye can sit at the table,' she said, leaning on the arm of the sofa.

Deirdre and Collins sat down by the table. A swarm of fruit flies began to hover around them.

'Do ye have guns?'

'Yes,' Deirdre said.

'Good,' Liz said. 'He can't stop bullets.'

'Who can't stop bullets?' Deirdre said.

'Him,' Liz said. 'Him. Don't make me say his name.'

'The man you used to work for?'

She nodded.

'A few weeks ago, you were going to work, everything was fine. What happened?' Deirdre said.

'Everything wasn't fine. He started asking me for sex.'

'And you said no.'

'Of course, I said no. We never had sex, he was my boss, never … never anything more. He lost it, he started shouting at me. He told me he was entitled to have sex, every man should be able to have sex. Women had no right to stop them.'

'What did you do?'

'I went home. He was ranting and raving. Then he texted me and said sorry, he didn't know what came over him. He asked me to go back, it would never happen again.'

'So, you went back.'

'Yes. I didn't know what else to do. It's my job, I thought it might have been a once-off. Then he was fine for a few days, he was nice to me. Then I went in one morning and he came down and … he tried …'

Collins looked at Deirdre. *Keep going.*

'He tried to rape you,' Deirdre said.

'Yes. But I screamed and he got a fright. Then I grabbed my bag and ran out of there. And I haven't been back since.'

'What happened after that day?'

'He started texting me first. About everything he was going to do to me. Sex things. He sent me horrible photos and videos. And some links to websites about how men were oppressed by women and refused sex. Then he starting phoning me. He'd told me he'd find me wherever I went, through my phones and computer. And he can, too!'

She stood up, agitated.

'Where are your phones? He can track your phones.'

'We turned them off, Liz,' Deirdre said. 'You wrapped them in tin foil and put them in the fridge, remember?'

'Oh yeah.'

'Was it he tried to break in here?' Deirdre said. 'Two weeks ago?'

'It was him, I know it was. Betty next door rang the guards and he ran off but I know he'll come again. I know he will.'

'You didn't tell the gardaí about him? That night?'

'No.' She began to sob. 'I didn't know what to do. I thought he might go away but he'll never go away. He says I owe him sex for all the money he paid me.'

'Do you have all the texts and photos on your phone, Liz?' Collins said.

'No. He deleted them, he can get into any phone. That's what he does. He gets into computers and phones are just computers. That's his business, working with companies to protect their computers.'

THERE WAS a pause. Collins wasn't sure what to do but they had to move forward. This woman clearly needed help.

'Liz,' Collins said. 'We're here now so nobody is going to hurt you. Is that okay?'

'Yes,' she sniffed. 'But what about when ye go away again?'

'First of all,' Collins said. 'Now that we know about him, his behaviour will change. These people are cowards deep down. We've just been out to interview him about another case, another woman.' Collins did not tell her that woman had been raped and murdered.

'What other woman?' she said.

'I can't tell you the details,' Collins said. 'But the net is tightening around him. I'd like you to talk to another garda, she will explain the situation and your options much better than we can. She's called a Family Liaison Officer and it's her job to advise people like yourself about what would be best for you to do. She can answer all your questions better than we can. She meets people like yourself every day and she's very nice, very kind. I'd really like you to talk to her. Will you talk to her, Liz? I can ring her now.'

'Okay,' she said. She broke down in tears.

CHAPTER 23

COLLINS USED Liz's landline to phone the station with the address and the urgent alert for Kate to come. He also requested an unmarked car to park near Ormsby's office to keep an eye on the place.

Kate arrived to the house after 1 p.m. and Collins briefed her standing outside the front door while Deirdre reassured Liz inside. He and Deirdre left the pair to talk alone.

He was glad of the fresh air as they stood by the car – he didn't know which made him more uneasy: the oppressive and fetid breathlessness of the house or the sense of terror that Liz had exuded. Maybe it was the combination of both, the way they accentuated each other.

He felt defenceless without his phone, and there was a lot to do. He borrowed one from a uniformed garda who had arrived with Kate. Then he and Deirdre briefed O'Rourke and Brennan with the phone on speaker in the car.

O'Rourke said that they would have to wait for Liz's formal statement before they could arrest Ormsby.

'What about bringing in him for questioning, ramping the pressure up?' Deirdre said.

'Let me talk to legal about that,' O'Rourke said. 'What do you think, Collins?'

'I'm afraid he's a flight risk. He's very wealthy by all accounts and we need to learn more about this incel cell, what that's all about.'

'Is somebody watching him?' Brennan said.

'Yes sir,' Collins said. 'There's an unmarked car outside his office.'

'What kind of a witness is she?' O'Rourke said. 'Is she credible?'

'She's very distraught,' Deirdre said. 'Looks like she's traumatised to me, sir. Almost paranoid. We told you about the phones and the place being in darkness and everything. I think she'll be okay after a while when she gets some medical attention.'

'Do you think she'll make a formal charge?' O'Rourke said.

Collins nodded yes to Deirdre.

'I do, sir,' Deirdre said. 'The trouble is that he appears to have deleted all the messages he sent to her phone, if we can believe what she said about that. She's a bit paranoid about phones.'

'What about his links with Helen O'Driscoll, Collins?' O'Rourke said.

'He denied being in contact with Helen, sir, but we found a recent message on her phone from him with a photo linking them. Now – that had been deleted, either by her or him, we don't know which, but IT were able to retrieve it. Unfortunately, it appears that Liz Howard has destroyed her own phone but if we can get the pieces of that, we might be able to retrieve the memory and the TU might be able to get something.

'This whole incel thing makes our case stronger for an arrest and charge but we'll still need something in the line of hard evidence for a murder conviction.'

'Okay,' O'Rourke said. 'Try to get a statement from her asap and we'll take it from there. Find out what you can about these incel nutters and see if we can use it. We've having a meeting at eighteen hundred hours, if ye can make that, be there.'

'Yes, superintendent,' Collins said.

A few minutes later Kate appeared at the front door and beckoned to Collins and Deirdre.

'She has agreed to talk to Bríd Crean and get legal advice,' Kate said. 'But I want to have her medically checked out, too. I think she's traumatised and doesn't really know what's fully going on.'

'Sounds good,' Collins said. 'But I don't think bringing her in to Pope's Quay is an option in her state.'

'I just phoned Bríd there,' Kate said. 'She'll meet us at a safe house they use on the back road to Glanmire. It's in the country and perfect for this. I'll try to persuade Liz to stay there for a few days and recuperate. She hasn't eaten in two days, for fuck's sake. I think she's dehydrated, too.'

'Not surprised with the heat in there,' Deirdre said. 'What do you want from us?'

'You and I will travel with her in the Audi. Collins, you and Mark follow on in the squad car. Is that okay?'

'Fine,' Collins said.

'Okay,' Kate said. 'Will you bring around the Audi, Deirdre, and I'll bring Liz out? She's packing a bag now. Do you have sunglasses? She hadn't been outside for weeks.'

Deirdre went to get the sunglasses.

'Is there no one to mind the house?' Kate said to Collins.

'There's another car with two of the Gurran lads around the corner, I didn't want the place to be crowded out here,' Collins said. 'I'll get them now.'

'Will you get the phones, Collins, when Liz comes out?' Deirdre said, handing her sunglasses to Kate.

'Sure. I want to talk to Melanie Ryan, too,' Collins said.

On the way to the safe house, as the uniformed garda Mark O'Hara drove, Collins checked his missed calls. One was from Melanie Ryan and he phoned her back.

'Ryan,' she answered.

'Hi Melanie, Tim Collins from Cork here, sorry I missed your call, we had a situation here. Do you know anything about the Helen O'Driscoll murder investigation?'

'I was just told by my boss that I'm to work with ye on it. I'll be heading to Cork tomorrow or Sunday to read the file.'

'That's great, we need all the help we can get. I just heard that a person of interest is on an incel list and I was given your name in connection with it.'

'Which incel list? There are a few, now.'

'I got the info from HQ, they said it was a list ye got from some fellow from Galway who was trying to get a child into his car and he had a printed list to try to get off. The name we're interested in is Blake Ormsby.'

'Oh. Yes, I know the one you mean.'

There was a pause. For a moment Collins thought the line had gone dead. They were driving along the South Link, heading for the Jack Lynch Tunnel.

'Hello? Are you there?' Collins said.

'Yes, can I ring you back, Tim? This list is classified and I just want to get approval before I say anything more. I don't think it'll be a problem, I'll ring you back.

'As soon as you can. This guy is a suspect and we just found out it isn't his first sexual assault. We need to nail him down before he kills again.'

'Okay,' she said. 'I'll phone you right back.'

COLLINS LOOKED at his watch. 14:08. He chatted with Mark, who was from Charleville. Collins rang the gardaí who were watching Ormsby's office.

'Hi lads, Collins here, anything else after the postman?'

'No, Collins, not a sign. But if he leaves should we follow him?'

'Yes, I'm going to ring the station there now and see if we can get another car to give ye backup in case he does a runner.'

'What kind of a threat is he? Can we use force?'

'No. He hasn't been charged or anything and isn't in the process of committing a crime. Just follow him at a distance and phone me immediately if he gets on the move.'

Collins checked his watch again when they pulled into the safe house to the north-east of the city: 14:40. Still no call from Melanie Ryan.

He had been there before. The building, at the end of a quiet country road, was new and large – it could accommodate seven women at a time. It had been purpose-built and funded by an anonymous benefactor. She also paid for its maintenance by Cork Refuge for Women, CRW. The centre, called *Suaimhneas*, was run by a woman called Emily Creedon whom Collins knew and had helped out in the past. It was not his first time seeing a traumatised woman arrive there.

Mark pulled the squad car to one side and Collins watched as Kate got out of the Audi and went around to help Liz, who stumbled when she stood up. Deirdre and Kate had to support her as far as the front door.

A woman came out through the entrance to meet them and all four went into the building.

Melanie Ryan phoned him at 15:30 as he was walking on the gravel under some beech trees. He had one eye on the door of the building but he knew better than to try to go inside. No men were allowed in.

'Melanie,' he said.

'Okay, I've cleared that with my boss. Sorry about that but you know the way.'

Collins did know the way but seldom followed it.

'Sure, no bother.'

'Okay. Here's what we have: Blake Ormsby was on that list but the guy we got it from is mentally unstable so we haven't really acted on it yet. We have infiltrated one of their chat lines and Ormsby's alias has cropped up on that, too.'

'One thing you should know about Ormsby,' Collins said. 'He's an expert on cyber security so he'll be covering his tracks big time online and he can hack a lot of systems, including people's phones. Is it illegal to be an incel member?'

'No. We're thinking of charging one or two of them with hate speech, but in itself it's not illegal to be involved. They don't have members as such, it's looser than that.'

'What can you tell me about incel?'

'Well, the idea goes back a long while – over thirty years – but it's only recently with the big jump in social media and conspiracy theories that the men are becoming more overtly misogynistic with a big sense of grievance and entitlement. If you can't blame the government blame women. Others are stoking up hatred online and then somebody is radicalised and goes out with a gun or whatever and kills people. Thankfully we haven't had that here yet but I'd say it's only a question of time. This guy Ormsby might be the first one, who knows?'

'How many are involved in Ireland, do ye know?'

'No, we have no idea, it isn't location based, it's mostly online.'

'How many are on this Galway list? Can I see it?'

'I'll take a picture of it and send it on. You mentioned that it might not be his first time, can you tell me about that?'

Collins told her what they had just found out about Lizzie Howard.

'Well, as a profiler, this makes a huge difference. I'm not sure when I'll get to Cork, but I'll see you soon. I'll send that list now.'

'Can you send it to another number, have you a pen? Because I met Ormsby earlier, I'm concerned he might be able to access my phone.' He gave her the number of a second phone he used which was pay-as-you-go.

Moments later his phone pinged with a text message and two attachments. Collins pulled out his reading glasses from his top pocket and put them on.

He opened the first image and enlarged it with two of his fingers. He scanned the list of six names in alphabetical order from Maloney to Young. The third name was Blake Ormsby with his incel alias 'Grand Gentleman'. He read the other names again but didn't recognise any of them.

He opened the second image and enlarged it. He looked down through it. Another six names in alphabetical order from Bateson to Jenkins. He gasped when he saw the second last name. It was William Hughes and his alias was 'Rogue1'.

'Jesus Christ,' Collins said. 'They're connected.'

He looked up and saw a car pull into the car park. It was Bríd Crean.

He approached her and she stopped.

'What can you tell me about her before I go in?' she said.

Collins briefed her.

'Can you get her to press charges?' he said. 'We need to get this guy off the streets, the chances are he'll attack other women.'

Bríd glared at him.

'I'll do what's best for my client,' she said. 'That's my job. Your job is to get the evidence to convict him.'

She turned and walked away. Collins did not reply.

He opened the lists on his phone again and looked down through them. He tried to make sense of what it meant.

DEIRDRE AND Kate came out of the building not long after Bríd Crean went in.

'How is she?' Collins said.

Kate said: 'Not great to be honest. The doctor is on her way from Mayfield to see her now. She needs to be sedated, God love her, she has a hard road ahead.'

Collins didn't reply.

When they said their goodbyes to Kate, Collins said to Deirdre: 'I have some news, Melanie Ryan sent me the list of incel names. There are two attachments, have a look.' He handed her his phone and unlocked the car.

Deirdre sat in and looked at the lists.

'Fucking hell,' she said when she saw the second list. 'That bastard Hughes.'

'Yes,' Collins said. 'We're not finished with him, yet.'

<<Private Chat Room 121/Max Level>>

Rogue1: The lack of quality of discussion on that public chat room is appalling.

Grand Gentleman (admin): They are the foot soldiers, we don't need them to be articulate, only willing. Armies are made of people like them.

Rogue1: I suppose, how was it?

Grand Gentleman (admin): It was amazing, more than I could hope have hoped for. Esp after I was interrupted the last time.

Rogue1: Did she beg, did she make a lot of noise? She was always noisy in bed with me!

Grand Gentleman (admin): Not much noise, she begged me to do it quickly but I couldn't oblige her. I found out since [from my surveillance] that her brat was hiding under the floorboards.

Rogue1: Is he a threat?

Grand Gentleman (admin): No, he saw nothing. When I caught her in the bathroom, she shouted 'PANIC'. That must have been a code for him to hide, I never saw him and he never saw me.

Rogue1: You monitoring their systems?

Grand Gentleman (admin): All under control. How about at your end, you still a suspect?

Rogue1: *My alibi is air tight, I made sure it would be. They have nothing and they cancelled their so called 'interview'.*

Grand Gentleman (admin): *Your links with her are unfortunate.*

Rogue1: *It was serendipity since they can't link the two of us. BTW is this chat secure?*

Grand Gentleman (admin): *Totally, there's nobody alive who can get in.*

Rogue1: *Good, have you the next one planned out?*

Grand Gentleman (admin): *All under control, maybe in a week or two when things calm down. After that, the panic will break out big time.*

Rogue1: *What's the plan, then?*

Grand Gentleman (admin): *Maybe after three or four, we activate the army, get the foot soldiers involved for widespread action.*

Rogue1: *Not so sure they're up to it. Most of them are only here for the porn.*

Grand Gentleman (admin): *Of course. But say 2 or 3 of them act out and that spurs another one. We can groom some of the weaker ones to pick their own victim. Imagine the ripple effect? Those bitches have had things their own way for too long.*

Rogue1: *That will put the fear of God in them.*

Grand Gentleman (admin): *It will put the fear of Men in them, that's what we really want.*

Rogue1: *They will all bow down eventually, like my wife (or as I call her, The Cash Cow).*

Grand Gentleman (admin): *The incel Rebellion begins here.*

CHAPTER 24

DEIRDRE REPORTED on the interview with Ormsby, the interactions with Liz Howard and the incel development to the group at the 6 p.m. briefing. Collins felt she again summed up the events brilliantly and he could see how energised the group was after she sat down.

'Okay, thank you detective,' O'Rourke said. 'Let's get everything we can on this Mr Ormsby. Obviously in relation to the murder investigation, but we'll want to nail him for the sexual harassment and assault of that woman. And we need to learn more about this incel crowd, too. I've contacted Superintendent Joe Mannix about the profiler Melanie Ryan to come down and join the team.'

'I think we should bring Ormsby in now,' Collins said. 'Before he gets lawyered up and gets his act together. I think if we go hard at him tonight he might crack and we could get a confession in the bag.'

'No,' O'Rourke said. 'We have no formal statement of assault or harassment and we have no evidence to link him with Helen O'Driscoll's murder. We'll keep an eye on him overnight and tomorrow and start building a case against him. I will issue you all with duties in the morning briefing.'

'With all due respect, sir, I think he's brittle and we need to go hard and quick or it could really drag out and we might lose our chance. He could attack another woman, too. We need to bring him in, right now.'

There was a shocked silence in the room and Collins realised he had gone too far, but he didn't care anymore. He felt a tap from Deirdre's foot to shut up.

'The decision has been made, detective. Last time I checked I was leading this investigation, not you. I'll see you in my office in ten minutes. This briefing is over, nobody is to go home for the moment, we'll need some of ye to co-ordinate the overnight watching of Ormsby. Tom will let ye know who will be involved. Seven a.m. here tomorrow if ye don't hear otherwise.'

O'Rourke stood up and left the room, flanked by Brennan.

'Jesus, what did you go and do that for?' Deirdre said, turning to Collins, shaking her head.

'He should have asked our opinion before making a unilateral decision. I really think we can break this guy if we isolate him and go hard. He'll dig in if we give him time.'

'Yeah, but that wasn't the way to go about it! You've shown O'Rourke up in front of the group and he can't back down now. We could have worked on him face to face.'

Collins could feel his face redden. She was right.

'He wasn't there to see the state of Liz Howard, a prisoner in her own home,' he said. 'How do we know there isn't another Liz Howard or two or three of them going through the same torture? We have to end this now.'

'Will you at least calm down before you meet O'Rourke?' Deirdre said, standing up. 'Can I go in with you and deflect some of the shit he's going to throw at you?'

'No, Deirdre, but thanks. This isn't my first time up in front of the headmaster and it won't be my last. It'll be fine. I won't do anything stupid.'

CHAPTER 25

ON THE way up to O'Rourke's office, Collins decided to eat humble pie and apologise. O'Rourke was one of the calmer superintendents he had worked with but he had a reputation for discipline. Collins didn't want to be taken off the case and that was a real possibility now.

He knocked on the door and heard 'Come in' from inside. O'Rourke was behind his desk tapping on a keyboard. Brennan was sitting to one side on his phone.

'i-n-c-e-l,' Brennan said, 'I only just heard of them now myself but the Dublin Castle have been monitoring them.'

'Sit down, Tim,' O'Rourke said, which Collins realised was conciliatory.

'I want to apologise,' Collins said, sitting down. 'I shouldn't have spoken out like that, especially in front of the group. It won't happen again sir.'

'Thank you,' O'Rourke said, looking at Collins calmly, the fingers of his two hands intertwined on the desk. He paused.

'Why do you think we should move on Ormsby now?'

Collins was taken aback, he had been expecting a bollocking. He gathered his thoughts.

'I got a sense of a lack of control in him today. That he was on the edge. I think he might break and his hatred for women might slip out. He was putting on a good show but then Deirdre asked him if he and Helen had a sexual relationship in college and he kind of lost it. I think he has triggers that if we push hard, he'll blurt everything out. Melanie Ryan told me today that these characters often go out with a bang if we give him scope. She said he could attack other women.'

O'Rourke nodded.

'Okay, I should have asked you how you think we should proceed and that was remiss of me. But you shouldn't have questioned my authority in the group, you should have spoken to me one-to-one after the meeting. You've led teams, you know how important authority is and how easily it can be undermined. If I lose that group of officers, the investigation will fail, so I need to do something about what just happened …'

The phone rang on his desk and he answered it.

'Yes, thanks for calling so quickly, assistant commissioner. Can I put you on hold for two seconds please, I have someone here with me?'

He pressed the hold button on the phone.

'Okay,' he said, fixing Collins with look. 'I'll bear in mind what you said and I'll talk to this man and a few others about it. In the meantime, I'm suspending you for two days without pay starting tomorrow. Report back for duty on Sunday morning, first thing. No arguments, clear?'

Collins didn't hesitate.

'Yes, sir,' he said, standing. 'Thank you sir.'

'Jesus, THAT's a bit harsh,' Deirdre said, when Collins told her about the suspension.

'Ah, it's only a couple of days. For a minute I thought I'd be off the case.'

'Still. Did you say something to him?'

'No. I apologised to him from the off. Then he asked me why I thought we should bring Ormsby and grill him straight away. He said he'd think about it and then he suspended me.'

'A bit odd, but you get two days off. What'll you do?'

'I'll probably go down to West Cork, give me a ring if anything happens. I'll be back Sunday.'

Part 2

No Place Like It

Chapter 26

Collins had been in a relationship with the Antrim woman Katie Cunningham for seven months. He met her in The Carbery Arms bar in Bandon when she had been its manager and Collins had been recuperating from a poisoning.

He had been delighted when, in April, she quit her job in the pub and opened a clothes shop in Dunmanway. She and her daughters Susan (17) and Zoe (14) had been living in the town for two years. Not running the pub in Bandon meant no commuting, more sociable working hours and a sense of normality.

Since then, he had been spending more and more time in West Cork with them, in their terraced house near the town centre. It was only a ten-minute drive away from where he had grown up outside Ballineen and that circularity was partly welcome and partly unsettling. His mother was only thirty minutes away in Bandon. She and Katie got on like a house on fire though he preferred to keep them apart as they ganged up on him.

His contentment in the domesticity of Katie, Susan and Zoe surprised him and he wondered why he felt so comfortable with them. Maybe he was getting old, maybe it was time to settle down with this ready-made family.

The living room of Katie's house was rectangular, with the TV at one end and a long sofa at the other. Zoe and Katie usually sat on the sofa together, the distance between them depending on Zoe's current level of umbrage with her mother. When not in her bedroom or out with friends, Susan sat in an armchair at the other end of the room tapping on her phone with her thumbs and sighing exasperated sighs.

Collins sat on one of the good table chairs near the sofa, trying to stay small. Trying also to understand the attraction of the various bake-offs, dance-offs, date-offs and build-offs on TV that seem to animate Zoe and Katie so much.

Susan treated him with the calm and knowing indifference that seventeen-year-olds can muster with ease. They spoke about art – Frido Kahlo, mostly, with whom she was obsessed – and Collins had loaned her some books which he didn't expect to get back. She had just finished her Leaving Cert and hoped to go to art college in Cork in September.

Zoe was sporty and moody. She liked to talk to Collins about Liverpool, their shared love, and her own Gaelic football with the school and the local club, Dohenys. Sometimes she blanked him. On the afternoon after his suspension by O'Rourke, Collins brought Katie a coffee to her shop and asked if there was anything he could do about the silences, or if he was doing something wrong. Katie was checking her orders behind the counter, in a big battered notebook.

'It's not you, it's her, Collins,' she said, writing furiously in the book. 'Shit, I thought I ordered those jackets.'

'What do you mean?'

Katie looked up at him. 'Don't take this this the wrong way but she's going through a phase where she's obsessed by sex.'

'What?' Collins looked at her, aghast.

'It happens most girls at some time or another. We had a big talk about it the other week. You probably notice how she's allergic to any physical contact between us and she's usually moody just before bedtime or first thing. And she blames you for us having sex.'

'Jesus!' Collins said.

'She'll get used to it,' Katie said, taking out her phone. 'I'm more worried about Susan, to be honest. That vegan stuff is doing my head in. I gave her the talk about boys but she's headstrong, that one. Luckily she seems to have gone off young fellas, she's too young for a bairn. We can't afford one, anyway.'

Collins held her eye.

'What?' she said. 'No, Collins, we had this conversation. You're not giving me money.'

'It's not giving, Katie,' he said. 'It's called contributing.'

She smiled at him and gave him a peck on the cheek.

'You keep contributing your little bit in the bedroom and that'll do me,' she said. 'Whatever Zoe thinks about it.'

'Hey, less of the little,' Collins said.

'I'm saying nothing,' Katie smirked. 'I'll tell you what, you can get the takeaway tonight, how about that? And a bottle of wine … or two. Now stop distracting me. Away out, you.'

FOR DINNER Katie insisted on them sitting at the table and asked Susan to set it beforehand.

'Why do we have to sit there?' Susan said. 'Why can't we sit where we normally do?' Collins had heard this argument before.

'Because,' Katie replied, 'there isn't enough room around the island for the four of us. What's the big deal? It's only twelve feet away.'

'The big deal is I don't like it. And I don't see why I should have to sit with you all, anyway, while you're all masticating dead meat.'

'Set the table, Susan, it isn't much to ask.'

'What's masticating?' Zoe said, looking on.

COLLINS WENT into the living room to phone Deirdre.

'Hi Collins, how are things down west?'

'Oh fine, any news there? Has Ormsby been brought in yet?'

'No, the super wants to hold off until Liz Howard gives a formal statement but Bríd Crean said she's still under sedation and won't be ready for a few days at least. Melanie Ryan is on her way so we might get more about incel from her and Ormsby's involvement. I think he should be brought in because of that alone.'

Collins smiled.

'I hope you didn't say anything to O'Rourke,' he said.

'Haha, very funny. He did sign off on my trip to London. I got hold of Lea Thompson and she'll meet me there on Tuesday. I'm flying out first thing, back that evening. So, you'll have to hold the fort then.'

'Well done, let's talk about that on Sunday.'

'Grand, I have to go here, see you then.'

AFTER DINNER, Susan went out to meet her friends. Katie said she had to be home by eleven to which Susan rolled her eyes. She wore leggings and a crop top which showed her bellybutton, which – she had announced some time previously – she was going to have pierced on the day of her eighteenth birthday, as well as getting her first tattoo – of many.

'We're playing O'Donovan Rossa in the West Cork Final next Saturday,' Zoe said to Collins. 'Will you come and watch us?'

'I will of course. Don't forget what I told you, now.'

'I won't,' Zoe said.

A friend of hers arrived with a football and they went to the GAA pitch, which was nearby. Zoe asked him to complain to the men in the club that they took up all the pitches and didn't let the Under 16 girls' team any place to train.

'I dunno,' she said, putting on her boots as her friend waited. 'Can't you, like, arrest them or something? That's discrimination, which is basically illegal. Isn't it?'

Collins said he'd see what he could do.

'You can open that other bottle, is what you can do,' Katie said. Collins looked out the window by the kitchen sink, at the blue sky above and sunlight on the roofs. He wished there was more light in the house and a garden. *Don't react if she says no,* he thought.

When they were settled in front of the TV on the sofa, he waited for an ad break and said: 'I was wondering if you'd think about a bigger place.'

'I can't afford it, sure,' Katie said. 'We're grand here, anyway.'

'I know we talked about this but I think it's time I helped out a bit,' Collins said. 'Financially, I mean. I'm staying here so often, I think I should.' He looked at her, waiting for a reaction. She looked back at him. She placed her hand on his arm, leaned over and kissed him on the lips. She sighed.

'Thanks, Collins,' she said. 'But that would change everything. You know it would.'

'Is change such a bad thing?' he said.

'No, but what's the set-up, then? What are *we*, then, Collins?' She paused the TV and her expression became more serious. He knew that look well.

'We're a couple,' he said, shrugging. He regretted now not preparing better for this, not having planned something more definite to say.

What was she looking for? Some kind of long-term commitment? Surely not a proposal. He couldn't tell.

'Are we now?' she said. 'That's nice.' She snuggled against him. Collins said nothing. He'd keep chipping away at her.

AFTER AN hour Zoe came home and went upstairs.

'Don't you be on your phone all night, young lady,' Katie said.

'I won't.'

COLLINS LOOKED at his watch. It was getting late. He worried about Susan.

CHAPTER 27

A MONTH earlier, Collins drove Susan to Cork for an interview in the Crawford College of Art about the portfolio she had submitted in April. Katie had given him the 'heads up' that Susan wanted to talk to him about something.

LATE IN March, one Saturday night, Susan had arrived into the house after 1 a.m. Unusually, Collins and Katie were still up, having a cup of tea after a party they had been invited to by one of Katie's customers. When Susan walked into the living room she burst into tears. Collins went upstairs and Katie told him later that Susan thought there had been a sexual assault at the party she had been at the night before.

'Is she okay?' Collins said. 'It wasn't her, was it?'

'No, no, a classmate of hers.'

'Did Susan witness it?'

'No. She didn't see anything; her friend Aoife thought she did, but she'd had a lot of drink. Anyway, the two of them got out of there and came home. I don't know, what do you think?'

'What did Aoife see?'

'She thinks she saw another girl in a bedroom with some boys who were having sex with her. The other girl, their classmate, Ruth, was very drunk and high on something.'

'For fuck's sake,' Collins said. 'And this was last night?'

'Yes,' Katie said. 'There's nothing can be done for the poor girl now, anyway, but Susan feels guilty she didn't do something at the time.'

'Getting out was probably the safest thing she could have done.'

'That's what I told her.'

Collins made some enquiries to local gardaí and got a phone call from a Bandon sergeant who had been given an anonymous tip-off that there was an 'incident' at a party outside Dunmanway the previous weekend. Collins suspected that Aoife or Susan had made the call. The garda, a woman, interviewed the victim who didn't want to make a complaint. She said that nothing had happened. The garda felt sure that she was lying and tried to draw her out but her parents weren't having any of it.

SUSAN WAS nervous before the art college interview and wanted to make sure that she had the full copy of her portfolio and everything else she needed. Collins knew how much going to art college meant to her and how hard she had worked on the portfolio. Katie was at the shop, her assistant had phoned in sick that morning.

Outside Enniskeane, Susan said, in a panic: 'I think I forgot something.'

Collins pulled in.

'What is it?' he said.

'It's the copy of the Frida Kahlo drawing I based my first set of sketches on. I need it for the interview.'

She riffled through her folders but couldn't find the drawing.

'We have to go back,' she said.

'Okay, Susan,' Collins said. 'But your meeting is at three and it's after two, now. If we turn around, you'll be late and I don't think that's the best thing to do.'

'But I need it!'

'Okay,' Collins said. 'Is it a famous drawing?'

'Yes, it's the one of the "The Two Fridas".'

'So, the woman you're meeting will know it. She's an artist herself, she'll be very familiar with it, you can tell her about it and she'll know it.'

'No. I need to have it. I have to show her the two hearts!' Susan's face was bright red, she was close to tears. Collins had to calm things down.

'Okay, I have a suggestion,' Collins said. 'But we need to get going, will you let me run with it?'

'Okay,' Susan said and she began to cry.

'There's a library in the college, right?' Collins said.

'Yes,' Susan said, wiping her eyes.

'And they will have a lot of books about Frida Kahlo. One of them is bound to have a copy of the drawing you need.'

'But they mightn't give me the book for the interview.'

'But they can photocopy the drawing for you. Why don't I phone them and ask them to do that?'

'Okay,' Susan said, unconvinced.

Collins phoned the library and not only did they have the drawing, but the library assistant knew it and would have a copy for Susan when she arrived and wouldn't charge her for it.

At Inishannon, Susan asked Collins to pull into a Centra to get some water. She didn't feel well and was afraid she might get sick.

Collins said he'd get the water and told Susan to get some fresh air in the garage forecourt. He phoned Katie and asked what he should do.

'Distract her, Collins. Tell her about some famous painter you know. I don't know, come up with some oul' shite or other. Give her a wee pep talk, gee her up, like.'

Fuck's sake, Collins thought. *How do you give a pep talk to a seventeen-year-old artist?*

When they pulled out, Collins talked about some of the great museums he had been in like the Louvre, the Prado and his favourite, the Hermitage in St Petersburg, but he didn't think she was engaged.

A few miles later, Susan said: 'I want to ask you something.'

Thank God, Collins thought. *A distraction.*

'Okay,' Collins said. 'Fire away.'

'Remember the night I came home upset?'

'Yes,' Collins said. It wasn't the distraction he'd been hoping for.

'Well, I know Mam told you about what happened that night and I wanted to ask you how can they get away with it? How can that happen, that five of them rape her and they just get away with it?'

'Oh, Susan, that's really hard to explain and I'm not sure I can.'

'But you're a guard, can't you do something about it?'

'I … there's not much I can do, I'm afraid. I wish I could have a better answer, but let me explain. To prove a sexual assault, you need to have proof, right?'

'I know that. But Ruth didn't even do her Leaving Cert, she dropped out of school and everything. Her life is ruined and I'm going to college and all my friends are going to college and it's not fair. Some of *them* are even going to college.'

'It isn't fair,' Collins said. 'No, it isn't, but maybe she can get help and she might go to college too, sometime, if it's what she wants.'

'It is *so* wrong,' Susan said.

'It is. The reason the system is so much in favour of men, even men who attack women, is that men set up the system. Who do you think make laws?'

'I don't know, lawyers or judges or somebody like that?'

'It's actually politicians who make laws. They get lawyers like the attorney general to help them but it's mostly politicians and politicians are mostly middle-aged men like me. Even now there are very few women in the Dáil but some of the laws covering criminal and sexual assault are decades old and there were almost no women politicians then or any awareness of issues like consent or #MeToo or anything like that.

'So, the burden of proof has to fall to the victims, who are almost always women, and because we have a presumption of innocence, it's very difficult when it comes to sexual consent. If two people go into a room and close a door, it's often her word against his and it's almost impossible to prove lack of consent.

'If your friend's case went to court, the barrister defending those boys would argue that Ruth went into the room voluntarily and wanted to have sex with one or more of the boys. And then she changed her mind and made a false accusation of being raped.'

'That is *so* stupid, who'd want to have sex with the five of them and anyway she was too drunk to consent to anything.'

'That's all true,' Collins said. 'But the onus is always on the victim to prove it and there are so many decades of misinformation about women and sex that it's very hard to undo. It's all wrong but I don't have any solutions, I'm sorry to say. I'd like to change the system but as it is, the vast majority of attacks go unreported because the victims know they have very little chance of justice and they are forced to relive the experience in court in the public eye, which many of them can't face and I don't blame them. It's a mess.'

'Poor Ruth,' Susan said.

COLLINS DROVE into the city, the Crawford College was on the south side, he could drop her at the door. Katie would kill him if Susan was late or upset when they got there.

'You said earlier that they're getting off,' he said. 'But maybe you can actually do something about that.'

'Me? What can I do?'

'You're an artist,' Collins said. 'You can make art. What if you make a painting or a piece of sculpture in a few years and it's called "Ruth" and it's bought by the National Gallery and generations of people see it there and see what it contains. What if that happens?'

Susan turned to him, her mouth wide open. She turned away.

'Thank you,' she said.

'For what?'

'You're the first person who called me an artist. Even if I amn't yet, I do want to be one.'

'You are one, you will be one. And tell the lecturer you're meeting today that.'

'I don't know if I'll even get in. That's why she wants to interview me. Maybe she'll even tell me I'm not good enough, that I didn't get in.'

She started crying again. They had passed UCC, he'd have to drop her off soon.

'You keep calling it an interview, but I read the letter she sent you. It didn't mention anything about an interview; it said she wanted to talk to you about your "impressive submission".'

'Yeah, but she was just saying that.'

'These people are academics, they choose their words carefully,' Collins said, pulling into the small college car park. He turned the engine off.

'Oh Jesus,' Susan said. 'What if I don't get in?'

'You're getting in,' Collins said. 'You have a few minutes, yet, and I wanted to say this earlier. Let's say a hundred people apply to get in here every year. And they only take sixty. So, they get a hundred portfolios, from all over Ireland, right?'

'Right.'

'Now thirty of them haven't a hope, they didn't put the work in, their portfolios were a mess. You're not one of them, right?'

'Right.'

'Fifty will get in no bother, you're one of them for sure, but three or four of them are absolutely outstanding, they are the students these lecturers dream of working with every year. And these are the four they invite to meet, and you know why?'

'Why?'

'Because they are afraid those four might get a better offer elsewhere and they want to make sure ye come here to this college. That's why she wants to meet you, she wants to make sure she'll get to work with you for the next four years.'

Susan inhaled deeply. She nodded.

'One last thing,' Collins said. 'Tell her about what happened to Ruth in April and about all the Ruths out there. Tell her about all the art you're going to make for them.'

'I will,' Susan said, her eyes afire. 'I will.'

'And don't forget to call into the library first, Collins said.

'Oh, I forgot.'

'Susan?' Collins said. 'For the next hour you aren't influenced by Frida, you are Frida. You *are* Frida, do you hear me?'

Susan stared at him.

'Say, it, Susan.'

'I am Frida,' she said.

'Keep saying it until the meeting is over.'

'I am Frida,' Susan said. 'I *am* Frida.'

She picked up her bag, tried to smile, and got out of the car.

THE ART lecturer had confirmed to Susan that she would be accepted to the college if she got the requisite points, which weren't high. But Collins worried if he had should done something more about the sexual assault at the party and how it had affected Susan, let alone the victim. It galled him that those boys had gotten away with a blatant rape.

'No SIGN of Susan,' Collins said to Katie on the couch. It was well after eleven.

'That wee one is getting on my wick,' Katie said and sent her a message. A beep came back immediately.

'She'll be home in ten,' Katie said.

'How's she doing?' Collins said. 'About the party, I mean?'

'I think she's okay. She still feels guilty but what could she have done? If she went in there, they might have turned on her. She's excited about going to college, which reminds me. You don't know anybody with a flat or digs in Cork, do you?'

'Leave it with me. I know a couple of lads with properties around UCC.'

'Good man,' Katie said and kissed him again.

Chapter 28

The following day, Collins visited his mother in Bandon. She was in better form than the last time he had met her. There had been some good news from the consultant, he expected a full recovery and she could begin physiotherapy.

They went for a drive to Kinsale and he wheeled her around the town. They had lunch outside the Bulman, which she enjoyed, even having a glass of rosé.

She snoozed in the car on the way home and Collins could look at her properly, seeing her frailty. He knew her irritability was because of worry about her future mobility and independence, and he felt sorry for her.

After an early dinner, Collins and Katie went for a walk up into the hills above the town. The landscape quickly transformed itself to rock and heather and the views to the south and west changed moment on moment as the sun went lower. He wasn't sure why the grey limestone attracted him so much: whether it was because it seemed to exemplify West Cork and its differences to other places or it had something to do with how rugged it was.

Katie complained about the steepness of the hill and how unfit she was. Collins liked the feeling of sweat breaking out on his back under his t-shirt. He would never be fit again but he could walk forever, that's one thing he could still do. He'd learned how to walk on his first year on the beat in Dublin. You simply put one foot in front of the other and keep doing it. But doing it all night on rainy nights in Dublin dealing with public order offences by kids out of their heads on drugs was one thing. Doing it beside this sparkling woman in one of the places he loved best in the world was another.

At a sharp bend near the top of the hill, Collins and Katie moved aside to let a slow-moving car pass by. A Mercedes with a Dublin 09 registration, two men in the front seats. He looked at the driver and was about to salute him, as all locals do in West Cork. A thin man in his late twenties, wearing a black John Deere baseball cap.

Collins recognised the passenger. For a moment, he couldn't remember wherefrom but he knew immediately he was a criminal. Then he had a flashback to a small courtroom in Spain. Sun streaming in a window and a young man in handcuffs smiling at him and slowly drawing his forefinger across his own neck.

'Jones,' he whispered, as the car passed.

He froze. Instinctively, he felt to his side, but he was wearing a t-shirt on a sunny evening's walk. He didn't have a weapon. He had nothing. He noted the car registration.

'What?' Katie said. 'Are you okay, Collins? You look like you've seen a ghost.' She put her hand on his arm. He realised he was staring after the Merc. He looked around for a rock or a stick.

'We should go back,' he said.

'Why?' she said. 'We're nearly at the grotto. Who are they, did you know them?'

He shook his head.

'It's not safe, Katie,' he said, meeting her eye. 'They're killers and they shouldn't be here.' He looked up the road, the car had disappeared around another bend.

'I couldn't give two fucks who they are,' Katie said, her northern accent growing stronger. 'I'm finishing my walk.' She strode on.

'Jesus, Katie,' he said after her. 'They know me. If they think ...' But he knew she wouldn't change her mind. He followed on and took out his phone.

He found the number quickly. Detective Superintendent Ronan Buckley of the Serious Crimes Squad based in Dublin Castle. The call went straight to voicemail.

'Ronan, Collins here. I just saw Eddie Jones on a small byroad two kilometres north of Dunmanway. 09 D 20341, a black Merc. Ring me back as soon as you can.'

He remembered Spain when he and Buckley had gone out there to bring Jones home to face charges of murder and aggravated assault. Charges they couldn't convince the Spanish judge of – he had been bribed, they found out later.

THE ROAD widened at the grotto and Collins half-expected the car to be parked there. No sign. The road after the grotto straightened and Collins could see it was empty for the best part of a kilometre. Maybe Jones hadn't seen him or recognised him, but he couldn't be sure. Katie weeded the flowers in the garden in front of the grotto, something she did every time they walked there. She had hidden an old gardening trowel behind a bush. Collins checked his phone for reception.

'We should really go, Katie,' he said. 'Honestly, if they come back it mightn't end well.'

'Catch yourself on, Collins. Youse forget where I'm from. I know what killers are like and I don't run away from them, the wee shites. I tell you one thing: I could murder a pint when we get back to town, it's some hot.'

'This isn't funny. We're in the middle of nowhere, here.'

Katie looked around her and up at the sky.

'It's nice, though, isn't it? Quiet, like.'

Collins' phone rang. It was Buckley.

'Ronan,' Collins answered. 'I thought Jones was in Dubai or Qatar or somewhere.'

'He was, as far as we knew,' Buckley said. 'You sure it was him?'

'Almost certain, unless he has a double. Isn't there an extradition warrant out for him?'

'There was after that drugs find in Rosslare,' Buckley said.

'What do you mean, "was"?'

Buckley sighed.

'Well, our main source on the find went missing and then he recanted his statement, so we had to drop the extradition warrant. Listen, there's been another development, too. Can we meet?'

'Where are you, Ronan? What's going on?'

'Actually, I'm in Clonakilty, could we meet tomorrow? I know it's Sunday, but ...'

'Are you on holidays or something?' Collins said.

'I'll tell you tomorrow, can you meet me? Inchydoney Hotel? Noon?'

'I'll be back on a murder case in Cork, Ronan, so I can't meet you tomorrow.'

'I'll phone Frank O'Rourke now and square that away, I need to talk to you, Tim, and it can't wait.'

'Sorry, Ronan, no can do. I'm needed back in Cork.'

Collins looked at Katie, squatting over some lilies. A strand of hair had fallen out of her bandana over her right eye. She pushed it back. Collins wondered how Buckley had known who was leading the case. Maybe he saw it on the news.

'Don't make me pull rank, Tim,' Buckley said. 'But I will if I need to. I have to go. Noon, Inchydoney Hotel, tomorrow.' He hung up.

'Fuck,' Collins said.

As he and Katie walked down the hill, he got a text from Tom Brennan:

Superintendent O'Rourke says your return to case put back 24 hours until Monday 7 am.

'Fuck,' Collins said again.

'Will we go to The Arches or the Southern Star?' Katie said, ignoring his bad mood.

Chapter 29

Collins parked by the beach and walked up to the hill towards the Inchydoney Hotel, thinking about Buckley and how to deal with him.

Detective Superintendent Ronan Buckley was a celebrated character in the recent history of the gardaí, especially in Dublin. He had received most of the credit for breaking up the Sheils gang which had terrorised the north inner city for decades. He had soared up through the ranks in the previous ten years, going from detective sergeant to inspector to superintendent in record time.

A native of County Tipperary, he was unusual in that he was more a rugby fan than a hurling one. He had attended a boarding school in Roscrea and played for the first fifteen alongside some future internationals, whose names he liked to drop in the right company. When Collins first met him, working out of the Drugs Unit in Pearse Street, Buckley had been a young ambitious detective carefully planning and plotting out his career. His slightly upper-class accent and good clothes had marked him out at the time and didn't go down well with some of the more down-to-earth upper echelons in the force. So, he learned to tone that down and to play the senior gardaí at their own game, chatting about hurling and Gaelic football and learning about whatever interested them.

Collins spotted him sitting at the periphery of the dining area in front of the hotel. He looked as fit and hale as ever, with the sandy complexion of his father, a gentleman farmer outside Holycross. Collins recalled that his nickname had been 'cleft' among the female trainees in Templemore. It was a prominent feature of his long narrow face along with a slight bend in his nose from an encounter with a set of Limerick studs at the bottom of a ruck.

Buckley was sporting Ray-Bans, a straw fedora hat, an expensive looking (pink) polo shirt and tan chinos. Collins smiled – Buckley like to cut a dash, as his father used to say. Collins was glad he had dressed down with a battered old Neil Young t-shirt, jeans and sandals. Katie and Zoe had gone to walk the beach, Collins didn't want him to know any more of his business than was necessary.

But Collins knew too that behind the arrogance and ambition, there was a serious, hard-working and tough garda, who had made a huge difference in many people's lives for the better. Buckley couldn't understand Collins' lack of ambition – not because of the extra money, he'd argued on the night of a rugby international and after a few too many beers – but because he could achieve so much more as a higher ranked officer and he could lead others and bring them on.

Buckley saw Collins approach and smiled and stood up. They shook hands.

'Collins,' Buckley said. 'Looking good, man.'

Collins smiled, such a Buckley thing to say.

'Hi, Ronan, how are ya, boy? Welcome to God's country.'

'I'm very well, why wouldn't I be, down here in this beautiful place?'

'Yeah, nice spot all right. Don't tell me Dan Joe is forking out for this hotel?' Dan Joe was Dan Joe Cunneen, the deputy commissioner who was Buckley's boss.

'God no. I'm staying in a B&B in Clon. I'm just here for the weekend, Jessica came down. Her folks are minding Jack and Tess for a couple of days.' Collins nodded. Jessica was Buckley's glamorous and rich wife, her father was some kind of property magnate.

'Nice one,' Collins said. 'And the weather held up too.'

'And …' Buckley leaned forward conspiratorially. 'I hear you're spending a lot of time down around here yourself these days.' The grin betrayed Buckley's joy in knowing that Collins never liked to talk about his private life.

'I am indeed,' Collins replied. 'Back to my roots, as it were.'

'Oh yeah, I forgot that.' A waitress appeared. Buckley never seemed to have a problem getting quick service.

'Will you have something?' Buckley said.

'Just a coffee, please, I had a late breakfast.'

'And a sparkling water for me,' Buckley said. 'Do you have San Pellegrino?'

'Yes of course,' the waitress said and addressed Collins. 'Would you like a cappuccino or …?'

'Americano, black. Sorry, I should have said,' Collins replied. The waitress looked at him more closely.

'Aren't you Susan Cunningham's …?' The young woman looked for a word but couldn't find it. She began to blush.

'That's right. Are you a friend of Susan's?' He didn't recognise her but all Susan's friends seemed to look the same to him.

'Yeah, we're in school together,' she replied.

'Good stuff,' he said and nodded. 'What's your name?'

'Kellie,' she said. 'Kellie Tobin.' She blushed again and scurried off. Buckley's eyes twinkled. 'Susan?'

'She's Katie's eldest girl. Seventeen. Zoe is fourteen, so I have my hands full.' Collins shrugged, he didn't want to talk about this.

Buckley laughed. 'You should see your face, Collins! Wait until I tell the lads, the great Tim Collins having manners put on him by two teenage girls.'

'Ah they're good kids, Susan's big into art, Zoe into football.'

'Hey, a ready-made family, how bad? No changing nappies and all that mess. I don't miss that, I can tell you. Jessica either, we were just saying last night.'

'How are your two?'

'Oh, full of it. They have it too easy. I tell you: I'd send Jack to boarding school, toughen him up, if I could get away with it. Still,' Buckley said. He took out his phone and found a photo. Two beaming children with a cocker spaniel in sunlight. Jack the older, maybe twelve, with his father's thin face. Tess more like her mother, a beautiful smile and a head of blonde hair.

'Jack's getting tall,' Collins said. 'He's a Buckley. Tess is more like Jessica I think.'

'Spoiled rotten, she is,' Buckley said. Then he noticed the time on his phone. 'Shit, this case,' he said. 'I'm having lunch at one.'

'Okay,' Collins said, sitting up.

Buckley pulled his chair closer to Collins and looked around him.

'Right,' Buckley said. 'We got a phone call to the West Cork Confidential line about two weeks ago.' Collins made a mental note of whether or not they had traced the number, even though it was illegal to trace calls to the Confidential line. He would have, for sure.

'A man told the operator – who is based out of Skibbereen as you know – that a truck on the N71 between Pedlars Cross and Bandon, heading for Cork and then to Limerick had a consignment of drugs hidden in it. The drugs were stashed in the diesel tank of a digger on the back of the truck. Oh, he gave a detailed description of the truck as well and the registration number and the name of the driver, a man by the name of Derek Webb.'

Buckley paused, just as the waitress arrived with the coffee and water. Collins smiled and nodded at her.

After she'd gone, Buckley resumed.

'Clon picked it up in an unmarked car just outside the town and followed it to Cork city. We set up the checkpoint on the

Commons Road. And sure enough, we found twenty kilos of good quality stuff. Mostly N-Bomb, cocaine laced with fentanyl and ecstasy laced with fentanyl. But the N-Bomb was a variety we hadn't come across before. It was home-made, according to the lab and dangerously strong. The whole lot was worth about €500,000.'

Collins nodded again. He had heard about the find, it was all over the newspapers. Now he had several questions.

'We traced Webb to a house a few kilometres outside Drinagh. He has a small farm and a few diggers and trucks, he does deliveries and repairs. An ideal front for transporting drugs, lots of places to hide it. He's thirty-five, single, has a girlfriend who's expecting, no record. Got in with the wrong crowd who offered him some easy money. He folded straight away, gave us chapter and verse, the name of his contact, the works.'

Collins couldn't resist any longer.

'Who's the contact?'

'Paul Phelan. Well known to us, did a spell in Limerick a few years ago.'

'Works for Chancer?' Collins asked. 'Chancer' was the nickname of Charlie Drummond, who was almost seventy now but had his fingers in every criminal pie from Killarney to Cork and as far north as Limerick. Nothing happened west of Cork city without his approval, tacit or otherwise.

'Yeah, or used to, anyway. Could be Chancer has gone in with Eddie Jones in manufacturing and shipping. Jones has the technical know-how from the Middle-East and Asia, Chancer has the local contacts, premises, logistics, means of getting his hands on the ingredients and the ability to recruit couriers like Webb.'

'Do you know who made the initial call?' Collins asked.

'No, it was the confidential line and Larry won't bend the rules on that.' Larry was Chief Superintendent Larry Murphy who was head of the Cork West Division.

'What else did Webb give ye?'

'Well not much and I don't think he's lying. It was a tight arrangement. Phelan recruits him, gets the stuff to him, tells him where to go and that's it.'

'Do you think it's being manufactured locally? That's not far from the Hill.' Derryglan Hill, mostly known as the Hill was about ten kilometres from where Webb was located, by Collins' reckoning. It was an infamous place, full of drop-outs and vagrants from all over Europe who had set up communes and built a kind of crusty shanty town on its southern slopes in the early 1990s. Most of the initial settlers had grown older and moved out by now but new iterations of the settlement kept springing up, despite the best efforts of the local gardaí and social services. It would be an ideal location to develop a drug manufacturing industry with one narrow winding rutted road leading up and down from the place.

'I don't think it's the Hill, we have a lot of sources there and we've rattled their cages good and not a smell of anything.'

Collins nodded again. He had to ask the most obvious question.

'Why are you involved, Ronan? Why isn't this being led from Cork or Killarney? And don't tell me Jones being in West Cork and you being in West Cork is a coincidence. You *knew* he was here and you followed him down.'

Buckley shook his head. He looked at his watch and then behind him.

'This isn't about Jones, it's about the drugs and the kids who will take them and the families fucked up as a result. Webb said that Phelan told him he'd have two deliveries a week for him for the next six months. Now, he or Phelan could have been lying or exaggerating about that. But that's over a tonne of this shit. And, it *is* shit. Absolutely lethal. Our people reckon if this got into schools and they kept the price down, we could be taking about multiple deaths. And if they can set up a huge production unit in the wilds of West Cork (no offence Collins), they could do it anywhere. They could have two or four or ten set up all over the country. So, Number One decided that we should take the lead and shut this one down and nip it in the bud. And if Jones is around, we know he's behind it and we know it's big, which makes it even more important to shut it down.'

'Number One' was the nickname senior gardaí likes to give to the chief commissioner of the gardaí, Sinéad Gilson. Collins had tried not to take offence at Buckley's comment about 'the wilds of West Cork'. He knew that, for Buckley, Jones was the one that got away and he never let a grudge go.

'If she's so interested in shutting Jones down, why not shut down West Cork? You know as well as I do that the dead bodies are going to start piling up now if that fucker is on the loose. Get a hundred new recruits in and set up roadblocks all over the place. Get Jones' picture all over the news, nip the whole thing in the bud.'

Buckley replied: 'You know as well as I do that's not going to happen. In the middle of the tourist season? We'd be hung, drawn and quartered. No, we have to do this the smart way, track down his associates, this has to be an intelligence-led operation.'

Collins didn't react to the bullshit jargon. He was getting a bad feeling. Buckley hadn't invited him over here on a weekend off with his wife to brief him or catch up on old times. The man never did a single thing without a purpose.

'No,' Collins said, more loudly than he intended. A few heads turned. 'No, Buckley, I'm assigned to a murder in Cork, I have a partner, I'm not doing organised crime any more. I won't do it.'

Buckley smiled apologetically and shook his head. He held up his hands in the surrender sign.

'No,' Collins said, with more venom behind it. 'Fuck you, Buckley. I won't do it, full stop.'

Buckley licked his lips. He lost the smile.

'It's already done, Tim. I'm sorry.'

Collins glared at him.

'Listen, Tim …'

Collins stood up and looked around. He felt helpless and he didn't like the feeling, he wasn't used to it. But walking away would change nothing.

Buckley stood up and leaned into him.

'Jesus, calm down, Tim. Just calm down for one minute.'

Collins tried to control his breathing. He sat down again and glared at Buckley, who spoke in a kind of harsh whisper.

'You're local, you're an experienced detective. You know how these fuckers operate, you know how they think. You got rid of Dorgan and Molloy and I hear you've put a dent in the Keaveneys, now, too. We *need* you, Tim. *I* need you. If this shit gets out into the festivals and the schools and colleges when they're back, we're talking multiple deaths. *Multiple.*'

Buckley looked at his watch and stood up.

'I have to go, Tim. I'll see you tomorrow at the station in Clonakilty, don't do anything stupid, now.'

Collins glared at him as he walked away.

He caught up with Katie and Zoe on the beach. He tried to make the sand feel good under his toes. Zoe told him she had done fifty-one keepie uppies with a soft football she'd found.

'You okay, Collins?' Katie said.

'I'm grand, why?' he replied, trying to smile convincingly.

'Your face is all red and you couldn't have gotten sunburn in that time.'

'Tell you later,' he said. 'Buckley had some news. All set for the match later, Zoe?'

'Have we any hope against Kerry?' Zoe asked.

'There's always hope, but it's hard to beat them down in Killarney.'

THE PHONE call came at 4 p.m. after they had returned to Dunmanway. Collins was sitting in the back garden, listening to the football on the radio. Katie was sipping a white wine spritzer and sunbathing, the straps from her top pulled down over her shoulders.

'Collins,' he answered, having seen the name on the screen.

'Collins, Frank O'Rourke, here.'

'Hello, superintendent.'

'I believe you met Superintendent Buckley earlier,' O'Rourke said. Senior gardaí almost always give full titles when referring to peers or more senior officers.

'Yes, superintendent, but I don't want this transfer. With all due respect, I want to see our case out with Detective Donnelly and the team. We need to do right by Helen O'Driscoll.'

O'Rourke paused before replying. Collins was expecting a bollocking, but he didn't care.

'I respect that, Collins. I do, and I wouldn't expect anything less. I'm not happy about this either, and I made that known too. You're a good detective and I need you to help close this case. But my … complaint fell on deaf ears. You're being moved and that's that. This goes to the top, nothing we can do about it. My advice is to make the best of it and the sooner ye sort it out, the sooner you can be back in Cork. I have to go.'

'Yes, sir,' Collins said, and he was about to have another try to change his mind, but O'Rourke had already hung up.

Collins stood up. He asked Katie if she wanted a top-up and she said no.

'That your boss? Is it formal?' she said, having heard one side of the conversation.

'Yeah. I need to tell Deirdre before anyone else hears. I think I'll have that beer after all.'

DEIRDRE PICKED up on the second ring. She was glued to her phone, that woman.

'Collins,' she said. 'I think you might be right about that college link, what you said yesterday. There's something iffy about the files. Reading between the lines, I think there's a chance Ormsby was harassing her too. If we had proof of that, we'd have the fucker.'

'Hi Deirdre, still at it, don't you ever take a break?'

'Oh, I just wanted to go over a few things so I came in to look at the file. I think we need to put some serious pressure on Ormsby.'

'I've a bit of news,' Collins said.

'Oh,' Deirdre said.

'I've just heard I've been transferred to another case.'

'What case? This is bullshit, just as we're starting to make progress.'

'It's a drug manufacturing thing in West Cork. A big one, they're saying, making some dangerous stuff.'

'And why do they need you? Can't the locals do it? Fuck's sake, Collins, this is murder. These incels are the scum of the earth.'

'I know, but they think Eddie Jones is involved. The locals aren't running it, it's being run by Serious Crimes, out of Dublin.'

'Oh.' This would be big thing for Deirdre, Collins realised. High profile, senior officers, Dublin Castle.

'I told them I didn't want in. I wanted to finish our case. I told O'Rourke, too, when he rang me just now.'

'Who is leading it?' Deirdre said. Straight to the point.

'Ronan Buckley. I used to work with him in the old Drug Squad in Pearse Street, maybe that's why he came looking for me. He knows I'm from West Cork. I'm really sorry, Deirdre, I didn't want this. If there was any way …' Collins didn't tell her the reason why Buckley had been alerted to him. He realised now that if he hadn't seen Eddie Jones the previous evening and called Buckley, that he'd still be on the murder investigation in Cork.

'Oh, okay,' she said. 'Well, it is what it is.'

'Hopefully this thing will wind down quickly. Anyway, I think we have our man in Ormsby, only a question of time before he cracks,' Collins said.

'Yeah, we're going to nail that fucker.'

'Will you keep me informed on the case? All set for London?'

'Will do. Jesus, that reminds me, I have to find my passport.'

'Safe trip, I'll ring you Tuesday.'

'Bye, Collins.'

COLLINS GOT a text just before dinner from an unknown number:

> *Hi Det. Collins. This is Insp. Jim Heaney, working with Supt Buckley. Briefing tomorrow Monday morning 08:00 sharp in Clonakilty Station, Incident Room 1.*

He racked his brains and couldn't place Heaney. He'd have to check him out with some of his Dublin Castle contacts. He replied after thinking some more about his options: *Thank you, Inspector. I'll see you there.*

In truth, he knew he didn't have any options. O'Rourke had gotten orders from on high and orders are orders in the gardaí. For some people anyway.

No point in thinking about it now, he decided.

Chapter 30

Deirdre got into the station early. She saw Melanie Ryan in the corridor with Brennan and made a beeline for her.

'Hi, Melanie,' she said, shaking hands. Melanie smiled and gave her a hug. She still had the distinctive long blonde hair and the glasses. To Deirdre, she looked more like a young academic or a PhD student than a garda. She still dressed like an academic, too, in loose jeans and a frayed T shirt. Deirdre wished she had the confidence to dress so casually.

'Deirdre! How are you? I only found out yesterday that you were transferred to Cork, how's it going?'

'Oh, fine, hectic enough with the investigation, can we grab a coffee?'

Melanie glanced at Brennan and said: 'Sure, how about 10:30?

'Do you know where the canteen is?'

'I'll find it, see you then.'

Deirdre made sure to be in the canteen early to get a table away from anything else. Melanie arrived ten minutes later.

'I'll get these,' Deirdre said. 'I'm starving, would you like a scone or anything?'

'No just the tea, thanks. I pigged out on breakfast in the B&B.'

After she'd brought the scone and teas Deirdre sat down again. How Melanie managed to look so young, she'd never know. She, herself, had always dressed formally to appear more serious and older.

'How are you doing?' Melanie said.

'I'm grand, they partnered me with Tim Collins, don't know if you've heard of him.'

'Oh, everybody knows him, how's that going?'

'Fine, really. He's a bit old school but not as bad as people say.'

'He was transferred to another case?'

'Yeah, a drugs ring in West Cork. Eddie Jones, apparently.'

'So, I heard,' Melanie said, frowning. 'Had to profile him a while back, a total sociopath. I also heard I've you to thank for being part of this investigation.'

'Well, I remember how you helped close out the Kylie Mc-Ilvanney case. I thought you might be able to help us again. Have you read the file yet?'

'Almost done, now. Superintendent O'Rourke is a bit of a criminal psychology sceptic, I hope I can prove him wrong.'

'What are your thoughts so far?'

Melanie paused and took a sip of her tea.

'Okay, this is all first impressions, you won't repeat them?'

'I promise.'

'First thing to note is the involvement of incel. That's a big factor. There are two types of main sexual assault offender profiles: specialists and generalists.'

'Could you explain those terms?' Deirdre said.

'Okay. Most sexual assaults are carried out by generalists, who offend as part of their general tendency to engage in all sorts of deviant and criminal behaviour. In other words, most sex offenders will be well known by the gardaí, with long records of all kinds of offences.'

'And specialists?'

'The specialist model of sex offenders assumes that they are not likely to commit other types of crime. Broadly speaking, those sex offenders are exclusively to be found committing sex offences of one sort or another. I think this offender could be a specialist, especially if he's in incel, which I think he is.'

'Because of the list?'

'Partly because of that but partly because I have infiltrated some of their chat rooms, using the pseudonym Rodger. I used that alias because the mass-murderer Elliot Rodger is one of their heroes. The level of hatred towards women in there is stomach-churning. If one per cent of them act out some of their fantasies, the carnage will be massive. But there's a lot of private chat rooms I can't get access to, so I don't know the full story.'

Deirdre wanted to know how Melanie infiltrated them, but knew better than to interrupt.

'I think Ormsby could be one of the organisers of incel in Ireland, because he uses the alias Grand Gentleman and he's one of the administrators. They call it the Safe Place.'

'What's it like?'

'Oh, you can imagine, full of pure hatred. The main characteristic of incels is that they blame women for their lack of sexual success. Hence the hatred. They go online to what they call the "Manosphere" and find likeminded people and many of them are then radicalised and act out on their perverted "principles". They don't refer to us as women, by the way, that's too humanising. They call us "Foids" which is short for "Female Humanoid Organism" or "FHO". They use a lot of acronyms. They also refer to women as "Stacy" or "Becky" depending on the woman's appearance.'

'Jesus.'

'I know. Then you have the so-called "Pick Up Artists" or "PUAs". These go around harassing women and sharing "techniques" online about how to sexually overcome women. It's a multi-million-dollar industry, you can take out subscriptions to forums where you can learn tips and strategies to be sexually successful with women. There are hundreds of videos online which you can watch – mainly for a price. Again, the women in these forums are looked upon as more or less subhuman.'

'How about the type of assault? The use of an object, for example.'

'Yeah, that's more common than people think. It's a way of de-humanising the woman, of objectifying her. You and I know that rape is not about sex but juries and judges don't get that. It's also another indicator of a specialist, especially if the perpetrator knew the victim. Given that Ormsby has no record of other crimes, and that he knew Helen O'Driscoll personally, he fits the profile. He also lives alone, after a broken marriage. Another characteristic of specialists is that they are repeat offenders, once they begin, they can't stop.

'Sexual violence is far too common in Ireland with only a tiny percentage being reported, but sex-related homicide is very rare. In sexual assault about 50 per cent of perpetrators know the victim but in sex-related homicide the percentage is much higher at 87 per cent. Some cases, like Sister Philomena Lyons in 2001, are opportunist in nature, but this doesn't follow that pathology at all. The profile for this offender is somebody who knew the victim and is fixated on sex.'

Melanie took another sip of tea.

'Which points to somebody like Ormsby,' Deirdre said. 'Wow, that's really impressive. How did you get into the incel chat rooms?'

'Oh, I made up a fake identity with an PPS number and every-thing.' Melanie looked at her phone's clock and stood up. 'I'll be briefing the team tomorrow morning, will you back me up?'

'One hundred percent, Melanie. Will we have dinner later? I can give you my impressions of Ormsby then.'

'For sure, give me your number there and I'll call you later.'

CHAPTER 31

THE DRIVE from Dunmanway to Clonakilty took Collins about thirty minutes. He knew the way well, a winding undulating West Cork road, full of shadow and light in the early morning sunshine. He had left Katie's in plenty of time as he usually did, being a stickler for timeliness. He also didn't want to give Buckley and Heaney a stick to beat him with.

He picked up a coffee from a kiosk on the wonderfully named Tawnies Grove. He parked on the road outside the station, an old pebble-dashed two storeyed building on a hill overlooking the town. *It must have been imposing in its time*, Collins thought, as he walked through the arched entrance.

He was no sooner in the door when he heard 'Timmy Collins!' and turned to meet an old sporting rival, Declan Kerr, a local sergeant. Only people who knew him since his childhood called him Timmy and he liked it when they did so.

Declan was going to the briefing and they walked together, chatting about the hammering Cork had gotten the day before in the Munster Final and how soft the team was.

Declan was stocky, barely fitting into his uniform. He liked a pint, and Collins knew there wasn't much hair underneath his cap. He was as garrulous as ever, very popular in Clonakilty town.

'You got roped in?' he said to Collins as they approached the meeting room on the first floor.

'For my sins,' Collins replied, adding nothing. 'Is there a big team?'

'Getting bigger all the time, as you'll see now.'

They entered the noisy room and Collins saluted some local gardaí he knew. Eight gardaí sat around a large table. They were talking in groups of twos and threes, hence the noise. The room quieted when Collins entered and he heard somebody say something about 'bringing the big guns in'.

There was a smaller table at the top of the room which was raised on a higher level. Three empty chairs behind it.

Declan sat down beside a young female colleague who had been keeping a seat for him. He said something to her and she immediately turned and fixed Collins with a wide-eyed look. He locked eyes with her, keeping his expression neutral and forced her to turn away. Declan resumed talking and their heads were close together so that nobody else would hear. Filling her in on Collins' past, no doubt, from which he would never escape.

IT WAS immediately clear that the room was too small and three more men and a woman had to stand at the back on Collins' left. The woman looked familiar, she was an inspector out of Limerick, he thought, but he couldn't remember her name. Beginning with 'L', Lally or Lehane, something like that. Collins nodded to the man beside him, whom he didn't know.

'Tim Collins,' he said, putting out a hand.

'Pat Joyce,' the man replied in a Galway accent, shaking hands.

Collins surveyed the room. It was getting hot and clearly the old windows were stuck shut. Collins could already smell body odour – some male gardaí were not known for their grooming skills. How many of these briefings had he attended? He dreaded to think. So many crimes, so many years. He felt a sense of weariness and waste. He told himself to cop on. He took another sip of the coffee, it really was good.

Two minutes later the clock over the door ticked to the hour and three men entered and walked up the steps to the top table. The last of them, whom Collins recognised as the local superintendent, Seán Brophy, nodded to one of sitting uniformed officers to close the door behind him. She jumped up and closed the door.

Collins' face remained impassive, he only had eyes for Buckley. Heaney was a smaller man, mid-fifties, he must just have barely met the height requirement.

Buckley, with the file spread out before him, introduced the case and laid out where they were at. He emphasised the need for being thorough, hard-working and going by the book. If Collins had heard similar introductions, he didn't let on. In fairness to Buckley, he was a skilled communicator and could process large amounts of information quickly and thoroughly. Something occurred to Collins and he put his empty coffee cup on the ground and took a small notebook out of his pocket. He wrote: *Source of arrest info*.

He thought he noticed Buckley taking note of him doing so. As if on cue, Buckley said: 'We have four new officers here today and I'd like to welcome them to the team. They are all standing at the back so you can have a good look at them. On the far right, we have Inspector Nuala Leahy from the Limerick Division. In the middle Detectives Sean Dineen and Pat Joyce from the Drugs Squad working out of Store Street. Beside them, on the left, Detective Tim Collins from the Cork City Division.

'Thank you all for being here and now I will hand over to Chief Superintendent Brophy to say a few words. We're very grateful to the chief superintendent who has been so generous with his staff and facilities.'

BROPHY GAVE a short speech on the evils of drugs and the need to protect our young and he emphasised again the scourge of drugs in society. Collins kept his face impassive. Brophy said he'd let them get on with the briefing and he left the room. This time he did close the door behind him.

Heaney then got to the point of the whole thing: what they were going to do and who was going to do it. Then he conferred quietly with Buckley, who nodded. Heaney continued: 'Now, we had a development last Saturday evening around 20:00 hours and I'd like to ask Detective Collins to describe that. Detective?'

Collins was taken aback, but he gathered himself and spoke: 'On Saturday evening last, while walking in the hilly area about two kilometres north of Dunmanway, a black Mercedes Benz passed me in the direction of Coppeen. It was going very slowly up- hill on a bad bend in the road. Registration number 09 D 20341. There were two men in the front seats, nobody in the back. The driver was a man, late twenties, early thirties, dark hair and stubble, wearing a black John Deere baseball cap. Thin face, sharp jaw, sunglasses, probably medium height. In the passenger seat was Eddie Jones, who is best known for his involvement in the so-called Dundrum Heist of 2010. I immediately informed Superintendent Buckley.' Once Collins had obviously finished, the room broke into a hub-bub of conversation.

Heaney spoke up: 'now, we are proceeding on the assumption that Jones could have a connection with the drug seizure in Black-pool three weeks ago and the information we received from that. Until recently there was an arrest warrant for him but that was dropped in April because a witness changed his story. This means that we are now broadening the investigation to include Jones, his associates, his travel pattern, his haunts and his recent history. We already have some details on the car. He has access to the kind of technology and people who could develop the type and quality of drugs we seized in Cork, so it fits. It could be nothing, but we must rule it in until we can rule it out.'

'Some of you know Jones of old and his track record of violence and mayhem. We're dealing with a very dangerous and volatile character here and we should treat him accordingly, if and when we will be confronting him.' Heaney then teamed up the four new people on the team, the two Store Street men with each other and Collins with Inspector Leahy.

Buckley closed the meeting and referred the team to Inspector Heaney and Sergeant Declan Kerr who would give them any further information they needed. He asked Inspector Leahy and Detective Collins to follow him.

CHAPTER 32

COLLINS AND Nuala shook hands in the corridor and followed Buckley who went into the first office on the right.

She looked about forty, with short dark hair. She wasn't tall but she looked fit and strong, casually dressed, in jeans and a light blouse, with expensive but plain walking shoes. Wedding band and engagement ring. He knew she had restructured a few stations in Limerick, which meant stepping on a lot of toes, but the word was she was as shrewd as she was determined to make it work. Which it did.

He couldn't figure out why she was here, especially as a field investigator, not an administrator. Or why Buckley had paired her with him. That could be to keep him in check, but there could be several reasons. Everything about her flashed 'formidable' and Collins was immediately on his guard. He also felt overdressed, with his jacket over his arm. He should have worn a short-sleeved shirt, too. He'd regret that before the day was out.

The office was small but long. A bank of filing cabinets lined the wall on the left. On the right a huge window through which sunlight poured. The window was thankfully open and the room was airy. Buckley sat behind his desk and beckoned them to sit also.

'Do you two know each other?' he said.

'No,' Nuala said. 'But I might as well get this out of the way.' Collins looked at her and she faced him.

'I guess you're wondering what I'm doing here. I don't know how to address you. Is it Tim, or …?'

'Everybody calls me Collins.'

'Okay,' she said. 'When I heard about this operation I immediately asked to join it. I wanted to raise my profile with

Superintendent Buckley here and the Unit and Dublin Castle, too. I also wanted to be involved as an investigator. I lack experience in that area and if I'm going to lead teams of detectives, which I will, I need to get my hands dirty, and to learn what it's all about. Which is why I asked to be partnered with you.'

Collins eyes widened. It wasn't just the frankness and openness of what she had just said. It was the way she said it – as naturally as if she had been telling somebody about the kind of breakfast she'd just eaten. Collins glanced at Buckley who was grinning at his discomfort.

Collins laughed.

'Sorry, but I wasn't expecting that,' he said. 'Well, I hope I don't disappoint. *We* don't disappoint. I've heard about what you did in Limerick with the restructuring. Has made a big difference people tell me. Very impressive.' He turned to Buckley. He had made up his mind to warn Buckley that a major show of strength would be the only hope against Jones, but he changed his mind.

'I'd like to start with Webb and the tip-off. I'd like to interview him, with Nuala of course, but I'll need to read everything you have, first. And I'd like to do some background checking myself. Last night I made some enquiries and there's somebody local to him who could be a big help. I was hoping to talk to him today.'

'All fine with me,' Buckley said. 'I was going to use you as a wild card on the case, let you do your own thing. Some of the others won't like it but I think we have everything else covered. But I will have to be kept informed – fully informed, Collins – on a daily basis if not more often. Is this okay with you, Nuala?'

'Fine with me,' she said. 'Will we get started?' She stood up and Collins stood in response.

'Last thing,' Buckley said. 'I know you didn't want this reassignment Tim, but are you fully on board? Can we count on you?'

'Fully,' Collins replied. 'Main thing now is we nail that bastard.'

'One hundred per cent,' Buckley said.

COLLINS AND Nuala leaned over a laptop on the large table of the incident room where the briefing had taken place. Four others of the team were sitting behind laptops around the table and three others were hunched together on chairs at the top of the room having a conference call on a mobile phone. The young garda who had been sitting beside Declan Kerr at the briefing had her forefinger poised over the mouse. Her name was Fiona Deane, she was from Tipperary, 'the home of hurling', as she had told him earlier.

'Again?' she said.

'Again,' Collins said and he tried to hear something in the message over the noise in the room. There was another detail in there, but it eluded him:

> There's a Scania truck on the road from Pedlar's Cross to Clon. 13 C 5332. There's a load of drugs in the diesel tank of the Hitachi 130 on the back of it. I sent ye some of them last week. After Clon, it's going to Cork and then Limerick.

'Hold on,' Collins said and took out his phone. He opened the Voice Memos App and held the microphone close to the laptop speaker. 'Again,' he said. Fiona played the recording again.

'You happy enough with that?' he asked Nuala. She nodded.

'Can we see the note and the package?' Collins asked. He had only just learned about that and was annoyed.

'I have a scan of it here,' she said. 'Will that do?'

Collins looked at Nuala. She shook her head.

'Where is the actual note and package?' she said.

'It's in the evidence room, I'll bring ye.'

The note was on a sheet of lined white paper from a spiral notepad, encased in a clear plastic sleeve. The writing was in blue biro ink. Large blunt letters.

THERE IS A LOT OF DRUGS BEING MADE IN WEST CORK. YE BETTER WATCH OUT FOR THEM MOVED AROUND. I WILL TELL YE WHEN.

The drugs, which had been tested, consisted of about fifty grams of white powder with small blue tablets mixed among them. They were in a Centra shopping bag, one of the reusable ones, cellotaped at the top and wrapped into a small parcel addressed to 'Clonakilty Garda Station' and under it the word (in the same style as the note) 'Drugs'.

'Any prints or residues?' Collins asked Fiona.

'Nothing apart from the postman who brought it straight here when he found it in the letter box.'

'Which letter box?'

'Oh, outside Skibbereen, on the road to Baltimore, near the rowing club. On the side of the road, no houses around or CCTV or anything.'

Twenty minutes later, Collins and Nuala were sitting in sunshine at a table outside The Yellow House, a small café on the road to Coppeen. They were the only customers outside. Nuala was having French toast, Collins a bacon sandwich. She was drinking latte, he was having his usual double expresso with a shot of boiling water.

'This French toast is really good. And the coffee,' she said.

'Yeah, it's a great spot, she does it all herself from scratch. The milk and bacon come from over the road. What were your first impressions about the recording?' Collins said. 'You were taking a lot of notes.'

Nuala took her notebook out of her handbag and opened the relevant page. Collins noted it was hardcovered and looked expensive. His own battered small brown thing seemed shabby in comparison.

'First thing: a man. Obvious, I know, but that rules out half the population. Not too old or young. So, between twenty-five and sixty, say. Second, a local, or so it seemed to me, you'd have a better take on that. Thirdly, an outsider – I mean somebody not in the drug trade; somebody not involved. Four, he seemed to know a bit about trucks. Five, he was correct, so he knew the exact spot where it would be and when. You?'

Collins thought for a moment.

'I agree with all that. He might be involved, but in a peripheral way, but he didn't seem experienced. I'm not sure why I say that, maybe the use of the term 'a load of drugs'. Now, down here a load can mean a load as in a load of hay on the back of a truck. But it can also mean a lot, or many. If he were involved he might say shipment or stash or delivery or something like that.' He took another sip of coffee.

'He also refers to drugs in the plural, which wouldn't be common I think, for those involved. To them it's product or gear – a single entity. The note shows a lack of education, but it could be a ruse, too. And the way they lumped everything in the one bag, that's unusual, too, I think.

'But there's something in the voice I'm not quite getting. Some speech impediment or flaw. Mainly I wanted to hear it so many times that I will know the voice again when I meet the man. Which I will do, sooner or later. Listen to it again, listen out for something wrong. It could be he had a cloth over the receiver or his mouth to distort it but I don't think so. What do you think?' He took out his phone and played it again.

> There's a Scania truck on the road from Pedlar's Cross to Clon. 01 C 5332. There's a load of drugs in the diesel tank of the Hitachi 130 on the back of it. I sent ye some of them last week. After Clon, it's going to Cork and then Limerick.

'I don't get an impediment,' Nuala said, 'but there's something all right, apart from the bad phone line. I think he was reading it out. He wrote it all out so he wouldn't say something wrong.'

'I agree,' said Collins. 'The way he said the registration number. So, he's not stupid, that was a smart move. I agree about the impediment, but there's something in the way he talks, some kind of uncertainty, as if he's not used to it, or he's not comfortable doing it. I might be reading too much into it, though.'

'That's always a danger. No hint of motive, either, no emotion in either message and he didn't give away Webb's name. He might not have known it.'

'Not in either message, but there *is* a motive, whatever it is. But we'd be guessing. You ready to go? I want to get there before lunch time. A lot of the people around here have their dinner at 1 p.m. and you don't want to clash with that, it's sacrosanct.'

'How far is it?' said Nuala looking at her watch. It was just before 11 a.m.

'About thirty minutes,' Collins said. 'We'll split this? Otherwise, we have to remember whoever paid the last time.'

'Good idea,' Nuala said.

COLLINS HEADED north on the R588 towards Ballineen and Enniskeane. He and Nuala chatted for a while about their backgrounds, she from outside Kilmallock, he from outside Ballineen. It was a good road but busy.

'Tell me about this Eddie Jones character,' Nuala said. 'I heard you came across him when you were in Dublin.'

'Yes, myself and Ronan tried to have him extradited from Spain but the judge said we didn't have enough. We found out after that he was corrupt, Jones had bought him.

'Anyway, Jones is a piece of work. Unusually he came from a good middle-class background, both his parents were teachers and all his siblings are professionals of some kind. They all disowned him long ago. His behaviour got worse after primary school and he ended up in Oberstown for serial offences, where he met some other gougers and it all went downhill from there.

'Thing about Jones is that he isn't a professional criminal for the money or the status. Everything is for the thrill of it. He really doesn't give a shit what he does or what the consequences are. The sky's the limit. He's smart and ruthless but in my opinion he's been lucky so far, and that has to run out some day.'

He passed out a tractor loaded with silage on a straight section.

'If this were a novel or a film there's be some sob back story for him and he'd be glamorised in some way to make to make him "a rounded character". But he isn't rounded, he's just a piece of vermin who needs to be put down.'

'You mean put away,' Nuala said.

'Yeah, right, put away,' Collins said. 'One last thing: he's a sexual deviant. He likes young girls, and there was credible evidence he was funding a paedophile ring in Spain.' Collins shuddered. 'It was horrific, I won't go into the details.

'Our biggest hope is that his impulsiveness will make him go too far. He's bound to fuck up at some time and we have to be there when he does.'

Collins changed the subject.

'Notice anything about the traffic?' he said.

'It's a busy road,' she said. 'A lot of trucks and tractors.'

'Yeah, I always notice when I come back down how many trucks there are on the road. And big vans with trailers and tractors and trailers. That's why having Webb as the mule was such a good idea.'

'Everything in the investigation should be revolving around him, I think,' Nuala said.

'What did you think of his statement?'

'Load of shite,' Nuala said. 'More holes than a sieve. See the way he gave up Phelan but wouldn't say anything about him or his location or where the drugs were being made or how he developed links with him? I think it was a rehearsed statement, agreed in advance, in case he was caught.'

Collins nodded.

'Bang on,' he said. 'I think you know a lot more about investigating that you're letting on. I'll bet the Phelan thing is a red herring to put us off Jones' scent. What we need now is the link between Webb and Jones and the drugs.

'I made a few phone calls last night and my mother's sister was married to a man from near enough to Webb's home place so I rang her last night to find out who would know everything about the townland. A man called Michael Pat Murphy fits the bill. He's a retired teacher and a history buff – he actually wrote a book about the War of Independence in this region, the locals are very proud that they fought the Brits. He's a fierce talker, my aunt said, so we'll have to keep him focused.'

CHAPTER 33

THE HOUSE was a neat bungalow on a flat straight stretch of road, near a bridge over the River Bandon. It had a low picket type fence at the front, an ornate gate and a recently tarmacadamed drive to the side and around the back of the house. That was where country people usually parked, preferring to use the back door instead of the front.

There was a lay-by at a farmer's gate across the road, so Collins pulled up there. He saw a small, thin man tending to a flower border by the fence. Very fit looking, neat hair going to grey. Collins put him at about sixty. Michael Pat Murphy, no doubt.

'We'll tell him we have to meet somebody in Drimoleague at one o'clock or we'll be here all day,' he said.

'Gotcha,' Nuala replied.

Murphy noticed them when he heard the car doors closing and stood as they approached.

'Michael Pat?' Collins said when they reached the gate.

'Guilty,' he replied, warily.

'I'm Detective Garda Tim Collins, and this is Inspector Nuala Leahy. We're not bringing any bad news, don't worry, or anything to do with you. I was told that you're the man to talk to around here for any information about the locality. I'm actually a nephew of Maura Goggin, who is married to Donie Noonan from Cloonties North, I'm sure you know him.'

Murphy's face broke into a smile and he strode forward, his hand out.

'Tim Collins, my God is it yourself? What an honour, what an honour. Lord save us and guard us, I don't believe it.'

Murphy hurried them up the drive, reciting some of Collins

most famous hurling matches. At the corner of the house, he wavered.

'She'll kill me stone dead if I bring ye in the back,' he said, shaking his head. 'Would ye mind going over by the front door and I'll let ye in there? I won't be a minute. My God, Tim Collins, the man himself.' He beamed at Collins. 'One minute,' he said and he trotted away.

Nuala raised her eyebrows. 'Do you get this kind of adulation everywhere you go in Cork?' she said, as they walked to the door.

'Sometimes. It's worst in pubs, when people have drink on them. No boundaries at all. But you get used to it. Some fellas can't go out at all, to weddings or any social event. They can't bear it. Okay if I take lead on this?'

'God, yeah. Though you'll have your work cut out to get a word in.'

ONCE THEY were settled in the sitting room Collins eventually managed to get them on track. Michael Pat's wife, Bridie, had to be reassured a few times that the visit had nothing to do with their son in Brisbane. Collins and Nuala had refused tea, saying they were just after a cup of coffee.

'We'd like to talk about the Webb family,' Collins said. 'Do ye know them at all?'

Michael Pat's face darkened and he squirmed.

'Yes, of course,' he said. 'I heard about Derek's arrest. The whole parish is in shock, not to mention the family. I should have known that's why you were here.'

'He's an only son? One older sister, Margaret, in England?' Collins asked and he saw the man flinch as though struck.

'Ah, well. Yes,' Michael Pat said, squirming. 'You see … well…' He looked at Bridie for guidance. 'I'm not sure if …'

'I believe,' Collins said before they decided, 'that Derek got caught in something that he didn't intend to do. He has no track record of any crime or anything to do with drugs and he may even have been coerced. Anything you can tell us might help his case, we believe there are some sinister people behind all this, not part of this community.'

There was a long moment of silence.

'We have to tell them, love,' Bridie said. 'I'll do it.'

CHAPTER 34

BRIDIE MURPHY shifted to the front of her seat and began.

'Mary McAuley was my best friend, we were joined at the hip. I called her Mary Mac. We lived very close by to each other in Dunmanway. She was in Sackville Street, I was in Main Street around the corner.

'When we were small we used to walk to school together and we'd often call in to people on the way. That's how it used to be back then.'

'Everybody knew everybody else and doors were as often open as they were closed, or the key would be in the front door. We walked in and out of all our friends' houses as though they were our own. We'd be fed, too, or given out to by other mothers if we were bold. We weren't really bold but when we'd call to people's houses on the way to school – and these would be elderly people now, or we thought they were elderly, anyway – they might send us for a message to the square or Mr Maloney might send us for a paper. And you just did what you were told those days. So, we'd be late for school and the nuns would kill us. But we didn't care. Mary was fearless as a child and her smile would melt you. Melt you, it would.

'Anyway, in secondary school she always had a boyfriend. She was so lovely, the boys fell for her left right and centre. I was jealous, I must admit. I was very shy too, but Mary would chat away.

'Something happened when she was going out with the boy of the Stokes. She would have just turned seventeen at the time. He was tall and handsome but he could be very cruel. I saw him beat up another boy one day in the old schoolyard, left him half dead. He turned out bad, after – he died in prison in England.

'Mary changed then, she grew fierce quiet. I tried to find out what was wrong but she wouldn't tell me.

'Next thing we knew she was gone. They said she had been moved to a boarding school in Dublin or was living with an uncle in the civil service there, but I found out after she was pregnant and was actually living with a nice couple in North Cork who looked after her until she had the baby. She was lucky she wasn't sent to one of those Mother and Baby Homes, at least she didn't have to endure that. She wrote me a letter a few months after she left, pretending she was in Dublin and that hurt me a lot after when I found out the truth.

'I ... should tell ye the circumstances of the baby.'

Michael Pat moved on the couch beside Bridie, he held out his hand and she gripped it. She took a deep breath and sighed.

'It turns out that – that man – wasn't satisfied in having sex with Mary, but he made her do it with his older brother too, while he watched. Then he'd be jealous and give her a terrible time of it. Then after a night in the pub she was raped by five of his friends and got pregnant.

'Well, she had the baby – a boy – and she came home, but she was never the same at all. Her mother and father gave her a terrible time of it. Her father especially. She hardly ever left the house or anything. By then I had done my Leaving Cert – she never did – and I was training to be a nurse in Cork, where I met Michael Pat.

'I came home one weekend and there was a letter from Mary begging me – begging me, now – to visit her, that I had to visit her. So, I did. By then I was driving and I drove out to Dromkeane, that's where they were then, they moved out of the town to where an uncle of hers used to live.

'Well, to say I got a frosty reception when I went into the kitchen would be an understatement. Her mother and father hardly looked at me. I knew something was badly wrong then and Mary told me the full story.

'Her baby, a boy, Derek as he became known – though she didn't give him that name – was taken off her only a day or two after he was born. And he was given to her aunt, her mother's sister Peggy who had no children of her own. She was married over near Drinagh to man called Jerry Webb, I think he was from Castlehaven originally but married into the land.

'Mary had to pretend that her child was her cousin. Only a few people around knew, but nobody ever talked about it.

'Then they married Mary off to Patrick Farrell in Tournafulla and he was a good bit older but he was kind to her, I have to say. I don't think she ever loved him but she was grateful to be out of that place and she told me after she had some nice neighbours up there and a few years after that, she had Bobby and then Ted and she doted on them both, she really did.

'I visited her in the Bons after she had Bobby and it was like my own Mary was back to me again.'

Bridie hesitated and grimaced.

'Will we take a break?' Michael Pat said. 'I think we will.'

'No, love, I want to finish this.' She sat up straight and continued.

'Anyway, when the boys were still very young, Mary got breast cancer. She was only forty-five when she got the first dose and she died at forty-seven, that's about ten years ago now, it was in August, the fifteenth, I'll never forget it. Ted was still in school, is that right love?'

'Yes,' Michael Pat said. 'I'd say he was doing his Leaving.'

Collins sensed that Bridie had aged in the few minutes she had been speaking.

'Anyway,' she said. 'Patrick was never the same, he kind of gave up the ghost. I heard they nearly took his cattle off him, he was neglecting the farm so much. Then he got a stroke and died not long after, it was a release really. There was a row between Bobby and Ted about the land I heard but I think I've said enough now.'

Bridie stood up and repositioned the framed photo of her son on a cabinet.

Nuala stopped taking notes.

'Thanks for telling us,' Collins said. 'It must be hard to relive that again.'

'Mary had a sad life,' Bridie said. 'But it's over now.'

MICHAEL PAT looked at Collins. He had an accusatory expression and Collins couldn't blame him. *So much misery out there,* he thought, *and my job is to tap into it.*

Bridie sat down again. She gazed at the window, with a faraway expression.

'Can you tell me anything more about Derek Webb and Bobby and Ted Farrell?' Collins asked. They had to see it through, now.

'I can,' Michael Pat said. 'If you're wondering do they know they're all brothers, I heard the answer is yes. But you'll have to talk to somebody else to get the full story of that. I'll give you her name and details before ye go.'

He stood up.

'Where exactly is Tournafulla?' Collins asked.

'I have a map, I'll show you before you go. It's above beyond Drimoleague, into the mountain,' Michael Pat said. 'A God-forsaken place, if you ask me, but maybe that's just, what do you call it? Pathetic fallacy?'

'Another sad story?' Collins said.

Michael Pat exhaled loudly.

'Yes. Ted. Well, nowadays he'd be called special needs or on a spectrum but it isn't as simple as that. He's …' Michael Pat hesitated. 'He was the strangest boy I think I ever taught. He was actually quite bright academically but he had – has – no social skills at all. None whatsoever. Couldn't relate to boys or girls his own age. Which meant he got a terrible time of it at school. He speaks strangely, which makes him sound as if he's mentally impaired – I don't know how else to put it. But he's quite intelligent. I'd say … I'd say there's a lot going on in his head and most of it isn't good at all.'

Michael Pat went to the dresser and brought a notepad back to the coffee table. He checked his phone and wrote a phone number.

Collins took out his own phone and opened the ViewRanger App. An Ordinance Survey map opened and he located where they were on it. He moved the cursor to north-west of Drimoleague and asked Michael Pat to show him where Tournafulla was. After a minute of moving the map back and forth, Michael Pat found the location.

'That's where Bobby and Ted are?' Collins said.

'Yes, up that cul-de-sac.'

Collins took a screen grab of it.

'I heard that things aren't great between them,' Michael Pat continued. 'Mary and Patrick didn't have a will, which is a disaster when there's land or houses involved. There was a legal dispute and the bloody land was divided between the two brothers and neither has enough to make a go of it. A complete mess, but to get the full rights of all that you need to talk to their cousin, Mamie Sheehan, she'll fill you in on the full story. She's a piece of work, now, so watch her.'

'How do you mean? Collins said.

'She's very bitter. Her husband William has dementia and she's very angry about it. To be honest, I think she was born angry. She might not even talk to ye, but she's a nosy divil too, so she'll be itching to find out what ye have and she'll try to get it out of ye.'

'Can you show me where she lives?' Collins said, passing over his phone again. It wasn't far away from Tournafulla, just a mile closer to Drimoleague.

Bridie stood up suddenly and left the room. Michael Pat's eyes followed her, anxiously.

'One last question, and we'll go,' Collins said. 'What does Bobby Farrell look like? Michael Pat described him as mid-sized, thin, with dark hair and a narrow face with a prominent chin. Almost the exact description Collins would have given of Eddie Jones' driver the day he'd seen them on hill outside Dunmanway the previous Saturday. Nuala put her notebook in her bag. The interview was clearly over.

Collins stood and shook hands with Michael Pat who walked them to the front door and closed it quickly after them.

CHAPTER 35

'STRONG WOMAN, the way she told that story,' Collins said as they walked towards the car.

'Yeah, Mary McAuley, too, getting on with her life. A lot of women had to do that.'

They didn't speak for a while. Collins drove west and Nuala checked her notes.

'Can you run that by me again, the connections between Derek Webb and Bobby and Ted Farrell?' she said.

'Okay. Mary McAuley had a baby when she was young, and he was given up for adoption to her aunt. That's Derek Webb, right?'

'Right.'

'Then Mary was married off to Patrick Farrell and had two children, Bobby and Ted Farrell. So, Bobby and Ted are full brothers, but they are also half-brother to Derek Webb who was arrested in possession of all the drugs in Cork. Got that?'

'So are we going to interview ...' Nuala consulted her notes. 'Mamie Sheehan, now?'

'What do you think?' Collins said.

'I think we should. No point in confronting those two without all the information we can get in advance.'

'I agree. We might want to brief Buckley and the team, too, before we decide on how to do that.'

Nuala nodded. She took out her phone and checked her messages.

'Speak of the devil,' she said and opened a call.

'Buckley?'

'Jim Heaney, which is the same thing,' Nuala said. She told Heaney where they were and what they were doing. She gave him the two names Bobby and Ted Farrell to check their records. She turned to Collins.

'When will we be back in Clon?' she said.

Collins looked at his watch. 'Before four,' he said.

She repeated the time to Heaney and hung up. She made another call, to her husband. One of their children had a cold and she told him to give her 7.5 ml of Calpol.

In Drimoleague, Collins pulled into the car park of Centra.

'I need to use the loo here, do you want a coffee or anything?' he said.

'I'll have a latte and a croissant,' she said. 'Be sure to wash your hands.'

THEY SAT in the car drinking their coffees and eating their croissants.

'Did you hear the way Michael Pat described Bobby Farrell?' Collins said. 'It was an exact description of the man I saw driving Jones outside Dunmanway. I think it's him. And I think that Ted Farrell was the man who gave the tip-off about the drugs.

'I was wondering if I should have played the recording of the tip-off to Michael Pat, to see if he recognised the voice as Ted's. What do you think?'

Nuala considered it.

'Not yet,' she said. 'We'll be meeting the same man so we can judge that for ourselves. I wouldn't play it for Mamie Sheehan, either, you never know what might get back.'

'I agree. I didn't want to do it without running it by you.'

She looked at him.

'I thought you were famous for your solo runs? Doing your own thing, whatever the consequences. Have you started toeing the line, Collins?'

'Don't believe everything you hear.'

'Fair enough,' she said. 'But you have a lot more experience than me in the field too, so I'd defer to that, unless it was something illegal or off-the-wall.'

'I don't do "illegal", Nuala,' Collins said. 'People exaggerate out of all proportion.'

'Yeah, right,' she said. 'How are we going to play it this time? Will you take lead again? Will they be all over you, like Michael Pat? The great GAA hero honouring us with his presence?'

Collins gave her a warning look. He was enjoying working with this woman.

'I think this will be a bit different,' he said. 'But yeah, if it's okay with you, I'll take lead. I have an idea what the bould Mamie will be like, so we'll keep this one a bit more formal and distant.'

'Fuck it, I know I shouldn't say it, but I'm really enjoying this. You have no idea how boring admin is, Collins. You really don't. Come on,' she said, putting away her coffee cup in the side panel of the door. She rubbed her hands together. 'Let's do it.'

COLLINS AND Nuala were sitting in the Sheehan kitchen, waiting for Mamie to come down from her daily 'upstairs lie-down'. Collins winced when he heard that, she would not be in the best of form having been deprived of her snooze. The kitchen was bright and airy and sunlight poured in through a large conservatory adjoining it. The range was on, which seemed strange in the middle of summer but he didn't have time to think about the heat, he had to concentrate on the interview.

Mamie's son, Liam, was still fawning over Collins much to his embarrassment and Nuala's pleasure. Liam was a scraggly rangy man in his mid to late forties. He had a peaked nose and a narrow, stubbled chin. An unruly head of reddish hair was sprouting above jug ears and his gnarled hands stuck out from overalls that were a size too small. Everything seemed elongated about him, Collins thought. He had never seen such long arms, except maybe in a few Kilkenny hurlers.

Liam seemed intent on telling the full story of the county junior hurling final of 1992 in which he had played, against Glen Rovers. He knew the names of not only his own St Mary's team but the Glen team too. He was mid-way through the second half when the inside kitchen door opened and a small fat woman with a walking stick shuffled through. She was wearing slippers, black trousers and a voluminous knitted green cardigan. Liam jumped up and went to her.

'This is the hurler Tim Collins, Mam, he's a detective. And this is detective …' he struggled to remember Nuala's name.

'*Inspector* Nuala Leahy,' Nuala said as Mamie made her way to her armchair beside the range. She plopped down into it and said: 'Thanks be to Jesus,' with a sigh.

She looked at the two gardaí and for a moment the room was quiet. Collins could see the intelligence behind the rheumy eyes. She looked closely at him, making no effort to disguise the scrutiny.

'You'll have tea,' she said in a clear but reedy voice.

'I already offered it,' Liam said. 'They won't.'

Mamie raised her eyebrows.

'We're just after coffee in Drimoleague,' Collins said, by way of an apology. 'Thanks very much for agreeing to speak with us.'

'We don't have visitors any more,' Mamie said. 'Let alone detectives and inspectors. Does that mean you're his boss? Does he have to do what you tell him?' She smiled but Nuala did not return it.

'It means I'm a more senior officer, but I'm not Detective Collins' boss,' she said. 'His boss is a superintendent, he doesn't answer to me. He is also a much more experienced investigator than me, so if anything, I'm his apprentice during this investigation.'

'We want to talk to you about the Farrells, above in Tournafulla,' Collins said. That got her attention.

'What did they do, now?'

'What do you mean, now?' Collins replied. 'Has there been some trouble?'

'They're fighting like cats and dogs the whole time,' Mamie replied. 'Didn't they have a big row in a pub in Bantry last summer?'

Again, Nuala was taking notes.

'What's that about? Do you know?' he said.

Mamie gave an exaggerated snort.

'What's it about? What do you think it's about? Land, of course. That's the only thing that matters around here. And money, which is the same thing.'

Liam, who was standing to the side said: 'I've to go,' and he went out to the yard. Mamie glanced after him. As if on cue, an old man entered the room through the same door that Mamie had used. He was clearly Liam's father with the same thin and lanky look. He appeared confused and stared at Collins and Nuala but didn't speak.

'Liam was looking for you,' Mamie said. 'He needs a hand with the yearlings.'

The old man muttered something that sounded like 'I must, I must.' He made for the door, then turned. 'Where are my boots?' he asked Mamie.

'Outside the door in the porch,' she said and he left.

'Where they have always been, for the last fifty-seven years,' she said to Collins and Nuala. 'That's what I have to put up with.'

'Sorry to hear it,' Collins said. 'About the Farrells?'

'Are you Jerry Collins' son?' Mamie asked.

'Yes,' Collins said. 'You have me, now.'

'Your mother is one of the Twomeys. A lovely family altogether, very sad about her father.'

Collins' grandfather had taken his own life, an act which haunted his mother, she still blamed herself even though the man had a long history of mental illness. Collins sometimes wondered if he had inherited some of it.

'She's in Bandon now,' Mamie said. It was a statement, not a question. 'How is she?'

Collins was annoyed but he hid it as best as he could. He wanted to get to the point and get away. This woman was so like his own father's mother: cold, snobbish and cruel.

'She's good, thanks. But she had a fall in March and broke her hip.'

'Oh dear,' she said. 'Tell her I was asking for her.'

'I will of course.'

'The Farrells,' Mamie said getting to the point. She took a shaky sip from a glass on the table to her left. Collins wondered if she wanted shot of him and Nuala as much as he wanted to be away. He wondered if she was hiding something, herself. Probably.

'Ye know the story of Bobby's mother?' she said.

'We did hear something, but if you could tell us your version, that would be very helpful,' Collins said.

'The first thing ye have to realise about Mary is that she was tough out. Patrick was as soft as putty. He couldn't run a business – and farming is a business in case ye don't know. *You* should know that, anyway,' she said pointing at Collins. He did not react.

'Not for love nor money. They ran rings around him at the mart and the contractors, too. And he loaned a lot of money to his useless brother who drank it all. She was the spine there.

'When she had Bobby she doted on him, she was cracked about him altogether. Ted was a bit of a surprise, when she had the one, we thought that'd be it, Patrick was a good bit older than her.'

Collins thought about telling her to get on to the brothers, but decided against it. She could clam up if she wanted and they would get nothing.

'She got breast cancer very young. I think there was a *dúchas* there, her mother died young too. Then Patrick fell apart altogether, he was as much drunk below in Daly's as he was sober, the land went to rack and ruin. Him dying in his sleep was no surprise.

'Anyway, there was war about the land after. It got very bitter. Ted was only seventeen and I think his solicitor – he's a blow-in in Skib – took advantage of him. He's a greedy cur the same man. It took five years to settle it and by then Ted and Bobby were mortal enemies. I heard they haven't spoken a word to each other in years and they living side by side.'

'How does the living situation work, are they in the same house?' Collins said. He was thinking of how to approach them both separately, when the time came.

'No. Mary and Patrick built a new house on the other side of the yard not long before they died. Ted moved back to the old house when that happened and it's in an awful state, leaky roof, draughts all over the place – he doesn't even look after it. He ran me out of it one day but I saw enough to know it's worse than a pigsty. Bobby's in the new house and that was another thing that had to be in the settlement.' She tut tutted at this and shook her head.

'So, the hundred acres was split and Bobby got the better land because he was farming it for longer. He was milking at the time but Ted wasn't, which means Bobby had a much better income. Ted does some contracting for the Flynns in the summer or he'd be on the breadline, I'd say. Bobby and his cousin, Derek Webb – the fella with the drugs and the reason ye are here – are fierce pally and I heard that Bobby does some driving for Derek.'

Collins did not react.

'I'm only surprised ye weren't up to Tournafulla the day after. Or were ye?'

Collins ignored the question.

'Is Derek up there much?' Collins asked. 'Have you heard of any unusual activity up there, recently?'

'What do you mean "unusual"?'

'Any activity? Strange cars, people coming and going?'

'Funny you should say that. The postman told me a couple of weeks ago he was up there delivering and he saw a Chinese fella in the yard.'

'Chinese?' Collins said.

'That's what he said. He has one of those new electric vans and it's fierce quiet. He pulled into the yard and there was a Chinese fella smoking a cigarette by the barn and he ran off when he saw the van.'

'What's your postman's name?'

'Jim Kearney, he lives in Dromore, over near the GAA pitch.'

'Was it a big surprise here when ye heard about Derek Webb?' Collins asked.

'Nothing surprises me, anymore. Sure, those drugs are everywhere. How did ye know about him, to stop him, I mean?'

'I can't say,' Collins replied. 'Is there anything else you can tell me about Derek, Bobby and Ted?'

'I heard that Bobby is a fierce man for the racing. Horse racing, I mean. I heard he's often in at the bookies in Dunmanway and at race meetings in Mallow, Killarney and so on. I heard that Derek's girlfriend is expecting, but you'd often hear that about a girl and it mightn't be true at all. He's going out with some girl from Dripsey.'

'Could you describe Ted and Bobby?' Collins asked. It was Bobby he was most interested in, but he didn't want to give anything away to Mamie.

'Well, Ted, God love him, looks like his father. He's stocky and smallish. He has big lips and a flat nose and he speaks in a monotone voice. He never looks people in the eye and you can't hear what he says because he's always half turned away. Bobby is like a darker, smaller version of Liam. Thin face, he looks a bit like Derek, actually; well, they are half-brothers. He's full of himself, cocky out, and I heard he was hanging around with a bad crowd from Bandon.'

'How do mean, "bad crowd"?' Collins said.

'A rough crowd, living in one of the council estates there. Fellas in trouble with the guards, that kind of thing. *Ye* should know.'

Collins cast a look at Nuala to know if she wanted to ask anything. She shook her head, almost imperceptibly.

'Thanks very much for your help,' Collins said and he stood up. 'We won't take up any more of your time.'

'Do you think Bobby is involved in this drugs thing?' Mamie could not resist a final effort to learn something.

'We're just talking to everybody we can at this stage,' Collins replied with a false smile. 'Thank you so much for your help, all the best.'

'Thank you very much,' Nuala said. 'You've been most helpful.'

As THE car left the farmyard, Collins paused.

'What?' Nuala said.

'I want to check out Tournafulla but if we go up there and they see us, it'll tip them off. But I think they're in danger from Jones and we should probably get to them sooner rather than later.'

'Why do you think they're in danger from Jones?'

'Somebody informed on Derek, but how many people knew where he would be and where the drugs were hidden?'

'We have no way of knowing, unless one of them talks, which is unlikely.'

'I want a good look at Bobby to confirm it was him I saw driving Jones at the grotto that day. If Ted is the one who did the informing, he's definitely in danger. What do you think?'

Nuala paused before answering.

'I agree we need to interview them both as soon as possible. Maybe even later today. But maybe we should report back first and then decide? A few hours surely can't make much of a difference, surely.'

'I hope not,' Collins said, heading the car back for Clonakilty. 'I hope Liam or Mamie don't give them the heads up about our visit. But I can't see either of them running. Where can they run to? And we don't have any proof of anything yet. Although that Asian man in the yard is strange. We'll need to talk to that postman, too. And get a search warrant. Would you mind phoning Ronan and trying to get a meeting in an hour? I think we need to move quickly now.'

CHAPTER 36

IN HIS office, Buckley and Heaney listened to Collins as he retold the encounters with Michael Pat Murphy, his wife Bridie and Mamie Sheehan. Heaney took notes.

Collins summed it up: 'We don't have the evidence yet but my thinking now is that it was Bobby Farrell I saw in the car with Jones on Saturday outside Dunmanway. I'll know that when I see him. Could be he roped Webb into the whole thing, or Webb roped him in.

'What I'm worried about is Jones' reaction to seeing me, which I'm sure he did. As it happens it was a coincidence, but do you think he'd make of it?'

Buckley paused before answering.

'He'd think you were down there investigating him.'

'I agree,' Collins said. 'And don't tell me he doesn't know that you and Dublin Castle are already here, hunting him down. The question is what he will do with that information and I don't think it'll be anything good.

'I wouldn't be surprised if there was some type of a lab up in Tournafulla after what the postman saw. And I'm fairly sure that it was Ted Farrell who sent us the sample of drugs and made the phone call about Webb transporting the drugs.'

Buckley nodded.

'Okay,' he said. 'But as you said we still need to prove it. We should interview them both as soon as possible.'

'I want to talk to Webb, too,' Collins said. 'We might be able to use them against each other and Jones. Webb and the two Farrells are in great danger, but they probably haven't a clue what he's capable of. Could be they're about to find out. You know how he likes to clean up any messes.' Collins addressed the last point to Buckley who returned the look.

There was a moment of silence as they digested this.

Collins turned to Nuala.

'Have you anything to add, Nuala? Anything I left out or got wrong?'

'Not really,' she said. 'We have motive, means, opportunity and the rest but we need to keep an open mind too and keep our options open. There's a lot we don't know.'

'Fair enough,' Collins said.

'Okay, here's what we're going to do,' Buckley said. 'We have enough to bring Bobby Farrell and Ted Farrell in for questioning. We'll be able to hold them twenty-four hours, get them to sweat a bit, see what we find out. When would be the best time to bring them in?'

'The sooner the better,' Collins replied. 'There's only one road in and out of there so we should get eyes on the place asap, but we'll have to be discrete in case they run. Bobby especially, if he hasn't already.'

Collins took an Ordnance Survey Map out of the side pocket in his jacket which was draped over the back of his chair.

'I'll just show ye Tournafulla here.'

He unfolded the map on Buckley's desk and pointed out the location.

'It's at the end of that grey line there. You go past a lake and take a left there. That's Rowan Hill behind. Now if we can get a couple of people up there with scopes we can see everything going on below. As far as I know, Ted's place is on the western side and Derek's is on the east. If we have a car here,' he paused and pointed on the map, 'and here, we can cover ingress and egress, but they will stick out like a sore thumb on such a quiet road.'

'Okay,' Heaney said. 'I'll get some lads up there. Some locals in plain-clothes who know what they are doing. We might have an ESB van or something they can use.'

'I'll talk to "legal" about bringing in the Farrells,' Buckley said. 'It might have to be in the morning at this stage.'

'I'd like to talk to Derek Webb,' Collins said. 'Is he on remand in Cork?'

'Yes,' Buckley said. 'Can you get one of the lads in Cork to set that up for him, Jim?'

'No problem, Counihan can do it. Do you know Tom Counihan?' Heaney asked Collins.

'Yes, I'll talk to him straight away.'

'Okay, we have a plan,' Buckley said.

COLLINS DROVE quickly from Clonakilty to make the 6 p.m. deadline for interviewing prisoners in Cork Prison, located in the heart of his beloved city's Northside. Nuala spent much of the journey talking to her two children and her mother who was in a nursing home in Kilmallock. That suited Collins fine, he wanted to think about how to approach Webb and how far he could go in pushing him. He also didn't want to tip Webb off that they were on to Ted and Bobby Farrell – he could get a message out easily. That limited his options until Ted and Bobby were also pulled in for questioning – hopefully in the morning.

The call from Tom Counihan that the interview could go ahead only came through as they were crossing the city in heavy traffic. Webb had waived his right to have his solicitor present, which gave Collins some hope that he was ready to talk.

On Summer Hill North, Collins and Nuala discussed the interview.

'I might take lead on this, if you don't mind,' he said. 'I don't expect to learn much, I just want to get a sense of him and to shake him up a bit. We can't give away anything we know.'

'That's fine,' she said. 'You have a lot more experience of these situations.'

'I'd appreciate your sense of him, his state of mind and what kind of pressure you think we can apply later,' Collins said. 'He needs to know he's a dead man once Jones gets to him, but I don't want him to know we know about Jones and the Farrells yet. When he hears about us bringing in the Farrells he might put two and two together, but today it's just a scoping exercise and I'm going to rattle his cage big time. I'm going to accuse him of killing Paul Phelan and we'll walk out soon after that. In and out in a couple of minutes. You okay with that?'

'Yeah, makes sense. And you never know, he might be ready to give us something, too.'

'Not yet I'd say, we need to raise the stakes and put the fear of Christ into him. It's his first experience of being inside and that affects some fellows badly. The thing about first offenders is they don't know the system yet or how to put down the time. Unfortunately for him, he'll learn, but he probably doesn't know that yet, either.'

COLLINS TOOK out his badge as he pulled up to the security gate and Nuala gave him hers.

'How are you doing? We're here to see a remand prisoner, Derek Webb,' he said and handed over the badges.

'Yeah, no bother, I just got the call,' the security guard said in a strong city accent. 'How's it going, Collins? How's the form, boy?'

'Good, how are you? Long-time no see.' Collins was bluffing, he couldn't recall ever meeting him before. The security guard grinned and tapped at a keyboard.

'Not too bad, like. Come here, the Glen will bate ye out the gate on Sunday, boy.'

'We'll see about that.'

'Ye haven't a pup's chance,' the security guard said, smiling. He handed back the badges. 'Park over there in Section C. Do you know the entrance? Just press the button by the door and somebody will come out. I'll call them now.'

'Sound, thanks a million,' Collins said.

'You've been here before?' he asked Nuala as he parked.

'No. First time.'

'It's brand new, as you can see. The old one was across the road, a Victorian dump. Horrible conditions for staff and prisoners.'

Nuala smiled.

'So, you're not one of the "let them rot in hell" brigade?'

Collins shook his head.

'I'm all for longer sentences but if anybody does want to make a new start, we have to try to make it happen. They're mostly kids, with a long way to go. Every time they reoffend there's a new victim and a whole new cycle of misery.'

'I agree,' Nuala said. 'I often thought about being a community garda in the early days. They do great work.'

Collins nodded and pressed the bell at the entrance.

He recognised the prison officer who led Webb into the interview room. Martin McCarthy, who was the brother of a former Na Piarsaigh teammate of Collins. In Cork, there was always a connection.

Webb was thin; his cheekbones sharp above a few days' stubble. Collins knew he was thirty-two but in other circumstances he could have appeared boyish and handsome, with a rakish tint in his brown eyes. His hair was dark and short and his skin was brown from being outdoors. He was wearing a grey t-shirt, jeans and Nike runners.

Webb was putting on a strutty air, as though he didn't have a care in the world, but Collins wasn't convinced. Something behind the eyes that seemed to indicate a bluff. A bluff Collins was about to call.

McCarthy sat Webb down, removed the cuff from his wrist and attached it to the ring in the table designed for that purpose. Collins nodded to McCarthy, who nodded back and then sat in a seat in the corner of the room. Collins paused for a moment. He wanted Webb to become even more uneasy. Eventually Webb raised his head and looked boldly at Collins and Nuala. For a moment Collins thought he might be high on something. That would make him easier to manipulate if they got him at the right time.

Collins pressed the video record button and spoke.

'Garda Inspector Nuala Leahy and Garda Detective Tim Collins interviewing remand prison Derek Webb in an interview room at Cork Prison. 5:45 p.m. on June 24th, 2018. Also present is prison officer Martin McCarthy. Mr Webb has agreed to be interviewed without legal representation today. Can you please confirm that, Mr Webb?'

Webb did not respond. The silence in the room intensified. Collins could see McCarthy shuffle in his chair. Collins gave him a look that said: 'Don't speak'. Eventually, he said to Webb: 'You have to say yes.' He did not want to use his name, yet, let alone his first name. That would send the wrong signal altogether.

Webb looked up.

'You have to say yes,' Collins repeated. 'That you agreed to meet us without a legal representative.'

'I don't need a solicitor,' Webb said. 'I've nothing to say to you.'

Collins let the silence drag out again.

'Okay. Well, I have something to say to you. Something for you to think about. First, you said you didn't know the drugs were in the digger. Then you said Paul Phelan made you transport them.' Collins paused for dramatic effect.

'Here's how this is going to go down. We are going to charge you with the murder of Paul Phelan. You're in charge of this whole operation. You tried to put the blame on Phelan after you killed him. That's a life sentence, you're going down for life, Webb. Life.'

'What?' Webb said. 'What are you on about? He isn't dead, he's in Tralee or somewhere.'

'He's dead all right, and we have proof. And we can prove that you two fell out over the deal and you killed him. Do you still have nothing to say?'

'No. That's bullshit. We never fell out. We put the stuff in the digger and he drove off.'

'"He drove off." Listen to yourself, Webb. Nobody believes that. The reason you gave us his name is that you knew he was dead and he couldn't deny his involvement. End of interview, Detective Collins is now stopping the recording.' Collins pressed the STOP button on the recorder and stood up.

'We're done here,' he said, glaring at Webb. 'Next time we come here, you better not be trying to bullshit us, Webb. I don't have time for this.'

Nuala stood up. Webb sat looking at them, his mouth wide open.

'No,' he said. 'I didn't kill nobody. I didn't do it.'

'Save it for the judge,' Collins said walking out the door. 'You're going away for life, Webb. You're fucked.'

CHAPTER 37

IN THE car park outside, Collins asked if Nuala would drive back, he had a few calls to make.

'No problem,' she said. 'But can I ask you a few questions about what just happened?'

'Fire away,' Collins said, handing her the car fob.

'You did warn me,' she said, unlocking the car. 'Sort of. I'm not complaining, but I want to get a better handle on what just happened in there.'

Collins sat into the car.

'Did you ever hear of a man called Bob Rotella?'

'No, who's he?'

'He's a sports psychologist, he mostly works with golfers.'

'Never took you for a golfer, Collins. Not that I've anything against it, my husband plays a bit.'

'No, I'm not a golfer – not really – they have to drag me out onto the course. But Rotella has written some books about sports psychology, which is the same for any game, really.

'Anyway,' he continued. 'Rotella was playing a fourball one day with a very famous professional against two college kids and the kids almost beat them – almost beat the pro. And they asked Rotella afterwards how that was possible. This pro had won the US Open and was one of the best golfers in the world. Rotella asked the kid if he could walk along a six by two-inch plank if it was laid out on the ground. There's a garage on the South Link just after the Elysian, will you pull in there please, I want to get a coffee?

'So, the kid said of course he could, six by two? No problem. Okay, said Rotella, could you walk it if it was a hundred feet up in the air? And the kid didn't answer. What we just did, Rotella

214

said, was walk along a plank on the ground, anybody can do that and they'd be relaxed doing it. But what if it's the final four holes in the US Open and the best players in the world are at your heels and your whole golfing life has led up to this moment? What if your entire career depends on the next shot and the one after that? The world is looking on, a couple of million people watching on TV and millions of dollars on the line?

'The point is that if you're relaxed and comfortable you can do almost anything. You can certainly follow a plan. And that's what Webb is doing. Jones coached him what to say if he was picked up. And what not to say. He's comfortable that he'll get a couple of years for a first-time offence, the barrister will make a strong case that he was duped by this Phelan or even intimidated into it. There'll be character witnesses, the local parish priest and a politician, blah blah. All Webb has to do is say what he's been told and he'll get through it.

'So, I'm raising the stakes. Knocking him off his stride. He's feeling alone now, that Jones has double-crossed him and set him up. Now he's a hundred feet up in the air and it's a long fall down. Next time I'll raise the stakes again. I'll pull the plank right from under him. There's an old saying that no plan survives contact with the enemy. Well, I'm the enemy and I wanted the little shit to know it.'

CHAPTER 38

As THEY were stuck in traffic on the Brian Boru Bridge Collins felt his phone vibrate. It was Deirdre.

'Hi Deirdre, how're things?'

'Good, Collins, how's it going down there?'

'Hotting up a bit, we just interviewed a hard chaw in Cork prison, totally in above his head. There are a few amateurs after getting involved with Jones, one of them should crack if we ramp up the pressure. Hopefully I'll be back to you in a few days. Any developments with Ormsby?'

'That's why I'm ringing you. Quick question. What do Liz Howard and Helen O'Driscoll have in common?'

'Both victims of Ormsby?' Collins said.

'Yes, but before they were victims.'

Collins thought about it. It came to him. *You good thing, Donnelly.*

'They knew him,' he said. 'They both knew him. Helen was in college with him and Liz was his secretary.'

'Exactly,' Deirdre said. 'It seems he targets women he already knows.'

'Did ye ever track down the ex-wife?'

'That's another thing,' Deirdre said. 'Her family told Clancy she went to Australia and changed her name and cut all ties with them and everyone else. They don't know where she is or anything, they get a postcard every six months saying she's still alive and is fine, but they blame Ormsby for her disappearance, that she was afraid of him. He's the one, Collins.'

'Yeah, but we still must prove it. What are you thinking?' Collins said.

'Two things. I'm off to London in the morning to interview Lea Thompson to see if I can find any link. And the super has agreed to putting all our energy into Ormsby, see if we can find other victims or near-misses. I bet you there's more, we just have to find them.'

'Sounds good,' Collins said. 'But even if Thompson doesn't know him, he could still be the one. He could have seen her in Tesco's and followed her home or whatever. He's also an expert in hacking, so he could have tracked her online, on social media and stuff.'

'Right, I'll ask her about social media. Anything else I should ask her?'

'Not really, you know the drill. Maybe ask if she knows anything about incel, or if she knew Helen or had any connection with Liz Howard. What age is she, could she have been in college around the same time with Ormsby?'

'Helen was forty-one, I think Lea is a bit younger, thirty-five.'

'I'd record the interview, too,' Collins said. 'If she agrees. Listening back often helps. One last thing, have a chat with Kate Browne. I know you've interviewed rape victims before but she has a good insight on how to talk to people with trauma.'

'Good idea, I'll let you know how it goes.'

'By the way, has anybody spoken to Evan Murphy yet?'

'Oh, yes, I meant to tell you. Kate and Lorraine briefed the team this morning. They met him yesterday with his dad and grand-mother.'

'And?'

'Nothing. They think he's blocking the memory. Suppressing it, was the term Lorraine used, it's called … motivated forgetting – apparently it's a defence mechanism. And the family didn't want to press him too hard, understandably.'

'Will he remember it eventually?'

'Clancy asked the same question. Lorraine said it might be triggered by something eventually, but it could take years. Maybe it's the best thing for the poor lad.'

'Maybe, but we still need evidence.'

'That reminds me. Melanie Ryan is here, going through the file. She's briefing the team shortly but I had a good chat with her earlier.'

'What's her take on it?'

'Ormsby fits the bill, completely. I won't bore you with the details but there are two kinds of sexual assault offenders: those who break the law in all kinds of ways, and those who only commit sexual assault. They're called specialists and she's convinced that whoever killed Helen O'Driscoll is one of them. That's why Ormsby has never come up on our radar. She also has more proof he's in incel, she infiltrated one of their chat rooms.'

'Wow, impressive.'

'She really is. O'Rourke isn't convinced – yet, but I think he'll come around. Word is he's under fierce pressure. If we don't make an arrest soon, he'll be replaced.'

'Any sign of Ormsby being brought in? Even for an interview?'

'Could be tonight, could be when Liz Howard makes her statement. But Melanie thinks that Ormsby has done this before and he'll do it again. That's why Lea Thompson could be vital. Have to go, here, Collins, good luck with Jones.'

'You too, in London. Let me know how it goes.'

'Will do.'

CHAPTER 39

AFTER THE stop for coffee, Collins rang the Clonakilty station and got the number of one of the two gardaí who were sent to overlook the farms at Tournafulla, Denis Grandon. Collins rang him twice, leaving messages. Then he texted.

The third time he phoned, Grandon picked up. *Typical garda*, he thought, smiling. *Never answer a call when you don't know who it's from.*

'Hi, this is Tim Collins here, is that Denis, are ye in position?'

'Yes, we're a few hundred yards on the hill above them. We have a scope and binoculars.'

'Anything moving down there? Any comings and goings?'

'Ted Farrell came in on a quad a while back, I'd say he's having his tea in the house now. No sign of any action from across the road in Bobby's place.'

'Any vehicle in Bobby's yard?'

'There's a tractor and a couple of trailers. A muck spreader but no car.'

'Right,' Collins said. He had a bad feeling about Bobby Farrell. 'How long have ye been there?'

'We're here about an hour, we had to go around by the Macroom road so we didn't pass up past them where they might see us.'

Collins looked at his watch 18:30, plenty of daylight left.

'Okay, thanks Denis. Will you give me a ring if anything happens? If there's any sign of Bobby, especially, I think he might have done a runner.'

'Will do.'

Collins phoned Buckley and briefed him about the interview with Webb, that it hadn't yielded anything, that he had shaken him up a little. Buckley said they almost had the go-ahead to bring in the Farrells for questioning and they would have a search warrant for both premises in an hour or so.

'Nice work,' Collins said. 'How did ye manage that?'

'Ways and means, Collins,' Buckley replied. 'Ways and means.'

Collins rolled his eyes. 'I was just talking to Denis Grandon,' he said. 'No sign of Bobby, and nothing moving in his yard. I know he isn't milking anymore so that might not mean anything but I think he's either done a runner or Jones might have got to him.'

'Hmm,' Buckley said. 'What do you suggest?'

'Unless he shows up in the next hour or two, I think we should move in at dusk, between half nine and ten.'

'Leave it with me,' Buckley said. 'I'll talk to Jim and Superintendent Murphy. Are you coming back here now?'

'I was going to head up to where Grandon and O'Sullivan are on the hill and have a look first.'

'Okay, but don't get seen and do not go near the place until you get approval from me first. Are we clear on that, Collins? No solo runs on this.'

'Perfectly clear.'

'Put me on to Nuala,' Buckley said.

'She's driving,' Collins said. He grinned at Nuala.

'Give her the phone, Collins.' Collins handed it over.

Nuala took it in her right hand put it to her ear. 'Detective Superintendent,' she said.

'Right,' she said after a moment. She glanced at Collins. 'Will do. No, I'll go with him. Bit of fresh air will do me good. Okay, bye.' She handed back the phone.

'Have I a new babysitter?' he said.

'Haha,' she replied, neither confirming nor denying it.

'Do you have a better pair of shoes for it?' he said.

'I've proper walking shoes in the B&B.'

'Okay, we'll head there first. I'll ring Denis and ask if they need a sandwich or anything. We better get something for ourselves, too. This could be a long one, either way.'

Collins rang the station again and got the number for Pat Horan, one of the gardaí on the road from Drimoleague to Tournafulla. He rang the number and Horan picked up straight away. Horan said the road was very quiet since they got there. Their location wasn't great, but they couldn't go any closer, he said.

'Okay,' Collins said. 'Ring me if anything happens.'

Chapter 40

After twenty minutes of climbing Rowan Hill, Collins had to take a break. Nuala was clearly much fitter, she wasn't even breathing heavily.

'God, it's beautiful here,' she said. 'No wonder people flock to West Cork.'

'The view on the other side is spectacular,' Collins said. 'You can see Bantry Bay and Whiddy Island, Sheep's Head to the south and the Beara Peninsula to the north. You keep yourself fit.'

'I used to be very fit, but three kids and a desk job doesn't help. I still jog a couple of times a week, usually in the early morning this time of year.'

'Fair dues,' Collins said, his days of jogging long behind him.

After another twenty minutes, he could make out Tournafulla at the foot of the hill and Drimoleague in the distance. He took out his phone and rang Denis.

'Where are ye in relation to the stone hut with the red galvanise on the roof?' he asked.

'Okay,' Denis replied. 'I can see ye now. Go across as far as that broken fence and come straight downhill from there, we're in the gorse.'

Collins put away his phone and walked on.

'Across this ridge,' he said to Nuala. 'Then down. They're in there.' He pointed to a large patch of flowering gorse to the south of a small rushy upland bog. His father hated what he called furze with a passion, he wouldn't have thought much of any farmer who let it spread to where sheep could have been grazing. He'd probably would have tried to reclaim the boggy area, too, much good it did him on his own farm, with his illness and the land sold off by Collins' mother as soon as he died.

'Why did you want to come up here?' Nuala asked as they skirted and old stone wall. 'When we already have eyes on it? Wouldn't we be better off in the station, planning our next moves?'

'I wanted to get a sense of the place,' Collins said. 'I have a map on my phone from the Land Registry Office marking out the two farms, how the land was split. I wanted to see it for myself before I talk to them.'

He stopped and took a few deep breaths.

'Can you spot the lads from here? They got an ideal location, in fairness.'

Collins pointed again and her eyes followed.

'Oh,' she said. 'I'd never have seen them.'

Collins scanned the den-like structure the gorse had grown into, with a natural tunnel through which the two gardaí were looking down on the farms. It was perfect. He surveyed the view to the east. The hills and valleys and river plains of West Cork. The town of Dunmanway in the distance. The road from Coppeen to Kealkill to the north, heading for Cousane Gap. Cullen Lake in the foreground, its surface limpid and dark in the low evening light. To the south, he thought he could make out the ocean, foregrounded by wind farms beyond Drimoleague.

They descended.

DENIS GRANDON, from Dungarvan, and his colleague Tony Quinlan, a quiet Kenmare man, had little to report. They ate their chicken rolls and filled Collins and Nuala in on what they had seen. Or not seen. Grandon was impressive, intelligent, willing to ask questions, full of initiative.

Quinlan was from a farming background and said what Collins had feared. 'There's always something to do on a farm, even a dry farm like this,' he said. 'Ted Farrell is coming and going the whole time, bringing feed and getting ready to spread slurry tomorrow. But there's no sign of life at all in the other yard. Cattle need water most of all, but if he has calves or yearlings, you have to check on them all the time. I don't get it.'

'You think Bobby isn't around?' Collins said. He looked at Quinlan, who was nervous and unsure of himself. He'd have to lose that, Collins thought. Gardaí need to have the appearance of knowing what they're about, even if it isn't true.

Quinlan shrugged.

'If he is, we haven't seen him. You see the third field from the house, where the Friesian bullocks are? It's a different colour from the others?'

Collins picked up the binoculars and looked at the cattle.

'They're all near the ditch,' he said.

'That's because there's good grass in the other field and nothing in theirs,' Quinlan said, finishing his roll and balling up the grease-proof paper. 'They're going to break out soon. We can't hear them from here, but I'd say they're making some racket.'

Collins took out his phone and phoned Horan. Again, he picked up on the second ring. He must be bored, Collins reckoned.

'Tim Collins here again, Pat. Any activity?'

'Ted Farrell is out and about the yard for the last couple of hours,' Horan said. 'I sneaked along the ditch to Bobby Farrell's yard and it's very quiet.'

'Any sight or sound of anything?' Collins said.

'Some cattle making a racket and some bawling from one of the sheds but apart from that, nothing.'

'Thanks, Pat, give me a ring if anything happens.' He hung up.

'Yeah, those bullocks are hungry. Some animals in a shed, too. No sign of Bobby,' Collins said to the others.

'There's Ted now,' Grandon said. He moved aside to let Nuala look through the scope.

'Looks like he's heading into the other yard,' she said. 'He's filling that tank from a tap.'

'I'd say he's watering the cattle in the shed that Pat was talking about,' Collins said, looking through the binoculars again. 'If they're stuck in there in this heat they must be parched. Bobby's gone and he didn't plan it, or else he left in a hurry. Why would you have cattle indoors this time of year, anyway?'

Collins phoned Buckley, who didn't take the call. A text arrived from Heaney to say he'd ring back in five. The air began to chill and Collins watched the sunline recede across the land below.

'Come on,' he said and stood up. 'We have enough.'

The call from Heaney came ten minutes later. The body of a man had been found in a cul de sac near Union Hall. Looked like he'd been badly beaten and then shot in the back of the head.

'Bobby Farrell?' Collins said. 'Or Phelan?'

'We don't know yet.'

'Can we move in on Ted Farrell, now?' Collins said.

'Yes,' Heaney said. 'The super said ye can bring him in and search both premises. It's a murder investigation now, the gloves are off. Can ye be there before nine? I'll be overseeing it.'

'Yes,' Collins said. 'We will meet ye at the junction by the bridge on the road from Drimoleague at 8:45.'

COLLINS HUNG back in the operation at Tournafulla. He wanted his first meeting with Ted Farrell to be in a holding cell, when he could dominate him from the beginning, with more information than he had now. Standing in the near dark by one of the four cars that had been parked in the farmyard, he watched Heaney talk to a shocked Farrell in his doorway and lead him away.

Ted Farrell was strong looking and overweight. He was wearing a pair of corduroy pants kept up by braces, the kind you normally see on older men. A pale long-sleeved shirt was not tucked in to his pants giving him a dishevelled air. Even from a distance, Collins could see that he was stooped and bent in on himself.

Collins' therapist Abigail would have a lot to say about Farrell's posture.

Two cars left with Farrell and three stayed behind. They had decided to do a quick search of the house before a thorough forensic examination in the morning. Collins put on a pair of latex gloves and, nodding to Nuala, went through the back door.

The hallway was grubby, with clods of dirt and cowshit on the tiled floor. Wellington boots to one side and three sticks leaning in the corner.

'Look for his mobile phone first,' Collins said loudly. He went into the kitchen. Again, messy, with unwashed ware and cutlery by the sink and two dirty plates on the kitchen table. There was dirt on everything: the microwave, the counter tops, the floor. The rubbish bin was overflowing as was a large black plastic bag beside it. No phone.

'In here,' somebody said and Collins entered the living room.

It was Denis Grandon. He pointed to the phone on the arm of an armchair. Collins flipped the black cover open; the phone was on and unlocked.

'Bingo,' Collins said. He went in to Settings, Display and Brightness and changed the Auto Lock to *Never*. Then he changed the Passcode to his own one.

'Can you do that?' Nuala said.

'We have a search warrant,' he replied. 'It includes the phone. The information on this phone could save lives, especially his own, if that body in Union Hall is Bobby.'

She didn't reply. He stared her down. Denis Grandon held out an open clear plastic Ziploc bag and Collins put the phone into it. Then he put the bag into his jacket pocket, Nuala watching him all the time.

They found nothing of interest in Ted Farrell's house. Then they searched Bobby Farrell's house, the back door of which was open, but that wasn't unusual in the country. It was not as dirty but again nothing of interest, nothing to indicate his involvement with Jones or in drug dealing. That would have been too easy, Collins surmised. There was a newspaper from the previous day, indicating he had left either late on the day before or that morning.

JUST AS it got dark Collins met Nuala and Tony Quinlan smoking in Bobby Farrell's yard. Denis Grandon was with them, showing a photo on his phone to Nuala.

'I smoke the odd one,' Nuala said guiltily, stubbing it out on the ground as Collins approached. She picked up the butt. Collins shrugged, he couldn't have cared less.

'What's on the phone?' he said to Denis.

'Oh, my girlfriend … fiancé,' he said, embarrassed. He held it out.

'Wow,' Collins said, looking at a photo of a beautiful smiling young woman on a sunny beach. 'You're punching above your weight there, boy. What's her name?'

'Áine. That was the day we got engaged, in Tramore.'

'Nice one,' Collins said. 'Any date yet?'

'No, probably next year.'

Denis took the phone back and put it away.

'Has anyone looked around the sheds?' Collins said, putting on his latex gloves again.

Tony Quinlan shook his head.

'We didn't think there was much point until the morning,' he said.

'I'll have a quick look around,' Collins said. Somebody had been smart enough to bring a powerful torch and he turned it on and moved towards the dark buildings at the rear of the house.

'I'll go with you,' Nuala said and scurried after him.

The sheds were old, as they are in most farms. The animals they saw Ted watering earlier were in a shed in a different part of the yard and Collins could hear the familiar shuffling and lowing sounds from them. It gave him a powerful sense of his childhood.

He opened the door of each of the four sheds. The hinges on the first three were rusted and the doors had sagged, making them stick. The sheds contained the usual farm detritus: old bits of machinery, fence posts, tools, old bales of wire and drums of oil and chemicals. The fourth one was different. It was larger than the first three combined, over thirty feet by twenty, with a high galvanise roof. And it was completely empty. The door had been repaired and the hinge swung without complaint – well-oiled. At one end there were two wooden shutters that could be opened for air. There was a faint smell of surgical spirits or formaldehyde, Collins couldn't quite place it.

'Do you know that smell?' he said quietly.

Nuala shook her head. 'Alcohol or paint, maybe?' she said. 'It was used for something recently, that's for sure, not a speck of dust.'

'I think this was the lab where they made the fentanyl, or whatever they used to enhance the drugs,' he said. 'Remember the postman saw a "Chinese man"?'

'We need forensics in here,' she said. 'I'll ring Buckley now and let him know.'

Collins closed the door and locked the latch behind them. He noticed a tractor nearby with a claw grab raised and remember how he had buried rubbish and dead animals when he was young on the farm. Nuala was on the phone to Buckley reporting the find. Collins, pointing to the tractor, said: 'I'm just going to check this, can you shine the light on me?'

He stood on the front wheel of the tractor and pulled himself up. Then he stepped on the arm of the tractor, like he'd done hundreds of times before, and peered into the grab.

The smell of chemicals from it was overpowering.

'Pass me up the torch,' he said. 'There's something in here.'

Broken glass and black rubbish bags. Some liquid glistened at the bottom. Plastic containers and powder were half-submerged in the liquid. He shook his head in anger and lowered himself to the ground.

Nuala closed the call and said: 'Anything?'

'It's full of glass and chemicals and laboratory stuff. Farrell got lazy, any ID on the body yet?

'They think it might be Phelan, it looks like it was done a week or so ago.'

'I just hope Bobby did a runner and didn't go to Jones looking for forgiveness. If he did, we'll find his body next. Jones never hides the bodies. Warnings to others, not that those fools ever listen. Where did they take Ted? I want to talk to him as soon as possible.'

'He's in Skibbereen,' Nuala said and she pointed to his jacket. 'Are you going to hand in that phone, by the way?'

'I will when I'm good and ready,' Collins said. 'It's time we stopped pussyfooting around. Jones is making a pure fool of us and I'm not having it. Fuck him, coming down here to West Cork and manufacturing drugs.'

He walked away towards the cars.

CHAPTER 41

IN CLONAKILTY Garda Station, just after midnight, Buckley briefed the team from the top of the room. Eight gardaí, including Collins and Nuala, sat around the table looking up at him. He had removed his tie, Collins noticed, but apart from that he looked as fresh as though he'd just awoken from eight hours of restful sleep. Collins had always been jealous of Buckley's energy.

'Okay,' Buckley said. 'To sum up: Bobby Farrell is missing, we have the remnants of drug manufacturing found in his farmyard. Paul Phelan is dead, having been tortured and shot about a week ago. Ted Farrell is in custody in Skibbereen station and we have a lot of work to do tomorrow, including interviewing him and searching those two premises with a fine-tooth comb. So, unless you've been allocated specific duties tonight, go and get some rest, we'll meet here again in the morning at oh seven hundred and plan the day. Keep your phones charged and close by in case we need anyone. Good work everyone, we made great progress today.'

People began to chat and stood up to leave. Collins made eye contact with Buckley who pointed towards the hall. Nuala noticed the gesture and they went outside.

'My office,' Buckley said, walking past them.

As they entered the office and before Buckley had even sat down, Collins said: 'I want to interview Ted Farrell in the morning, I think I'm the best person to do that.'

Buckley sat down, looked at him and shook his head.

'I don't think so, Collins. We'll go easy with Ted tomorrow and see where that gets us. No point in burning bridges at this stage of the investigation.'

'Burning bridges?' Collins said, raising his voice. 'Jones has burned every bridge from here to Allihies and he's fucking laughing at us. Where did going easy ever get us with that animal, Ronan, will you tell me that?'

'Calm down, Collins, you always take these things too personally. This is a major investigation with many different strands and we're going to roll it out professionally and as a team.'

'I'm perfectly calm,' Collins said, holding up his hands as if to prove it. 'Look. It's not about taking these things personally. The fact is we failed Phelan, we failed Webb and we are failing Bobby now. We need to lock down West Cork, maybe the whole county, and Kerry too. I told you that before but you didn't listen.

'Bobby will be transported alive first and then killed. We need twenty-four-hour protection for Webb in Cork prison, too. Not to mention Skib. Is there ASU outside the station? I wouldn't put it past Jones to have a go at him. And you know as well as I do that he only responds to one thing: a show of power.'

'Okay,' Buckley said. 'First thing is this: we *have* an armed presence in Skibbereen station, overseeing Ted Farrell. You're not the only one around here to realise his potential in this case.'

This threw Collins but he didn't show it.

'Secondly,' Buckley said retaining his calm. 'You know as well as I do that there are 12,000 kilometres of roads in Cork and we'd need the whole force to patrol them, let alone Kerry. I'll arrange that protection for Webb, too, that's a good idea. Any other suggestions? I was thinking you might talk to Webb again tomorrow, now that Phelan is dead, I understand that was the focus of your "interview" today.' Buckley made the 'quote' symbol with two fingers of each hand when he said the word.

Collins resisted the temptation to glare at Nuala who must have told Buckley.

'I think it's better if I talk to him on my own tomorrow, man to man, as it were.' He glanced to Nuala. 'No offence, Nuala, but I think he might be a bit more accommodating if I was on my own.'

Again, Buckley shook his head.

'It'll all be recorded, anyway, Collins. Let's do this by the book, I don't want any bounce back or complaints. And remember what I said about solo runs.'

'Anything else?' Collins said. He wanted to get working on Ted's phone. He had already texted Hega about what to expect.

'Nuala,' Buckley said. 'Can you give myself and Detective Collins a moment alone please?'

Nuala left the room.

Buckley leaned forward, his eyes hardening.

'Okay,' he said. 'We go back a long way so I'm cutting you a bit of slack here. Next time you try to undermine my authority or dismiss me, you're off the case and you won't be back in Cork either, you'll be doing drunk-driving detail somewhere in the middle of fucking nowhere. Are we clear?'

'Sorry I bruised your ego,' Collins replied, quietly. 'And in front of a woman too. Boo, fucking hoo. Grow up, Buckley. You wanted me on this investigation because you thought I could get you results and make you look good. I don't give a fuck about your career or your rise to the top. I only want Jones and I thought … I *thought* … you wanted the same thing. If I guarantee you that whatever I do won't blow back on you, will you let me take the gloves off? You won't ever have to know. I don't appreciate the baby-sitter, either.'

Buckley smiled and clapped his hands slowly.

'Great performance, Collins, well done. You set yourself up as the only one who cares, the Jack Reacher of Cork, cracking heads and breaking rules as he goes along. You're not the only one who cares and you've isolated and weakened yourself time after time. You depend on people like me to give you assets and access to suspects. You look down on me from that great big fucking white horse of yours but you need me a lot more than I need you. And you know it, too. So, let's quit the pretence and stop swinging our dicks around. Have you got the phone? Don't deny it if you have.'

Collins nodded. Buckley had surprised him again.

'Okay, get what you can from it and let me know. I don't need to know how, in fact I'd prefer not to. Okay?'

'Okay,' Collins said. 'Can I go now before I say something I'll regret?'

'One last thing,' Buckley said. 'Nuala isn't your baby-sitter. She's a bloody good garda and start treating her like one. She wants to learn field-work before she goes any higher and she will go higher, Collins, I guarantee that. She's headed for the very top and she could be very useful to you when she gets there. If you're still around the place, that is.'

'Okay,' Collins said. 'Message received. I'll interview Webb with her. But I do need to see Ted. The only thing that will work with him is shame and guilt. Coming on the heavy won't do any good, men like him aren't intimidated by that, he's been dealing with it all his life.'

'Okay, I'll think about it,' Buckley said.

Collins rose to leave. He turned around by the door and said, smiling: 'Isn't this the part where you say you missed working with me and I say I missed you and we hug and go out and kick ass?'

'Fuck off, Collins.'

AT THE front door of the station Collins told Nuala he was going to check out the phone and then hand it in and she asked to tag along. He suggested she head to the B&B and get some sleep.

'I'm going through the phone with you,' she said, and folded her hands across her chest.

Collins thought for a moment and said: 'Okay, meet me in the Incident Room in ten minutes, I need to get coffee and a laptop.'

She nodded.

'Want anything?' he asked.

'Camomile tea, if they have it,' she said.

Fifteen minutes later the Incident Room was empty apart from Collins and Nuala. He handed her the tea.

'Where d'you get that?' she said.

'Somebody in the hotel owes me a favour,' he said. 'They're always open. Sandwich?' He put two wraps on the table.

'Wow,' she said, reaching for the one labelled 'Salad'. Collins' one was labelled 'Chicken'.

'Okay,' he said, taking the laptop out of an old Umbro duffel bag. 'Do you know the architecture of a mobile device?'

'No, of course not.'

Collins placed the phone on the table, still inside the Ziploc bag. He put on another pair of latex gloves.

'Me either. For me to be wading around in a complex computer like this iPhone would be a complete waste of time. So, I get somebody to do it for me. Somebody who does know their way around. I can tell them what to look for and they can find it.'

She nodded.

'And I don't need to know who this person is?'

'He's an IT expert I work with, completely above board. He's on the books in Anglesea Street as a consultant.'

She nodded and took a bite from the wrap and then a sip of tea.

Collins opened the laptop and turned it on. He took the phone from the bag and connected it to the laptop with a cable. He plugged in the laptop and typed in the Wi-Fi password for the station.

'This wrap is really fresh,' Nuala said. 'They have actual balsamic dressing on the salad.'

'Oh, they know what they're doing down there.'

He took out his own phone.

'Hi Hega,' he said. 'Congratulations, boy. How's married life treating you?'

'Howya, Collins,' Hega said. 'Ah, sure, grand. Been on the piss since. One minute, I need to go into my control room.'

'What's that in the background?' Collins said, not wanting to give away too much to Nuala. It sounded like a party.

'Oh, just a few of the gang here, nothing major. Jen is staying with her Mam for a few days, she's wiped. Okay, I see your laptop now. Open the App, did I give you version 3.0?'

'Yeah, that's what is says on the logo.'

'Grand, is the Wi-Fi any good there?'

'No idea.'

'Okay it's downloading now. Looks like it'll take twenty-five minutes. Not too bad, what do you want me to look for?'

'The usual. Where he went in the last week, calls, texts, WhatsApp, social media. I need it now is the only problem.'

'No bothers boy, I'll ring you back in a while.'

While they waited, Collins and Nuala ate their food.

'How many coffees do you drink a day?' she asked.

'Depends how many I need. Not many, unless I'm on a case like this. I like to sleep the odd time.'

'Will you drive back to Dunmanway tonight?'

'Naw, takes too long and something might happen. I'll sleep here in the station, they have lots of spare rooms.'

'Don't you need a bed?'

'Not really. I have a sleeping bag in the car. I was expecting a few long days.'

She raised her eyebrows.

'So, you have a few people who owe you favours?' she asked, smiling.

'You know, a small act of kindness every now and again goes a long way,' Collins said. 'I know that doesn't fit in with my image, so don't tell anyone.' He took a sip of coffee and checked the download.

'Twelve minutes,' he said. 'One of the mistakes that some people make – and by people I don't only mean gardaí – is to treat everybody the same. Especially if they get into trouble. There's a huge spectrum of offenders, from Jones at one end to the immigrant mother who takes a bread roll for her hungry child at the other end. Now you can put her in the system and throw the *Theft and Fraud Act* at her, but how will that help her child? Who's the victim here, Tesco or a hungry child? Where is the greater good served? If we get her a night job in a hotel making tea and sandwiches, it's a win-win situation.'

'Is that what happened?'

He shook his head.

'No comment. But you get the idea. It's like what you said about community gardaí earlier. I hope when you get to Number 1 up there in the Phoenix Park you'll remember that.'

'Yeah, right,' she said. 'But speaking of promotion, why haven't you ever wanted to go up the ladder? You know you could make a huge difference if you were a superintendent leading a unit. You'd walk in there if you wanted it.'

Collins sighed. This wasn't his favourite topic of conversation and other senior gardaí had asked him the same question.

'I don't know. I haven't ruled it out, but there never seems to be the right time. I very nearly quit the force a couple of years ago. Then I got dragged back in and there were … consequences for that.'

'The Butcher Case.'

'I'm not fond of calling it that, but yes.'

'You think it should be called the Murphy case?'

'No. Fuck him. The media, who never mention the victims, glorify those bastards. Do you know the names of his victims?'

'No,' Nuala said. 'No, I don't.'

'Paddy Crawford was the first one. He was fifty-eight, from

Castlelyons. His mother is in a nursing home in Fermoy. He had two sisters and a brother. Then there was Paul Sheehan, he was only twenty-five, but he'd been sick for a while. He was English, from Bradford, his parents are from Dublin originally.' Collins winced, this was regurgitating bad memories for him. He spoke about it rarely, except to his therapist.

'Sonny Grogan was killed running away from him, fell off a wall. Then Kathleen Creedon and Tom Davis, they were a couple, they were hoping to get married. At least they died together and not alone. So, I don't know what the case should be called. They were all homeless but they were people too with families and hopes and dreams.' The laptop gave a beep. The download was complete. Collins stood up.

'My contact will take an hour or two to process the data. He'll ring me then. I'll tell you everything in the morning. I don't know about you but I'm wrecked.'

Nuala nodded.

'See you in the morning. I'll be in at six, that briefing is at seven,' she said, gathering the coffee cup and sandwich wrapping.

'See you then,' Collins said. 'I'll hand in the phone now, we don't need it any more. I'd like to interview Farrell first thing if Buckley gives me access. Otherwise, we might leave for Cork around 08:30, they don't open in the prison until 9:30. We might have to wait until later if Webb wants a solicitor this time, but I don't think he will.'

CHAPTER 42

THE CALL came at 03:30 when Collins was in a deep sleep under a desk. His phone rang and showed *Hega The Great!* on the screen. Somehow he could change the name that came up on other people's phones when he rang them.

Collins stood up, answered the phone and shuffled out of the sleeping bag.

'Yeah,' he said.

'This is a good one, Collins,' Hega said. He sounded excited. Or high. That probably explained why it took so long.

'What is?'

'Ever hear of an App called TrackIt?'

'No. Why?'

'He had it on his phone. It's used to track things, there's a small device and you can follow it by GPS on the App. It's shit hot, Collins, I'm going to order three or four of them.'

'What was he tracking?' Collins was wide awake now.

'Cars. Three of them on the account, at least.'

'Jesus. Can you get in and see where they are?'

'Sure, I'm looking at them now. One of them hasn't moved in a few days. It's in that guard compound in Mayfield, you know the one?'

'Can you get the reg from the devices?'

'No, but he has names on them all.'

'What are the names?' Collins sat down. He flicked a lamp switch on the desk and looked for a pen and paper.

'The one in Cork is called "Webb". That's W-E-B-B.'

'The other ones?'

'The other ones are called "Bobby" and "Maeve".'

'Where's the car called "Bobby"?' Collins held the pen over the paper.

'Down in west Cork. Near a place called Goleen?'

'Have you the exact location?'

'Of course. I can send you the coordinates.'

'Since when has it been there?'

'One second. Today, sorry yesterday, at 14:28.'

'And the car marked Maeve?'

'In an estate in Clonakilty, didn't move in two days.'

'Okay, I have to go, here. Get as much information as you can about where that "Bobby" car in Goleen has been in the last couple of weeks. Check Saturday evening first, around 7 p.m., okay?'

'I'm knackered, Collins. Can't we do this tomorrow, maybe around two or three?'

'*Do not* go to sleep, Hega. Just don't, right? I'll be ringing you every half an hour and if you don't answer you'll have a squad car blaring all over you in minutes. You hear me?'

'Okay, all right boy. Take it handy, I'm only saying. I have something here I can take, it'll keep me going for a while.'

'I'll be ringing you in about twenty minutes. Talk then and thanks, this is great work.'

'No bother, boy,' Hega said and Collins hung up.

COLLINS HAD first driven from Clonakilty to Skibbereen in a squad car, with Nuala. The Armed Support Unit had taken control then. There was a convoy of three Audi 4x4s, with two unmarked garda cars behind.

Collins didn't enjoy fast driving. He especially didn't enjoy being a passenger in a speeding car. So, he sat in the back of the second Audi and talked to Hega. The driver was Ray Halloran of the Armed Support Unit, Nuala was in the front passenger seat. The vehicles powered west towards Goleen.

Sitting beside Collins was another black uniformed ASU garda, called Bill Hammond. He was built like a tank with a shaved head – straight out of central casting – and he was sound asleep despite the blaring alarms and flashing lights. Collins had an internal light on above his head and was trying to take notes from Hega about where Bobby Farrell's car had been over the previous week.

First of all, he confirmed the car had gone around close to Dunmanway the previous Saturday, so it had been Bobby Farrell driving Jones that evening in the Merc – which wasn't registered to him. The car had gone on to a house in Carrigaline where it remained for two hours – some kind of meeting, Collins guessed. That house would have to be raided immediately.

Then the Merc returned to the Aldi in Skibbereen where it stopped for a minute – dropping off Jones, no doubt – before returning to Tournafulla. That was disappointing; Collins had hoped to get a location for Jones but he was too smart to let Bobby know where he was based. On the Sunday, the car went down to Drimoleague town around nine in the evening and was parked there until midnight and then went home. Probably to a pub, Collins thought, he'd have those checked out, too, in case Bobby had met anyone. On the Monday – the previous day – the car drove to the address outside Goleen and had been there since. Jones had probably told Farrell to meet him there and had killed him, or had one of his henchmen do it.

In the previous six days before Collins saw the car outside Dunmanway, Hega rattled off a list of locations. He could only give the street or approximate location, not the exact address. But they sounded like drug drops and local gardaí would be able to identify those.

'Okay, thanks,' Collins said. 'Will you text me all those locations and times? And have you any information about the location in Goleen?'

'Oh yeah, I meant to tell you. I looked up that on the live satellite feed for 3 p.m. today. I could see the car and another one nearby. That was grey, I think.'

'What do you mean, live satellite feed?' Collins said.

'Oh, I have access to that, did I not tell you? Now, it's no good at night or when it's cloudy but today it was clear so I'll take a screen grab and send it on. Looks like some type of forest, or something, a lot of trees anyway. When I checked the feed at 5 p.m. the other car was gone.'

'Okay send it on, thanks again.' Collins hung up.

'Ten minutes, ETA,' Halloran said from the front and turned off the alarm.

'Roger that,' Hammond said. He turned on the passenger light on his side and began to examine his automatic weapon. Collins took out his SIG Sauer and did the same.

Hammond looked at the pistol and scoffed: 'Fucking pea-shooter, Collins. Stay out of our way, boy.'

'How do you sleep with all that racket?' Collins said.

'I just don't hear it,' Hammond said. 'A bit like my old doll doesn't hear me when I tell her how shit Liverpool are.'

'Good one,' said Collins. 'Leeds, isn't it? When's the last time ye won anything?'

'That close to the Playoffs last year, Collins.' Hammond held up his thumb and forefinger just apart. 'New manager now, Christiansen, definitely going up next year.'

'Dream on,' Collins said.

'Jesus, what are ye like?' Nuala said, turning around.

Hammond and Collins shared a glance, like small boys caught misbehaving by an adult. Collins' phone pinged. He turned it to silent. The satellite picture, clearer than he expected.

'Ray, I have a satellite photo of the location, you should see it before we go in.'

'Roger that, we're pulling in up here to co-ordinate.'

Hammond took Collins' phone and looked at the image.

'I'm told the second car left the scene before 5 p.m.,' Collins said. But it looks like this dirt road here ...' he enlarged a section of the picture ... 'is the best way in.'

COLLINS, NUALA and four other gardaí stood around in a clearing by the cars while the ASU headed off to secure the car and the area around it.

When they had pulled up there quietly, ten minutes earlier, Nuala, as the most senior officer, argued that everybody should proceed to the car site. Halloran replied that his people had night vision goggles and radio units and they had trained for situations like this. Eight of them were more than enough to manage and untrained people could pose more of a danger to each other than 'hostiles'.

Nuala had turned to Collins in the back seat and he nodded: he knew how things could go badly wrong in the dark with too many armed people in a heightened state of anxiety. There wouldn't be anybody else in the car in any case, apart from Bobby Farrell. He was sure of that.

He could see the first sign of dawn over the spruce trees to the south east. He could sense the sea nearby. A breeze had picked up; they would be glad of it later, another sunny day had been forecast. Three weeks now since any meaningful rain and the land was parched.

'Collins, a quick word in the car,' Nuala said and she moved back toward their Audi. She sat in the front passenger seat and Collins sat in the driver's.

'What is it?' Collins said. Nuala looked uneasy.

'These situations,' she said. She was looking ahead and not at him. 'Confronting armed criminals with weapons ...' Collins could see she was getting upset.

'Okay,' he said. 'First thing you need to realise about the four men standing out there is that they are afraid at this moment. They are shitting it and so am I. Even the ASU people are nervous and I've talked to Halloran about this. They don't want to die, they don't want to kill anybody, especially one of their colleagues, which can happen very easily. So, we're all in the same boat here. Never forget that. Anybody who isn't nervous or anxious in this situation is either a fool or a psycho. I used to vomit with nerves before hurling matches, for fuck's sake. Bloody matches.'

She turned to him just as the car light went off. He was glad she had the dark. He could hear the quickening of her breathing and she swallowed.

'And that never changes,' he said. 'In fact, I'm getting more jittery the more of these kinds of situations I have to deal with. I was delighted when Halloran insisted the ASU go in alone.' He paused. He didn't want to patronise her.

'What you need to learn – and this took me a while – is how to hide it. How to fake the calmness that you think you're seeing in others. The other thing is that the training does kick in. Trust it. You've been well trained by experts and you must focus on that and draw it out. What's the best thing to do in *this* situation, *that* situation. It'll be right there when you need it, trust me.'

He thought he saw movement in the distance and the four standing gardaí turned to face it.

'Last thing to remember is to breathe. That always helps. If you just breathe, your body will do what it needs to do. You'll do just fine, Leahy, I know that for a fact.'

He opened the door and the light came on. He didn't look back at her. He said: 'Looks like the hard chaws are back. Let's go and see what another dead body looks like.'

THEY HAD shot him through the mouth, that was clear from the

photo on Halloran's phone. Which usually indicated that somebody had talked to the gardaí.

'Look at the next one,' Halloran said. Collins scrolled forward
on the phone.

Farrell's body was arranged face up in the boot of the car and
lying on his chest was a dead rat.

You're some fool, Bobby Farrell, Collins thought. *Thinking you
could handle Eddie Jones.* Collins passed the phone to Nuala and
she winced.

'That him?' she said.

'Yep, that's the man I saw with Jones outside Dunmanway,' he
replied. 'You know what that rat means?'

Nuala nodded.

Collins looked at the tall trees all around. The forest was ready
to be felled. Collins had always though he'd like to be a forester,
what a great place to work.

Dawn had come, the sunlight was inching down the hill above
them.

'When are forensics getting here?' Collins asked Nuala, who
had just informed Buckley.

'They're over in Union Hall now, finishing up. Probably get
here around eight or nine.'

'Okay,' he said. 'No point in us hanging around. I need coffee
and some food. There's a good place in Ballydehob, I'll ring ahead.'

'The super said he wants to meet us in Skibbereen station as
soon as possible,' Nuala said. 'Looks like you might get your crack
off Ted Farrell after all.'

'Good,' Collins said. 'And then we'll head to Cork to ramp up
the pressure on Webb.'

'You okay to eat in Ballydehob?' Collins asked Halloran. 'Or do
ye have to stay here?'

'We're leaving two of ours here to look after ye,' Halloran said.

'The rest of us are heading back to Skib to watch the station.'

'Very dangerous place, West Cork,' Collins said. 'Keep a good look out. And will you send me those photos, please?'

Chapter 43

Deirdre exhaled as the plane touched down in Heathrow Airport. She had never liked landings.

The flight has been quiet and she'd managed to sleep for a bit in her window seat.

She felt the Oyster Card in the front pocket of her jeans, from her last time in London. She picked up her bag from under the seat in front of her. Passport, wallet, phone (fully charged), notebook. She turned off the Airplane Mode on the phone.

She took another breath and opened the notebook with the instructions how to find Lea Thompson's house near Shepherd's Bush. Piccadilly Line towards Cockfosters as far as Acton Town, nine stops. Then the District Line towards Upminster as far as Stamford Brook, four stops. Then a twelve-minute walk to Bassein Park Road. Forty-three minutes in all, thank God for Google Maps.

She looked at her watch: 07:55. Giving herself thirty minutes to get out of Heathrow without baggage, she would be at Lea's house before 09:30. She'd make the 16:45 flight home easily.

The street was like any other suburban street in London. Terraced houses with pale brick frontages. A small food store at the corner, cars parked either side, trees giving shade. She found the house quickly and went down some steps to the front door as Lea had instructed her. There was a spy hole in the middle of a newish red door and a small camera on the wall above.

A big dog barked when the doorbell rang.

'Who is it?' a woman's voice in the intercom.

'Detective Sergeant Deirdre Donnelly from Cork, Lea. We spoke on the phone.'

The rattling of locks opening and a chain being removed. The door opened back.

A small woman in a sports top and tracksuit bottoms appeared, holding back a brown, mastiff-like dog. Her fair hair was in a ponytail. She wore a Fitbit on one wrist and a rainbow bracelet on the other.

'Come in,' she said and Deirdre walked through. The room was dark and long – a living room, with dressers and bookshelves at either side and a sofa and armchairs to her left, a coffee table. Some prints on the wall: pictures of Joni Mitchell, Joan Baez and Carly Simon. Some landscapes and a few abstract posters. A large collection of CDs in wooden racks and piled up on the dressers.

She likes her music, anyway, Deirdre thought as Lea closed the door, locking one of the mortice locks with a large key.

'Sit down there,' Lea said. 'I'll just put her out the back.' She pulled the dog by the collar, saying, 'come on Janis, treat, treat, treat.'

Deirdre sat down in an armchair and put her notebook and phone on the table. She opened the notebook to the list of questions she had prepared and glanced through it. She found the Voice Memos App on the phone and activated it. She checked the volume and battery and did a test recording.

'Tea or coffee?' Lea called from the kitchen which adjoined the living room.

'Coffee would be great, thanks.'

Deirdre looked around. A lot of the books on the shelves beside her were about psychology and psychiatry. A whole row of self-help books. The room was neat, no sign of anybody else living with her.

She recalled the advice from Kate Browne, of the Family Liaison Unit, not to badger or press Lea too hard. The big danger was that she might shut down.

'You mustn't lose sight of the fact,' Kate had said, 'That this will bring the most horrific moment of any woman's life back right into focus. She must dread having to talk about it and she'll have to deal with that trauma all over again now.'

Kate had told Deirdre to keep the interview as light as possible. *How the hell was she supposed to manage that?*

Lea placed a cup of coffee and small jug of milk on the table. She sat on the sofa opposite Deirdre, leaning forward. She sipped from a glass of water. She looked fit and healthy, Deirdre thought. Her skin was clear. She was pretty, if a bit tired around the eyes. A good bit older than her file photos, but that was understandable given what's she's had to deal with since.

'Is this about the murder of that woman in Blackrock?' Lea said. Her voice was neutral, almost no accent.

'I'll come to that in a minute Lea, but can I ask you first if I can record this? I'll just use it for my own notes, otherwise I'll be sure to get things wrong.'

'Okay,' Lea said nodding. 'But can you send a copy to my solicitor in Cork? I'll give you her details. She actually suggested I record it myself, so you'll have saved me the bother.'

'No problem,' Deirdre said. 'And I understand completely how hard this is for you, and I appreciate you agreeing to talk to me.'

'With all due respect, I don't think you can understand, but that's fine too. I'm glad you can't, to be honest. My main motivation is that this might do something to bring about justice for Helen O'Driscoll and myself. You answered my first question by not answering it.'

This took Deirdre aback, she had under-estimated Lea Thompson; she had stamped 'victim' on her forehead and had seen nothing else besides. She knew that Lea was training as a psychotherapist but this was still impressive.

'Okay,' Deirdre said. 'Can I ask if you have any memories or any sense at all of the man who attacked you?'

'None, I was struck from behind in my kitchen and when I woke up later, I was half naked on the sofa in agony, covered in blood. I have no idea if he was tall or short, dark or light, old or young. Nothing.'

'Could you have known him? Any sense of that?'

'I was unconscious when he …' she hesitated. 'When he did that to me. I have no idea, but of course I have thought about it a lot.'

'And?'

'And I dated one or two pricks but I never got the sense that they were predators or that they would rape me.'

'Okay, I've read your statement but after all this time is there anything to add? Any suggestions for us or anything you've thought of since?' This was weak, Deirdre knew, but she was really just leading up to the question about Ormsby.

Lea sighed and put her head into her hands.

'It's hard, you know,' she said, teary eyed. 'The worst is the self-blame but I'm working on that, I have had a lot of therapy and now training to be a therapist for other victims gives me a sense of healing. I know, objectively, that I did nothing wrong or to be ashamed of, but it's still there.'

She stood up.

'I'm just going to bring Janis in, is that okay? She won't do anything, and she loves company.'

'Of course,' Deirdre said.

The dog trotted in wagging her tail and Deirdre rubbed her ears.

'Another coffee?' Lea said.

'No thanks.'

'There is one thing that bothers me,' Lea said. 'He got in my front door, which was locked. How did he open it? I never got an answer to that.'

'Do you remember what kind of lock it was?' Deirdre had wondered how Ormsby had gotten into Helen O'Driscoll's house, too.

'It was called a Yale Nightlatch. There was a switch on the inside I could have pushed up and he wouldn't have been able to open it. That is one thing I regret. Now I do use that safety switch, but I also have two mortice locks which I make sure are locked at all times, whenever I come home or go out.'

Deirdre wrote in her notebook: *Check lock in Ardlea.* Lea glanced at the clock over a mirror on the wall.

'I want to tell you a few names,' Deirdre said. 'And if they mean anything to you.'

'Okay, what are they?'

'Did you ever have contact with Helen O'Driscoll? Ever hear of her before?'

'No, I'm fairly sure.'

'Ever hear of a woman called Lizzie or Liz Howard?'

Lea took a moment to think.

'No, who is she?'

'She's popped up on our radar, I can't give you the details yet.'

Deirdre took a deep breath. *Here goes,* she thought.

'Blake Ormsby, ever heard that name?'

Deirdre watched her closely for a reaction. Lea grimaced and shook her head.

'No. It's a strange name, I'd have remembered it.'

'William Hughes? Lives in Dublin?'

Again, Lea shook her head. She closed her eyes and sighed.

'Shit,' she said. 'I raised my hopes again, I'll never learn.'

'I have four photos I want you to look at.' Deirdre took the envelope out of her bag and passed them over.

'Are they the four you named?'

'Recognise any of them?'

Lea looked at them closely and threw them on the table. She stood up and walked away. The dog followed her. She turned and said: 'For *fuck's* sake.'

'Lea,' Deirdre said, standing.

'I thought you had something. I thought you'd found him, that you had proof. I wrote out my impact statement last night. Look! Look at *them*!'

She strode forward. She pulled up the sleeves of her top and Deirdre could see the scars on her wrist and her arm.

'I have more on my thighs, want to see them? I'll fucking show you if you want.'

'No no. Lea, sit down. Please. I'm not finished.'

'Do you have proof or not?'

'No. I don't. I want to be straight with you, but we're gathering proof and we think this case and yours might be linked, but we're not certain. Not yet. I'm sorry … I'm sorry your hopes were raised. Sit down, please.'

'Are those two men suspects in Helen O'Driscoll's murder? Are they? Are they?'

'Sit down, Lea. Let me finish. I'll tell you what I can, but I can't tell you everything. I just can't…'

The dog whimpered and jumped up on Lea.

'It's okay girl,' she said, sniffling. She rubbed the dog's head. 'It's okay.'

She sat down and readjusted her sleeves. She wiped her face with her hands.

Deirdre sat down and made a decision.

'Ok, I'm going to tell you something I shouldn't and I'm asking you not to divulge it to anyone. Do you agree? If it gets out it could damage our case against the bastard who killed Helen.'

'Okay, I won't tell anyone.'

'It isn't in the papers yet, but Helen was sexually assaulted before she was murdered and we think that the nature of the assault was similar to yours.'

Lea recoiled as if she had been struck. She bent and leaned her head forwards and pressed her hands to the top of her head. She groaned and rocked herself backward and forward.

Deirdre felt she had to press on.

'I have one more question. Have you ever heard of incel?'

Lea raised her head and sniffled.

'The men who think they are entitled to sex? Do they have something to do with this?'

'We don't know yet, there might be a link. Did you ever have any dealings with them or know somebody who was involved?' Deirdre could feel some desperation in her voice, she tried to calm down.

Lea shook her head.

'No, not that I know of. I only know about them because of that murder spree in Wales and it was all over *The Guardian*.'

NOTHING, DEIRDRE thought, after Lea had locked the door behind her. She walked up the steps onto the street. *Absolutely nothing, a waste of time. Not to mention raising Lea's hopes.*

She closed the gate behind her. She breathed in and out. She thought about the scars on Lea's arms and thighs. All the other scars of all the other victims – inside and outside. All the memories they are carrying, all the horrible nights they have put down and will always put down. She thought about Helen O'Driscoll's body on the bed in her own house, where she should have been safe.

You're going to nail this bastard, she thought, walking towards the train station. *You will not let her down. No way.*

CHAPTER 44

SKIBBEREEN GARDA Station was a much more modest building than the one in Clonakilty and its unsuitability for holding Ted Farrell immediately struck Collins as he approached it. Single storey at the front, finished in plain brick, it resembled a suburban home more than a police station, despite the two garda badges on the front wall, the defibrillator to one side of the door and the high telecommunications mast behind it. At the back, it was split level with a single cell on the ground floor.

The media presence outside was no surprise even though it was still before 8 a.m. Once the news of a second murder would get out, the number of camera crews and reporters would treble. A feeding frenzy.

An RTÉ reporter, Brigid Moloney, and another from Cork city, John McLaughlin, made for Collins and Nuala when they got out of the Audi.

'Collins,' McLaughlin said. 'Is it true ye found a second body?'

Collins shrugged as if it was news to him and he walked on. So, the news was out. Inevitable, but it still annoyed him. But the main thing was that he'd be the one breaking the news to Ted Farrell. He nodded to the ASU officer stationed outside the front door: Karen Costello.

'Hi Karen,' he said. 'Hope you like an audience. It's going to be mental here before the day is out.'

'Nice to see you, too, Collins. The minute you arrive back west the bodies start piling up.'

Collins grinned. He liked that woman; she could floor pints too, and sing 'The Boys of Barr na Sráide' as well as anyone he'd ever heard. When he noticed the facia board had rotted above Karen's head, the grin left him. It was symbolic of the poor funding of the gardaí by successive governments. Then when people like Jones cut loose, the politicians start flinging blame for their own failures.

Buckley and Heaney were conferring in the wide corridor. Buckley waved Collins and Nuala into the office on the right, which was already stifling hot.

'Jesus, wouldn't they open that window?' Nuala said pulling at the latch.

'It's stuck, don't waste your time. Welcome to Shkib,' Collins said, pronouncing it as a local would. 'Good news is the meeting room at the back will be cooler.'

'Somebody leaked about the second body,' she said.

'Yeah, this place is going to be like Grand Central Station by lunchtime. We'll have to get Ted to Cork, to Anglesea Street or somewhere within a couple of hours.'

Buckley walked in and sat down behind the desk. He looked angry. Collins and Nuala sat opposite him.

'I've just had a new one ripped open by Number One,' Buckley said.

'Why?' Nuala said, a little naïvely, in Collins' opinion.

'Why? Why? Because I've only been down here a few days to sort out a drugs operation and now we have two murders on our hands. The Minister for Tourism gave her a bollocking an hour ago and she felt the need to pass it on.'

'Good job you're down here, so,' Collins said. 'It showed you were fully justified in taking charge.' He knew it was what Buckley wanted to hear, but he didn't care. He badly wanted to get at Ted Farrell.

'That's what I told her!' Buckley said and he calmed down. 'Anyway, it looks like Jones did for Bobby Farrell. The fucker is probably on his way to Spain already.'

'No,' Collins said. 'He won't run. When did he ever run, even when we had three witnesses on the go that time in Cherry Orchard?'

'Yeah, but it's like looking for a needle in a haystack in West Cork, if he's even still here. And we have zero evidence – none – that he's involved.'

'Hold on a minute,' Collins said. 'I saw Bobby Farrell and Jones in a car together outside Dunmanway last Saturday, just a few days ago. And we have a known drug dealer murdered outside Union Hall. And now Bobby Farrell is killed, too, execution-style, the exact same way. We have the records of the tracking device which show that Bobby Farrell's car was exactly where I said it was last Saturday. And we have two people in custody, one arrested with a huge shipment of drugs who is intimately connected with one of the murder victims.'

'Okay,' Buckley admitted. 'That's well put, but we still have to find him.'

'First things first,' Collins said. 'The main priority is to protect our assets now: Ted Farrell and Derek Webb. Whatever else, we need to keep them in custody and isolated. And we need time to work on them, Webb especially. He's a cocky little fucker but I intend to knock that out of him soon.'

'What's your approach with Ted Farrell?' Buckley said. 'His solicitor is in with him now and you have history with her.'

'Oh,' Collins said. 'Is it Eleanor Sheehan?'

'It is.'

'Well, well,' Collins said.

'Who is she?' Nuala said and Buckley smirked.

Collins sighed.

'I was involved for a time with Eleanor Sheehan. But, more importantly, she represented a man I was accused of trying to kill two years ago. We're not on best terms, to put it mildly.'

'Still want to have a go at Farrell?' Buckley said.

'I do, and to answer your question, my approach is this: if he leaves our custody, he's a dead man. He's a recluse and a bit of an oddball but I have information that he's far from stupid. She will have told him we have nothing to charge him with, but that's not true. He put a tracking device in three cars that we know of and that's illegal, under the *Non-Fatal Offences Act*.'

Buckley nodded. 'Yes, but even if we charge him, we'll have to release him, unless a judge says otherwise, which they won't.'

'I can't imagine he'll give us anything this morning, *she'll* have reassured him enough to keep his mouth shut. He'll also feel guilty about Bobby's death and that'll shake him up badly. I'll work on the guilt angle big time. He had no idea what he was getting into and what kind of a monster was behind it all. I'll try to distance him from the solicitor.'

'Okay,' Buckley said. 'But this isn't about you versus your ex, so don't make it into something personal. I know how you can hold a grudge.'

'Fair enough,' Collins said. 'Do you know what might help? If Nuala came the heavy in there and I played the good guy, appearing to take his side, getting all pally with him. I think he'd be far more shook up by getting a hammering from a woman.'

Buckley shrugged and looked at Nuala. It was up to her.

'Yeah, she said. 'I can do that.'

'Right, so,' said Collins. 'Let's go.'

'WE SHOULD clean up a bit before we go in there,' Nuala said in the corridor. Collins noted she had a small overnight bag with her.

'Sure,' Collins said. 'Meet you here in five?'

'Make it ten.'

Collins went to the main desk.

'How're you keeping, Collins?' the sergeant behind the desk asked him, smiling. Collins recognised him, one of four Beecher brothers, all gardaí, from Macroom – great fishermen.

'I'm good,' Collins said. 'How are all the Beechers?'

'Yerra, only middling. We preferred it quiet down here, boy.'

'Me, too. Wish I was heading out from Baltimore with a few rods and some cool ones.'

'Oh, now. What can I do you for?' The sergeant had a bemused look about him, but Collins knew he was as smart as a whip.

'You wouldn't have a spare razor and a tie in a drawer, there, anywhere?'

'Indeed and we do. Now: would you prefer the blue, or the green?' He reached into a drawer and took out two folded up ties in clear plastic bags. If nothing else, this garda was tidy. He smiled, looking Collins up and down. 'The blue, definitely with that jacket.'

'You're very good,' Collins said, taking the tie.

'And here's your razor and a bit of gel,' Beecher said, opening a small toilet bag and removing a disposable razor and a small bottle of shaving gel. 'Aftershave? I've a bit of Brut here. You'll be only gorgeous for that lovely solicitor.'

Collins chuckled.

'Face the child to Macroom,' he said. 'And you'll never rear a fool.' It was a saying his Nana Kitty was fond of.

'Now you have it, Collins,' Beecher said, sitting back down. 'Now you have it, boy. I want everything back except the razor.'

CHAPTER 45

COLLINS CONCENTRATED on Ted Farrell when he entered the interview room. He had steeled himself not to react to Eleanor, no matter how well she could push his buttons. Nuala looked like a business executive, however she had managed it. Collins had long given up on trying to fathom the transformative power of women.

The room was cool and dark, at the back of the station and on the ground floor. Ted Farrell was wearing the frayed red jumper he'd had on when they took him from Tournafulla the night before. He had clearly been crying, his eyes were rimmed and Collins could see the remnants of a tissue in his massive left hand. Which meant that Eleanor Sheehan – the good solicitor that she was – had told him about Bobby's death, depriving the gardaí of the leverage breaking such news would give them.

Nuala was closer to the recording video and she pressed the button. 'Interview in Skibbereen Garda Station on the 25th of June 2018. Present are Mr Ted Farrell of Tournafulla, County Cork, Garda Detective Tim Collins and Garda Inspector Nuala Leahy. Also present is Mr Farrell's legal representative, Ms...' Here she paused and waved to Sheehan to name herself. *A nice touch*, Collins thought.

'Eleanor Sheehan of Sheehan, Brady and Comyns,' Eleanor said, a bit too stridently.

'Thank you Ms Sheehan,' Nuala said. 'I was only looking for your name, not the company you are employed by. That is hardly relevant.'

'*Excuse* me ...' Sheehan began but Collins cut her off.

'Ted,' he said, leaning forward. 'I just want to begin by giving you my sincere condolences for your terrible loss. Superintendents

Buckley and Brophy have specifically asked me to convey their condolences, too. It's terrible what happened, terrible.'

Farrell looked at Collins, shocked, and then lowered his head. He muttered a 'thank you'.

Collins continued: 'Now, more than anything else, we want to find out who did this terrible thing and bring them to justice. That's what we want more than anything and Bobby would have deserved that. Your mother and father, too. Now, Inspector Leahy will ask you some questions and it's vital – vital – that you tell her what she needs to know. Is that okay, Ted? Can you do that?'

'My client …' Eleanor began.

'Ted Farrell, where were you yesterday between the hours of twelve noon and 5 p.m.?' Nuala said loudly. 'I'm asking you a question!'

Ted looked at her in horror, his mouth a wide O.

'Excuse me!' Eleanor said. 'My client has not been cautioned, let alone charged with anything. This is …'

'Ted.' Collins leaned forward again. 'Ted. Listen. We need to rule everything out and everything in at this stage. So, if you tell the inspector where you were, we can clear this up.'

'Who was Bobby Farrell's next of kin?' Nuala said. 'Mr Farrell? Who will the farm go to when your brother died? Will it go to *you*?'

'What?' Ted said, recoiling. Even Eleanor Sheehan was taken aback. Then she countered.

'This is outrageous, is my client seriously being accused of murder?'

'Ted, Ted,' Collins said. 'Look at me, Ted. Where were you yesterday? Were you on the farm or what? We have to get this out of the way.'

'I was, I was,' Ted said, imploringly.

'Did you go anywhere?' Collins said, knowing well he had.

'I went into Drimoleague around one o'clock to get some ham and some bread and a … a … bit of dinner.'

'Good,' Collins said. 'What shop did you go to?' Important to get him flowing.

'The Centra.'

'Good man, that's grand, their cameras will prove that.'

'I never, I'd never hurt Bobby.'

'And when did you come back to the farm?'

'Around 2. Yes it was near 2, the Joe Duffy show was on.'

'And after that? Did you have a bit of grub?'

'I had a sandwich. And then I went out to the Low Field and … there was a broken ballcock, one of the bullocks broke it.'

'Jesus those bullocks would break anything. Were you able to fix it?' Again, Collins knew the answer.

'I had to weld it. I had to drag the welder out there and find a new rod.'

'That's a dose. How long did that take?'

'I wasn't finished 'til near four and I had to drag water over the weanlings, there's no water in that field.'

'Good man. That took you until … after five?'

'It did.'

'Detectives,' Eleanor Sheehan said, 'since my client has not been charged with any crime, I insist this interview be terminated and he be released immediately.'

'*Inspector*,' Nuala said. 'You will address me by my proper title, Ms Sheehan.'

'Oh, for God's sake.'

'Ted,' Collins said. 'Did you know Bobby was involved in drugs? Did you know that?'

'Don't answer that, Ted,' Sheehan said.

'Ted, we need to catch who did this. You have to help us, for

Bobby's sake. What would your late mother, Mary, God rest her, have wanted you to do?'

Ted Farrell put his head in his hands and began to weep and rock backwards and forwards.

'I'm terminating this,' Eleanor said. She stood up and reached for the recording controls.

Nuala intercepted her, grabbing her hand.

'You're interfering with garda equipment,' Nuala said. 'You're trying to prevent us doing our job. You do not touch garda equipment, is that clear?'

'I'm leaving,' Eleanor said, gathering up the sheets of paper before her. 'This is over. Ted, the interview is over. You are free to go.'

Ted looked up at Collins.

'Am, I, Collins?'

'Ted,' he said, shaking his head, sadly. 'Why don't you and I have a chat, face to face, without anybody else being present? We don't even have to record it, if you don't want to. Just a chat between the two of us, man to man, and we can clear all this up. What do you say?'

'Ted, as your legal representative I advise strongly against this.'

'I know Collins,' Ted said to her. 'That's Tim Collins. He played for Cork, you know.'

'Yes, but it's a trick, Ted. When he gets you on your own, he'll ...'

'I'm not a child!' Ted stood up and bunched his fists. Collins wondered for a moment if Ted would attack Eleanor and if so, would he be able to subdue him; probably not. Ted Farrell clenched his eyes, began to shake and it looked for a moment that he was having an epileptic fit. Then, just as suddenly, he inhaled and exhaled deeply, looked at Eleanor Sheehan and said to her: 'You can go. If I need your services again, I will let you know.'

'Good man, Ted,' Collins said. 'Will you have cup of tea or anything? Did they give you breakfast yet?'

'They offered it but I wasn't hungry.'

Collins sat down and Ted Farrell did likewise.

'Would you have a breakfast roll? They do a good one in Field's.'

'I would. I'd nothing since last night.'

'How do you take your tea?'

'Mr Farrell,' Eleanor tried, but Ted held up his left hand in dismissal.

'For the record,' she said. 'And this is on video tape. I have formally advised my client not to proceed with this course of action.'

'Drop of milk?' Collins said. 'Any sugar? Will you look after that, Nuala? And the full breakfast roll for Ted. I'll just have a coffee, please.'

'I know what you're up to, Collins,' Eleanor hissed. 'And you won't get away with it. Nothing he says will stand up in court.'

Collins stood up, smiled and reached a hand out to Eleanor. 'Miss Sheehan, always a pleasure to meet you. Please give my best regards to your mother. How is she?'

'For fuck's sake,' Eleanor said, ignoring the hand and leaving the room. Collins gave a meaningful look to Nuala.

'Ms Sheehan and Inspector Leahy have left the room,' Collins said. 'Now, Ted, let's get all this sorted out.'

IN THE first half an hour, until Ted had finished his breakfast roll and tea, they talked mostly about hurling and football. How Cork were useless against Kerry in the Munster Final the previous Sunday. They both gave out about the high price of calves at the mart and the low price of finished animals from the factories. The dry weather, the high price of water and car insurance; how the government were trying to cod farmers and the EU were worse.

Collins was sure that Ted knew he was being led along. He had remembered what Michael Pat Murphy had said about him not being stupid. Ted was playing for time, playing the fool. He had been doing that since childhood.

Collins looked at his watch. It was almost 8:30 a.m.

'I must go soon, Ted, but I want to ask you some serious questions now. Is that okay?'

'It is.' Ted looked wary, Collins sensed him calculating how much he could give away. He remembered that Michael Pat had said he was cunning.

'Did you know Bobby was dealing *drugs*?'

'I didn't. I swear to God, Collins. But after what happened to Derek Webb, I suppose it made sense.'

'We know you did, Ted. We know you knew about the drugs.'

'I didn't.'

'We know you phoned the gardaí in Clon. We have a recording of the phone call and that will match your voice, we can do that. We know it was you, Ted.'

'No, I didn't. I didn't.'

'You see, Ted. Every lie you tell us goes down against you. All this goes down on your record and it'll all come out in court.'

'I didn't do nothing.'

'We also know it was you sent the package in the post. We know where you posted the drugs from, too. We have a video of your car near Skib. the same day. We have your fingerprints on it, too. We know everything, Ted.'

Ted reacted to this, he must have worn gloves and felt confident that Collins was lying.

'No. I didn't. I didn't.'

'Ted we have two prints and they will match yours. You must have touched the bag before you put on the gloves. Juries love fingerprints, the chances of them being wrong are a million to one.'

'No. That's a mistake.'

'Ted, we can match your voice to the phone call and your fin-gerprints to the package. You're playing the fool here and I know you're no fool. Do you know who we were talking to yesterday about you?'

Ted shook his head.

'I was talking to Michael Pat Murphy, the teacher. And do you know what he told me? He told me that you were as smart as anybody in the class. You're no fool, so don't be playing the fool. This isn't a joke, Ted. This is real and it's about to get very real for you.'

'No.'

'We found the drugs in Bobby's yard, Ted.'

Ted shook his head again.

'You knew there were drugs being made there and you didn't tell us. That's an accessory after the fact. That's ten years in jail, Ted.'

'No. I didn't know nothing.'

'Do you know how we found Bobby's body in his car so quickly?'

'No. How would I know that?'

'Were you tracking his car?'

Ted reacted again. Very slightly, but it was unmistakable.

'No. How would I do that?'

'We have your phone, Ted. We know you tried to delete the App, but we found it there, we have technicians who can do that.'

'I don't know anything about that.'

'Ted. Don't insult my intelligence and I won't insult yours. The TrackIt App was on your phone and that's how we were able to find Bobby's car and his body. We used your phone. So don't deny it.'

'No. That's not true.'

'Do you know who killed Bobby?'

'No. How would I know that?'

'We do.'

'What? Why don't ye arrest him, so?'

'Don't get smart, Ted. You're not in a good place here. We have a lot of drugs and two dead bodies and there's a lot of pressure to solve these cases. We're going to put you away for a long time.'

Ted shook his head and Collins changed tack.

'Have a look at this photo on my phone,' he said, opening the screen with his thumbprint. He found the photos Halloran had sent him. He opened the longer shot with the rat.

Ted squinted to see it and leaned forward.

'Jesus!' he said, recoiling. He pulled his hands over his mouth. 'Jesus Christ.'

'You did this, Ted.'

'No! No, I didn't.'

'Do you know why they put a rat on him, Ted? That's because they think it was Bobby ratted them out, but it wasn't Bobby did that, it was you. You're the rat, Ted, and you got Bobby killed.'

Ted wouldn't look at the phone. Collins pushed it closer. Ted hung his head and closed his eyes.

'That's what got him killed: you ringing the gardaí and sending the drugs. The man running the drugs ring did this. He also killed another dealer by the name of Phelan. We found his body yesterday near Union Hall. Who do you think he's coming for next, Ted?'

'No. I didn't do it.'

'He knows you're here. When we release you, he'll come for you. He has killed between fifteen and twenty people that we know of. What's one more, Ted? You think you'll be safe in Tournafulla? Where will you go? He'll follow you wherever you go. He'll find you in prison, he'll find you in London. Doesn't matter.'

'No, no.' Ted was rocking back and forth again.

'I'd say your mother must be proud of you now. You had your

brother killed and you're either going to prison or you'll be killed yourself. The land will be sold off. You'll be remembered forever in West Cork as the man who had his brother killed. They'll be talking about you for a hundred years. "Ted Farrell, the man who killed his own brother".'

Ted curled up into a ball in the chair and began to moan. This was it. Collins had to close out the deal. He stood up.

'Stand up,' Collins said.

'What?' Ted looked up at him.

'I said stand up, you sack of shit.'

'No,' Ted was pleading now.

'We're letting you go.'

'What?'

'We're letting you go. You're free to go. But we'll be telling everyone in Drimoleague and Dunmanway what you did. Fuck off out of here, you piece of shit.'

Ted stood up. He staggered and he had to hold on to the desk to stay upright. Collins went to the door and opened it. The corridor was empty outside. Collins knew that everyone was looking at the whole thing on the big screen in another room.

'Out. Get the fuck out!'

Ted looked at the door in horror and then at Collins. He swallowed and sat down.

'Yes, I tracked him,' he said, his voice guttural and raw. 'But he wasn't the only one I tracked. I tracked Jones too. The fucker who's running the show. I know where he is, too. I want a deal.'

Collins closed the door and sat down.

'Start from the beginning, Ted,' he said.

CHAPTER 46

THEY GAVE Collins and Nuala a round of applause when they got back to the Incident Room in Clonakilty at 2 p.m. Collins was embarrassed and stood leaning against the back wall.

'Jaysus you should get an Oscar for that, Timmy,' Declan Kerr said, grinning. 'Best show I've seen since the one with Liam Neeson, what's it called again?'

'What about the Beast of Limerick, here?' Collins said, pointing at Nuala. 'I was scared, let alone Ted Farrell.'

'Very scary,' Declan said. 'But you trying to be nice was a bit scarier. I thought your mouth would fall off with the smiling.'

'Very funny, Declan,' Collins said, lamely.

Buckley came into the room with Heaney and they sat down. The gardaí went quiet.

'Okay,' Buckley said loudly. His voice was almost trembling with excitement. 'We found the second phone in the barn, where Farrell said it would be and we have what he says is the location of Eddie Jones. Can you turn on that projector there, please?'

The projector lit up and a map became clear on the wall behind Buckley.

'This is the location of one of the other cars that Farrell was tracking. According to what he said – thanks to the good work of Nuala and Collins here – this is the place. Apparently Farrell had eight tracking devices on the go, including the one we think will give us Jones.

'If we zoom out we can see it's in the hills north-east of Glen-garriff at a very remote location. It's also very inaccessible which is why we have to plan this carefully. The ASU will take lead and we'll have army backup. It looks like there are four vehicles parked there, two cars and two SUVs, so Jones could have several men with him, and they will be heavily armed.

'Needless to say, it needs careful planning. We don't want a bloodbath but we especially don't want any casualties on our side. The ASU and some army people will go across country later this evening and move in at 3 a.m. tomorrow morning. We will provide logistics by bringing in those in custody and back-up on the roads around the area and we'll pick up any pieces if there's fall out or if some of Jones' gang escape. Any questions?'

'When do we get our individual assignments for tonight?' Sean Dineen asked.

'We'll reconvene here at eighteen hundred hours and we'll have them, then,' Heaney said. Collins' phone vibrated on silent and he checked the caller. It was Denis Grandon. He killed the call and texted him: *Call you in 10.*

'Anything else?' Buckley said.

'Has Ted Farrell been moved to a more secure location?' Collins asked.

'We're a bit busy with this operation now, Collins. To answer your question, yes. We've moved Ted Farrell here to Clonakilty, under armed guard,' Buckley said. 'Anything else? If not I suggest that those of you involved last night get some rest between now and six o'clock. It's going to be a long night.'

COLLINS CALLED Denis outside the station. Nuala had gone to her B&B to have a nap. Collins decided to drive out to Inchydoney and do the same in his car.

'Hi Denis, Collins here.'

'We found something here,' Denis said. 'Well, Tony did.'

'In Tournafulla?'

'Yes, I'll put him on. He'll explain it better.'

'Is that Collins?' Tony said.

'Yes, go ahead, what did ye find?'

'I think there's a false room upstairs in the house. There's a gap.'

'A gap? What kind of gap?'

'I measured the two bedrooms upstairs and they come to twenty-four feet. But when I measured the wall along the hall it's nearly thirty-two feet.'

'Oh. Is there any explanation for that?'

'The only explanation is either there's an eight-foot-thick wall between the bedrooms or there's another room up there.'

'Did ye try to find an entrance to it?'

'We did, and we think we have it. It's through the wardrobe in the spare room. I was a bit suspicious when that was empty. I think there's a false panel there and I think it will come out. We just wanted to let you know before we tried to get in there.'

'Okay, good move. Put on gloves and try to get in. Don't touch anything. Give me a ring when you find something. I'll be there in less than thirty minutes.

COLLINS BOUGHT a coffee at the garage on the main road west out of Clonakilty. He took a sip of it in the car park and realised he couldn't drink it; his stomach wouldn't allow him any more coffee that day. He counted back. He had drunk eight cups since the first one that morning when Hega had phoned him at 3 a.m.

He brought the coffee back into the garage and gave it back to the young barista.

'Is it okay?' she asked him.

'It's fine,' he said. 'I'm just coffee'd out. I'm not looking for a refund, I just didn't want to put the full cup in the bin.' He bought a large bottle of water. He drank deeply from it in the car and fought the urge to close his eyes. He turned on the radio loud at a classic hits station and sang along to songs he didn't like as he drove towards Drimoleague. When he joined the main road from

Dunmanway, he knew he'd be okay, his body had found something, somewhere. His phone rang on the hands free. He answered.

'Collins, you're not going to believe this,' Denis Grandon said excitedly.

'What is it?'

'He's some kind of a pervert. A peeping Tom for sure.'

'What did you find? Describe what's you're looking at. I'll be there in fifteen minutes.'

'It's a small room, maybe eight-foot by six. First thing you notice are all the photos on the wall. A man and a woman having sex.'

'Porn?'

'I'm not sure. I don't know, you'd have to see them.'

'What else is in there?'

'A laptop and a desk. Two large printers. All the photos were printed on them, I'd say. They're big pictures, A3 size. There are three or four cameras and telephoto lenses and some scopes like the one we had on the hill when we were looking down on the farms. Like I say, this guy is some kind of a peeping Tom.'

'Did you try to open the laptop?'

'Yeah, there's a password.'

'Okay. Is there Wi-Fi in the house?'

'Yeah, it's good actually.'

'Right. I'm coming into Drimoleague now, do ye want anything from the Centra?'

'One second,' Denis said and there was a pause on the line. 'Yes, three large hot chicken rolls, two with butter; one with Mayo. Two Cokes, one Seven Up.'

Collins smiled, some things never change.

CHAPTER 47

COLLINS PHONED Hega as he pulled out of the Centra, the three chicken rolls cooling on the passenger seat.

'Collins,' Hega said. 'Perfect timing, boy, I'm just out of bed. Did ye get the car?'

'We did, Hega, thanks again. Listen, we have a laptop here, but it's password protected. Can you get in remotely?'

'Sure, no bother. Just connect it to your phone and ring me again and I'm in. But use the good cable I gave you, none of those cheap ones.'

'Okay, I have that in the boot here. I'll be on to you in twenty or thirty minutes.'

Collins hung up and then phoned Declan Kerr.

'Hi, Declan, Collins here. I meant to ask you earlier; did ye follow up on that address in Bandon? Where the tracker showed the third car?'

'We did indeed, I'm just back.'

'Was there a Maeve?'

'Yeah, her name is Maeve Hunt, she's twenty-eight and she was Bobby Farrell's girlfriend up to a few weeks ago when she broke it off with him.'

'Did she say why?'

'She said she didn't like who he was hanging around with. She wouldn't elaborate, but I guess it was Webb and the like.'

'Did ye find the tracker on her car?'

'We did, even though it was well hidden. She hit the roof over that. Wanted to know who put it there. She suspected Bobby, and we didn't tell her he was dead, either.'

'She'll find that out soon enough. Is she on social media? I'd like to see a picture.'

'She is. Facebook and Instagram, I'll text you one there, now. Hold on, why do you want a picture?'

'The lads found some photos in Ted's house, I want to check if it's her. Looks like he was fixated with her. Maybe he was jealous of Bobby or something.'

'For God's sake.'

'I'll let you know.'

The photo pinged through as Collins was parking the car in the farmyard. He looked at it. A dark-haired, attractive woman, whose life was about to take a turn for the worse.

In the room, he was quickly able to confirm it was her. The pictures were of poor quality and they seemed to be stills from videos. The man didn't hold the video camera, it was pointing down at the bed from a few feet away. She didn't seem to know it was there, no photos showed her looking at the camera.

How Ted Farrell got the photos or videos was another question. But if he had gone to the trouble of following her, it made sense why he would want them.

Collins connected his phone to the laptop with the good cable and phoned Hega, who picked up immediately.

'Okay,' Hega said. 'Are you connected to the laptop?'

'Yes,' Collins said. He had set the phone to speaker mode. The screen of the laptop was open and it showed a password prompt in the middle of a blue background.

'Give me a minute,' Hega said. 'I should be able to see the laptop there. Okay I have it. This shouldn't take long, Collins. I'll tell you when you can hang up.'

Collins looked at the lurid pictures on the walls. There must have been twenty of them and they were on all four walls and the back of the door. The smell in the room was musty and Collins didn't like to think about what Ted Farrell had been up to in there. There were some details of the room in which the photos had been taken. The wall colour was light blue and the bed's headboard was some type of soft beige material. He tried to remember the beds in Bobby Farrell's bedroom across the yard. Easily checked.

Collins' eyes were drawn to the laptop. The screen burst into life and lines and lines of fast-moving white text began to scroll up on it.

'Okay, I'm in, Collins. You can disconnect the phone now.'

'Can you get past the password?'

'Done. I'm in the hard drive now. In a minute it will boot up with a new password, 0000.'

The screen showed the laptop rebooting and Collins typed in the four zeros. He searched for 'Maeve' on the C Drive and a folder called 'Maeve Slut' came up. He opened it. Six videos. He opened the top one. It began with an empty bed. Then a couple fell on to it, laughing. Maeve Hunt and Bobby Farrell. Soon they were tearing off their clothes and Collins closed the video and phoned Hega.

'Hega, will you have a look through the hard drive?'

'No bothers. I'm having a quick sconce at the browser history there. I should have done that with the phone too.'

'What does it show?'

'Well, a lot of porn sites but he was on the TrackIt website a lot too. I was able to login into his account because he set the site to remember his password. You should go in there, there's two cars being tracked live. One called "MH" and the other is called "Jones".'

'How do you mean being tracked live?'

'Well, the cars are on the go, they're moving, like.'

Collins' felt his heart race. If Jones wasn't at the house near Glengarriff, the whole raid tonight was worthless.

'Shit, can I log in now and see where they are?' he said.

'Sure, just open the Google Chrome App and type TrackItLive. The password should be remembered.'

Collins did so. He saw five streams at the top of the screen. Two of them were flashing. He clicked on the one called 'Jones'.

A map opened and he could see a red moving dot blink on and off. It was moving what looked like northwards. He clicked on a 'minus' button and the map zoomed out. He was shocked to see Drimoleague to the south. Then it dawned on him. The car was moving towards Tournafulla. It was two kilometres to the west, just approaching Cullen Lake. If it turned left there, it would be heading straight for them. He watched, mesmerised, as the car reached the turn off by the lake. It stopped, the light blinking red all the time. Then it went left. It was minutes from them.

He phoned Heaney first as he rushed down the stairs. Thankfully, he answered on the second ring.

'Detective,' Heaney said.

Collins was at the back door.

'I'm at Tournafulla with three others. I have just found out that a car, which I suspect contains Eddie Jones and others, is approaching us from the Drimoleague road. They will be here in less than five minutes. Send armed members and do it now. Send the ASU from Skibbereen too. I'm telling the lads to run, they won't have weapons.'

Collins ran to the two squad cars parked in the yard. The three gardaí were eating their rolls. Tony Quinlan and David McNulty were sitting in the front of one car. Denis Grandon was sitting in the back. All four doors were open.

'Do ye have weapons?' Collins shouted. 'Do ye have any weapons? Jones is coming up the road.'

Denis shook his head. He had just taken a bite of roll.

'No,' he mumbled.

'Get out,' Collins said. He thought he heard a car approach.

'Heaney?' he said, into the phone.

'Backup units heading your way now,' Heaney said and Collins put his phone into his inside jacket pocket.

He took his weapon from his holster and turned the safety to OFF.

'Ye'll have to run, there's nothing else for it.'

'What?' Denis said, getting out of the car. He was still holding his roll. All three gardaí were standing now.

'Jones is coming straight here. That's him,' Collins said, pointing. He saw two vehicles pass a gateway fifty yards down the road. 'He's going to be armed. Ye need to run now. I'll try and keep him off.'

'I'm not running,' Denis said, putting the roll on the roof of the car. 'We don't run from the likes of him.'

'Listen,' Collins said. 'I don't have time to argue. Get out of here, take cover.' He moved towards the entrance of the yard and crouched down behind the squad car. He pointed his weapon towards the road as two vehicles turned the corner. One was a dark grey SUV, there were three men inside, Eddie Jones in the passenger seat. The second car reversed out of sight behind the ditch and so did the SUV.

Collins glanced behind him. Thankfully, the three gardaí were running away. They were all young and fit.

CHAPTER 48

COLLINS WONDERED if Jones would retreat, having seen the squad cars. He heard three car doors close. Time seemed to slow down. Then both vehicles surged into the farmyard, making straight for him. Collins couldn't see the driver of the SUV, he must have been crouching down. He fired twice aiming for just below the steering wheel. He retreated behind the second squad car as the SUV smashed into the first one.

'Armed gardaí!' Collins shouted. 'Drop your weapons and put your hands up!'

He had a clear line of sight to both drivers' doors but he couldn't see either man. He noticed movement near the entrance to the yard and bullets thudded into the car in front of him. He took cover. An automatic weapon, he was seriously outgunned.

'Collins? That you, Collins?' Jones shouted from behind the ditch. 'Drop your weapon and you can walk. We came to take something that's ours and then we'll be gone. Drop the gun and I'll give you thirty seconds. Nobody gets hurt.'

Collins ran towards the sheds at the rear of the yard and took cover behind a high concrete wall. He tried to think. *What, two or three minutes since he rang it in?* Surely it would take at least twenty minutes before an armed unit would get there. He had to hide.

He had his bearings from the previous night and from looking down on the buildings from Rowan Hill. He immediately dismissed the two stalls with cows and calves. Calves were too curious and cows with calves too aggressive. The next stall was open, they would check that one for sure. There was a round bale of hay in the corner, ideal for hiding behind, so he discounted it. The one where the drugs had been manufactured was empty, no good. On the other side of that, three dry cows stood placidly chewing cud and staring at him. If somebody came in and wanted to check the bale, he would have to pass by the cows on the other side of the bars.

Collins closed the metal stall door made from galvanised sheeting. It gave a slight groan. He grabbed three large hanks of hay from the bale and threw it on the ground before the cows, who began to eat them. He tried to calm his breathing and think. If Jones was there looking for a stash of drugs, would he come looking for him? How could he get out if they came through the door? What would he do if they found one of the others?

He climbed over the bars, careful to not drop his weapon, and moved behind the cattle, wary of a kick. There was a feeding trough and a tank that he could hide behind. He hunkered down behind them. The cows chewed noisily. He couldn't tell how much time had passed. How many rounds had he fired? Three, four? That meant he had eleven or twelve left. He checked the mechanism of the gun, it was fine.

He repeated the mantra his weapons trainer had drummed into him. 'Do the job in front of you. Hit the torso and keep shooting.' He listened out for the sound of footsteps. Nothing. He closed his mouth and breathed through his nose.

AFTER A few minutes, he heard a door banging, then a triumphant 'Ha, come out you fucker.' A Dublin accent.

'Collins! Come out, come out wherever you are!' It was Jones, Collins would know that voice anywhere.

'Collins! Come out or I'll fucking shoot him. I'm not joking. I'll put a bullet in him if you don't give yourself up.'

Collins climbed the gate and sidled along the wall. He looked through the gap at the side of the door. Jones and another man were standing in the middle of the farmyard, maybe thirty yards away. Denis Grandon was on his knees beside them, his eyes shut.

Jones had a black pistol pointed at Denis' temple. The other man had a sawn-off shotgun pointed down at his back. Collins recoiled away from the gap.

'Jesus,' he whispered. He didn't know what to do. He pressed his cheek against the wall's rough concrete. If he went out, Jones would shoot the two of them. If he replied, Jones would find him. He tried to think. He'd have to give himself up.

Surely Jones was bluffing, even he wouldn't be mad enough to kill a garda.

He looked again through the gap. Denis had lowered his head, as if bracing for the impact.

'Now, Collins! Last chance saloon!' Jones shouted.

'*Do something!*' Collins whispered but his feet wouldn't move.

The blood was churning in his head. His breathing sounded raw and ragged. He couldn't stop looking but was unable to move a muscle. He forced his left hand down to the handle of the door and gripped it, watching through the gap all the time. He tried to turn the handle but his hand wouldn't move.

He willed Jones to run away without shooting Denis. Then he realised that wasn't going to happen. He stopped breathing. Time no longer existed.

The deafening sound of a gunshot and a spray of red. Denis' head whiplashing to the right and his body flopping to the ground.

Jones gave a whoop of glee and turned and ran. The other man ran too.

Collins swung the gate open and burst out into the yard, his gun pointed. He fired a shot. Another cheer from Jones as he rounded the corner. Collins shot again but they were out of sight. He ran to Denis, his blood pooling on the concrete. He was lying on his back, his legs bent at a strange angle underneath him.

'Denis,' he said as he reached the body. 'Denis!' He knelt down and lifted Denis' head. There was a neat entry wound just above his eyeline on the temple. The exit wound was a gaping hole. A spatter of red on the ground and blood flowing into a deep crack in the concrete. He lay Denis' head back on the ground.

'Oh, no,' Collins said. 'Oh, no.' He put his two hands on Denis' chest and tried to feel for a heartbeat.

'Denis,' he said. 'Denis.'

He saw Tony Quinlan peer out from a doorway and walk into the yard.

'Denis!' Tony shouted and ran towards them.

Collins heard a strange whine come out from his own throat.

He took his phone out and phoned Heaney.

'Denis Grandon has been shot dead,' Collins said. 'He's dead, where's the backup?'

'What?' Heaney said.

'Denis has been shot in cold blood. Jones did it. He's gone.'

'Oh, Jesus,' Heaney said.

Collins stood up. 'I can track them on the laptop,' he said, his voice hoarse. 'I can track them and tell you where they're going!'

'Do it!' Heaney shouted. 'Do it!'

'Tony, get a blanket. Cover him,' Collins said and he ran away.

Chapter 49

Collins staggered up the stairs, smearing blood on the bannisters. He rushed to the laptop and sat down.

'I'm at the laptop,' he said, into the phone, trying to catch his breath. 'Okay, I see them. There were two vehicles, they might split up. I think there's a tracker in only one of them, don't know which one. Right now, they are driving north on the L256 just after Cullen Lake. In a few kilometres that road turns west towards Kealkill. I wonder if they are heading for the hideout we were planning on raiding tonight.'

'Okay, let me relay that to our mobile units. I see it on the map there. Are you sure he's dead, Collins? Did you check for a pulse?'

Collins groaned. 'I'm sure. It was point-blank to the head.'

Collins heard Heaney hiss. 'He's sure,' he said, to somebody else, probably Buckley. 'Point blank. I'm putting you on speaker, Collins. I've Ronan here with me. We've sent out three units from Bantry. I think they will be able to intercept around Cousane Gap. We've cars from Macroom, Killarney, and Kenmare on their way, too.'

'They're heavily armed,' Collins said. 'One short barrel shotgun and at least one automatic weapon. Four to six men, I think. One car is a grey SUV, I think it's a Mitsubishi. The second car is black. Looks like an old Mondeo but I can't be sure. A saloon for sure. I didn't get any regs.'

Collins continued to direct Heaney where the cars were going. As expected, they were heading west towards the Beara Peninsula where the 'safe house' was located. They were taking back roads, hoping to avoid any checkpoints but eventually they would have to cross one of the main roads or the coastal road near Ballylickey.

It was decided to intercept them at a junction between Kealkill and Ballylickey but the gardaí had to rush to get there first. They had a 'stinger' with them, a spiked device to immobilise the first car. But they had to pick a place where it wouldn't be seen in time.

Collins heard sirens in the distance and then closer. Cars pulled up outside, doors slammed. Then the sound of footsteps.

Somebody shouted downstairs: 'Anybody here?' It sounded like Declan Kerr.

Collins replied: 'Tim Collins, come up.'

Steps on the stairs. Then a head poked around the corner. It was Declan.

'Timmy, I just heard. Where is he?'

'Down the yard, Tony Quinlan is with him. I told him to get a blanket,' Collins said. 'I'm on to Inspector Heaney now. We're tracking a car.'

'Are you hurt?' Declan said. 'There's blood on your hands.'

'No. It's Denis'.'

Declan went down the stairs.

'Collins, Ronan here. How did it happen?'

Collins didn't feel like retelling it. 'Jones and another man captured Denis somehow, I didn't see how. They brought him out into the yard and made him kneel down. Jones called me out and said he'd shoot Denis if I didn't come out.'

Collins stopped. *The side of Denis' head. His mother and father. His fiancé.*

'And?'

'I didn't come out. I didn't come out, all right! I fucking didn't. And Jones shot him in the side of the head.' Collins groaned. He made that strange whine again. He started to weep.

'Jesus. Jesus,' he said.

'Okay, Collins. Okay,' Buckley said. 'We're going to get these fuckers. What can you see on the screen?'

'They are still heading towards Kealkill,' Collins said. 'It's a long straight stretch of road.' He sniffled.

Ten minutes later he saw the cars stop on the screen's map before a junction.

'I can see them stopped now, just before the junction,' he said.

'Okay,' Heaney said. 'Now we wait. Nothing else to do.'

Collins stood up. He wanted to rip those bloody photos off the walls. He heard somebody come up the stairs. It was Declan Kerr again. Declan shook his head.

'Terrible,' he said. 'Terrible.'

'Is Tony okay?' Collins said.

'He's very shook. David, too.'

Collins closed his eyes, but all he could see was Denis' body crumpling to the ground.

'Any news about the cars?' Declan said.

'We intercepted them outside Ballylickey,' Collins said. 'Just waiting now. I have Inspector Heaney here on speaker phone.' He pointed to his phone on the desk.

'Collins,' Heaney said through the phone.

'Yes?'

'One car intercepted, "stinger" deployed.'

'Did they get him?'

'Four detained, Jones wasn't with them.'

'Shit,' Collins said. 'We have to find him.'

'Oh, we will. You may be sure of it,' Heaney said. 'I'm hanging up now.'

'Okay,' Collins said and he looked at the photos on the wall.

'Farrell,' he said.

Chapter 50

Collins went down the stairs. He turned on the tap in the kitchen and washed the blood from his hands. He washed his face in the running water. Then he drank from it. He wiped the blood off his phone with an old tea towel.

This is on you.

He went out into the farmyard. Declan followed him, not speaking.

Tony and David were standing around the body with some other gardaí.

'Did they get them?' David said.

'They got four of them, but not Jones,' Collins said.

'Fuck,' Tony said.

'Was it Jones did it?' David said.

'Yes,' Collins said. 'It was.'

'I heard him calling you to come out,' Tony said.

'Yeah,' Collins said. 'But I didn't, did I?'

Nobody spoke for a while and they moved aside when the forensic team arrived and started taking photos and videos.

When the ambulance entered the yard, Collins left and went back to his car. He pulled out onto the road. His phone rang. It was Nuala. He let it ring out.

He drank the rest of the water from his bottle as he drove away from Tournafulla. As he was approaching Clonakilty, the phone rang again. Nuala. He answered on the hands-free.

'Tim, it's Nuala. I just wanted to say how sorry I was to hear what happened. That's a terrible thing to experience.'

'Thanks, Nuala,' Collins said. 'Are you in Clon by any chance?

I wanted to interview Ted Farrell again, I wonder would you sit in, too?'

'Yes, I'm at the station.'

'Okay, I'll be there in ten minutes. You couldn't phone his solicitor, could you? She'll have to be there if he wants her.'

On the outskirts of the town, there was a garda checkpoint. *About fucking time*, Collins thought.

The garda was startled when she saw Collins behind the wheel. He had met her once, she was from Mallow. He couldn't remember her name. She put her hand out to him and he shook it.

'I'm sorry for your loss,' she said.

'Thanks,' he said. 'We all lost today.'

COLLINS SHOOK hands with two local gardaí outside the station. Inside there was a tangible sense of shock. There were no media yet, and he was glad of that. Only a question of time, but he was afraid what he'd say to them.

He went straight to Buckley's office and knocked on the door.

Heaney answered and he shook hands with Collins. Buckley came around the desk and did likewise.

'Are you okay, Tim?' Buckley said.

'I've had better days.'

'You should take some time off after that.'

Collins shook his head.

'Thanks, but I think it's better to keep going while I can. When we get Jones, I'll take a day or two. I think Farrell might know more. The drugs being at the farm, for starters. I was hoping to interview him again. Webb in Cork, too. They're hiding stuff from us and we need to know it all.'

Buckley didn't answer for a moment.

'Sit down,' he said.

Collins did so. His legs were weak for some reason. Buckley pulled up a chair beside him and sat down.

'Are you sure you're up to it?' Buckley said. 'That must have been a horrible shock.'

'I think so,' Collins said. 'I've spoken to Nuala and I've asked her to interview Farrell with me. She phoned the solicitor in Skib too. Did you raid that house outside Glengarriff yet?'

'The ASU just arrived, looks like there's nobody there apart from two Asian men. They found weapons and drugs but no sign of Jones.'

'Right,' Collins said.

'Okay,' Buckley said. 'I've informed the commissioner and he's briefed the minister. The commissioner has informed the family and is on her way to Dungarvan to meet them. As his commanding officer, I should be at that meeting too. I'm leaving in five minutes. Jim will be in command until I get back later.

'There will be a state funeral, obviously, this is the first one since Tony Golden in 2015. I think the minister wants that on Saturday but it depends on the family, too.'

Collins didn't want to think about meeting Denis' family, what he'd say to them. He said: 'when forensics are finished with the laptop, it should be checked in case there was another tracker in the car that Jones used. Any news of that?'

'Nothing,' Heaney said. We have thirty checkpoints up already and a hundred officers are being deployed here immediately, from all over the country.'

Buckley said: 'GSOC will probably do a public interest investigation and there will be an internal investigation, too. So, you'll have to appear before those.'

'Yeah,' Collins said.

'I was thinking about what you said earlier,' Buckley said. 'When Jones called you out. If you went out, he'd probably have shot you and Denis as well. You did the right thing, Tim. We know he was capable of it and he's had it in for you since Spain.'

'We'll never know,' Collins said. 'I'll never know. Can I go now?'

'You sure you're okay?'

'Only one way to find out.'

HE AND Nuala had to wait another thirty minutes for the solicitor to arrive from Skibbereen. They sat on a bench outside the interview room as several gardaí entered the corridor and shook his hand. Some of them cried as they did so. Collins cried, too.

Pull yourself together man. You have a job to do here.

Nuala told him about a phone call from her youngest who had won a star at school. He would have preferred silence but didn't have the heart to tell her to shut up.

'Are you going to lead with Denis' murder and the drugs?' Nuala said, when she had finished the school star story.

'I was thinking of using the photos first and see where we get with those. If we hammer him with the death of a garda, he might clam up. I dunno, what do you think?'

'Probably a good idea,' Nuala said, 'you have it in your pocket if you need it.'

He was disappointed when he saw the solicitor acting was Eleanor again. She was good at her job and would advise Farrell to tell them nothing. He had hoped she might have handed him over to a colleague after what happened earlier.

She surprised him when she put out her hand for him to shake.

'I heard the news about your colleague, I'm sorry for your loss,' she said. 'You, too,' she said to Nuala and shook her hand.

'Thanks Eleanor,' Collins said.

'Thank you,' Nuala said.

'I need a few minutes with him before ye come in,' Eleanor said. She entered the interview room.

Collins could see a look of shock on Ted Farrell's face when they went in. So, Eleanor had told him about Denis. In fairness, it was her job. But Collins had decided to go hard from the beginning.

'Mr Farrell,' he said, loudly, 'do you know a woman called Maeve Hunt?'

Eleanor glared at Collins because she didn't know where this was going. She was expecting Collins to bring up Denis.

'Do I have to answer that?' Farrell asked her. Collins watched him closely. Ted knew by now that they had found the room – hence the question.

'Probably better if you do. Where is this going, detective?'

'Do you know Maeve Hunt?' Collins asked.

'She used to be going out with …' Farrell hesitated '… with Bobby.'

'That's right,' Collins said. 'And you were jealous of him.'

There was silence for a moment.

'Isn't that correct, Mr Farrell? You were jealous, isn't that right?' Ted Farrell lowered his eyes.

'I have just come from your house, Mr Farrell. Where I saw thirty – thirty! – large pictures of her on your walls, having sex with your brother.'

Collins let that sink in.

'But the pictures were only of her; why is that, Mr Farrell?'

Farrell did not respond. Eleanor glanced at him, trying not to show her disgust.

'Do you think it was okay to destroy her privacy like that? To *degrade* her?'

'Detective, is there a point to these questions?' Eleanor said. Collins looked at her coldly.

'Where did you get the videos? Did you film them?'

'I didn't film nobody. *He* did it.' Collins could feel Farrell's anger and jealousy bubbling under the surface. *Good.*

'And how did you get them?'

'He had them on his phone. He's a disgrace.'

'And you wanted them. You wanted to look at her and imagine it was you with her.'

'He had her!' Farrell shouted. 'He had her and he had no interest in her, no more than the man in the moon.'

'And you didn't?' Collins said, quietly.

'She wouldn't look at me. When I met them in Daly's she wouldn't even look at me. She was afraid of me, he must have told her lies about me.'

'And then he got involved with Derek Webb and drugs.'

'Haha, when she found that out, she was gone.' Ted Farrell was going inside himself. Collins could feel his loss of control.

'He had no interest in her,' Ted said. 'No interest, he didn't even try to get her back.'

'You showed him,' Collins said.

'I fucking did! I fucking showed him. She wasn't good enough for him. Tournafulla, the land; nothing was good enough for him! The bollox.'

'He called you names, I heard.'

'He called me "freak". "Do this, freak. Do that freak."'

'You fucking showed him.'

'By Jesus I did.'

Eleanor looked at Farrell. Collins wasn't sure why she didn't intervene.

'Ted. We might take a break. Will we take a break?' she suggested.

'We fucking won't. And that fucker, Webb, too. He was laughing at me. He isn't laughing now. By Christ he isn't. In jail in Cork, the bollox.'

'So, you put the trackers on all the cars that came into the yard. And Webb's truck.'

'I did. They thought I was stupid.'

'They're sorry now, I bet.'

'You can be sure of it.'

'And then you rang the station in Clon and you sent the package.'

'I did. I fucking showed them.'

'Fair play to you. But they must have threatened you not to say anything.'

'They did. Bobby came over with a gun one day. And that bollox Jones threatened me, too. In my own house, the fucker.'

'What were they doing over in his yard? In the back shed?'

'They were making drugs, what do you think they were doing? Them two Chinese fellas. They're chemists.'

'How long were they doing it for?'

Collins was waiting for Eleanor to interject. She didn't.

'Since May, I think. It started in May. In Tournafulla, anyway. But there were queer fellas visiting Bobby a good bit before that. Since Christmas, I'd say. Webb brought some of them.'

'Would you have any photos of those, fellas, Ted? Or registration numbers? It would be a big help to our investigation and to your situation, too.'

'What situation? I didn't do nothing. Sure, didn't I tell ye about it?'

'I'm not so sure, Ted. You were paid to keep quiet, weren't you?'

'I wasn't! They never gave me a penny.'

'I'm not talking about money, Ted. You were paid in videos, weren't you?'

Farrell winced and shook his head. Collins knew he was right.

'Bobby knew you were jealous about Maeve; that you were obsessed with her. And he gave you those videos as payment.'

'Don't answer that, Ted,' Eleanor said.

'We have the videos on your computer, Ted. We have the photos on your wall. You breached that woman's privacy and you put trackers in her car. And you took payment to keep your mouth shut about the drugs manufacture in Tournafulla.'

Ted shook his head.

'Do you know what the inspector and myself have to do after this interview, Mr Farrell? We have to drive to Bandon and visit a young woman there. She lives with her elderly mother, did you know that? You probably did, since you were stalking her. We need to remove a tracker from her car. Then we have to tell her about the five videos on your laptop and the thirty photos on your wall. She will have to watch those videos, Mr Farrell. She will have to tell her mother about them. She will need to testify about them in court and all her family and friends will know about them. Thanks to you.'

Ted Farrell began to groan and rock back and forward as he had done in Skibbereen earlier that morning.

'And do you know what she will ask us when we tell her all this? I'll tell you what she will ask us.' Collins leaned forward over the table and lowered his voice.

'I think that's enough, detective,' Eleanor said.

'While she's crying her heart out she will ask us: "What kind of a man would do all that to me? What did I ever do to him to deserve this?"' Collins let that sink in. He was nearly done. Ted Farrell began to weep.

'Tell us what you know, Ted. Show her you're a better man than that. Show Maeve you're a better man than that.'

'I'll tell ye. I'll tell ye,' Ted Farrell said, wiping his eyes.

CHAPTER 51

DEIRDRE'S RETURN flight to Cork was delayed, so she didn't make the 6 p.m. briefing. She had phoned Superintendent O'Rourke from Heathrow and told him that nothing had come from the interview.

When she made it back to the station, after seven, Clancy was at his desk typing up a report.

He looked up.

'No joy?' he said.

'Nothing. How about ye?'

'Not really. The super is still holding off on interviewing Ormsby until Liz Howard is well enough to talk to us. Looks like that will be tomorrow morning. You and me will be heading down around half-nine to talk to her. If we can get past her Rottweiler, Ms Crean. She's already cancelled the interview twice.'

"Why isn't John going with you?"

'He's out with a bad back. He's crocked.'

'Okay,' Deirdre said, pleased. She had been afraid of being side-lined to menial work when Collins wasn't around. 'See you here at the morning briefing?'

'See you then,' Clancy said and returned to his report. He was clearly even less chatty than Collins.

SHE WENT to her desk and logged in. She wanted to check PULSE; there was something bugging her about Liz Howard's file. She found it immediately.

The previous November, Liz had been involved in a car crash with a woman coming out of a junction in Ballincollig. The other driver was at fault and her insurance paid out in full, and no charges were pressed against her. A minor traffic accident, but the file said that Liz had suffered neck injuries. Some medical expenses and treatments were added to the damages to the car, which the insurance company had not contested. The file just said 'neck injuries' which could be anything from severe whiplash to a slight sprain. The total figure was €14,500, which was standard for nothing major, or if somebody wasn't looking to make a killing.

What Deirdre wanted to know was that if Liz couldn't work, had somebody else been working as a secretary to Blake Ormsby? Now she would get to find out.

In the morning, the external gate of *Suaimhneas* was locked and Deirdre, who was driving, introduced herself and Clancy to Emily Creedon who answered the intercom. She met them in the car park.

'Come this way. You'll be meeting Liz and Bríd in the Visiting Room,' she said and led them around the back to a stand-alone building containing only one room which had a glass wall all along one side. There was a small office table in the middle of the room and some armchairs and a sofa against the wall on the right.

'This is the only room where men are allowed in *Suaimhneas*,' she said, addressing Clancy. 'Bríd and Liz will join you shortly, they're talking inside now. Liz is still very delicate, so please don't upset her, she's at a very sensitive stage of her recovery. And just to let you know we have a camera in the room, and we record everything. The two of you will sit on the other end of that table and Liz and Bríd will sit opposite you.'

They arrived ten minutes later and Deirdre could see how vulnerable Liz Howard was. She looked even smaller, thinner and paler than she had the previous week. When the two women sat down at the opposite end of the table, there was a tremor in her hands, which she tried to hide by putting them on her lap out of sight. She was wearing a loose black top and yoga pants. The black accentuated her complexion. Her eyes were bloodshot. Bríd handed her a bottle of water which she tried to open. Bríd helped her.

'Okay,' Bríd said, taking a file from her briefcase. 'My client has made a written statement which I have typed up. She will now read it from this print-out and then she will sign it in your presence. I have two more copies here which I am now giving to you. There will be no questioning about this today. At another time, when she is feeling more robust, my client will answer questions in my presence, but not today.'

She held up the two print-outs, waiting for agreement.

'That's fine,' Clancy said. 'As we agreed. My colleague has one question afterwards, but it isn't directly related to this matter or the statement.'

'Very well,' Bríd said. 'Can you read the statement, Liz? In your own time. And if you make a mistake don't worry. And if you want to stop at any time, we can stop. Or we can do this another day, too, if you prefer.'

Liz took sip of water and a deep breath. She read the statement haltingly.

It more or less confirmed what she had told Deirdre and Collins in her house. It was very carefully crafted by Bríd Crean and didn't contain any supposition or anything that could be taken apart by a defence lawyer. When she had finished, Liz put the paper down, took out a tissue, and wiped her eyes. At no point did she look up and meet the eyes of Deirdre or Clancy.

'Okay, Liz, well done,' Bríd said, putting a hand on her shoulder. She gave her a pen. 'Can you sign it here please?'

She did so and Bríd signed it underneath.

'Okay,' Bríd said, addressing Deirdre. 'You have a question?'

'Yes,' Deirdre said, trying to meet Liz's eyes. 'It's about the car crash last November, Liz. I'm just wondering when you were out sick afterwards if anybody else covered for you at work. Do you remember?'

Liz looked up momentarily and then back down again.

'Oh, yes. I'd forgotten about that.' She took a moment. Her eyes opened wide. She looked at Deirdre.

'Yes, there was a woman, but she left after a week. I never got the rights of it even though I rang the agency when I was back at work. I saw, after, that he paid for somebody for three weeks even though she only worked one. There was a huge backlog, there were loads of invoices to sort.'

'Do you remember the name of the agency?' Deirdre said, as nonchalantly as she could.

Deirdre thought about it.

'Yes. They're called RecruitUS. All one word, with the U and S in capitals at the end. You know, I wondered after why she only stayed a week, but he paid them for three.'

Deirdre nodded and wrote down the name.

WHEN THEY were driving back towards the city, Clancy looked up the recruitment agency.

'Would you believe it?' he said. 'Their offices are just across the road from the station on Copley Street?'

'Meant to be,' Deirdre said.

'You really think there could be a connection?'

'It's a long shot, I admit, but the only connection between Helen O'Driscoll and Liz Howard is they both knew Ormsby personally. I don't think he attacks women he doesn't know. If nothing else, this person will be able to tell us what he's like, we have almost no sense of him apart from when me and Collins met him.'

'I agree,' Clancy said. 'We can't leave anything undone.'

THE OFFICE was on the ground floor of an apartment block built about a decade earlier and they were immediately ushered through and met by the manager. The words 'Garda Detectives' and 'investigating a serious crime' usually mean the manager wants to be involved in any discussion. He introduced himself as Dave Hill and brought them through to his office.

'How can I help you?' he said. 'Is there a problem with an employee?' Deirdre wondered if he thought one of this contract staff had done something.

She replied: 'You placed a temporary administration or secretarial person with a company called Cyber Securities Ltd. This would have been last November. We want to talk to her.'

'I'll check,' Hill said and began scrolling and typing on his computer. Deirdre took out a folder containing the names of Ormsby's other companies, in case he had used one of their names.

'Ah, yes,' Hill said. 'I have it here. It was a short-term contract for 3-4 weeks, temporary admin. assistant. That could mean anything, in fairness.' He looked up at them. 'What's this about?'

'It's nothing to do with your company,' Clancy said calmly. 'Or the person you placed with Cyber Securities. It's in relation to a serious crime that we're investigating currently. Your employee isn't involved or anything, but we need to talk to her urgently. *Very* urgently. Can you give us her details, please? We need them now.'

Hill made a quick decision.

'Yes, of course. Anything to co-operate with the guards. Her name is Barbara Mulcahy but she no longer works with us. She terminated her contract a few months ago. And there's a note on the file here, too. It says she went out sick after a week with Cyber Securities and we couldn't find a replacement straight away. Then a Mr Ormsby paid in full by credit card and said he didn't want a replacement. That's a bit strange.'

'Do you have a phone number and address? For Ms Mulcahy?' Clancy said. 'And her PPS number, too.'

Hill hesitated. 'Under GDPR I don't think I can give you those details.'

'We can get a warrant,' Clancy said. 'But we're hunting a killer and if he kills again while we're waiting for those details, that's on you. And I'll make sure everybody knows it.'

Hill glared at Clancy and Deirdre. Then he looked back at his screen and began to call out the phone number and address.

Clancy took out a neat notebook with a small pen attached. He wrote down the numbers and the address. Deirdre watched how calm and in control he was. *Every day is a school day,* she reminded herself.

'I'D BE inclined to go out there now, what do you think?' Deirdre said to Clancy as they walked down the steps outside the office.

'Don't you want to ring her first?' Clancy said, which was exactly the reply she had wanted.

'I think it's best to catch people off-guard,' she said. 'They're inclined to give us more, then. You drive, I'll locate the address on Google Maps.' She handed him the car fob.

He took it without speaking.

She was aware how pathetic it was to have to want Clancy's approval, but she didn't care. It felt good.

THE HOUSE was on a long winding boreen off the Inniscarra Road about ten kilometres outside the city. It was the last of three the houses, well-spread out, in a cul de sac. No sign of life, no car.

They rang the doorbell, no response. They looked around. A kennel out the back but no dog barking. Everything well locked up.

'Try the phone number,' Clancy said, as they got back into the car.

Deirdre pressed the number. She had already added it to her contacts list. It began ringing – the long slow notes of a foreign call. She hung up.

'Sounds like she's abroad,' Deirdre said. 'Will I ring again?'

'Do. If she's away a long time, we'll tell her now – see if she has anything on Ormsby. If she's back in a few days, we'll hold off.'

Deirdre pressed the number again. It rang three times.

'Hello?' a woman's voice.

'Is that Barbara Mulcahy?'

'Yes, who is this?'

'This is Detective Sergeant Deirdre Donnelly from Anglesea Street Station in Cork. There's nothing wrong, we just want to talk to you about somebody you came into contact with through work. We'd prefer to talk to you in person, are you abroad right now?'

She glanced at Clancy to see if there was any signal from him but he looked straight ahead, driving slowly.

'Yes, I'm at a wedding in France, what's this about?'

'When are you back, Barbara? We'd prefer to not do this over the phone.'

'I'm home Sunday.'

'What time does your flight get in?'

"Em, late sometime, I think after ten.'

'Okay, we'll call Monday morning so, would that be okay? It's nothing to worry about, we just want to talk to you about a job placement you did a while back.'

'Okay,' Barbara said, doubtfully. 'Can you tell me what placement it was?'

'We'll talk to you on Monday, Barbara, you have my number there. My name is Deirdre Donnelly. See you Monday morning.'

'What do you think?' Deirdre said to Clancy again. She would have to stop doing that.

'It's a long shot, anyway,' Clancy said. 'But we need to check everything. Let's get this fucker Ormsby in and shake him up a bit. We'll talk to her on Monday, when she gets back.'

CHAPTER 52

On the morning after Denis' death Collins left the station and drove out the N71 towards Skibbereen. He was tired from the lack of sleep, but he knew he'd be able to keep going until it was over.

It was a beautiful morning and the road was quiet, partly because of the checkpoints, partly because of the sense of fear permeating West Cork.

He took a left at Owenahincha Cross and met the ocean at Little Island. He drove past the house he was looking for and went to the Fish Basket, a café beside Long Strand. He parked outside and looked at the beach, but it reminded him of Denis' photo of his fiancé and he turned away.

He ordered two coffees, four sausage rolls, and a double espresso. Colm usually had company this time of year. He drove back the road, eating one of the rolls and pulled in around a glass-fronted house overlooking the beach and out to Galley Head.

Two cars on the grass outside, Colm's van and a Toyota Auris.

Spot, Colm's dalmatian, and a collie Collins didn't know barked behind the big glass sliding door. Only Colm Stubbs could get away with calling a Dalmatian 'Spot'.

Collins slid the door open and let them out. The collie was wary of him until she realised Collins and Spot were old friends. The dogs ran around sniffing on the grass and relieved themselves. Collins entered the living room of the house.

'Stubbs,' he shouted up the open plan stairs. 'It's Collins. I have coffees and sausage rolls.'

Collins looked around. Beer bottles and the butts of joints in ashtrays littered the coffee table. Colm, a friend since secondary school, had moved in there and renovated the place when he sold his start-up five years earlier for €22 million.

Collins sat on the sofa and sipped his espresso, trying to enjoy the view, but all he could think of was the moment the gun went off and Denis flopped to the ground.

The collie came back in and sidled up to him.

'Hello there, girl,' Collins said. 'Will we get you a drink? We will.' He picked up the dog bowl by the door and refilled it at the sink. She lapped from it. Then she hopped up on the couch and leaned up against him.

'You're the best girl,' he said. 'You are.'

'Her name is Millie.'

Collins turned. A woman in her late-twenties, dressed in a faded t-shirt and shorts walked down the stairs in her bare feet. Collins stood up and the collie jumped off the couch.

'Tim Collins, I'm sorry for barging in like this, I didn't know Colm had company.'

'Fiona White,' the woman said, shaking hands. 'Can I have one of those?' She indicated to the coffees in a cardboard tray.

'Yes, of course,' Collins said.

'So you *suspected* there might be company. Which indicates a trend,' she said, picking up a coffee. She added milk from the fridge.

'You should be a detective,' Collins said.

'Elementary my dear Watson,' she said. 'Although I think you'd be more Holmes than Watson. Colm told me about you last night, when we heard about the guard being shot.'

Collins nodded.

'I'm here to pick up something in the garage. Please tell Colm I can't stay, we're busy right now.'

'Pity,' she said. 'There's a swell coming in this morning.'

'Charlie don't surf,' Collins said and felt foolish. *Is that where you're at now?* he thought. *Trying to impress young women with quotes from films?*

'Bye, Tim Collins,' she said. 'Or should I say Lieutenant Colonel Kilgore?'

Collins smiled in the doorway. 'Bye Fiona, bye Millie. Bye Spot,' he said rubbing the Dalmatian's ears. 'Can I close the door on her? She'll only follow the car.'

'What was he like?' Fiona said. Collins didn't understand. He looked at her for a clue.

'The guard who died?' she said, her features darkening. 'What was he like? I saw his name was Denis, my brother's name is Denis. He looked like my brother in the photos.'

Collins didn't know what to say.

'He was beautiful,' he said and slid the door closed.

THE KEY was hidden under a ledge between the back door and the garage. Collins knew that Colm kept the garage safely locked even if he left the house door open sometimes. Collins pushed the heavy metal door in and switched on the light.

His old red Puma gear bag was stuffed behind a small dinghy in the corner under a rusty metal bench. He took the bag out and placed it on the bench. It was reassuringly heavy and bulky. He opened the zip and took out the black shotgun, which was wrapped in an oilcloth. He could smell the oil. A Mossberg 590 Nightstick – pump action, custom-made. He checked the magazine was empty then filled it with seven cartridges from one of the boxes in the bag.

He put the shotgun and the oilcloth back into the bag, zipped it back up and placed it in the boot of the car. He drove back to Clonakilty.

LATER THAT day the gardaí simultaneously raided five addresses in West Cork based on Ted Farrell's information.

Two houses in Bandon, one in the hills outside Castletownbere, one outside Skibbereen and a caravan in Schull. The hope was that Jones would be hiding out in one of the houses, but there was no sign of him or the grey 4x4.

Collins took part in the raid of the caravan in Schull because Farrell had said there were some 'strange Englishmen' staying there. The caravan was empty but they learned that the 'strange Englishmen' were a group of young surfers who had been ordering hash and cocaine from one of the Bandon dealers and had since returned to England.

Six arrests were made at the other addresses, people all known to the gardaí, none of whom were inclined to talk. A waste of time. Nothing.

CHAPTER 53

COLLINS COULD sense the frustration in Clonakilty Garda Station. The inescapable truth that they were letting Denis down.

Three days later and all the road blocks, all the phone lines, all the questioning and the knocking on doors had yielded nothing. They didn't seem any closer to finding Jones. The feeling was that he had fled and was out of the country. Everybody was tetchy at the early briefing.

The funeral was looming and there was resentment among some of the gardaí about who was attending and who was not.

Collins had driven back to Cork the previous night to get his dress uniform. It was hanging in the car outside the station. He tried to think what he could say to Denis' family later.

When he learned that Tony Quinlan was rostered for active duty that day instead of attending his friend's funeral, he approached Buckley after the briefing.

'Quick word in your office,' Collins said and they walked through.

'Do you have something?' Buckley said. 'I thought you were a bit quiet in the briefing, the lads could do with a bit of a lift.'

Collins shook his head.

'No, it's about who's going to the funeral.'

'Jesus, don't start, Collins, I've a pain in my head from the complaining.'

'Listen,' Collins said. 'I want to go to the funeral and pay my respects to Denis and his family but I think I should switch with Tony Quinlan. Tony should go and I should stay here. What if something happens, today, anyway?'

'No. I want you to meet the family. Tell them what happened first hand, talk up Denis' bravery.'

'Yeah, but today isn't the day for that. They'll be in bits, Ronan.

I'll visit the family in a week or so, when things have settled down and we have Jones behind bars. Tony should be at his friend's funeral. He's already feeling guilty he was hiding when Denis was taken.'

Buckley thought for a minute.

'Okay, it would help morale a bit around the place. We could be in for a long haul if Jones has made it back to Dublin or out of the country.'

'Good decision,' Collins said. 'Will I tell Tony or will you?'

'Will you send him into me?'

'I will,' Collins said.

COLLINS MET Tony in the briefing room and told him Superintendent Buckley wanted to see him in his office. Tony walked off with a scowl, expecting a reprimand for having complained he couldn't attend the funeral.

'Change of plans,' he said to Nuala. He told her he was staying and Tony was going to the funeral.

'Okay,' she said. 'Probably a good decision. I'll be back tonight. Listen, don't get into trouble in the meantime, will you?'

Who, me?' he said.

HE PORED over the file in the briefing room for the rest of the morning, hoping to see something new, something he'd missed. He phoned Rachel Clifford, the garda in charge of the comms lines set up in Cork. Nothing useful. There were reports that Jones had been seen in Dublin Airport, Amsterdam and Malaga.

At 1:30 he knocked on Buckley's office door and Heaney told him to come in. He was leaning against the desk watching the funeral on the large walled TV.

'The mass is over,' he said. The screen showed six white-gloved gardaí in full dress uniform carrying Denis' coffin out of the church. There was a close-up of his mother and father and his fiancé, Áine, who was in tears.

Collins shook his head. He couldn't watch it.

'Nothing useful from the comms line people,' Collins said. 'I was just on to Rachel.'

'Yeah, we're going to need a lucky break or maybe a mistake from Jones,' Heaney said. 'If he's even still around. But we have to assume he is for now.'

'I was thinking of interviewing some of the scumbags we pulled in the other day,' Collins said. 'Try to scare something out of them. I think they're mostly being held in Cork. Maybe have another crack at Webb, too.'

'I don't have any better ideas,' Heaphy said, still watching the TV.

'I was just going to get a sandwich first, want something?' Collins said.

'Thanks,' Heaney said. 'Chicken and cheese on brown bread, mayo, no butter. It seems strange to be ordering lunch while that's going on.'

'I know,' Collins said. 'I can't watch it to be honest.'

'I know,' Heaney said, and he sat back down behind the desk and picked up the phone. Collins walked out, eyes straight ahead.

DOWNSTAIRS THE information screen in the foyer was also showing the funeral with the sound muted. They were placing Denis' coffin in the hearse.

The duty sergeant called Collins over to his desk and said: 'There's a fellow there looking for you, wouldn't say what it's about.' He pointed to a heavy-set man who was sitting in the waiting area. The man stood up when he saw Collins.

Collins approached him. He looked like a farmer, maybe fifty or so, with that ruddy complexion that farmers get from being out in all weather. He was medium height, with a cardigan over his shirt and old trousers tucked inside turned down wellington boots. He had a flat cap over what looked like a bald head, with long sideburns.

'Tim Collins?'

'That's me, who have I?'

'Lawrence Devereux, Reenascreena,' the man said, with a strong local accent.

'Anything to Victor Devereux?' Collins said.

'Isn't he my brother, wasn't it him told me to come here looking for you?'

'How is he, how's the sculpture going?' Collins said. He had often wished he could afford something by Victor Devereux although they were very big.

'Yerra, I haven't a clue, they all look like desperate yokes to me. All I know he's rolling in it, he's too busy to help me with the hay.'

'What can I do for you, Lawrence?' Collins asked.

The man looked uncomfortable for a moment. 'It mightn't be anything, I don't want to waste yere time.' He glanced at the funeral.

'Just tell me what it is and we'll take it from there. I'm just on my way out down to the hotel, will you walk with me?'

'Okay,' Devereux said and they walked out together.

'Tell me what you saw or heard,' Collins said. 'From the beginning.'

'Okay. I've a small bit of land up by Carrigfadda by the hill. I've a few sheep up there.'

Collins knew enough not to interrupt, though he didn't know where Carrigfadda was.

'Anyway, I was up there yesterday and there's an old holiday house off the road. You can't see it from the road but one of my fields looks down on the back of it. And wasn't there a grey car and some class of a van, what do you call them, camper vans, parked behind the house.'

'Describe the grey car,' Collins said.

'A big yoke, looked like a Pajero or something. Thing is, I know the woman who owns the house, she lives in Dublin. I phoned her and she said that some quare hawk rented it in May for four months in cash, all in advance. Never saw the like of it. She said she was going to ring ye herself.'

'Okay,' Collins said, trying to stay calm. 'Anything else?'

'I called in to Dinny Walsh down the road to know did he see anything and he didn't see hide nor hair of anything coming or going there for weeks. There's a big padlock on the front gate. But when I was above in the hill I saw some fella come out of the back door. Looked like he was working on the camper van's engine, the bonnet was open.'

'Could you describe him?'

'Not a hope, I was way up the hill, could have been a woman for all I know. I just thought I'd let you know.'

Collins stopped on the street. He made a decision.

'Where are you parked?' he said.

'At the SuperValu,' Devereux replied.

'Okay,' Collins said. 'Will you drive me out there? I just have to get something back at the station.'

'I will,' Devereux. 'I was awake half the night last night thinking about that young guard. They're burying him now, God love his poor family.'

Collins got the red Puma bag out of his boot and walked with Devereux to his car, a 00 Peugeot hatchback. He put the bag in the back seat and sat in.

Devereux started up the car and drove out the main road west.

'Terrible what happened that Dungarvan lad,' Lawrence said.

'I don't want to talk about that,' Collins replied.

There was nothing said for a while, then they talked a bit about farming and the price of lambs and Victor Devereux's English wife, the famous actress, whom Lawrence clearly didn't like.

They turned right off the road to Reenascreena and went on to Carrigfadda. Collins remembered it when they got there, a high hill with a scenic walk up to the top through a forest. After a church, Devereux turned right onto a narrow gravel road, which ascended.

'This the way up to that walk on the hill?' Collins said.

'It is, but we're not going that far,' Devereux said.

He pulled up by an ornate gate which led into a bare field with a rough path around a hillock which went out of sight. Sure enough, the gate was padlocked.

'The house is in there,' Devereux said. 'Behind that little hill. My fields are above beyond.'

Collins paused. A perfect location.

'Probably nothing,' he said. 'But I better check it out, all the same. Have you a phone, Lawrence?'

'I do,' he said, taking out an old battered Samsung.

'What's your number?' Collins said. He dialled the number and it rang.

'You have my number now,' he said. 'I'll ring you in a minute when I check out the house. Drive a bit up the road and don't come near the house unless I ring you. If I'm not out in ten minutes, dial 999 and tell them the whole story. Check the time now. That okay?'

'I suppose I don't want to know what's in the bag,' Devereux said. Collins met his eyes.

'There isn't any bag, Lawrence. So, you couldn't have seen one. We clear about that?'

'Right,' Devereux said. 'Right you are.'

'Have you anything in the boot to open that padlock?'

'Oh, I do. That won't be a problem.'

CHAPTER 54

COLLINS GOT out of the car and took the bag from the back seat. Devereux drove off. Collins got over the ditch by the gate and crouched down. He took a pair of latex gloves from a pocket and put them on. He took a bulletproof vest out of the bag and strapped it on. The shotgun felt light, he checked the chamber was loaded and the safety was off. He pressed the release button and locked the breech bolt. He checked that his SIG Sauer was fully loaded and the safety was off and put it back into his holster. He stuffed his jacket pockets with cartridges. He took his phone out and turned the volume off.

He left the bag by the ditch and walked down the path.

As the path curved round the hillock, the house came into sight. A plain pale bungalow, made from prefabricated pieces as part of the Bungalow Bliss template in the 1970s. Collins checked the safety again. His mouth was dry. He heard music, coming from a radio behind a camper van which was facing away from him. He approached the side of house and peered behind the corner. Nothing. A grey Pajero, very like the one he saw at Tournafulla, was parked at the other side of house, close to the wall.

He checked the path for any trip hazards and took the long way around the van, away from the house so that he'd be facing it.

As he rounded the van, he saw a man standing on a kitchen chair bent into the engine. The man, sensing something, looked up. It was Jones. He threw a spanner at Collins and jumped off the chair. Collins evaded the spanner and fired a round into the front of the van.

'Run, Jones,' he said. 'Make it easy for me.'

Jones glanced behind him, calculating how far to the house. It was obviously too far.

'Get it over with,' he said in his neutral accent. He grinned.

Collins could see the madness in his eyes, that crazed brightness. That same look he knew from that Spanish courtroom when, despite all the odds, Jones had found a way to bribe or blackmail a senior judge. The cockiness that would never leave him, even though he knew he was about to die.

It must all end now. And you must do it.

'The funeral is happening now,' Collins said. 'A state funeral, with thousands of people. How many will go to your miserable funeral, you piece of shit?'

'That's on you, Collins. If you were man enough to come out, he'd still be alive.' Another grin.

'So, you could kill us both? That's what you wanted, isn't it?' Collins could hear that his voice was hoarse with anger.

'You'll never know, will you? It'll eat at you forever.'

Do it, no more talk. This is what you wanted, he'll never hurt another living soul.

'You think there's a prison out there that can hold me? *Me?*' Jones started laughing, bending over. He straightened up and shook his head.

'You don't have the balls,' he said. 'You don't have it in you, you –'

Collins strode forward swinging the stock around. He smashed it into Jones' face. Jones went down. Collins pummelled the gun into his temple twice, grunting with the effort. He kicked him in the ribs.

Collins staggered back and had to lean against the van for support. His head was spinning, he could hear blood rushing in his ears.

'I didn't do it,' he said, hoarsely. 'I didn't.' He spat.

He looked at the house, he'd have to check it. With Jones unconscious on the ground, Collins walked to the back door which was kept open with half a concrete block. He checked Jones for movement, none.

On the kitchen table a black semi-automatic Beretta. Looked like a 9mm. He picked it up and stuck it inside his belt at the back. He went into the hall. A quick left into a bathroom and a small bedroom beside it. He looked in to the other rooms and went out the back door. Jones hadn't moved. Collins placed the Beretta on the concrete path behind the kitchen chair by the van.

He sat down unsteadily on the chair facing Jones and the house. He turned off the radio. He tried to stop his legs from shaking.

It's still not too late. You could use the SIG and put the Beretta in his hand. You owe it to Denis.

He heard himself whine. He closed his eyes and saw Denis' body whiplash after the shot, the spray of blood. He moaned.

'Do it!' he said. 'Fucking do it!' He was crying, now. His hands were shaking. He held the shotgun tight. '*Do it,*' he whispered, but he knew he wouldn't.

He noticed a sledge hammer to his left, leaning against the house wall. He stood up and walked to it. He leaned the gun carefully against the wall and picked up the hammer, felt its heft. He walked to Jones and stood over him.

They would be at the graveyard now, he thought. *The coffin would be flanked all the way by gardaí in salute.*

He adjusted the hammer in his hands so that its handle was vertical. He stepped over Jones so that he had one foot planted on either side of him. He held the sledge over Jones' left collar bone and smashed the hammer into it. The satisfying sound of a crack.

He held the hammer over the right collar bone and crashed it down again. Another crack.

There would be sobbing as they lift the coffin out of the hearse. Shock and silence permeating the still air.

Collins stepped away and looked at Jones' hands. The right one was flat on the concrete path, the palm facing up. He hammered the sledge into the four fingers. The right hand was at an angle. He smashed the hammer into the point just above the thumb.

Collins looked at Jones' feet, in strong boots. His right foot was upright, but his left one was splayed on the gravel at an angle. He smashed the hammer into a point just above the ankle. A dull thud. He crashed it down again.

The sound of shoes on concrete as six gardaí carry Denis to his grave. A priest intoning prayers.

Collins walked to the wire fence beside the Pajero. He threw the hammer into the long rushes in the field. He picked up his shotgun and sat down again on the chair. His legs and hands were no longer shaking. He looked at his watch. It said 14:33.

More sobbing as they lower the coffin down. Then it would be over.

CHAPTER 55

COLLINS TOOK out his phone and rang Ray Halloran from the ASU who he knew was still in Skibbereen and told him some of the story. He gave him directions from Reenascreena church and described the ornate gate.

'Is the location secure?' Halloran said.

'Yes, just me and Jones and he's unconscious. One bystander.'

'Outstanding, on our way.'

Collins phoned Lawrence Devereux and told him it was safe, he could come down.

'I heard a shot,' Lawrence said.

'It was just a warning,' Collins said, 'nobody was shot. Will you do me a favour? Will you bring the red bag you never saw with you, it's on the ground just inside the gate on the right?'

Collins phoned Heaney.

'Are you after forgetting my sandwich?' Heaney said.

'You know, I am, but I have something better for you.' He told him some of the story. Heaney said he was on his way.

Collins looked at Jones on the ground. His breathing was laboured, must have punctured a lung. Collins phoned Halloran again and asked him to bring an ambulance with him.

He went behind the van to vomit, but nothing came up. He took off the bulletproof vest and dropped it on the ground.

He heard some banging at the other side of the house. Lawrence was breaking the padlock. The Peugeot slowly came into sight and pulled up behind the van. Lawrence lowered the car window.

'If I was you, I'd have her facing back out by the hedge,' Collins said. 'A lot of garda cars and an ambulance are going to be coming through here and you'll be stuck all day.'

'Right you are,' Lawrence said and he turned the car and parked it. He got out and stood beside Collins. He handed over the bag. Collins put the vest into it.

'That the fella who killed the young lad?' Lawrence said.

'That's him.'

'Is he dead?'

'Unfortunately, not,' Collins said. 'You did well to tell me about this place.'

'Sure, I only called into you because I had to get some nuts for the dogs and they have an offer in SuperValu. Didn't I come away after, without them?'

'You'll have a good story for Victor and that actress.'

'By Jesus, I will,' Lawrence said and he rubbed his hands together. 'Are you sure he isn't dead? Is that him wheezing?'

'Certain,' Collins said. 'Didn't he fall off the chair when I fired into the van and hurt himself?'

'He didn't!'

'He did. Took a right fall.'

'You fecker, you're codding me.'

Collins sighed. He loved West Cork people.

They talked about the land Lawrence had on the hill and how dry the weather was. Collins heard the croaking of a raven in the distance – his favourite bird. He looked towards it, two black specks in a blue sky.

'Is the land above any good?' Collins said. He wanted to just talk now. About anything.

'Any good? Desperate altogether. Sure, there's no good land in West Cork.'

'I suppose,' Collins said, thinking about the land he farmed with his father as a boy. How his father used to say the same thing.

'But it's home, anyway,' Lawrence said.

'It is,' Collins said and he looked again at the hill in the distance.

'No place like it,' Lawrence said.

'No, then,' Collins said.

After some time – he couldn't tell how long – he heard sirens. He stood up and put the shotgun and the cartridges into the bag. He put the bag into the boot of Lawrence's car. He put the gloves into his pocket.

He leaned against the bonnet of the car.

The edges of his vision clouded.

He had never been so tired in his life.

CHAPTER 56

THERE WAS a lot of paperwork and questions to be answered. Collins knew the score, he'd been through it all before.

Buckley gave him a bollocking about the extent of Jones' injuries.

'Could you not have just restrained him? Hit him in the head and leave it at that?' Buckley moaned, when he got back to the station from the funeral. 'The fucking do-gooders, not to mention his barrister, will make a big deal of it.'

'I had a choice between shooting him or restraining him,' Collins said. 'I'm sick of this. You and I both know the Beretta is the murder weapon, even the DPP can't fuck that up. It was a frenzied attack, right? By a man who murdered a garda in cold blood, right? Fuck the do-gooders and fuck the barrister. And fuck you, Buckley, I'm off.'

Walking away, he knew that Buckley would have preferred Jones dead – they all would have, including him.

It wouldn't have been hard to fake a suicide with the Beretta. Let alone shooting him with the SIG, planting the 9mm, claiming self-defence.

Collins knew, too, that he was angrier with himself than he was at Buckley.

HE LEFT the station at 6 p.m. and took the main road to Dunmanway and he was at the GAA grounds just before half-time. He didn't go in the main entrance; he parked on the Clonakilty Road, went through the back gate, and walked across the training pitch.

The main pitch in Dunmanway had a steep bank on one side, with trees at the end farthest away from the entrance. Collins stood about half-way up the bank beside the trees. He would have a good view of Zoe in the second-half when Dohenys would be attacking the goal right in front of him.

The scoreboard read: Dohenys (Dunmanway) 0–5, O'Donovan Rossa (Skibbereen) 1–2. A draw. He looked around the ground. A small crowd, as would be expected for an Under 16 girls' game. Most of the crowd was at the far end, even though they were looking into the sun. Katie and the other parents would be over there, too.

In the second-half, scores were hard to come by. Both defences were strong. Zoe got the ball three times and was fouled by her marker every time. Eventually the referee blew his whistle. Collins resisted shouting at him. Zoe kicked the free herself, from the hand, and scored.

O'Donovan Rossa got the next four scores and were leading by three points with about ten minutes to go. The coach shouted at Zoe that they needed a goal. Zoe won the next ball well, on Collins' side of the pitch. As she turned to head for goal, her marker stuck out her elbow and caught her on the side of the head. Zoe went down and there was a howl of outrage from the home supporters. The referee gave the defender a yellow card, when it was a clear red. Zoe stayed down and was attended by one of the selectors.

Collins moved away from the trees and into the open. He was only thirty yards away from her.

'Get up Zoe Cunningham!' he shouted. He could see heads turn towards him. 'Get up!' he shouted again and Zoe got to her feet. She looked towards him.

'You know what to do,' he said, loudly enough for her to hear. She nodded and took the free and it went inches wide.

'Next ball, Zoe,' he shouted again. 'Plenty time.'

O'Donovan Rossa dominated possession for the next five minutes but didn't score. Dohenys scored a breakaway point; Zoe's friend Lauren finishing well. Just two points between them. With two minutes remaining, the big Dohenys centre-back won a high ball and, as Zoe ran into space to win the clearance, she swung her left arm into the neck of her marker who stopped in her tracks. Zoe caught the ball, ran through and buried it low to the net. Now the O'Donovan Rossa players and mentors complained, but the referee had not seen the infringement. He blew the full-time whistle soon afterwards. Dohenys had won by a point.

Collins smiled as he watched Zoe jump around with her team-mates. Families and friends ran on to the pitch to congratulate them. He walked away towards his car. When he was about fifty yards away, he heard a shout behind him.

'Wait!' she shouted as she sprinted towards him.

He stood and smiled and held out his arms. Zoe slammed into him, and pressed her head into his chest. He held her tight.

'You came,' she said and she looked up at him. She was sweaty, red-faced, and joyful.

'Course I did,' he said. 'I promised I would. Well done, great goal. Nice elbow, too.' He held out his arm.

'I did what you said. I fought my corner. I got even instead of getting mad.'

'You did. I'm proud of you.'

She heard someone shout her name and turned.

'I have to accept the cup,' she said and brushed her hair back from her forehead. Her mother had the exact same habit, Collins realised. They were so alike.

'Don't keep them waiting, then. And well done again, you were the winning of it.'

'We're going to the Arches later to fill the cup,' she said.

'Enjoy it, girl. Ye deserve it.'

She nodded and hugged him again and ran towards the pitch. He watched her for a moment and turned away. At the car, the exhaustion hit him again. He thought about his colleagues in DeBarra's in Clonakilty drinking pints in memory of Denis. He should be there with them. Maybe there would be music. Then he thought about the bed in his apartment in Cork city. He started the car, swung it around and took the next left, which brought him across the Bandon River and on to the Cork Road.

The first number he dialled was Buckley's.

'Collins. I'm on the way back to Dublin, I hear there's a gang going to DeBarra's; wish I could have joined you. We'll sort that about the injuries. Fuck him, as you said.'

'Actually, I'm ringing to ask you if I can return to Cork and resume working on the Helen O'Driscoll murder case.'

'Oh. Well, you'll have to give statement for the book of evidence, but there's no rush with that. Or the GSOC inquiry. Yes, that's fine, you can tell Superintendent O'Rourke I said you were okay to go back.'

'Thanks, I appreciate that. I want to get this fucker.'

'I'm sure you will.'

'Tell Jessica I was asking for her. Take care, Ronan.'

'Take care, you, too. Great work. Get some rest.'

He ended the call. He phoned Nuala.

'Hi Collins. Listen, sorry I meant to ring you. I need to head back to Limerick. We'll have those pints some other time, okay?'

'For sure, Nuala, we'll do that. And it was a pleasure working with you.'

'The pleasure was all mine, Collins. I learned a lot.'

'Me, too, safe driving.'

'See you, Collins.'

A text came through and he looked at it. From O'Rourke: *Welcome back, see you 07:00 Monday.*

Another text, from Katie: *Thanks for that, don't be a stranger. Heard ye arrested somebody, hope it's over now* ☺

CHAPTER 57

ON A bend outside Dunmanway, he found the next number.

Abi, Therapist, it said.

He pressed it.

'Hello, Tim,' she said, answering immediately.

'Hi Abi, how are you?'

'I'm fine. Just about to sit down for dinner. Are you okay?'

'I am, but I'd like to talk to you as soon as I can. Would that be okay? I'm heading back to Cork now.'

'Is it urgent?'

'No, but I should talk to someone about it.'

'What happened? Are you all right?'

'I'm fine. I didn't kill him, Abi. I could have and I thought I was going to, but I didn't. I didn't do it. I didn't kill him.' He had to pull over on the side of the road. He was crying and he couldn't see clearly.

'Stay on the line, Tim. I'll be right back.'

Collins went looking for a tissue in the glove compartment. Katie always had a packet of tissues in there. At the thought of her, he pressed his head into the steering wheel and began to sob. Somebody beeped him as they passed, he wasn't stopped in a good place.

'Fuck,' he said, through gritted teeth.

'I'm back, Tim,' Abi said. 'Just take a moment and try to breathe. It's okay. We'll talk this through.'

Collins looked in the rear-view mirror and pulled out the car. They began to talk.

LATER THAT night, he was sitting in his father's armchair, looking at the young people gathered on the steps of St Mary's church across the river. The sun was setting in the north-west above Gurra-nabraher and the steps were in shadow.

He was drinking lukewarm white wine, the only thing he could find in the apartment. The celebrations would be going strong in the Arches pub in Dunmanway, why wasn't he down there with Katie and Zoe and the others? He wasn't sure.

He dialled his brother Paul's number in New York City.

'Timmy!' Paul answered. 'You'll never guess where we're headed.'

'Yankee Stadium?' Collins said.

'Did I tell you? I don't remember telling you.'

'Just a guess, must be a hot one.'

'Hot as Hades, brother. Say hello to Sally here.'

'Hello, Sally, how are you?'

'I'm fine. We're gonna whup the Red Sox tonight.'

'Good stuff. Who's on first?' There was a pause. Collins smiled.

'What's on second,' Sally replied.

'I Don't Know's on third,' Collins said. 'You remembered, well done Sally.'

'Pop helped me,' Sally said.

'That's what Pops are for. How's school?'

She laughed and spoke to her father. 'Uncle Timmy said, "How's school?"'

'Oh, he did?' Paul said. 'Well, tell him.'

'It's very quiet, Uncle Timmy, because we're on vacation. So, the school is very quiet.'

'Good answer,' Collins said. 'Last question: what are you going to have at the game? To eat, I mean?'

'Oh, oh, oh. Em … I think I'm gonna have some fries and some Coke. Large fries and a large Coke. Byeee.'

'Looks like there's a D train pulling up,' Paul said. 'Any news? How's Mam?'

'She's fine, much better. No news, just ringing for a chat.'

'Everything all right, little brother?'

'Oh yeah, fine. A bit knackered, long day. I might look up that game online and we can WhatsApp. If I can stay awake that long.'

'That would be great. Here's our train, gotta go. I'll send you a picture.'

'Do that. See you, Paul.'

Collins hung up. He thought about pouring another glass of wine and decided he didn't need it. He wouldn't be able to stay awake so there was no point in putting the baseball on. He placed the phone on the table top. He closed his eyes and thought: *I just wanted to hear the voice of somebody I love.*

Part 3

A PRAYER FOR HELEN

CHAPTER 58

COLLINS STEPPED out on to Lavitt's Quay. He had slept badly until he went to the toilet at six. Then he went into a deep sleep and woke groggy at nine. Even a blazing shower hadn't revived him, he needed fresh air, coffee and the *Examiner*.

He turned left towards Cornmarket Street and De Calf Café, which was his regular haunt. He had never returned to The Tavern since he was poisoned there the previous year. As he passed the Vibes and Scribes second-hand bookstore (another regular haunt) a small boy passed him on his right and handed him a piece of paper. He took the paper and read it. It said: *Don't speak to him. Outside Opera House now. Hega.*

The boy looked back and Collins recognised him. Cian, Hega's soccer-mad nephew. Collins had met him a few times at Turner's Cross, at Cork City games. Collins swung around and walked back the way he came.

Hega was slouched against a pillar of The Crawford Gallery beside the Opera House. As Collins approached, Hega put his forefinger to his lips in the universal 'don't speak' symbol. He took a series of A4 sized cards from under his denim jacket.

The first one read: TURN OFF YOUR PHONE

Collins reached for his phone in the inside pocket of his jacket.

Hega showed another card: OFF OFF

Collins turned off his phone and waited for another card. Hega seemed to have several. Instead Hega said: 'We're fucked, Collins.'

'Can we talk now?'

'Yes,' Hega said. 'As long as we stay outdoors and away from street cameras.' He pointed to the cameras mounted on poles near Christy Ring Bridge.

'Want to explain all this?' Collins said.

'He's after hacking everything.'

'Who's after hacking everything and what's everything?' Collins was getting impatient, and he was hungry. Hega was such a drama queen.

'Ormsby, who do you think?'

'And when you say "everything"?'

'Everything. The whole garda system. PULSE. All the case files. All the HR, CAB, every fucking byte of it, man.' Hega shook his head and his eyes grew wet. *Jesus, don't cry, Hega,* Collins thought.

'Okay, let's calm down and you can tell me everything from the beginning,' Collins said. 'But I need coffee first.'

Hega sighed dramatically and shook his head again.

'All right,' he said. 'I could do with a Red Bull.'

They walked to the Cork Coffee Roasters on French Church Street. Collins got a double espresso and Hega had a Lucozade Sport, they didn't have Red Bull. They stood by the wall on the narrow street outside. Hega couldn't understand why Collins wouldn't get a coffee in Costa or Starbucks which were nearer to the Opera House.

'I don't get it, Collins,' he said. 'A coffee's a coffee, man. What's the difference?'

'That's like saying a football club's a football club. Who do you love more: Cork City or PSG?'

'City of course.'

'There you go. How's Jen, when's she due again?'

'September, all good, man.'

'Great stuff. Tell me about this hacking,' Collins said quickly.

'Okay, three days ago some of my alarms starting going off,' Collins said.

'Alarms?'

'Some of my firewalls started to drop – turn themselves off. That triggered a shutdown before anything could get in, but I'm still offline.'

Hega let an elderly man walk by before resuming.

'But it was the links with the CGS that were hit first. That meant the malware came from there.'

'CGS?' Collins said.

'Central Garda System. So, I went into Anglesea Street to have a look and the whole thing is riddled, every bit of code is fucked. Everything will have to be deleted and the backup will have to be re-initialised.'

'What does that mean?' Collins said.

'They will have to shut everything down and reboot it all using a backup.'

'Is that a big thing?'

'D'oh,' Hega said, rolling his eyes. 'Huge, man, it'll take weeks.'

'Have they started it yet?'

'Yeah, but they're keeping it quiet and doing it bit by bit.'

'How do you know it's Ormsby?'

'Hah, he's not as smart as he thinks he is. I got hold of some guy in Switzerland that he pissed off and showed him the code. Ormsby's company specialises in something called HIDS, which stands for…'

Collins waved his hand for Hega to move on.

'Any way yer man in Switzerland, Gunther, showed me how the viral code that he uses to test his defence systems is the same that's after infecting the GCS and tried to get into my systems.'

'Can you prove it?' Collins said.

Hega shook his head.

'Probably not. Gunther swears it's Ormsby but he has a grudge against him.'

'And our phones are affected too?'

'He can get in anywhere. I just wanted to make sure before I told you. If you give me your phone, I'll check it for you.'

'When can I have it back?'

'In the morning,' Hega said. Cian turned the corner from Paul Street and walked up to them.

'Uncle Philip, I have soccer training,' he said.

'I have to go, Collins,' Hega said, picking up the cards he had leaned against the wall. 'I'll call to your gaff at nine in the morning, okay?'

'Okay,' Collins said, trying to figure out how he'd manage a whole day without his phone. 'Will you give me those cards? I'll probably need them.'

He finished his coffee and headed for Anglesea Street.

Chapter 59

Deirdre answered the door in her dressing gown. She wasn't expecting Collins, holding up a card which said TURN OFF YOUR PHONE.

After she had complied and he had explained, they sat in the kitchen. Jake was out for a run.

'I was just about to have a boiled egg and toast, would you like some?' she said, glad she'd had her pyjamas on.

'I will, please. I was on my way to breakfast when I got the news about the hacking and these yokes.' He pointed to the cards.

'That guy is a valuable resource.'

'Hega? Don't I know it? Thank God I was able to get him past HR.'

Deirdre remembered about the shooting and that she hadn't spoken to Collins since. The word was that he had taken it badly, couldn't even go to the funeral or the pub the night after.

'I was very sorry to hear about young Grandon,' she said. 'It must have been awful.'

Collins winced and took a moment to reply.

'Yes. Thanks for your text,' Collins said. 'If you don't mind, I'd prefer to not talk about that.'

'Sure,' she said. 'How do you like your egg?'

'I don't mind,' Collins said. 'Any news about Ormsby? How was your trip to London?'

'Okay,' Deirdre said, glad to be talking shop. 'Well, Lea Thompson was impressive, I must say. Getting on with her life as best she can. Still has … issues. We *have* to nail this fucker, Collins.'

'Any link to Ormsby?'

'Not that I could find. She used to go on a lot of online dates but she didn't recognise the name or picture. Hughes, either, I still think he's involved.'

'Did she know Liz at all?'

'I asked her, but no.'

'Or Helen O'Driscoll?'

'No connection, I asked her about everybody involved. But there was one thing. Her attacker and Ormsby had got past a locked door. I check the door in Ardlea and it was a simple door lock. Somehow he can open them. We need to figure that out.'

'Anything more on Ormsby?' Collins asked, buttering some bread.

'Now that you mention it, yes. I think I have another woman who knows him. Or I should say he knows her. Well, she used to work for him.

'Is three minutes okay?' she said, pointing at the saucepan.

'Fine, thanks. The woman?'

Deirdre was getting annoyed with Collins' quick-fire questions. It was like being interrogated. She told herself to calm down, that he'd been through a shitty time.

'I found out that Liz Howard had been out sick last November and a temp. had covered from her, with Ormsby. I tracked her down to a recruiting agency, her name is Barbara Mulcahy. She's abroad now but back tonight.'

She paused. She had to tell Collins she was partnered with Clancy now.

'Oh, I just remembered,' she said. 'The super has paired me with Clancy since you were gone. O'Regan is out with a bad back. Me and him are interviewing this woman tomorrow morning first thing.'

Collins buttered his toast and took a bite.

'I met O'Rourke in the station, just now. O'Regan is okay again, so you're back with me. Sorry about that.'

'Good stuff,' Deirdre said. 'There's something funny about all this, Barbara Mulcahy was supposed to be working three weeks but she left after only one, but Ormsby paid in full. We'll get the rights of it when we meet her. Are you sure that's done enough for you?' she said about the egg.

'It's fine, thanks Deirdre. Really. I appreciate this, I wanted to come straight here after Hega.'

'Will you have more toast?'

'No, thanks, that was grand.'

'Okay,' she said. 'What do you want me to do about my phone?'

'I'll ask Hega. If you've been in touch with that woman and Ormsby hacked it, he might know about her. But I can't believe he's hacked all our phones as well as the computers at work. Anyway, I'll head away, I've taken enough of your time.'

Deirdre was relieved when he left. There was something beaten down about him that she didn't want to think about.

CHAPTER 60

DEIRDRE THOUGHT Collins looked a lot better at the briefing meeting. He told her he had 'caught up on his sleep' the day before.

Now that they had the statement from Liz Howard, O'Rourke announced that the plan was to arrest Ormsby and charge him with harassment and attempted rape the following day, once the file was completed. Then to go heavy on him about the murder of Helen O'Driscoll.

'He'll get bail for sure,' O'Rourke said. 'But we'll continue to build evidence for the murder and he might slip up under interview. Maybe even confess – who knows? I think we can also get a search warrant, which might yield something useful.'

'What about Hughes and Ormsby being on that incel list?' Deirdre said.

'I've had some further legal advice about that list,' O'Rourke said. 'And we've been told to be wary of it. So, we can use it to further our enquiries but it might not stand up in court. Apparently the source of it has been admitted to a mental institution so we're on thin ice there.'

Collins brought up the issue of the hacking and Ormsby having access to everything on the computers and phones.

'We don't know that for certain,' Mick Murphy said. 'Yes, there's been a hacking and they are dealing with it, but everything seems to be working well, so far.'

'My information is the type of virus being used is the exact same one that Ormsby uses to test his firewalls with his clients.'

'Well, the head of IT, Ted Slevin, told me that it's more than likely some Russians behind it,' Mick replied. 'And they're going to look for a ransom.'

'But they haven't,' Collins said. 'Using the precaution principle, I suggest we don't put anything more about Ormsby or this investigation on the system until we know the hacking has been cleaned up. And we should all get our phones checked too. The IT consultant Philip Hegarty checked my phone on Saturday and found several pieces of malware on it.'

'Been at the porn again, Collins?' O'Regan said and laughed at his own joke.

'And isn't it a bit of coincidence,' Collins said, 'that in the middle of an investigation where the main suspect is a world-expert on hacking that our system is hacked?'

Mick Murphy shook his head.

O'Rourke said: 'I think we should proceed with caution on this. There's no harm in being careful what we put on the system and have our phones checked. Mick, will you get on to IT and set that up, please?'

'Yes superintendent,' Murphy said, making a note.

DEIRDRE AND Collins drove out to Barbara Mulcahy's house. They turned off their phones before they left the station in case they could be tracked. She remembered the way.

'Very isolated,' Collins said, getting out of the car.

'Lovely, though,' Deirdre said. She'd always wanted a house in the country. 'Look at the view.' To the south and west, there was a sweeping view of the river valley and lakes in the distance.

'Very nice,' Collins said. 'Will you take lead on this? We should probably be careful not to spook her.'

'Sure,' Deirdre said, resenting Collins' broad hint.

Barbara Mulcahy was a thin, stressed-looking woman of about thirty-five. She opened the door as they approached and said: 'I have to be at the child-minders by twelve.'

'Oh, we won't be long,' Deirdre said. 'It's just a routine enquiry.'

'Come in, we'll sit in the kitchen. My husband is asleep, he works nights and I don't want to wake him. So, please keep your voices down.'

They sat at the kitchen table and she offered them tea or coffee. Deirdre asked for tea, Collins asked for coffee, after he'd noticed the fancy-looking Smeg coffee machine in the corner. When she smelled the lovely aroma from it, Deirdre was sorry she hadn't asked for coffee, too.

'What's this about?' Barbara said. 'Is it about that queer hawk in Ballincollig? That Ormsby fellow?'

Deirdre tried not to react. She noticed that Collins didn't blink at the name.

'It is, actually, but why did you refer to him as "a queer hawk"?'

'What's he done?' Barbara said, making the tea.

'Oh, it's very early in the investigation,' Deirdre said. 'Why did you think it was him?'

'What investigation?' Barbara said, putting the cup of tea on the table. 'Sugar, anyone?'

'No thanks,' Collins said. 'We just have to follow up on these connections all the time, we got your name from your employer and we want to talk to you about when you were working with Blake Ormsby Research.'

'Can you tell us about your time there?' Deirdre said. 'How did you get the job?'

'I was temping with an agency at the time,' Barbara said. 'I work for myself now, mostly from home. I do admin and accounts, that kind of work.'

'You never told us,' Deirdre said, 'how you guessed it was him we wanted to talk about.'

'Oh, he was a total creep. Even thinking about him makes me sick to my stomach. What's he done?'

'When you say a creep, what do you mean?'

'Oh, he was fine the first few days, he more or less ignored me. Then he started looking at me when he'd pass by.'

'When you say "looking at me"?' Deirdre said.

'Kind of staring at me. I'm not sure how to explain it, but it was very odd. And then he'd start muttering to himself when he went up the stairs and after he'd close the door, he used to shout stuff.'

'Could you hear what he'd be shouting?' Deirdre said.

'It could be something like "For fuck's sake" or "Jesus Christ" or something like that, but it usually involved "They", whoever "They" are.'

'Could you give us an example?'

'Oh, it could be something like "They think they're smart" or "They think they know it all, they don't know anything!"'

'And the next time he'd come down he'd be as sweet as pie. He asked me out twice.'

'And what did you say?'

'I told him I was a married woman and that it was an inappropriate question to ask an employee.'

'What was his reaction?' Deirdre said.

'Oh, he stormed up the stairs and started shouting again. I often heard him shouting about "bitches" too.'

'When he was shouting about "they",' Collins said. 'What do you think he was referring to?'

Barbara thought for a moment and swept some crumbs off the table with her hand.

'I think he was talking about women,' she said. 'I think it was all about women. He couldn't look me in the eye when he was talking to me, but then he'd be standing there staring at me. And not in a good way. I complained to my boss three times but they did nothing, so I didn't go in the second week.'

'Did he ever make a physical approach, or touch you in any way?' Deirdre asked.

Barbara shook her head. 'I used to put a chair beside my desk so he'd have to move it to get around. Often they come around the desk to "by the way" show you something or other and then they'd put their hand on your arm or around your back or something. Or your breast.'

'Has that happened to you?'

'Are you kidding?' Barbara said. 'You mean it *hasn't* happened to you?'

Deirdre could feel herself blushing. Three times in Templemore and those two creeps in Store Street. She nodded.

'Would you be willing to make a formal statement, Barbara?' she said. 'If we needed one?'

'If you tell me what you're investigating, I will,' Barbara said. 'Is it a sexual assault?'

'We can't tell you,' Collins said. 'It might help his case.' Then he nodded, twice. *Nicely done, Collins*, Deirdre thought.

'Well,' Barbara said, having hesitated. 'Everything I told you was the truth and I'd be willing to say that to anyone, including a judge. I'm sick of those bastards, sick of them. And did ye find out who it was on Tuesday night? That gave us an awful fright.'

'I'm sorry,' Deirdre said. 'What happened on Tuesday night?'

'My neighbour, Kitty Keohane, saw a man walking down the road with a backpack and rang the garda station and then she rang me, giving me the fright of my life. I thought something had happened to Pat at work or something. Only for us going to France the following morning, I would have been on to ye.'

'And did you see him?'

'No, I didn't, I turned on the outside light and let the dog out and he took off up the road and then I heard barking but I was afraid to go out.'

'Has that ever happened before? Was somebody lost or something? A car breakdown?'

'Lost? Out here? And if it was a breakdown why didn't they call in to Keohanes or Barrys? I was nervous again last night alone with Fiachra, he's only three.'

AFTER THE interview, Deirdre turned the car and drove back the narrow road. When they were approaching the first house, a woman came out. She was in her sixties and was wearing an apron and wellington boots.

Collins opened the passenger window.

'Hello,' he said.

'Ye were down with Barbara,' the woman said. 'Was it about Tuesday night?'

'Are you Kitty Keohane?' Collins said. 'You made the call, is that right?'

'Yes. Did ye find him?'

'Not yet, they only told us about it today,' Collins said. 'We're detectives from the city, Ballincollig asked us to look into it.'

'I'm sick sore and sorry from ringing that garda station, and they passing me from Billy to Jack.'

'Can you tell us what you saw, Kitty?'

'For God's sake,' the woman said. 'The dog was barking around 3 a.m. and woke me and I looked out the bedroom window and there was a man walking down the road, bold as brass.'

'Could you describe him?' Collins said.

'I could. He was about the same height as Tony, my youngest, that's around five ten. He was a strong fella, hefty looking, he had a dark jacket and a baseball cap so I couldn't see his face but I think he had glasses on. He had one of those things, what do you call them, on his back.'

'A backpack?' Collins said.

'That's it, a big yoke, it was dark in colour, too, with some logo on the back.'

'I can't imagine ye have too many people coming down here in the day, let alone in the middle of the night,' Collins said.

'Are you joking me? I thought it might be Pat, Barbara's husband, but he's a good bit taller and thinner. So, I rang her straight away and she got the fright of her life. Why didn't ye send somebody straight away, she could have been murdered in her bed? Any of us could.'

'I don't know about that, I'd say they probably did send out a car, I'll find out for you.'

'Write down your phone number there and I'll ring you about it. I'm after complaining already to my local TD.'

Collins took out a notebook and wrote an 087 phone number on it.

'Here,' he said, tearing off the page and giving to her. 'Ring me any time, especially if you see anything suspicious.'

When they had driven off, Deirdre looked at Collins and said: 'Did you really give her your phone number?'

'I might have gotten a number or two wrong,' he said and she had to laugh.

CHAPTER 61

THE GRAND Gentleman finds himself in a field in the middle of the night. They think he is a fool but he isn't a fool. If he were a fool (not was, were, he knows his grammar), they'd have caught him already. Not only will they not catch him for his fun with Helen, they don't even have enough to charge him, it's obvious. That buffoon Collins and that bitch Donnelly, they'll be chasing him until the cows come home.

Even if they have something against him, the danger has to be faced down. The Grand Gentleman has an army to lead and a Rebellion to start. Leadership means sacrifice, everybody in a position of authority knows that.

It appears that these fields are some kind of corn or wheat. The Grand Gentleman doesn't know much about farming but if the yokels want to plant crops in the ground and cut them down, then let them. Somebody has to do the higher mathematics to invent the machines the yokels need and that's where the Grand Gentleman comes in. Much higher mathematics than basic engineering.

He isn't making the mistake of walking down the road again. He looked at the Google Earth images and there's only two fields to walk across to get the house. And every field has a gate, how else do the machines get in and out?

He has the taser for the dog and he'll taser the bitch, too. Easy to climb a fallen tree, who was it said that? He can hear a dog barking in the distance, but dogs bark in the night. That's what they do. The husband is at work again, The Grand Gentleman has tracked his phone. The bitch's phone is in the house, much good it will do her.

Everything is in the backpack. Fjällräven, best brand on the market, nothing but the best. The Swedes know their design. Fjällräven: the Arctic fox if he isn't mistaken and he usually isn't. His Trusty is all he needs, really. His Trusty will have fun tonight, it's been too long already.

He sees the gate, exactly where Google said it would be. What a bad idea Google is: so much information available to so many, when they don't know what to do with a fraction of it. He wonders if he could get inside the Google mainframes and hold them to ransom. He is sure he could.

The gate is open, careless yokel. He walks through and turns right. The Maglite lights his way. He knows the house is at the end of the field. He knows there's only a picket fence between the field and the house garden. He expects the dog to begin barking soon, much good it will do him.

He is in the garden, and the dog is quiet. Strange that, but let sleeping dogs lie. The house has three windows at the back and he tries all three: locked. Never mind, the universal key will open the front door, a basic Yale 60 mm backset, €20 on Amazon. The husband should have invested in something safer but then he's another fool, another Chad with another Stacy. Sex on tap for those guys but there won't be any more sex with this Stacy, will there?

He takes out the taser for the dog and has it ready. The gloves will protect his hands, Kevlar reinforced. The key slides in and the Grand Gentleman is aroused. If he could get a hard-on he knows he'd be rock hard now.

The lock turns, the door opens, and he goes into the hall. He knows the layout as well as his own house, the plans were easy to download from the planning office. He walks down the hall, there's a nightlight on – for the brat no doubt. He opens the bitch's bedroom door, the taser at the ready. Trusty is rock hard and Trusty will soon be having his fun.

CHAPTER 62

BARBARA MULCAHY is awake in the bed. Fiachra is asleep, at last, his breathing beside her is quick and steady. How quickly his heart beat as a baby, she could never get used to that. The doctors and nurses had to reassure her several times in the maternity hospital.

Must be 4 a.m. but she never looks at the clock any more, what's the point in knowing? With the little light on in the corner for Fiachra it's hard to tell if it's getting bright outside or not.

She thinks she hears something in the hall and she sees the door begin to open. She sits up, careful not to disturb Fiachra.

It's Emily, with a cup of tea, did she sleep out?

Emily sits on the side of the bed and gives her the tea.

'You told me to wake you if there's any news,' Emily whispers.

'Did something happen?' Barbara says.

'They caught him a half an hour ago, Deirdre just phoned me.'

'In my house?'

'Yes,' Emily says. 'It's over, Barbara. He's under arrest, you can rest easy now.'

CHAPTER 63

COLLINS, DEIRDRE, O'Rourke and Brennan were waiting in an Audi 4x4 in a little cul de sac a couple of kilometres away when the call came through from the Armed Support Unit. *Suspect in custody, proceed.* Gubbins and some of his forensic team were in a van parked behind them.

Deirdre started the engine and they drove to the house.

A couple of ASU vehicles were there before them, lights flashing. Armed men in black clothing stood around. A handcuffed Ormsby was in the back of a Volvo, his eyes closed as if he were trying to block it all out. Deirdre strode to the car and opened the door.

'Fuck you, Ormsby,' she said. 'You piece of shit.'

'Bitch,' Ormsby said, not opening his eyes.

Collins held Deirdre's arm and pulled her away.

'All right, Deirdre,' he said. 'All right, girl.' He closed the car door.

'THERE'S A backpack,' one of the ASUs said to Gubbins when he got out of the forensic van. 'We didn't touch it.'

Collins and Deirdre went to where O'Rourke and Brennan were being briefed by the officer in charge, Kieran Vaughan.

'We spotted him coming through the field at 03:18. He tried the windows at the back of the house first. That was a good idea not to leave one of them open, he might have suspected something.

'He got in through the front door, he had some kind of universal key or something. When he entered the bedroom, we took him down. Minimum force, he didn't struggle. He said something about 'his trusted' or something and he started ranting about 'those bitches'. We have a recording, we videoed everything.

'Will we bring him in?'

'Yes,' O'Rourke said. 'Good work, write it up in the morning.'

COLLINS TURNED to Deirdre. He wanted to do this in front of O'Rourke and Brennan in case they forgot. He gave a fist tap to her shoulder.

'Good work, detective,' he said. 'First round is on you. You made it happen.'

Collins thought back to how hard Deirdre had argued to convince O'Rourke that Ormsby was going to strike again and was going to target Barbara Mulcahy and to hold off his arrest. O'Rourke had given her two days.

How it was Deirdre's idea to bring Melanie Ryan down in the first place, and how she backed her to the hilt that Ormsby fit the profile. How she had browbeaten Collins and Clancy to support her and argue Melanie's case with the super.

The clincher was when Hega hacked into the highest levels of the incel chat line with Melanie Ryan and they saw in black and white that Ormsby was planning another attack.

O'Rourke's worries about entrapment until he got definitive legal advice that there was no inducement from An Garda Síochána. It had all paid off but it would never have happened if Deirdre hadn't pushed it so hard.

'Well done Detective Donnelly,' O'Rourke said. 'Collins is right.' He put out his hand and Deirdre shook it. Brennan did the same. Deirdre looked in shock, and Collins was afraid she would get emotional.

'Don't get a big head, Donnelly,' Collins said. 'I taught you everything you know.'

Deirdre laughed. She put out her hand and Collins shook it.

'Jesus, I'd murder a coffee,' Collins said. 'There's a fancy Smeg machine in there.'

'Do not even think about it, Tim,' Blessing Nzekwe said, walking past in her polypropylene suit, carrying a large plastic box.

'I hope there's something incriminating in that backpack,' O'Rourke said. 'I'll put pressure on Gubbins to let us know today.'

'Bound to be a rape kit,' Brennan said.

'Yes, but we want him for Helen O'Driscoll,' O'Rourke said. 'I said a prayer for her when we were parked in that lay-by.'

When Collins heard that, he knew he'd go into battle with a man like Frank O'Rourke. More, he'd follow that man into battle, however unlike each other they were in faith and personality.

Collins put out his hand. O'Rourke took it.

'Thank you for your leadership,' Collins said. 'She was lucky to have had you in charge.'

CHAPTER 64

PAUL GUBBINS pointed the remote at the laptop and a large photo appeared on the white screen at the top of the briefing room. The room was packed with gardaí, word had gotten out that forensics had something to nail Ormsby for Helen O'Driscoll's murder. Deirdre sat in her usual seat, Collins to her left and Melanie Ryan to her right, looking out of place.

Deirdre watched the rest of the team: O'Rourke and Brennan, with Mick Murphy. Clancy, O'Regan, Kelleher and Jim Murphy in their usual places. They had partied hard the night before and Deirdre was not feeling great, she could have done with some toast. Her tea was getting cold on the table before her. Melanie looked as fresh faced as ever, like she was after ten hours sleep, when in reality it must have been closer to four.

'We found this in Ormsby's backpack. We think this is the object he used for the sexual assault,' Gubbins said, pointing a red laser light at the screen.

'A Coke bottle?' Clancy said.

'The point is that we found traces of blood on it and if it's a match with Helen O'Driscoll's DNA, we have him,' Gubbins said. 'We also found this.' He clicked to the next slide. It showed a long piece of red cord.

'We believe,' he said, 'that this is the murder weapon he used to kill Helen O'Driscoll, it is a very close match to the pathology of her neck wound. We found traces of skin and blood on it, which we are convinced will match her DNA.'

'When will the results be back?' O'Rourke said.

'Two days,' Gubbins said. 'That's the fastest they can be. Science can't be rushed, I'm afraid. But there's also the possibility of more than one blood type on the bottle, if he's also used it on other women.'

'We have him,' Deirdre said.

'Any prints on it?' O'Rourke said.

'Yes, a match for Ormsby,' Gubbins said.

'*Yes!*' O'Rourke said and clenched his fist.

'How are the searches of his property and businesses going?' O'Rourke said. 'Anything incriminating?'

'There was a lot of pornography and literature from incel in his house,' Mick Murphy said. 'Some kind of Manifesto it looks like he wrote. And that expert is flying in from Switzerland today – we're hoping he can get into his computers.'

'What I'm wondering is why he didn't get rid of the porn and the incel stuff,' Clancy said. 'He knew he was a suspect. Why didn't he dump it?'

'Arrogance,' Collins said. 'Same reason he went after Barbara Mulcahy. He thought we were too stupid to ever pin anything on him. But there's something else. Can you bring up the old photos of when Ormsby and Helen were in college? The ones that Robbie Wilkins gave us? There was one taken in a pub.'

Mick Murphy went to the laptop and opened some folders. A photo of a young Helen O'Driscoll at a table in a pub came up. Then one with herself and Ormsby. It looked like they were both singing into empty Coke bottles as though they were micro-phones.

'That's the one,' Collins said.

Mick enlarged the photo to zoom in on the bottles.

'Bingo,' O'Rourke said. 'We have the fucker.'

The room burst into applause.

AFTER THE meeting, Collins told Deirdre he had to do something, he'd be back in an hour.

'Give me a shout when you get back,' she said. 'I want to talk to you about something.'

'Will do.'

He signed out an old unmarked car and put the flowers and vase into the boot. He headed out the South Link to avoid the Douglas traffic. On the road to Passage, he noticed people walking on the path by the water. He resolved to exercise more, to walk more. Which made him think of Katie. She had texted him the previous night: *Don't be a stranger, tough guy.*

He'd ring her later.

He turned right after the little roundabout and parked outside the cemetery. He wasn't sure where the grave was, but it would be one of the new ones, he guessed.

He found it quickly, the name on the little wooden cross at the top. *Helen O'Driscoll Loving Mother and Wife.* Some fresh flowers by the cross. Hard to believe it wasn't even three weeks. He put the vase of water on an even piece of earth and pressed it down. Then he put the flowers into it. He thought about their symbolism, he thought about Helen's eyes.

He heard voices behind him. A man, a woman, and a boy in a red sports shirt. The boy had a little dog on a lead. He recognised the man as Greg Murphy, the woman as his mother, Nora, the professor. The boy, of course, was Evan. He was talking to the dog.

Collins first thought he would walk away but they had seen him. As they approached, he realised that Nora recognised him. She shook his hand.

'Thanks for what you've done,' she said. 'Will he be convicted?'

'We believe so,' Collins said.

'This is one of the detectives, Gregory,' she said to her son. 'It's Tim Collins, isn't it?'

Collins shook hands with Greg Murphy and said: 'I'm sorry for your loss, we haven't met. I just came to pay my respects.'

'Asphodels,' Nora said. 'Are you a classicist, Tim?'

'Oh, no, although you did try to teach me some in UCC many years ago,' Collins said. 'My mother grows them.'

'Well, you clearly learned something,' Nora replied.

Collins crouched down to talk to Evan. 'Hi Evan, my name is Tim and who's this?' The dog, a young cockapoo, approached Collins warily, wagging his tail, and Collins rubbed his ears and back.

'Charlie,' Evan said, quietly.

'Is that a Munster jersey?' Collins said.

The boy nodded.

'Would you believe that I'm good friends with Sam Dunlea's Dad?' Collins said. 'And he's always offering me tickets for Thomond Park? Next time they're playing, why don't I get two tickets for you and your Dad and ye can meet Sam and some of the players?'

'Can we, Dad?' Evan asked.

'Course we can. That's very kind of you.'

'Maybe you can get four tickets,' Nora said. 'I wouldn't mind meeting some of those players, and you might come along yourself.'

'Yes, of course, I'd be happy to. How is … Jim?'

'He's fine,' she said. 'But he wouldn't be up to going to Thomond. I, on the other hand, love the place.'

'Good stuff,' Collins said. He'd forgotten the vitality of the woman, even on that dreadful night.

'I'll head away,' he said. 'Can I get your number, Greg, so I can contact you about those tickets?'

They exchanged numbers.

'See you, Evan,' Collins said. 'See you, Charlie.'

ON THE way back to Cork, he stopped into Gogo's on the Well

Road for coffee and scrambled eggs. He phoned Katie. She picked up on the second ring.

'What about ya, Collins?' she said, cheerily.

'Hi Katie, how are things?'

'Fine, except where the fuck have you been? My two daughters are thick with me, they have me killed to ring you.'

'Ah, we were finishing up that case in Cork, but it's looks it's more or less over now. I was thinking of calling down tomorrow, for lunch or something if you were free.'

'Sure, call to the house first and we'll have a ride. In fairness, it's been ages.'

Collins laughed.

'Will do,' he said.

'And then we might have a bite of something and look at a house or two out on the Kilbarry Road,' she said and paused. 'If you're still on for that.'

'I'm still on for it, girl. I knew I'd wear you down.'

'Haha, the trick was to let you think it was your idea in the first place,' she said. 'I'll ring the estate agent and set that up. I've a customer here, go way you now and I'll see you tomorrow at half twelve in the house. No pressure, Collins, but bring your A game.'

Collins laughed again and sipped his coffee.

A TEXT came in. From Paulo, his old hurling buddy: *Me & CC going to the game tonight in PUC, you on?*

Collins smiled and replied: *Big time, meet ye in Longboats at 5.*

Chapter 65

'Everything alright?' Superintendent O'Rourke said, looking worried behind his desk. Deirdre and Collins sat facing him.

'That message sounded a bit formal or something,' O'Rourke added.

'Oh, no, everything's fine we're working away on the file for the DPP,' Deirdre said. 'Great news about those DNA samples being positive for Helen O'Driscoll and two others.' She had heard the news when she got in early that morning, even though it was a Sunday. She was determined that the file would be immaculate and they'd nail Ormsby.

'I suspect one of the other samples will be from Lea Thompson,' O'Rourke said. 'What do you think, Collins?'

'Hopefully,' Collins said. 'But we must work on the third victim, too. Most victims of sexual assault never come forward as you know but now that Ormsby is going away for a long time, hopefully that woman will make herself known and can get justice. Which is partly what we asked to meet you about. Sorry for it being on a Sunday but we knew you'd be in.'

'Oh?' O'Rourke said. 'I'm intrigued, now.'

Deirdre took a deep breath.

'It's about this incel ring,' she said. 'And Melanie Ryan's list. I know you said we have to be careful with it but it needs to be fully investigated. And she has other lists, too.

'I did what you suggested yesterday and put the sixteen names on the list to Lea Thompson and another sixteen fake names. And we got a hit. Lea said she dated a man called Stanley Reynolds some years ago. That was one of the names on the incel list. We think the men are sharing information about women they know to other men who are then targeting the women. That way there's no connection between the attacker and the victim. I think it was a coincidence that both Hughes and Ormsby knew Helen. Talk about being unlucky. But we were lucky, too, and we might not be, the next time.

'The point is that Melanie has no resources – she's completely dependent on being called in by teams like us after a sexual assault or murder has been perpetrated.'

'You have a proposal?' O'Rourke said.

'Yes,' Deirdre said. 'Our view is that there's a tsunami of gender based sexual violence in Ireland right now and the force isn't dealing with it well enough. I'm talking about everything from a teenage boy bullying a secondary school girl into a feel, all the way up to Ormsby. And there's so much in between. Domestic violence, date rape, spiking drinks, coercive control, stalking, revenge porn, harassment, you name it. Did you know that 26 percent of women in Ireland have experienced sexual violence? That's one in four. We were thinking that with Ormsby in the news now the timing might be good.'

Deirdre's mouth was suddenly dry. The speech she had prepared all morning seemed to be drifting away and she wasn't sure if she was making any sense. However, O'Rourke was taking notes which she took to be a good sign.

'For a start,' she continued. 'We need to deal with the incel group and this list of names. Collins and I, or any Dublin based detectives can't deal with somebody in a position of power over women in somewhere like Sligo, some so-called pillar of the community. Those guys need to be dealt with locally, but the local members need some support and guidance nationally. And they need clout. This would have to be led by a superintendent or chief superintendent to have any hope of traction.

'We don't know if there are any other Ormsbys but it's likely there are, if that list is anything to go by, and they need to be nipped in the bud. Apparently, they all write Manifestos in case they are killed, outlining their warped philosophy, if you can even call it that. What's to stop one of them ploughing a car or a van into a feminist rally or even a group of schoolgirls? That's already happened in the States and these guys are being radicalised online. Some sickos are already trying to make a hero out of Ormsby on Twitter, for God's sake.'

Deirdre felt she had said enough. She looked at Collins for him to speak.

'I was talking to Inspector Nuala Leahy about this,' Collins said. 'And she has agreed to help with administrative assistance, she has a lot of experience in that, and her work in Limerick has been well received. As Deirdre said, it's not a question of if but when another Ormsby turns up. And it's too late after. We need to watch social media and infiltrate incel and any other groups out there. Melanie Ryan needs a team to lead.

'I know we're going to charge Hughes and some of the others with abetting now that we have access to the full chat rooms, but it's not just the likes of him. The level of violence against women is off the charts now.

'Nuala thought that setting up a pilot unit in two or three divisions would be a good starting point. We're not looking for additional resources, we know there's no hope of that. It's a question of real-locating current members to focus on this issue. Needless to say, it would be very popular with the minister, too, she is very strong on women issues. Can't hurt to have a woman commissioner, too.

'And that's it really,' Collins said. 'It was Deirdre's idea I have to say, she should get the credit, but I'd like to be part of it, too.'

Deirdre didn't know whether to be hopeful or not. She let a breath out. Having Collins' support could make all the difference, even if he only agreed as long as he got a go at Hughes.

O'Rourke looked at them for a moment.

'I think it's a great idea,' he said. 'Would you both be prepared to make this pitch to Assistant Commissioner Gallagher next week? If he likes the idea I think we might take it further up the chain. I'd prepare some PowerPoint slides if I were you and do some research if this has been done in any other countries. If I was ye, I'd bring Nuala Leahy along and Melanie Ryan, too.

'A few other tips. Don't be critical of the force, but this would give added value to the success we have already had, solving this case and breaking up the incel ring. Look up the commissioner's speeches and use some of the buzz words she likes to use. Final thing: don't ask for a new formal unit, that might need legislation and it would get caught up in all sorts of red tape. A task force might be a better option, especially in the short term; she could probably run that by the minister a lot easier.

'Meantime I'll talk to the Assistant Commissioner tomorrow and we'll take it from there. These things get tied up in red tape and there are all sorts of obstacles, politically and every which way, but if we don't try, it won't happen, that's for sure.'

O'Rourke was quiet for a moment. Then he said: 'Of course the naysayers will say that we nailed Ormsby without this kind of initiative.'

'That's true, sir,' Deirdre said. 'But that isn't much consolation to Helen O'Driscoll or her family, with all due respect. And what about the next Helen O'Driscoll? And the one after her?'

LATER, HAVING a drink with Collins in Meades, waiting for Jake to arrive, Deirdre felt ebullient. The case against Ormsby was getting stronger by the day, it was a slam dunk when Clancy tracked down a lockup he had rented and found a box containing a variety of women's clothing and underwear, some of it bloodied. Not to mention the bomb-making equipment. If that won't convince the commissioner to set up a task-force she didn't know what would.

A special unit to protect women would be a huge legacy and would have justified all the shit she'd gone through. She'd heard on the grapevine that there was an inspector post coming up in September, somebody was retiring, and she had a great chance of getting it, especially after her role in the Ormsby case. How proud her father would be, even if he was retreating further behind dementia, day-by-day.

As inspector there'd be no smart comments when she entered the room, no innuendos in the canteen. And, definitely no idiots thinking she'd go out with them, or worse.

She looked at Collins. Working with him had gone well, after all. In fairness, he completely backed her idea to O'Rourke and gave her the credit for it. She'd have to rein him in a bit when they got started, but she was confident she could manage it.

She wasn't sure if Collins was in a good place at all. Since Ormsby's arrest, she was sleeping well again, but he looked knackered. She saw his eyes close, he appeared to be falling asleep. The thing with Denis Grandon had probably taken its toll, but she told herself not to under-estimate him.

'Hey old man,' she said, nudging him. 'Don't fall asleep on me.'

His eyes opened and he smiled. He took another sip of his wine.

'I'm tired,' he said. 'But I wanted to say it's been great working with you, Deirdre. I've learned a lot. And it was you got Ormsby nailed, well done, girl.'

She put out her hand and he shook it.

'Thanks for backing me on that idea to O'Rourke,' she said. 'Meant a lot, and with the great Tim Collins behind it, it really has a chance. But don't be getting all maudlin on me now. *And* it's your round. Will we share a tapas plate? Jake should be in soon.'

'Why not?' Collins said.

Part 4

Coming Home

CHAPTER 66

IT COULD have been any street in any town in Ireland. The kind of houses you would see anywhere.

Collins was parked opposite a bungalow, with an extension at the front. Similar houses fanned out up and down the road. A van drove by, heading towards Cappoquin.

Just a suburban house at the edge of a town in County Waterford.

The pebble-dashed front walls needed a coat of paint. Maybe Denis used to do that job for them. Somebody else will have to do it now. The house name on a pillar: *Rosary*.

Collins closed his eyes and tried to breathe deeply as Abi had taught him.

He opened the car door and got out. He checked his dress uniform and took his cap out of the back seat.

DENIS GRANDON's father, Ned, came out into the front hall. He was tall like his son, but stooped and grey. His eyes were keen, though.

He opened the front door and Collins realised he didn't know what to say.

'Tim,' Ned said and he put out his hand. 'Thanks for coming. The days are long.'

'I'm sorry I couldn't come sooner,' Collins said, taking off his cap. 'And I apologise I wasn't at the funeral.'

'Good job you weren't,' Ned said. 'I heard what happened. Come in, come in.'

Ned hesitated before going through. He beckoned Collins to the side.

'Now. I just want to let you know. Elaine is very angry about what happened.'

Collins nodded.

'I'm angry too,' Ned said. 'But at the bastard who killed Denis. Elaine … well she's just angry, angry at everybody and everything; including the gardaí. Do you see what I mean?'

'I do,' Collins said. 'I don't blame her.'

THERE WERE brown carpet tiles in the long hall, wallpaper on the walls, closed doors on either side. Glass panels on the door of the kitchen on their right. A Sacred Heart on the wall above the table.

They walked through into the living room. Just another living room in just another house. Floral carpet on the floor and the walls covered in some type of wooden panelling.

Two women were sitting in narrow leather armchairs beside an unlit fireplace. One older, Denis' mother, Elaine. One younger, his fiancé, Áine. They had both been crying. Áine stood up, Elaine did not.

Collins reached down to Elaine and shook her hand.

'I'm sorry for your loss,' Collins blurted out. *Don't cry*, he thought. *Don't you cry on these people.*

'Thank you,' Elaine said. 'This is Áine.' She was about to add more but stopped herself in time.

Áine hugged him. She started crying.

'I'm so sorry,' Collins said. 'I'm so sorry, it should have been me.' His eyes filled with tears.

'You smell like him,' Áine said, smiling and sniffling. 'I suppose all those uniforms smell the same.' She looked at him. She was tall and her eyes were an extraordinary shade of blue, almost like robin's eggs.

'He worshipped the ground you walked on,' she said. 'I'm glad I got to meet you.'

Collins winced. He couldn't find the words to say. *You're useless. Useless.*

'Sit down, Tim,' Ned said. 'Sit down, will you have a cup of tea? Or coffee? Denis said you were fond of coffee.'

'Tea would be grand,' Collins said. 'But maybe we'll sit down and chat, first.'

He sat down. He held his cap on his lap.

'You broke our hearts in '93,' Ned said. 'We thought we had ye bate the same day in Thurles.'

'William Power gave an exhibition of hurling that day,' Collins said. 'I never saw the like. How is, he, I heard he had an accident?'

'He's good. He is down to one crutch now, I saw him below in the field at a match last week.'

'Was he brave?' Áine blurted out. 'Oh, I'm sorry. I'm sorry, he wanted so much to be brave.'

There was a momentary silence.

'At the end, you mean?' Collins said. She nodded.

'He was amazingly brave. When they started shooting I told the lads to run away and hide in the yard, and Denis wouldn't do it. "We don't run from the likes of them", he said. Now… they did all run away, he didn't do anything stupid, but they found him in one of the sheds. It was all my fault really, I'm so sorry.'

Elaine made a sound through her closed lips.

Collins continued, he wanted to get this out. 'He was a very fine young man, a credit to you all. We owe him a debt we can never repay. He died serving his country and his community and we'll never forget him. I'll never forget him. Never.'

Ned coughed to prevent himself from crying.

'We light a candle every morning,' Elaine said. 'And we say a Hail Mary. It's very hard to believe he'll never come home again.'

Collins looked at the candle and picture on the mantelpiece. Denis, handsome and happy, smiling in his uniform on the day of his passing out.

Áine started crying.

'He was very proud of you,' Collins said to Áine. 'He showed me your photo.'

'He did? Do you remember where it was taken?'

'He told me it was in Tramore,' Collins said.

She smiled.

'He liked that one,' she said.

'I think I'll make the tea now,' Elaine said. She left the room. Áine followed her.

Collins and Ned began talking hurling again until Collins interrupted it.

'I have to tell you, Ned,' Collins said. 'I'm very ashamed of this. Jones wanted me to come out. He called me out. I was hiding in a shed. He said he'd shoot Denis if I didn't come out. And I didn't come out. I didn't.'

'Sure, if you came out he'd have shot the two of ye,' Ned said. He reached out a big hand and put it on Collins' arm. 'He'd have shot the two of ye. And what do you think Denis would have wanted you to do? You know what he'd have wanted.'

Collins closed his eyes and tried to breathe.

'He was a credit to you,' was all he could manage.

'We were very proud of him, and we always will be.'

AFTER THE tea and apple tart, Collins said: 'I'd like to go to the grave, I wonder would ye come with me?'

Áine went in the car with Collins to direct him. She was quiet.

When they pulled up outside the graveyard, she looked at him and said: 'I'm pregnant'.

'Oh, Áine,' Collins said and he held her hand. 'That's wonderful. Isn't it?'

She smiled and wiped her eyes.

'It is, but I haven't told them yet. I don't know how.'

'Sure, they'll be thrilled, a new baby. It'll be like having Denis back again. It's a miracle, Áine.'

'That's what Mam said.'

'Do you want to tell them now?' Collins said. He didn't know where he was going with this.

'I do,' she said. 'When they told me you were coming today I told Mam I would. I nearly did it in the house but then I got afraid.'

'There's nothing to be afraid of,' Collins said. 'When we go to the grave I'll tell them you have some news and you just say it.'

She wiped her eyes again and said: 'Thank you.'

He picked up his cap from the back seat and put it on again. He put on his white gloves. He took a bunch of flowers out of the boot of his car. He took the plain glass vase his mother had given him. *You good thing, Grandon,* he thought and he smiled.

Elaine and Ned stood outside the gates of the graveyard waiting for them.

'Those flowers are lovely,' Elaine said. 'I don't know them.'

'They're asphodels,' Collins said, almost adding something more. 'My mother grows them in her garden, she gave me some, coming.'

As they walked towards the grave, a wave of realisation washed over him. That this was the third graveyard he'd visited in the last month. That there were three young people needlessly dead and buried within them. That Ned, Elaine, and Áine would mourn Denis for the rest of their lives and that Elaine's anger would grow inside her like cancer. That Denis' unborn child would grow up never knowing him. That Jacqueline Buckley had buried two of her children and may well have to bury a third. That Evan Murphy will never remember his mother and Greg Murphy will never forgive himself for not protecting his wife. And that Collins had failed them all.

He half-filled the vase at a tap they passed. He paused when they reached the grave. There was a plain wooden cross, with the words on a small plate: *Denis Grandon 1989–2018. Loving son and fiancé. He died for Ireland.*

He looked at the bare ground, still arrayed with funeral flowers. He looked at the sky. He bent down and pressed the vase into the earth near the head of the grave. He put the asphodels into the water.

He took a deep breath and tried to stand as tall as he could. He pressed his heels together and faced the grave. He saluted his fallen comrade. He held the salute for ten slow seconds before lowering his arm.

'God rest you, Denis,' he said quietly.

HE FACED Elaine and Ned who were holding hands and weeping.

He smiled and said: 'Áine has a bit of news.'

CHAPTER 67

IN EARLY August Collins drove through Dunmanway town. It was late in the afternoon and the Friday traffic was heavy. Another lovely sunny day.

He passed their old terrace house in West Green and turned right on to the Kilbarry Road.

He swung in to the new estate, with six large detached houses, surrounded by gardens. He parked by the gate and saw that Zoe was cutting the back lawn with the electric mower. He waved at her and she turned the mower off. He hugged her, which was a new thing they did since the football match against O'Donovan Rossa the month before. She was wearing football shorts, runners and a Cork jersey and her hair was tied up in the bandana he had bought her for her birthday.

'I don't see why I have to cut the grass while she's sunning herself over there,' she complained. 'Why do I always have to do it?'

'Because you're so good at it, Zoe,' he said. 'Plus, it gets your step count way up. You're as fit as a fiddle. All set for the county final against Mallow?'

'We have a challenge match in Bantry on Tuesday, will you bring me over?'

'Course I will, no bother.'

SUSAN WAS lounging in a deck chair at the side of the house, wearing sunglasses and tapping on her phone. Music was blaring from a speaker on the grass.

'Hi Susan,' Collins said.

'What about ya, Collins?' Susan said, in a perfect mimicry

of her mother's accent. Collins smiled and went into the kitchen.

Katie was washing potatoes at the sink. She kissed him when he came in, her face lined with concern.

'How did it go, hon?' she said, referring to the Garda Internal Review of Denis' death.

'It was long. They made me go through it, moment by moment. But it's done now.'

'Are you okay?' She put her hand on the side of his face.

'Ah, yeah,' he lied. The grilling had rattled him. Why didn't he come out? Why didn't he make the others run away over the fields to safety? Why didn't he stand his ground when Jones came into the farmyard and protect his colleagues? What was he feeling when Denis was on his knees, a gun to his head? What were his thoughts? Why didn't he do something, *anything*?

'I had a good session with Abi afterwards,' he said. 'That was a great idea of yours to set that up. I talked a lot, she says I'm making real progress.'

'Good man you are. Will you have a beer before dinner? We're having a barbeque.'

'Sure, I'll get the coals from the shed.'

As COLLINS was lighting the barbeque, Zoe came around the corner, pushing the lawnmower.

'Susan, that's my top!'

'You never wear it anyway.'

'Take it off, it's mine.'

'Chill out, girl.'

Zoe planted her hands on her hips.

'Take. It. Off. Right now!'

Katie shouted through the kitchen window: 'Zoe, keep it down will ya? They can hear you in Clonakilty. And you,' she said, nodding to Susan. 'Don't take your sister's clothes without asking. What are ye like?'

Zoe turned to Collins, tossed her hair behind her shoulder and said: 'That top is mine, I'm supposed to fight my corner, amn't I?'

Collins held up his palms and was careful not to smile. He put more charcoal on the barbeque.

How lucky you are, he thought, *to be part of these people's lives.* He thought of Denis and how he would never have a day like this.

He winked at Zoe as she passed. She smiled back, grateful for the acknowledgment of the injustice.

AFTER DINNER he and Katie went for a walk down by Kilbarry Church and they called in to the Cillín near the river, where Katie touched the hawthorn tree by the entrance as she always did. Then they looped around to Castle Street and walked up and down the town, saluting people. Out the Kilbarry Road again, past the recycling centre, the tyre repair company and the health centre. God, he loved that road, with those dramatic, sunlit hills to the north.

When they got back to the house, Susan and Zoe were sitting together at the patio table, peace having been restored.

Katie and Collins sat with them and Zoe brought out drinks. Katie lit a citronella candle on the table.

'That reminds me,' Collins said, addressing Susan. 'There's a Louise Bourgeois exhibition in the Museum of Modern Art and I'm driving to Dublin on Thursday. I could bring you, if you like. I'll be passing right by Kilmainham. Her spiders are incredible, you really should see them up close. I'll have a good car, one of the Audis, but we'll have to leave around 7 a.m.'

'Thanks,' Susan said. 'That'd be great, can Kellie come, too?'

'Absolutely.'

'What's so great about spiders? Zoe said. 'They're disgusting.'

'They're made from bronze,' Susan said. 'And they're, like, twenty feet high or something.'

'Yuck,' Zoe replied, making a face.

When it got cooler, Susan and Zoe went inside. Katie reached out her hand and he held it. She turned her chair and leaned over to kiss him.

'I've been meaning to say this for a while,' she said, 'and now is the time.'

'Is everything okay?'

'Everything is fine. I just wanted to tell you that I love you. And the girls love you, too. I know they do. We all love you, okay? And we love having you here with us.'

Collins was taken aback and didn't reply.

'Those girls never stop singing your praises. You're so good to them. Susan warned me last week not to mess things up, to be nice to you. I'll do my best, but I can't promise anything.'

She stood up and he followed her lead. She kissed him for a long time and then hugged him, her head pressing into his chest. He felt the tension of the past weeks slip away as he held her close.

'I love ye too,' he said and glanced to his left. Zoe and Susan were standing there, staring at them.

Zoe said: 'How gross is that?'

Susan held two fingers to her mouth and made a puking sound.

Collins laughed and gathered the girls under each arm.

ACKNOWLEDGEMENTS

Thank you to all at Mercier Press, Mary Feehan especially. Thanks to Dee Collins for all her great work on the book and Carina McNally for publicity. Thanks to Sarah O'Flaherty for the brilliant cover.

Thanks to Catherine Kirwan, Michael Harrington, Una Coakley and Ciara Coakley for reading this book and critiquing it for me. Thanks to my two writers' groups: who read and critiqued passages from the book. They are Anna Foley, Diarmuid Hickey and Eileen O'Donoghue; and Rachel Andrews, Madeleine D'Arcy and Arnold Fanning.

Thanks so much to the author Michelle Dunne for her lovely cover quote.

Thanks to everyone who has supported me in my writing, my wife Ciara especially.

Tadhg Coakley is the award-winning author of five books. His debut novel *The First Sunday in September* was shortlisted for the Mercier Fiction Prize and published in 2018 to much acclaim. His crime novel *Whatever It Takes* (Part 1 of the Tim Collins Series) was chosen as the 2020 Cork, One City One Book. *Everything* (a sports autobiography, which he co-wrote with its subject, Denis Coughlan) was one of the 2020 sports books of the year in *The Sunday Times*, *The Irish Examiner* and *The Irish Times*. His bestselling memoir *The Game: A Journey into the Heart of Sport* (2022) was described in *The Irish Examiner* as 'one of the most distinctive, original, beautiful and best books on sport this country has known'. It was shortlisted for the An Post Irish Book Awards. Tadhg's short stories, articles and essays have been widely published. www.tadhgcoakley.ie